SEVEN UNHOLY DAYS

A THRILLER BY

JERRY HATCHETT

ISBN-13: 978-0-9887012-4-3 (Red House)
ISBN-10: 0988701243

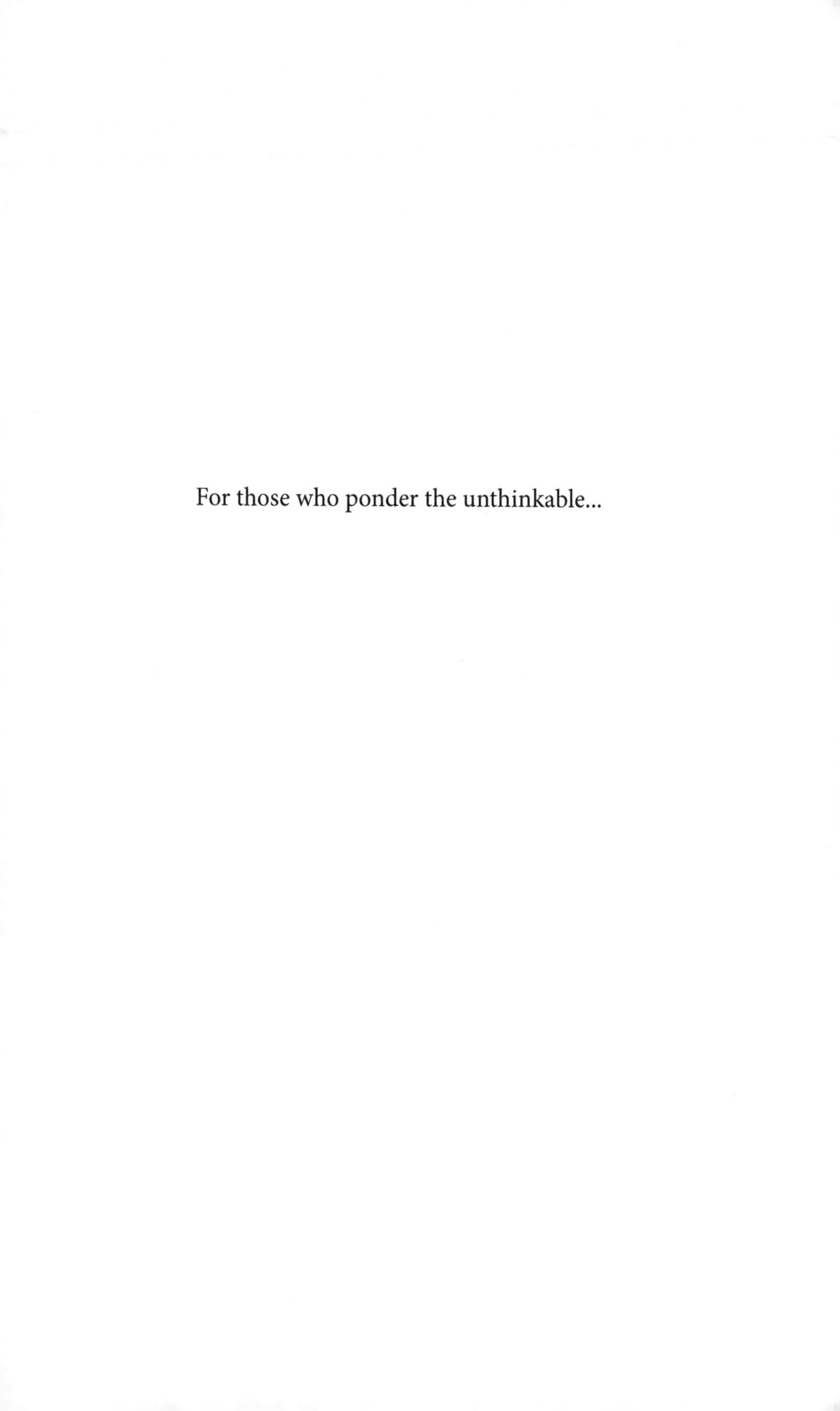

For those who ponder the unthinkable...

Cyber Attack on U.S. Electric Grid
"Gravest Short Term Threat" to National Security
—*ABC News*

MONDAY

Then God said, "Let there be light"; and there was light.
And God saw the light, that it was good;
and God divided the light from the darkness.
God called the light Day,
and the darkness He called Night.
So the evening and the morning were the first day.
Genesis 1:2-5

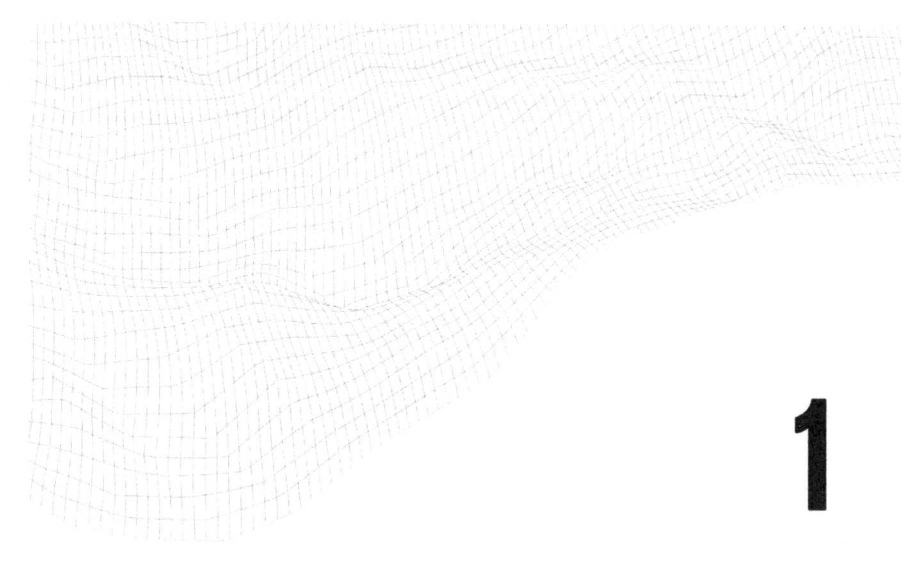

1

1:02 PM CENTRAL DAYLIGHT TIME (LOCAL)
GREAT CENTRAL ELECTRIC
YELLOW CREEK COMPLEX
NEAR IUKA, MISSISSIPPI

I felt trouble in Jimmy Lee Tarkleton's handshake. It was a little strong and a little long. This man liked pissing contests.

"The inspection is scheduled for next week, Decker," he said.

"If you have a problem, take it up with headquarters. They dispatched me."

"For what?" He was a bearish man, thick-chested and sturdy, and he showed no sign of moving.

"Three days of excessive grid fluctuations. I'm here to identify the problem and recommend a solution."

He yanked the handset from a wall phone and dialed.

"This is Tarkleton at Central. Put me through to the director, right now." He paced back and forth, tethered by the cord.

I looked into the fifty-foot-square nerve center of Great Central Electric. Acoustic walls, subdued indirect lighting in a high ceiling, big air-conditioning ducts. Fiberoptic cables fanned out to a long bank of servers and a crescent-shaped console held two rows of flush-mounted displays.

A ten-foot transparent display dominated the front of the room. I drew a deep breath and smelled the thunderstorm redolence of ozone, ever present in a room full of computers. This was geek nirvana.

Tarkleton fired questions at someone on the other end now. Under different circumstances I might have admired, even liked him. He was the first manager in a long time who didn't fall all over himself to suck up to me.

But after three weeks of flying around to inspect the four centers and reassure myself the facilities were up to par, along with a half-dozen useless meetings with government bureaucrats, I had no patience for Tarkleton's brand of staunch integrity.

I missed watching the sun sizzle into the Pacific at the end of the day, looking at the stars through crisp mountain air. I missed my dog, Norman. I wanted to go home, spend some time reading, watch a few movies, binge on Netflix. Norman loves good movies. He hates the kennel. I hate hotels.

Tarkleton hung up the phone and turned back to me. "Mr. Decker, I just spoke with the director and she confirmed the dispatch. You're welcome to proceed with your inspection, but like I told her, someone has bad information."

"How's that?"

"We haven't had any abnormal grid conditions."

"If that's the case there's something very odd going on with the reporting network, and it's not affecting the other three centers."

He shrugged and pulled a leather pouch from his pocket, from which he produced a pipe that he packed with tobacco and lit. "Inspect to your heart's content," he said through a cloud of aromatic smoke.

When the guy manning the code console looked my way and waved, I stepped into the control room.

"Mr. Decker. It is you!" He beamed. "I am Abdul Abidi, and I am pleasing to make your acquaintance."

He looked like an Abdul Abidi, and he was pleasing to make my acquaintance. A wiry little fellow with dark skin, big brown eyes, and likely a stratospheric IQ. If the team was in order he was the super-geek of the bunch, the real codeslinger.

The second guy of the three-man team squinted at me through thick glasses that he pushed up every few seconds. "You sir, on the analysis station, what's your name?"

"Harold Beeman." He sounded like a kazoo. I smiled and nodded.

The final crew member, manning the main bank of system monitors, didn't wait for me to ask. He turned in his chair and managed to look down at me without getting up. "Brett Fulton," he said. "But you can call me Mr. Fulton."

"Thanks, I'll bear that in mind." Every tech crew has at least one.

I drifted over to Abidi and we talked shop while I kept an eye on the monitors. I was pleased to see that he and the others continued working while we chatted, each man focused on his station, occasionally keying in an adjustment. The big display showed the sixteen states of the Central region glowing a uniform, reassuring green. Normal operation.

"Can you pull up a three-day flux graph, hourly intervals, please?" I said to Abidi. Seconds later, he had it on his monitor. I leaned down and examined it. To my surprise, Tarkleton was right. It was perfect. So was every other check I ran.

I straightened up, puzzled by the inconsistency, but satisfied that the problem wasn't here. "You're running a smooth operation."

"Very smooth," Abidi said with a big grin.

"Keep it up." I shook his hand and headed for the door. The reporting glitch could be diagnosed remotely, so I needed maybe fifteen minutes to wrap up my review and I'd be homeward bound. Tonight, I'd finally sleep in my own bed again. I was almost to the door when the room exploded in a hellish cacophony of light and sound.

"Alert! Grid failure! Alert! Grid failure!" The synthesized contralto voice blared in sterile monotone as an ear-splitting Klaxon wailed through its cycles.

What the hell? The steady stream of cool air from the vents slowed, then died, as the control center switched to standby power from an onsite generator. Display screens all over the room scrolled in sync to the alarm that still screamed: "Alert! Grid failure!"

On the big screen, the reassuring glow of seconds ago was faltering. I watched in stunned silence as Mississippi flickered and went black.

Tarkleton blew back into the room, a gray-haired twister looking for a place to touch down. "Decker, I didn't authorize any drills!"

I ignored him and started back to the console.

He put a heavy paw on my arm. "Where do you think you're going? I'm not letting you anywhere near the controls!"

"Alert! Grid failure! Alert!" The voice was relentless.

"Will somebody please turn that dang thing off?" Tarkleton bellowed. The alarms died and the twister focused on me again. He was still holding on to my arm. "Mr. Decker, I suggest you tell me exactly what you've been up to in my control room."

"And I suggest you let go of my arm," I said. "This is no drill, man. You just lost a state."

His hand dropped. He stood motionless, a spent twister. The room was unnaturally quiet in the aftermath of the alarms.

"Alert! Grid failure! Alert! Grid failure!" Hell broke loose again. This could not be happening. I looked up, unwilling to believe my eyes. On the screen, Alabama winked out.

I pushed past Tarkleton and returned to the console, where Abidi was already typing away, his fingers flying over the keyboard with uncanny speed. I leaned over, scanning the monitors. Grids don't fail without a damn good reason. I directed Abidi's search, telling him where to look.

Tarkleton's massive presence loomed over me. "It's a hundred and four degrees outside and a lot of air conditioners just quit. If we don't get the power back up, we've got a problem."

"Since we're exchanging suggestions, I suggest you let me do my thing," I said without looking up. I already had a problem of un-frigging-believable proportion. My company had designed every system in the room.

"You know what happened?"

"Not yet, but I intend to find out."

He was silent for a moment, relighting his pipe while he mulled this over. "Very well, then. Gentlemen! Mr. Decker has the floor. Give him your cooperation." He paused, and I felt the weight of his eyes on me. "It's your system, Decker. Fix it."

A secretary stuck her head through the doorway. "Mr. Tarkleton, North Mississippi Medical Center on the blue line. They have people in surgery and their generator failed. What do I tell them?"

"Lord Almighty. Tell them we're on it, but get that generator back up." He turned to me. "That's the largest hospital in the state. Stop twiddling your thumbs and get that grid back up."

"I need your station," I said to Harold Beeman. The room was heating up and he was already covered in sweat. He looked right at me, his eyes the size of golf balls through the glasses, but he didn't move. I motioned for him to get up and still he sat. I looked to Tarkleton for help.

"Harold, move your butt!" he said.

Beeman got up slowly, still staring at me. A big bead of sweat rolled off the tip of his oily nose. He finally cleared the chair and I slid into it.

I typed and clicked my way through analysis screens and grid models, looking for answers, finding none. Everything was normal, except for the two entire states that—

"Alert! Grid failure! Alert! Grid failure!"

Make that three. Tennessee faded. My career was disintegrating. I pictured a room full of reporters in bloodlust frenzy, jackals closing in on wounded prey. Mr.

Decker, what went wrong? Did you cut security corners when you designed this system? Was Decker Digital not ready for the challenge of such a project? Exactly how vulnerable are your systems, Mr. Decker?

Someone killed the alarms.

"I'll have to call Washington if we don't get them back up in a hurry," Tarkleton said. "Any chance these states went down independently?"

"Didn't happen," I said, working my way deeper into the system.

"I agree," Brett Fulton said. "The problem is here. With Decker's system."

I vowed to wipe the smug smile off his face as soon as I had the grids back up. And to fire the Decker Digital employee responsible for this gaffe.

The secretary was back. "Mr. Tarkleton, blue line again, Memphis International, they're screaming and cursing, demanding to talk to you."

Tarkleton grabbed a telephone handset and punched a large blue button on the base. "Tarkleton here ... Yes ma'am ... I'm sorry, I don't have a time frame for you ... I understand ... it won't help, but call him if you want to." He slammed the handset back into its cradle. "Decker, I'm in a world of hurt here."

"Perhaps it is not trouble with Matt Decker's system." Abidi looked up from his monitor. "I am seeing something most unusual in my lines of code. I am thinking cyber-bomb."

I leaned over and peered at the screen. "You're saying the server ordered all three shutdowns? You can't be serious. Too much redundancy, too many safeguards."

"It has happened. I am showing you here, and here, and here." He pointed to three lines of code. "These are the exact times Mississippi, Alabama, and Tennessee became dark. I assure you I am most correct."

"Fulton, run me a printout of the core system activity log," I said. "STAT, man, three states are down!"

He glared at me, then typed and clicked. Nerd Beeman waited across the room by the printer, ripped the sheet out as soon as it finished, and brought it to me. I found the three bold lines of print that marked the events in question and told Abdul to call out the times he had found buried in the program code.

"Eighteen-sixteen and thirty-seven seconds, eighteen-eighteen and fifty-three seconds, and eighteen-twenty-one and nine seconds, all Zulu times."

Yellow Creek was five hours behind Greenwich Mean Time, also known as Zulu, the world standard for matters technical. Abidi was right. The times the states went down perfectly matched the cryptic numbers he had found. "There's nothing wrong with my systems." I slapped the printout down on the counter.

"Come again?" Tarkleton said.

"Somebody tampered with the code." My code. Code engineered to be unbreakable.

Abidi cast me a worried glance. I could see he was already processing the implications, and he didn't like them. Neither did I.

"Can't we just do a manual override to switch this first grid back on and then deal with the others?" Fulton said.

This moron had obviously spent all of fifteen minutes studying the systems.

"Oh no no no," Beeman said. "CEPOCS is not designed for manual overrides. A stunt like that could cause terrible damage."

He was right. The grid switches were designed for

precise machine control, not manual.

"Up until sixteen minutes after one, everything was fine, right?" I said.

"Sixteen minutes plus thirty-seven seconds after one," Abidi said.

"Whatever. My point is that the shutdowns were rigged to occur at that particular time on the system clock. There's no reason we can't turn the main system clock back twenty-four hours until we can figure out what's going on here."

"I understand precisely to where you are traveling," Abidi said. "CEPOCS will return all parameters to the pre-trigger state. You are a computer hero."

Fulton snorted.

"I don't know about hero, Decker," Tarkleton said, "But if this works, you can call me Tark."

Swell.

Two minutes later we watched Mississippi, Alabama, and Tennessee sequence back to life on the display. Tarkleton wiped his forehead with a sleeve. Abidi was jubilant. Fulton dumped a BC powder onto his tongue and swallowed it dry. Beeman was too wired to stand still; he kept walking around peering at readouts. I watched him circle the room.

All states were back online and I could restore the CEPOCS code to its original state. Some P.R. damage control lay ahead, but I had friends in the media—along with a few vulnerable non-friends. I'd gotten off easy. Lurking in the rear chambers of my mind, however, was a nagging buzz: CEPOCS was Decker Digital's flagship project, and until I could find the hole and plug it, the system was vulnerable.

After three trips around the room Beeman eased into

his chair and hunched over the keyboard, his shoulders drawn in tight. Why was he still so worked up? He looked back and I caught his eye. I started toward him.

"Hey, Harold." He turned his back. His hand was on the mouse, clicking away with jerky movements. Closing programs. Purging files as fast as he could type and click.

I was behind him in two big strides. "Beem—"

He sprang from the chair, sending it careening into my shins. I fell back against a support column. He bolted from the room. I shoved the chair out of the way and went after him. A high-security program had just been hacked and here was a freaky-acting geek.

I made it to the parking lot just in time to see him whiz by, firing a panicky look my way as his car fishtailed past.

Tarkleton came up behind me, panting, his dead pipe still clenched in his teeth. "What's going on?"

I watched Beeman blow through the main gate and hang a hard turn onto the main road doing about fifty. "I'd say—"

"Matt Decker!" I turned around and saw Abidi in the doorway, motioning frantically. "Come here quickly!"

2

2:42 PM CENTRAL DAYLIGHT TIME (LOCAL)
YELLOW CREEK

Abdul pointed to the display. The sixteen states were gone. In their place was a black screen filled with bright red letters, a sickly animated font that seemed to drip and run down the screen like a bloody message on the wall of a murder scene:

SEVEN DAYS OF PERDITION

"You better get Washington on the line," I said to Tarkleton. "This is a nasty bunch."

"Looks like some kind of religious nut," he said.

"Hardly. There's a group on the Internet called the 'Sons of Perdition.' They claim to be environmentalists trying to stop mankind's 'damnation of the Earth.'"

Abdul nodded. "I have read of them."

"In reality," I said, "they're nothing but a gaggle of cyber-thugs who get off on hitting systems, the bigger the better. Corporate servers have borne the brunt of their attacks so far, but they're getting braver and the infrastructure is a natural target."

Tarkleton flicked a lighter and sucked the flame down into the bowl of his pipe. "If you say so, but perdition, even 'sons of perdition' for that matter, has biblical meaning too."

"Washington will bring in the FBI, and I'm sure they'll check all angles. If you'll get that ball rolling, I need to spend some time inside Beeman's station and the other systems. Our rollback was a finger in the dam. I want to close the hole for good."

He puffed and nodded.

"By the way," I said, "I think we should ask local law enforcement to bring Beeman in so we can find out what he knows."

"I know where he lives. After we get caught up here, let's go find him ourselves."

A knock sounded at the doorway and I looked that way. Standing there was the most beautiful woman I have ever seen.

"Mr. Tarkleton, you mind if I speak to Brett for just a minute?" she said.

Her voice was smooth, almost melodious. The sight of her, the sound of her, captivated me.

"Hey Jana," Tarkleton said. "Come on in."

She walked by on her way to Brett and smiled briefly as she passed. Shoulder-length blond hair, tan skin the texture of butter, eyes I can't find words to describe. They talked quietly for a moment, and he handed her a key.

Girlfriend or wife? On her way out she caught me off guard by stopping.

"Where have I seen you?" she said.

"On TV," Tarkleton said. "This is Matthew Decker."

"Really, the computer guy?" she said.

I nodded and smiled. She extended her hand. "I'm Jana Fulton. Very good to meet you, Mr. Decker." Fulton. Damn.

"My pleasure, Jana." Her touch was like everything else about her, and another of my senses flooded with unfamiliar feelings. Our eyes locked for the briefest moment and I didn't care that her jerk of a husband was fifteen feet away. I wanted to believe she didn't care either, but I couldn't trust my whirling psyche. She smiled again, and then she was gone.

I glanced toward Brett. He was oblivious.

4:30 PM CENTRAL DAYLIGHT TIME (LOCAL)
THE PEABODY HOTEL
MEMPHIS, TENNESSEE

Abraham Hart sat on the Victorian leather sofa in a white linen suit, dark hands laid neatly on his lap. Parked underneath coal-black eyebrows, his startling blue eyes flicked back and forth, looking first at Dane, then Riff. Both men looked hardcore military: sturdy frames, buzz cuts, Dane in blue jeans and a desert-camo fatigue jacket, Riff in black cargo pants and a painted-on black tee.

"Messers Christian," Hart said, "perhaps you can explain this to me," pointing a manicured fingertip at a lamp on an end table, unremarkable except for the fact it was on.

"Remember, sir, this was a test," Dane said, "and quite successful."

Hart slowly moved the pointing finger in front of his face, bringing it to his lips in a call for silence. "Mr. Christian, I never classified this as a test. I classified it as step one. My tests were carried out some time ago."

Another staring session, as Hart reflected on a series of mysterious power outages in the western states a few years earlier, and another more recent string of failures on the Atlantic seaboard. Mysterious to some, not to him. "You are handsomely paid. I did not hire you for a display of trial-and-error buffoonery."

Riff was turning red, his eyes narrowing. "Now look—"

Hart raised his finger back to his lips. "No." Civilizations rose and fell during the silence. Finally he resumed, punctuating each word with an angry tap of his finger on the table. "You look. My instructions were specific. Three states. Three hours. I got less than one hour. Why?"

"Sir, this is a minor asset problem," Dane said. "We have two people at Central, neither one aware of the other. Both failed to effectively limit Decker."

"I see."

Dane hesitated before continuing. "I must remind you that this game with Decker is—"

Hart drew a sharp breath and raised his hand. "Do not presume to lecture me. Simply explain how you plan to restore the primary code."

"I'll reinstall it myself. There's no indication our code has been discovered at the other three centers, but as a precaution I'm going with the propagation code on the reinstall. It will spread to the other three centers, as well as the archival code. By zero-hour, our code will be in place in all four centers as well as the archives, and the system will be locked."

"What about the failed assets?"

"Riff and I will deal with them. As for Decker—"

"I will deal with Decker." Hart tapped his lip. "Personally."

Dane nodded. "Everything will be in order, sir. We guarantee it."

Hart closed his eyes and drew a slow, deep breath through his nostrils. The eyelids slowly raised and he stared at neither man, instead gazing at the space between them. "Be very sure that it is, Messers Christian. Leave me now."

Hart sat alone in the lavish hotel room and evaluated the afternoon's events. The three states were of course a test, a very successful one and the last step before the Glorious Beginning, even though he dared not let the Christian brothers know. The flock deserved praise and encouragement. Barbaric mercenaries deserved nothing.

Decker had behaved predictably. He checked his watch and smiled—mere hours remained before the public's love affair with that silly little wunderkind would lurch to a halt. Over the course of the coming week, destiny would be fulfilled, and in the process he would crush Decker like a cockroach beneath his mighty sole. The next few hours, however, were critical. Perhaps a bit of diversion was in order, something to occupy Decker's mind until the plan was fully in motion.

Hart opened and booted his laptop, then established a link to his main personal computer seven hundred miles away. He composed an email, and through a series of tunneled commands, ordered the remote machine to rebuild and send the message via an elaborate network of anonymizers that would eliminate any chance for his crafty adversary to track its origin.

He shut down the laptop and switched on the television to CNN. File video footage of the Yellow Creek facility was playing while the anchor talked. "Join us this evening for in-depth coverage of today's blackout in the South. Up next, we take a look at televangelism. Is it about God or about dollars?"

Hart switched off the set, walked to the window, and looked to the sky. "God," he said with a sneer, "you had your chance and look what a mess you made. Prepare to step aside, old man."

3

8:40 PM CENTRAL DAYLIGHT TIME (LOCAL)
IUKA COUNTRY INN
FIFTEEN MILES SOUTHEAST OF YELLOW CREEK

I combed Beeman's station for clues and found none. Whatever he deleted, he did thoroughly. Nor did I find irregularities—beyond the one nasty bug—during an exhaustive check of every system in the plant. Plugging the hole presented a problem: I had to find it first.

Now, on Tarkleton's recommendation, here I sat in a closet-sized room at the Iuka Country Inn. He was due at nine-thirty for a trip to Beeman's house.

I showered, put on jeans and a tee-shirt, and powered up my laptop. My plan was to get in a bit of research on the GCE control crew, especially Harold Beeman, before Tarkleton arrived.

"You have new mail," the laptop announced. There

were only eighteen, so I decided to take care of them first. I moved through the list quickly, answering the ones that warranted it, filing some, trashing some.

Number sixteen broke the routine. It was from a gibberish Hotmail address and had no subject:

Return-Path: <i14_696938@hotmail.com>
Delivered-To: x7ijljAweRRv
-deckerdigital:com-x7ijljAweRRv@
deckerdigital.com
X-Envelope-To: x7ijljawerrv@
deckerdigital.com
X-Originating-IP: [66.156.171.40]
From: i14_696938@hotmail.com
To: x7ijljAweRRv@deckerdigital.com
Subject:

Never more horror, nor worse of days
Than those to come to he who stays.
Your filthy secrets Are in jeopardy.

The prickly hairs on the back of my neck stood up and a chill rippled down my spine. This was my private address; only a handful of people had access to it. No one accidentally emails x7ijljAweRRv@deckerdigital.com, and I did have some features in my past best left alone. Nothing that rose to the level of "filthy secrets" as far as I was concerned, but not good for business, either.

What the hell was going on? This didn't fit the Sons of Perdition. I could burn every one of them and they knew it. They wouldn't confront me directly.

WHAM! WHAM! WHAM! The knocks shook the door in its frame, and I jumped six inches off the chair. I went to the door and looked through the peephole. Tarkleton was early.

"Come in, Mr. Tarkleton."

"Thanks, but you're supposed to be calling me Tark now, remember?"

"Tark it is. Listen, I'm sorry we got off to a rough start today."

"Not a problem, it was edgy for all of us." He cocked his head and looked at me. "You sure you're okay?"

"Yeah, why?"

"You look a little pale."

"It's been a long day. I'm fine, really. Ready to go see Beeman?"

"I tried his cell phone about ten times. He's not answering. I'll get the sheriff looking for him."

"By the way, I think you're right. This doesn't really fit for the Sons of Perdition gang I mentioned earlier."

"What changed your mind?"

"Just thinking it over. Doesn't feel right."

We wrapped up the conversation and he left. I almost told him about the email, but I decided to keep it to myself for the time being. Tarkleton was beginning to seem like a nice enough fellow, but I've found it's best to build trust the same way you build a house of cards: very carefully.

Back in front of the laptop, I went to work backtracking the email. It was naturally from an anonymous email provider, in this case Hotmail. Fortunately (for me, anyway), a lot of these brand-name systems aren't as secure as they would have people believe. I was inside their traceroute log files within forty seconds, ready to see where the sender of that email came from when he logged onto the Hotmail server.

I found the IP easily enough and ran a quick trace on it. That was where I hit a brick wall. Whoever it was had the good sense to come into Hotmail from a cloaking service that hid his identity. I could punch through that brick wall, but it carried a detection risk and, depending on how many anonymizers they bounced through on the way to Hotmail, it could take a lot of time and crunching numbers. I decided it wasn't worth it. Yet.

Checking out Beeman was next on my list. CEPOCS wasn't my first government contract, and I had left a few back doors scattered about. It took two minutes to pull up a detailed dossier on Mr. Beeman from the Department of Public Utilities database. His DOPU file was unremarkable: a bunch of typical tech training and certifications, dependable worker, and no arrest record, not even a traffic ticket, IQ 121. Married, no kids. The file had a picture of his wife, Mary, who looked to be about the size of a Volkswagen. Harold better stick with the missionary position.

Abdul Abidi's research was more interesting. He came to the U.S. from Iran on a student visa and eventually became a citizen. He had more than typical tech training. He was Dr. Abidi, with a Ph.D. in applied computer science from none other than MIT. Noteworthy, to say the least. IQ 154, single, parents and a number of siblings still back home in Iran. Lots of speeding tickets, but nothing more serious. What was an MIT Ph.D. doing in the GCE control room? I downloaded his file to the hard drive for easy access and a deeper look later on.

The file on Brett Fulton was as shallow as he appeared to be. He had an associate's degree in information technology from Itawamba Community College, Fulton, Mississippi, not far from where I sat. Football star there in the junior college division, no 1-A scholarship offers when he finished his second year. Walked on at Ole Miss, got cut, took a swing at the head coach, got suspended from school and never came back. No IQ listed. Boring jock who wasn't even good enough at that. The bottom of each file had a row of thumbnail images of family members and one of them drew my cursor to it like a magnet.

I clicked to open it, and Jana Fulton's picture filled the screen. Twenty-seven, a trauma nurse, and *sister* of a prick. I stared at the picture for another couple of minutes, then saved her file to the hard drive, too.

It had been a hectic day and I was worn out, but I decided to go ahead and include Tarkleton in my brief investigation. "NO MATCH" was the surprising result of the search. I made a note to re-run the search later. There was obviously an error of some sort. Anyone associated with the power grid had a file. That included me, although my files were somewhat sanitized.

WHAM! WHAM! WHAM! The door shook just like last time, for good reason. Tark was back. I opened the door and he burst into the room, breathing hard, his pale blue shirt drenched with sweat and stuck to the big hairy belly underneath. I remembered that his name was all over the screen of my laptop, so I closed the lid as quickly and discreetly as I could. He was looking that way, but I couldn't tell if he saw anything or not. I hoped not.

"You're not gonna believe this," he said. "Harold Beeman is dead."

4

9:20 PM CENTRAL DAYLIGHT TIME (LOCAL)
MEMPHIS INTERNATIONAL AIRPORT

"Gulfstream two-one-six, Memphis Tower. Cleared for departure on runway three-six left, sir."

"Roger, Memphis Tower, Gulfstream two-one-six. Departing runway three-six left."

"Roger, two-one-six. Contact Memphis Center on one-two-eight-point-five, and have a good flight, sir. Looks like a beautiful night all the way."

"Memphis Tower, two-one-six. Airborne, contacting Memphis Center on one-two-eight-point-five."

The cabin of the twin-engine business jet was quiet by the standards of kerosene burners, immaculate by any measure. Only three months old, the aircraft's interior smelled of new leather and carpet. Hart swiveled his seat to face the window on his right as the pilot arched the G-V smartly upward, ascending out of Memphis airspace at two thousand feet per minute. The street lights below first became soft-edged amber-orange pools of light, then a glittering medley of interconnected and criss-crossing lines as the plane turned to a northeasterly heading while continuing to climb.

Twenty miles laterally and four miles vertically from Memphis, the city looked like a seething cauldron of hot coals laced with a thousand rivulets of molten lava. Hart returned his seat to the forward-facing position, musing to himself that Hell probably looked something like that from a distance, with its fiery lakes of brimstone. Except that Hell could not be turned off.

He moved to another seat, pulled his laptop from an attaché, and raised the lid. He connected to the Internet through the Gulfstream's satellite-connected WiFi system. Still no word from Decker. What was that hedonistic nightmare of a human being up to? He checked his watch. Less than four hours remained.

10:25 PM CENTRAL DAYLIGHT TIME (LOCAL)
IUKA COUNTRY INN

We were on our way back from the crime scene, where someone had broken poor Beeman's neck before tossing him in the Tennessee-Tombigbee Waterway. No suspects. No clues. Nobody saw a thing.

"Wonder where old Beeman is right now," Tark said as we headed back toward the opulence of the Iuka Country Inn.

"Zipped up in a black bag?"

"Nah, that's just his body, worthless as tits on a boar hog now. I'm talking about his eternal soul. It's all that matters in the end, you know."

Here it came, Jesus mumbo-jumbo, soul-saving in the Bible Belt, time for me to get right with God. Oh how I knew the song and dance. "I don't mean to be rude, Tark, but I'd just as soon steer clear of religion. I don't believe in it."

"Don't believe in religion, you mean, or don't believe in God at all?"

"None of it."

"What a shame."

"Not a shame to me, I'd just rather deal with the reality in front of me. And that reality just got a bit stranger, wouldn't you say?"

"What do you think is going on here, Matthew?"

"I think Beeman screwed with my code and it got him killed. You?"

"Hard to figure. I just don't understand what anybody has to gain by tinkering with the juice."

"I'd like to shore up the security in CEPOCS, put a few extra blockades in place until we can figure out exactly what's going on."

"You think they might try something else?"

The temptation to tell him about the email was strong but I had no way to know how he'd react. If I could track these people down without spawning twenty questions from the authorities about my past, so much the better. "You never know. I think they've proven they're serious."

"No argument there. What exactly can you do?"

"I can implement a total system lockdown."

"Class three?"

I nodded. He sighed. "That disables AGM," he said.

Automated Grid Maintenance was the CEPOCS feature that made it possible for three-man crews to keep fifteen to twenty states running smoothly. It monitored every grid, every switch, constantly making adjustments and rerouting flow. Without it, every bit of that was done manually.

"True enough," I said, "but that's the only way to guarantee no more modifications until we can get a handle on this situation."

"When did you have in mind?"

"Sooner the better. How soon can you have a crew in place?"

"It'll take a crew of at least twelve or we'll have fried switches all over the place."

"I'm aware of that."

"I'll go home and start working the phone. We'll shoot for first thing tomorrow morning; best I can do, Matthew."

"Morning it is."

The rest of the drive back was fairly quiet. It had been a long day and another lay just ahead. By eleven o'clock I was burrowed into my bed and listening to the soothing hum of the old air conditioner.

5

11:36 PM CENTRAL DAYLIGHT TIME (LOCAL)
IUKA COUNTRY INN

The urgency of needing to know where the email came from won out over fatigue; I got out of bed and fired up my notebook. Espionage and tiptoed malice were bad enough. Murder was an escalation that demanded answers. My quarry had made it personal and he needed a name, something for me to focus on. After staring at his email address for a bit I settled on "69" as a nickname for the bandit and penciled it in on the top of a legal pad, then drew a vertical line to split the page. On the left side I'd keep track of steps and clues. The right would be a list of any weaknesses I found along the way.

I logged into a shell account that hid my identity under a dozen layers of aliases and went to work. The first order of business was building more anonymity, thick insulation against intrusion detection that could be traced back to me. I did this by routing my activity through a series of servers in disparate geographical locations. Seattle to New Delhi, over to Madrid and back to New York, then to London by way of Taipei. Satisfied that I was sufficiently cloaked, I worked my way back into the Hotmail server and then into the first anonymizer service 69 had used. A commercial service, it was set up quite well, enough so to keep out 99% of those who might come knocking. Three minutes later, the details for the account holder scrolled into view on the screen. I penciled in JANE SMITH on the pad. Paid for the account with a money order sent through snail mail. Not good.

Stepping backward through the trail led me to another cloaking service, again commercial. JANE SMITH. The next leg of the journey was more of the same. JANE SMITH. The legal pad had plenty of entries on the left, and finally a couple of chinks in the armor for the right-hand column. I wrote in REPETITION, and directly underneath, COMPLACENCY. 69 was confident the three cloaking services provided unbreakable anonymity. I looked over the notes again to be sure I hadn't missed anything, and found more balance for the right side of the page. All three services were American companies. I penciled in USA, certain that 69 was inside the country.

The entry point into the third service was the end of the cloaking trail. This was the point of embarkation for 69's online journey. All that remained was to decipher his actual logon, a process in which thirty to forty hops through a chain of servers is not uncommon. I cracked my knuckles and let loose a lightning flurry of pings and traceroutes, separating the real hops in his logon from any spoofs he might've managed. There were nothing but clean routes; I had the bastard.

My heart pounded from the thrill of the hunt as I closed in. I keyed in the last few commands and waited for the system to show me exactly where he came from, the very place he jumped onto the Internet. What scrolled onto the screen sank my spirits.

According to the query report I was reading, 69 was a direct node on an AT&T fiber backbone, not logged on from anywhere, just a phantom on the Internet. There were only a handful of people in the world who could pull off a direct connection without leaving any fingerprint as to location, but there it was in blue and white. He was either an uberhacker or he had one working for him.

Exhaustion hit me in a big way, but I needed a plan before turning in. A very serious thug wanted me to pack my bags. Why? Anyone with this level of chutzpah surely knew investigative hell was about to be rained down upon their sorry ass. In the face of such an assault, what threat did I pose? There was only one logical answer. Terrorism was about to bare its rotten fangs again; they were planning another hit on CEPOCS.

Bailing out and going home was an attractive theory, but running leaves an aftertaste I don't care for. And as Tark said, CEPOCS was my baby. The thought of someone screwing with it pissed me off, and the ramifications of leaving it unprotected were staggering. An extended blackout across a whole state—or, perish the thought, across several states—could be catastrophic. Hospitals, traffic systems, commerce, communications, and air conditioners—no trivial matter in August—all dead.

I had to do something but this had crossed the line from hacking to murder and I was in over my head. The

FBI needed to be here. They probably already had a file open on the blackout but they needed more than that. It was time for a task force, wide open and full bore. I didn't want them nosing around that email, but who said they had to know about it at all? I had already proven it to be a dead end as far as finding its source, so there was really no reason to mention it. It could remain my little secret, and maybe I could draw out 69 myself. I opened the email, clicked REPLY, and started typing.

```
FROM: x7ijljAweRRv@deckerdigital.com
TO: I14_696938@hotmail.com
SUBJECT: DO I KNOW YOU?

If you have business with me, state the
nature. If not, keep your spam out of my
mailbox. I have no time for games or bad
poetry.
```

A click of the SEND button and it was on its way. I shut down my machine and burrowed into bed once more. This time sleep came quickly.

DAY ONE
TUESDAY

And I saw, and behold a white horse:
and he that sat on him had a bow;
and a crown was given unto him:
and he went forth conquering, and to conquer.
Revelation 6:2

6

12:06 AM CENTRAL DAYLIGHT TIME (LOCAL)
DOWNTOWN IUKA

The Christian brothers rolled through downtown Iuka in a rented Jeep. “Welcome to Pisswater! Let’s hope the second man followed instructions,” Riff said. “I know you told Hart we were reinstalling the code ourselves but we really don’t have time for that.”

“I’ll be sure to ask him before I kill him,” Dane said. He took an amber vial from his pocket, opened it, shook the last two Percodans onto his tongue, and swallowed them dry.

“He’s mine,” Riff said. “You got to do the other one.”

“That sawed-off little worm barely counted, but whatever. Tell you what, drop me off here and pick me up after you’re through with him.”

“Drop you off here for what?”

"I need to see the pharmacist."

"You need to see a doctor. You can't keep taking that crap like that."

"I don't need a lecture. I need to stop this jackhammer in my head. Stop the truck, there's a nice little drugstore right over there."

"Damn it, Dane, you're putting us at risk with this crap. You don't need to be breaking into a drugstore in the middle of this operation. We're bad short on time, and besides, we never do jobs alone."

"You can handle him just fine, baby brother. Call me when you're through and I'll tell you where I am." Dane stepped out of the Jeep.

He watched the Jeep until it turned a corner and then walked through the parking lot on the side of the Good Neighbor pharmacy. A narrow alley ran along the back of the building. He stepped to the rear door and examined it with a Mini-Mag-Lite. No sign of an alarm system. He pulled a pick set from his pocket and tried to open the lock but his hands were shaking too badly. A quick jab with his bare fist shattered one of the panes of glass in the old door. He reached through, unlocked the deadbolt, and stepped inside. A fast look around the inside doorjamb verified that there was no electronic protection. Stupid hicks.

12:12 AM CENTRAL DAYLIGHT TIME (LOCAL) FULTON RESIDENCE

Brett fought to free his wrists but the duct tape held his hands firmly behind the back of the chair. Riff stood in front of him, leaning over so they were nose to nose. "Fulton, I'm way short on time, I want out of Pisswater, Mississippi, and I don't have the energy for a lot of dramatics. So I'm not gonna bullshit you. You're about to die. You've been deemed a liability in a sector that's already been a trouble spot, and we can't take a chance by leaving you hanging around. But I can make it easier for you, if you'll cooperate. Interested?"

"Screw you," Brett tried to say through the duct tape over his mouth.

"Okay, tough guy. Have it your way. I really hate to do it like this, but if you won't tell me where the computer is you leave me no choice. I was going to be merciful and put a bullet in your brain before I light the house, but I guess you'd rather burn to death sitting in that chair, eh?"

Brett's eyes grew wide and he shook his head.

"You've had a change of heart?"

He nodded. Riff unsheathed a small stiletto from his thigh, slipped it between tape and cheek, and cut. He put the knife back in its sheath and with one swift motion jerked the tape from around Brett's head, taking clumps of hair with it. Brett let out a yelp.

"Talk."

"I left the computer in my locker at GCE after I ran the program this afternoon," Brett lied. He had loaned the computer to his sister, Jana, for a fundraising project she was organizing. His original plan had been to get it back from her in time to slip out to GCE and run the program as ordered, but that was before all hell broke loose this afternoon. After that, he decided he'd rather just give these people their five grand back and be done with it. He thought the program he ran earlier was designed to copy information out of CEPOCS, not put some kind of virus into the system. To hell with that. It would appear, however, that they were uninterested in refunds.

Riff brought blood from Brett's right cheek with a cracking backhand. He walked around the chair three times before stopping in front of it and starting to speak in a low growl that sounded more animal than human. "You were clearly instructed for that computer to never be out of your sight until we retrieved it from you." He walked over to a wall shelf and picked up a picture of Jana.

"Where's your little sister, Fulton?"

"How should I know? She doesn't live here." That was technically true. She lived in Tupelo but since taking a nursing job at the Iuka Hospital E.R. a couple of months go, she did spend a lot of nights at Brett's house. Thankfully she was working tonight.

"I know everything about her sweet ass, Brett. Maybe I'll go by the hospital and say hello." Riff smiled a wicked grin. "Maybe we'll even go for a ride." He gently kissed the picture, looked into Brett's eyes, and tugged at his crotch.

Brett had spent a lifetime blustering his way out of tight spots without having to get physical. The few times he had gotten as far as an actual fight, he had lost. It was time to win one. He worked up a mouthful of spit and unloaded into Riff's face.

The grin turned into a snarl as Riff threw the picture against the wall and brought both hands to his face to wipe his eyes.

Brett leaned as far back as he could, then slammed his head forward into Riff's face. He felt a sickening crunch of cartilage and bone and saw his stunned captor reeling backward from the blow. Knowing that any hesitation would result in instant and lethal retaliation, he lunged to his feet with the chair still wedged between his arms and spun around so that his back was to Riff. He bent down as far as he could and flung himself backward with every ounce of strength he could summon. Two feet later, he hit Riff and kept pumping his legs until they crashed into a wall. The tension on his arms eased as the chair cracked into a dozen splintery pieces.

Riff grabbed him in a stranglehold from behind. Brett stomped Riff's right toes as hard as he could and the hands dropped from around his throat. He took two steps forward, whirled around, and landed a solid kick to Riff's crotch. Riff crumpled to the floor in a guttural moan. Brett strained every muscle in his arms and shoulders, and duct tape gave way to adrenaline. Riff was pulling himself back up, blood and mucous from his mangled nose covering his face. Brett kicked again and caught him squarely in the throat.

With Riff holding his throat and gasping for air, Brett bent over him and first slipped the stiletto from the sheath on his thigh, then pulled a Colt Government Model .45 semi-automatic pistol from his waistband. Advantage established, it took Brett about five seconds to decide whether his next move would be to exact revenge, run, or both. It felt great to ram the narrow knife into the asshole's chest.

He left the house with tires bawling, headed to his parents' farm out on Highway 25. His father would know what to do. Find a lawyer, something like that. After he got there he'd call the hospital and warn Jana to stay away from his house.

Or maybe he'd better call her now. He pulled the cell phone from his pocket but it hadn't fared well in the fight.

The face was shattered and dark. The speedometer needle was nudging one hundred miles per hour when he gave up and threw the phone onto the seat beside him. He looked back to the road and screamed as the car hit the shallow curve a mile short of the farm. He slammed his foot on the brake but it was too late. The car left the road, nosed down into a drainage ditch, and began flipping end over end. Brett was not wearing a seat belt, and he was thrown through the windshield midway through the car's third somersault. Death was instant.

12:13 AM CENTRAL DAYLIGHT TIME (LOCAL)
IUKA HOSPITAL

"You're sure you don't need me to stay?" Jana Fulton said to the supervising E.R. nurse.

"Go on home, we've got it. If we get busy, I'll call."

"Thanks. I'll see you tomorrow." Jana walked through the exit and made her way across the parking lot to her car, happy to get an unexpected night off due to a scheduling foul-up that resulted in an extra nurse on a slow night. She wasn't sleepy and with any luck she'd be able to finish laying out the brochures and flyers for the Nurses' Auxiliary fundraising auction that was coming up in two weeks.

Halfway between the hospital and Brett's house she dialed his cell. "The wireless customer you are calling is not available. Please try your call again later," squawked the recording. She dropped the phone into her purse and drummed her fingers on the steering wheel while she waited for a traffic light to change.

Three minutes later she turned into the driveway and parked behind a Jeep she didn't recognize. Brett's car was gone. She walked to the door, unlocked it, stepped inside, and turned on the light.

12:13 AM CENTRAL DAYLIGHT TIME (LOCAL) GOOD NEIGHBOR PHARMACY

Dane took the time to bandage the hand he sliced when he broke the window, then left the drugstore with a bag full of painkillers. Percodan, Percocet, Vicodin. The dimwits even left bottles of Dilaudid and Oxycontin on a shelf instead of in the Schedule II safe. He could survive for months. He slipped to the corner of the building and looked around it. The parking lot was clear and there was no traffic on the street. Riff sure was taking his time for a simple job; he'd been gone a good twenty minutes. And he wasn't answering his phone. Odd.

According to the Pisswater map the Fulton house was only two blocks away, so Dane started walking. Even past midnight, the August air was humid and sticky. As he turned the corner at a convenience store a raucous band of teenagers came out, loaded into the cab and cargo bed of a pickup, and left the parking lot of the little store shouting and singing, being teenagers. He stopped for just a moment and watched, marveling at the exuberance of their youth, thinking about how they saw the future as endless and unknown, and almost saddened as he thought about the reality of their brief remaining time. The feeling passed soon enough.

He was angry at Riff for breaking communication, but

a couple of the Oxy should ease his frustration. There really wasn't time for a fight, and besides, his brother could be nasty on the other side of an argument. The truckload of teenagers flashed through his mind again.

He felt the oxycodone begin to work and looked at his watch. 12:17. He only had an hour to meet up with Riff, get to GCE, and take care of business. Where is that silly brother of mine? Sometimes the pills didn't work like they were supposed to, but this was a good night and the searing pain in his forehead was easing. As he turned onto Fulton's street, he remembered having once been a teenager himself. A year older than Riff, he remembered his first vehicle, a raggedy old Ford pickup.

The nostalgic buzz ended as he neared the house. The Jeep was in the driveway with a car parked behind it. He walked to the driveway and felt the hood of the car. Hot. Over the chirping cicadas and rustling of the leaves in the old oak trees that lined the street, he could hear the metallic tick ... tick ... tick ... of the car's exhaust system cooling.

Just as he touched the knob on the front door, a blood-curdling scream shrieked from inside. Instinct took over as he drew his gun and kicked open the door. Charging through the broken doorframe in a semi-crouch, weapon-forward stance, he took a rapid survey of the zone. Nine o'clock, clear ... twelve o'clock, clear ... three o'clock, what the hell? A woman, he'd seen her picture before, Fulton's sister. She stood shaking, gasping for breath, little broken sobs, tears rolling down her face. At her feet was the only human being on the planet he cared for, his lifelong companion. Riff lay with his feet out and his back propped against the wall. The front of his black tee-shirt was wet, glued to his body by blood that poured out from around the blade of the knife in his chest. His eyes were open, locked in a look of surprise, hands covered in his own blood. He would've tried to pull the knife out. Somebody's going to pay for this.

"Lady, start talking or I'll send you where my brother is."

She kept crying, but said nothing. Dane took three steps and stopped in front of her. "I'm not a patient man."

The sobs were easing, the tears drying up. "I don't have any idea what happened. I just walked in and found the place like this. And him sitting there like that. Who are you?"

"Where's your brother's laptop?"

"In my car."

"How long has it been there?"

"It's been in my car since this afternoon, but I borrowed it about a week ago. Why?"

"Damn it!" Dane rubbed his forehead. "Let's ride."

"Why do I need to go?"

"I'm short on time and I figure you know your way around. And trust me, going with me beats the alternative."

"What's that?"

"You're not dumb, lady, so don't insult me by acting it."

"All right, let's ride."

12:40 AM CENTRAL DAYLIGHT TIME (LOCAL) YELLOW CREEK

Getting into the GCE control room was easy enough in the middle of the night. The place was so automated that there was only one man on duty to keep an eye on things at night, much easier to deal with than the three-man day crew would have been. Dane did take time out to shoot the security guard at the front gate, but shooting a man was no big deal. He had done it many times before and it came as naturally as getting a drink of water. In fact, he did get himself a drink of water from the security hut right after shooting the old fool who was fumbling with an antique-looking revolver that was stuck in its holster.

He was prepared to kill the control monitor if need be, but the idiot did himself a favor by being asleep. A sturdy clip to the base of the skull ensured he'd stay that way for an hour or so. Reinstalling the code into CEPOCS proceeded without a glitch but it was a step he hoped he wouldn't have to do. He checked his watch. *We never do jobs alone.*

You can handle him just fine, baby brother. Working in the dim lighting in the control room, he slipped a cordless electric screwdriver from his pocket and removed the screws holding a cover panel in place on the base of the big display at the front of the room. With the panel removed, there was an empty space inside the cabinet large enough to hold something the size of a small footlocker. He stepped into the hallway and wheeled in a dolly with two metal boxes on it. One was a faded green color. The other looked like a giant high-tech briefcase.

Jana watched him work the briefcase box into the space in the bottom of the cabinet. She considered running, since she wasn't tied or handcuffed, but after thinking about the way he killed the poor old security guard she decided to stay put.

He raised the lid on the case and a chill rippled down Jana's spine. The device was obviously a sophisticated bomb, the interior of the case loaded with electronics and a shiny metal sphere. Soft beeps sounded as he keyed in numbers. A long beep sounded and he shut the lid on the case. He looked carefully at his watch, and then began reinstalling the panel on the cabinet, leaving the contraption hidden without a trace.

"Why are you doing this? What have these people ever done to you?"

"Not a thing. This is business."

"Your business is killing innocent people?"

"I do what I'm paid to do. I don't ask why." He tightened the last screw on the cabinet.

"Yeah, I'm sure you were 'told' to kill Mr. Stevens."

"He pulled a gun."

"All you had to do was tell him to stop. He was an old man, you cold-hearted bastard."

"Can the chatter, lady."

"Or what, you'll kill me too?"

"I'd rather not." He winked and smiled.

"Keep dreaming; you'd definitely have to kill me first."

Dane slapped her so hard she saw white flashes and her knees buckled. The urge to cry was overwhelming but she refused.

"Let's get a move on. I still have work to do," he said. He wheeled the dolly out of the control room and into a dark corridor, then opened the door to a supply closet and looked around. He grabbed Jana's arm and shoved her inside, then closed the door.

Jana heard the dolly rumbling down the hallway outside. As soon as the sound faded she pulled on the door handle. It moved, but only slightly. There was no lock on the door handle but he had obviously tied the door shut. She braced her feet on the wall, got a good grip on the handle, and yanked hard. She'd need another plan. After a bit of fumbling she found the light switch and flipped it on. The door opened in and to the right. To the left was a tall industrial shelf filled with an assortment of janitorial supplies. She settled for a broom and an industrial sized aerosol can of tub-and-tile cleaner, put them on the tallest shelf she could reach, and started climbing the shelves. They were metal, and clanked and clattered as she made her way up, but not knowing how long she had, speed trumped quiet.

The top shelf was covered in a thick layer of dust that clogged her nose and burned her eyes, but it was empty. She lay on her stomach, reached down to the shelf underneath, and retrieved the two items she had placed there. The broom handle was just long enough to reach the light switch and turn it off. She pulled the broom back, unscrewed the handle, and laid the head aside. Then she waited, crouched in the dark, the broom handle in her left hand like a spear and the aerosol can in the right, listening for the sound of the dolly coming back down the hallway.

After a few minutes her thighs started cramping and her eyes poured tears from the dust. It took every ounce of concentration she could summon not to sneeze. Should she try anything at all, or was it suicide? Her fighting spirit had been high earlier, but the darkness and dust and cramps were sapping it more by the minute. And the minutes crept by like days.

She flinched when she heard something outside the door. Had her attention lapsed and caused her not to hear the dolly approaching? Maybe it was a janitor mopping the floor outside, someone who could help. Or get killed like poor Mr. Stevens. The urge to scream for help at the top of her lungs was overpowering but she resisted. Then the door opened and her heart sank. It was him.

He was backlit by the dim light outside and she had a good target as he stepped into the closet. Now or never. She pushed to spring herself off the shelf and found out that her right foot had gone to sleep. The uneven pressure caused her to come off the shelf at an angle and instead of a clean dive into him with her broom handle spear, she fell on top of him in a tangle of arms and legs. He fell to the ground under her weight and she with him. She fought to get up without letting go of either weapon but it was impossible. He had the other end of the broom handle in one hand and her right foot in the other as she struggled to free herself.

"You little bitch!"

She let go of the broom handle and dove for the doorway but he still had a solid hold on her foot. On her stomach now, she grabbed the edge of the door frame with her left hand and pulled hard but his grip was too strong. She pushed herself up onto her left hand, then aimed the aerosol can blindly behind her with her right and pushed the button. He screamed and let go of her foot, and she scrambled on her hands and knees through the doorway and into the hall. She looked back just long enough to see him wiping the caustic white foam out of his eyes, then jumped to her feet and ran.

As she stepped into the control room she heard his footsteps pounding the floor, coming fast. She made her way through the room and was six feet from the front door when she heard the sound of a pistol being chambered.

"Take another step and this one will be your doing."

She stopped and looked back.

He was standing over the man he had hit in the head earlier, the gun pointed at his head. "As it is, he'll wake up with a bad headache. Or you can go through that door and he'll never wake up at all." He pulled the hammer back.

Jana slowly raised her hands and said, "Please don't shoot him."

"Don't try another stunt like that unless you want to be shot yourself. Got it?"

She nodded. "What next?"

"We're going to bury my brother, then take a trip."

"Where?"

"A nice open field. He never liked being cooped up."

"I mean, where are we taking a trip to?"

"You'll find out soon enough."

"Why take me anywhere? If you're going to kill me, just do it here and be done with it."

"I'm trying to save you from being—" He paused. "Never mind."

"From being killed? By that nuke you planted?"

He arched his eyebrows in surprise.

"I'm not stupid. There's only one kind of bomb that looks like that. You think I want to live somewhere else while that thing murders everyone I love? I don't."

"You're confused. I'm not running a democracy and I don't give a shit what you want. I sure as hell can't leave you here to blab to the cops. That leaves me with two options, kill you or take you with me. So save the lip and be glad I'm choosing the latter."

"Did you hear a word I said? I don't want to—"

Dane grabbed her by the arm and pulled her toward the door. "You talk too much."

Back in the Jeep and in search of a suitable place to bury Riff, Dane tried to make sense of what he was doing. Once he found the woman inside the house, he had no choice but to do something with her. But what? The professional thing was to kill her and move on, but he couldn't.

Losing Riff changed everything. Born a year apart, they had been partners in life. Dane the level head. Riff the impulsive. Together, it worked. He fed off Riff's cold aggression, using it to stay focused when doubts crept in. His mind kept drifting back to the teenagers in the pickup. And the woman. Riff would've had no problem taking care of the her, innocent or not. "Business is business, big brother," he would've said.

But Riff wasn't here, only Dane and the woman, and things didn't seem so cut and dry anymore. They were confusing as hell.

"Hello, am I alone in here?" Jana said as she nudged Dane on the knee with her foot—after her attack and attempted escape at GCE, he bound her hands with nylon wire ties—and startled him from his reverie.

"What?"

"I was talking."

"Imagine that."

"Please go back and turn that bomb off before it's too late."

"Lady, don't start up again. I'm not in the mood."

"How much are you getting paid?"

"Enough for this to be my last job. Ever. Happy?"

"Happy? Your bomb might kill every family member and friend I have, and you want to know if I'm happy?"

"Sorry I asked."

"Who do you work for?"

"You'll find out soon enough. The whole world will."

"What's that supposed to mean?"

"It means there's one hell of a week ahead, lady."

"My name is Jana."

"Whatever."

2:14 AM EASTERN DAYLIGHT TIME
CABIN, GULFSTREAM 216

For years Hart had dreamed of the Glorious Beginning, and always the dream had been to witness it from this one awesome perspective. The road had been long and filled with obstacles, the complexity overwhelming. Now the moment had arrived. His psyche was operating in two distinct modes, one of frenzied anticipation, another that matched his outward appearance; serene, beyond petty emotion. One wanted to revel in what he had personally accomplished, and what was to come. The other was driven to accept his role, great though it was, as a pawn in a grand universal scheme of destiny over which he had no control. The former gave him the drive he had needed to put the plan together. The latter afforded him the ability to rationalize and justify the atrocities that would unfold over the next few days.

The luxury jet flew lazily at six thousand feet above New York City. The late hour provided few other planes in the clear night air to contend with, but the view of the city that never sleeps shone true. No other place on Earth could offer up such a view from the heavens, such a testimony to the accomplishments of modern man. There were other cities in the world that covered more ground, but none had the breathtaking prowess of the islands of light below as they lay shouldered against the blackness of the water along their shores.

Visual symbolism aside, certainly no other city wielded the tangible power over the rest of the Earth that did New York. Other cities could affect economies globally in a technology-driven world, but there was none other that could essentially shut them down. There were cities that had more people, but the Grand Lady below was alone in her diversity. She was a snapshot of the modern world. Other cities were important to the modern world. New York was crucial. It was the one and only logical vantage point for Hart as the beginning of the end arrived. She and her people had proven resilient before, but this time they would acknowledge defeat and yield to a superior power.

He watched the timer on his wristwatch count down the last few seconds, vowing to kill those responsible should the timing be amiss and ruin the moment for him. There would be no need. As the digits reached zero, it happened. It was so startling a thing to witness that the plane momentarily bobbled side to side as the pilot jerked.

In one instant, the massive presentation of lights below was gone. New York City was as black as the waters around her. Chaos would soon reign on the ground, but from the nighttime skies above, it looked as if the nerve center of the world had just died. He couldn't see them from the Gulfstream, but he knew reconnaissance satellites above the United States were already transmitting even more staggering images: New York City was not alone. In the blink of an eye, the mainland of the United States had just gone dark. All of it.

Hart gazed out the window for about thirty seconds, closed his eyes in a euphoric state of satisfaction and said quietly, "It has begun."

7

2:12 AM CENTRAL DAYLIGHT TIME (LOCAL)
IUKA COUNTRY INN

WHAM! WHAM! WHAM! My eyes popped open and I shook my head. Not again. I fumbled with the switch on the lamp beside the bed but it wouldn't turn on. It was too dark to see anything through the peephole so I left the chain in place and cracked the door. Tark.

It suddenly hit me that the power was off. My boxers clung to me with sweat. I let him in.

"Matthew, we've got huge problems."

"I see that. How much dropped?"

"All of it."

"Good grief, the whole state again?"

"Not just this state, Matthew. All of 'em."

"All three?"

"All sixteen," he said.

"The hell you say!"
"The heck I say."

We found the security guard lying in a puddle of congealing blood inside the little guard shack at the entrance to the complex. "Tark, we're bad out of our league. We need to call in some help, and I don't mean the local sheriff. The FBI needs to be here."

He took the guard's gun from its holster, which was already unsnapped. "That's fine, but in the meantime we'll have to fend for ourselves. You know how to shoot?"

"I can shoot."

"Good." He spun the pistol on his finger and handed it to me butt first. "You take this one. I brought my own."

He reached into his pocket and pulled out a blue Smith & Wesson Chief's Special. Five shots, snub nose, .38 Special. Very nice personal defense weapon if you liked small revolvers. I prefer good automatics with triple the firepower. I had a stainless Beretta fifteen-shot 9mm at home, but I was a long way from the Oregon coast. The guard's gun would have to do, a Colt that looked to have been handmade by old Samuel himself.

Inside the control room, the night monitor was sitting on the floor beside his console, conscious but groggy. He had no idea what happened, only that he had a killer headache. Tark did a walkthrough of the building and found what looked like the scene of a scuffle in a janitor's closet, but nothing else looked out of place.

I went to the code console where Abdul Abidi spent his days and started digging into the code where the crack had been hidden that caused the earlier failure. This time wasn't going to be quite as easy. That module of code had been encrypted and asked me for a password, which was bizarre. If they wanted to flat out deny access, all they had to do was encrypt it and leave it at that. Why set it to pop up a password prompt?

"Matthew, I just pulled this out of the CEPOCS wire." Tark handed me a sheet of paper. I literally stopped breathing for a moment when I read it.

```
PRIORITY COMMUNIQUE
FROM: GREAT AMERICAN ELECTRIC
TO:
GREAT EASTERN ELECTRIC
GREAT CENTRAL ELECTRIC
GREAT MOUNTAIN ELECTRIC
GREAT PACIFIC ELECTRIC

BEGIN MESSAGE - AT 2:16 AM EASTERN
DAYLIGHT TIME THIS DAY, THE POWER
GRID OF THE UNITED STATES WENT INTO
A STATE OF TOTAL FAILURE. ADVISE ALL
CONTROL CENTERS TO COMMUNICATE VIA
SECURE ELECTRONIC MAIL ON EMERGENCY VPN
FROM THIS POINT FORWARD TO MINIMIZE
CONGESTION IN TELEPHONE SYSTEM. TAKE ALL
APPROPRIATE MEASURES TO RESTORE OPERATION
AND ADVISE THIS HEADQUARTERS OF ANY
SUCCESS. A NATIONAL STATE OF EMERGENCY
HAS BEEN DECLARED BY THE PRESIDENT. STOP
```

8

9:45 AM CENTRAL DAYLIGHT TIME (LOCAL)
HART COMPLEX

Jana watched Dane stow the single-engine Beech Bonanza in the hangar, then swallow a couple of pills as he walked back outside.

"What now?" she said.

"We wait for the boss. When he gets here, we stick to the plan."

They sat on the ground beside the hangar and waited, neither speaking. Within a half-hour the Gulfstream appeared on the horizon. Three minutes later, the pilot floated the sleek jet onto the runway and taxied to the hangar.

"Why is this woman here?" Hart said as soon as he stepped off the plane and saw Jana standing beside Dane.

"She's a nurse. We lost the one we had on staff here, so I brought her with me as a replacement."

"Brought her from where, Mr. Christian?"

"Mississippi."

"I see." Hart turned to Jana. "Within the realm of medical technology, what does the term CBC refer to?"

"Complete blood count." Something about Hart's eyes terrified her.

"And within a complete blood count, what primary parameter might return a value of fifteen thousand?"

"White cell count."

"Assuming a white blood cell count of fifteen thousand, what might we infer about the patient?"

"They probably have an infection of some sort." Did the man never blink?

"Very well. What is your name?"

"Jane Ashley."

"I assume it is Miss Ashley?"

"Yes, sir." Dane seemed to soften a bit en route, but not enough to land the plane and let her go. He explained the ruse and advised her to be convincing if she wanted to live. She couldn't use her real name for fear Hart would know of Brett's involvement and recognize the name. Jane Ashley would be easy to remember; Ashley was her mother's maidn name and she had spent a lifetime saying, "It's Jana, not Jane." According to Dane, Hart also didn't allow married workers or volunteers, no room for distractions from pure loyalty. Since she was indeed a nurse there would be no problem with that aspect; she only hoped Hart didn't find out it was Dane who had given the order for the existing nurse to be transferred immediately to what he referred to as the L.A. branch. All she wanted was to survive long enough to escape the nightmare she had fallen into.

"Your social security number, Miss Ashley?"

"Excuse me?" Her mind reeled. She couldn't give him the real thing or he could find out who she was. But what if she made up one and he checked on it? Surely he wouldn't go to that much trouble. Dane looked calm.

"Your social security number, Miss Ashley. It is not a difficult question for someone of your intelligence."

"Four five nine—"

"Let me see your identification."

"She didn't have time to bring anything, sir," Dane said.

Jana tried to hide the fear that made her want to break out in a desperate run. She held her hands together in an attempt to stop the trembling. Hart looked down, then grabbed her hand and examined it.

He released her hand and turned to Dane. "Come with me, Mr. Christian." Dane followed him into the hangar.

The woman's wrists are chafed. She has been tied up. Who is she and why is she here? Lie to me and you will die this day."

"Her brother was one of the Mississippi assets. It was too risky to leave her behind."

"And why did you not simply eliminate her?"

"I'm not sure, sir. I just didn't."

"I am beginning to question your mental well-being, Mr. Christian. Although I typically do not say such things, it is a fact that until very recently your performance was exemplary. Of late, there have been a number of what I can only deem to be mental lapses. You could have put everything at risk. I do not know what is wrong with you, but I demand that it be corrected forthwith. Is that clear?

"Yes sir."

"Lock the woman away. After the sun sets this evening, take her to the back of the property and dispose of her permanently." Hart walked to the waiting white Humvee and got in on the passenger side.

Dane massaged his temples. Hart had not asked where Riff was. Just as well. One crisis at a time was enough. *You can handle him just fine, Baby Brother.*

A short drive later, Dane turned onto the drive that led to the security gate. Less than a hundred people had the credentials necessary to make it through the gate and to the center of the two thousand acre spread, but if anyone could have approached the buildings at the core, their innocuous appearance would have raised no alarms.

Situated on flat terrain, the large metal buildings looked like nothing more than storage barns. Farm construction projects don't garner a great deal of attention in the Midwest, and Hart had gone to great lengths to see that his was no different. The fields abounded with pampered soybeans and cornstalks, and a smattering of tractors, combines, and other agricultural equipment decorated the grounds near the three buildings. There was even a barn and corral with horses milling about, including a spectacular solid white one. The illusion of an ordinary farm in the heartland was convincing.

Dane touched his key fob to a reader, entered a seven digit code into a keypad and stepped up to a retina scanner. Hart waited with hands clasped in front of him as mammoth doors slid quietly back into the walls to provide a walkway into the hardened command center. Dane stepped aside for Hart to enter first, Street Sweeper—fully loaded with a dozen 12-gauge 00 buckshot rounds—hung over his shoulder, eyes scanning for the slightest irregularity. Once Hart was safely in, he stepped inside with Jana in tow and pressed a large red button that closed the concrete doors behind them. Once inside, the cozy farm illusion gave way to a different reality. The corrugated metal walls served only as a shell for the reinforced concrete structure inside.

Every wall, every square inch of floor, and every visible fixture was black. A black valance ran the upper edge of the walls, concealing hundreds of feet of neon tubing that cast a hellish orange glow against the black girders and electrical conduits above. Visibly energized by the transition from the placid faux farm outside to the techno-fervor within, Hart closed his eyes for a moment, drew a deep breath, then walked to a small tower in the middle of the cavernous room.

While he made his way up the short stairway, an eerie quiet spread over the facility as seventy-three workers—all clad in black lab coats—turned their attention away from the black consoles and computer screen and to their leader on the elevated platform.

He stepped to a microphone and began to speak. "Faithful servants, I am here to thank you for a job well done. The Glorious Beginning was glorious indeed." He paused briefly as a crescendo of cheers began to erupt from those gathered around him, then raised a finger to his lips, silencing the captive flock. "Operation White Horse was a resounding success.

"You have all been trained for what lies ahead, and I am confident you will conduct yourselves admirably. Security is to be at maximum during these remaining seven days. No contact whatsoever between this facility and the outside is to take place, beyond what is directly necessary for implementation of the distraction events. Thank you all."

He stepped back from the microphone and made his way down the stairs amid a clamor of cheers and applause. On the floor, he walked through the facility, shaking hands with some of the volunteers, hugging others, working his away through the crowd like a campaigning politician until each one had been warmly greeted.

The inner diameter of the concrete tube was five feet, the pneumatically driven elevator inside it built on the same principle as the hard plastic cylinders that whisk back and forth between bank tellers and their drive-through customers. No cables to break. No gears or pulleys to be exposed to topside trauma. The air compressors that pressurized the chamber for lift and controlled descent were buried deep below the surface, along with the generators to power them and everything else in the subterranean fortress. Huge underground tanks were filled with enough diesel to run the generators for years if need be.

The transport tube was an ingenious design, with redundant radio transmitters inside the elevator-cylinder to control the entire mechanism. Iris-style aperture doors built of inch-thick steel plates were stationed every hundred feet, automatically closing to seal the tube as the cylinder passed them on its downward trek, and automatically opening when it came up.

The mechanisms to drive these safety diaphragms were located below, eliminating exposure to any aboveground risk. The walls of the shaft were two and a half feet of heavily reinforced concrete. At the bottom of the shaft, a quarter-mile under the topsoil of the Nebraska farmland, lay Hart's private chambers.

With his loathsome parents out of the way and an unlucky gardener convicted of their murders, young Abraham had begun to seek his destiny, feeling, knowing, that he was to be a part of something great, something so wondrous as to change the very course of history. A multi-billion dollar inheritance provided a great deal of freedom for destiny seeking.

The nightmares went on for years, several of them recurring: pieces of his parents reassembling themselves on the kitchen floor and chasing him through the house, a serpentine razor strap that talked in his father's voice as it slithered on the floor, and most frequently, being chased through a void of darkness, able to see a brilliant point of light in the distance that he could never reach no matter how hard he ran toward it. Over time he came to understand that the dark/light dream was not a nightmare at all, but rather a divine revelation, pieces of a puzzle that would somehow be a part of his glorious future. Darkness and light, darkness and light. Keys. Power.

He studied intensely and traveled the world in search of something that would trigger the metamorphosis from random bits and pieces into a solid understanding of what lay ahead.

During an extended visit to Las Vegas, he reluctantly agreed to take a visiting executive from his company to a Siegfried & Roy performance. As far as he was concerned, tawdry American tourists were something to be observed, not actually associated with up close as they sat with mouths agape at the sight of parlor tricks. The man was a valued employee, however, one that he could trust to covertly establish connections for certain technology and materiel if need be. Abraham hadn't needed such things yet, but you had to be prepared.

As expected, the few moments of Siegfried & Roy "magic" that he did watch bored him beyond description.

What he had not expected, however, was that the experience would be the catalyst to gel everything about his future, everyone's future, into a vision of crystal clarity. The appearance of the showroom itself had started the final melding process in his mind and soul that evening. A dome-shaped room, the Mirage Theater was black. Very black. Black floor, black walls, black ceiling. The housings of light fixtures were black, as was the multitude of sound reinforcement gear that hung on black chains, almost invisibly, from the dome above. All the seating was black, though the welting cord around the edges of the black upholstery on the V.I.P. booths was made of gently glowing fiber optic material that added to the sci-fi ambiance of the room.

With the houselights down, it was as if one had stepped into a boundless void, suspended in space. He instantly felt at home and his mind began to work. The show began within minutes, but while his stupid associate marveled at elephants disappearing and whores being sawn in half, he sank deeper and deeper into himself. His thoughts raced as all the years of frustrated attempts to understand his place in the universe collapsed into clear understanding of what he had to do.

He closed his eyes and reveled in euphoria while the applause went on around him in response to the show. When his excited guest repeatedly tapped him on the shoulder and insisted that he should see the final scene on the stage, Hart's first thought had been to show his irritation by using the base of his palm to drive the idiot's nasal bone into his tiny brain, then watch him spasm quickly into death. Exercising restraint, he instead elected to open his eyes and look at whatever it was that was supposed to be so interesting.

The beauty of the sight illuminated his mind and solidified the vision that had been developing. Two dozen gorgeous white tigers sat perched on bubbled outcroppings of a clear acrylic dome in the middle of the stage. Their striking white color represented purity and justice in the blackness of the world around them, their strength the natural order of control.

At that moment, the vision became solid, the puzzle-piece fragments of the years coalescing into an intricate understanding of who he was and what he would become. A transition was in order, and the name was a good place to start. Abraham Hardier would become Abraham Hart, the old making way for the new, the past surrendering to the future. He had delivered himself. Now he would deliver the world.

Since that night, he had worked methodically toward the fulfillment of The Plan, and sought to recreate the ambiance of the Mirage Theater whenever possible. His passion was only fueled when he heard one of the majestic tigers had dragged one of the silly showmen off the stage by his throat. It all fit. Light. Dark. Power. Ferocity. The overwhelming predominance of the color black in the underground bunker/residence served as dramatic testimony to his effort to recreate that seminal room of inspiration.

His obsession with the paranormal, the supernatural, and everything in between was reflected in the trappings of the main room. Books and historical documents were everywhere. Nostradamus shared shelf space with a dozen other prophets of lesser notoriety but similar genre. A large group of works by and about da Vinci detailed the many years he spent in search of a hidden code in the text of the Bible. A much later publication by Michael

Drosnin told the story of the code finally being found by Israeli mathematician Eli Rips, launching a series of the same ilk by numerous unknowns. No less than a hundred UFOlogy books were there.

More astonishing than all the other categories combined were the enormous variety of Bibles. Bibles from every era, every denomination, and every translation. One copy sat conspicuously in a lighted glass display case in the middle of the room, a thousand-year-old copy of The Torah in its original Hebrew text. The ancient version of the first books of The Old Testament would have been at home as the pride and joy of a Judaic museum. To be certain, it had been, but money in sufficient quantity can buy many things from a multitude of nefarious sources.

At the moment, while his followers above worked like drones, Hart sat huddled over a large King James Version of the Holy Bible. Though he knew them all by heart, he pored over the words of its apocalyptic final book, absorbing them into his very soul, becoming one with the prophecies.

Without warning, like an explosion inside his head, he thought of Matthew Decker. His stomach seethed with acid and bile climbed the back of his throat. Hardier North America, the U.S. subsidiary of Hart's company, Hardier Enterprises, had been the early front-runner to capture the design contract for the power grid control infrastructure. Then Decker's bought-and-paid-for politicians stepped in and cried foul because Hardier wasn't a "real" American corporation.

Congressional hearings went on for months. Hart refused to attend personally but teams of lawyers argued on his behalf while lobbyists doled out his money in the backrooms of Washington. When the chicanery was done, Decker Digital had the contract. Monies spent chasing the contract were for naught. The loss in potential revenue was enormous. The humiliation of having the coveted contract publicly stolen from him was worse, and the delay it introduced into the master plan was unforgivable.

The infantile American media covered the progress of the affair ad nauseum and treated Decker like a celebrity afterward. "Join us tonight, when our special guest will be technology wizard Matt Decker." "Up next, Matt Decker. Will his name join the likes of Steve Jobs and Bill Gates?" "Don't miss Matt Decker tonight."

Vile blather it was, even reliving it as a memory, but he closed his eyes and took deep relaxation breaths, shaping his hatred for Decker into worthwhile passion. Decker failed to comprehend what the Glorious Beginning was even about, much less stop it. Now it was time to toy with Mr. Decker, to enjoy his demise the way a beer-drinking American slob might enjoy a football game.

The irony was a thing of beauty: Decker would play the game, trying uselessly to stop the Distraction Events. And while he lost battle after battle, time would march inexorably toward the spectacular *real* conclusion.

9

10:20 AM CENTRAL DAYLIGHT TIME (LOCAL)
GREAT CENTRAL ELECTRIC

Trying to break into my own code was an unnatural experience, like knowing someone was trashing my house while I stood locked outside. Abdul showed up about an hour after we got there and had been rattling the keys alongside me ever since.

Simple fixes wouldn't work this time. The malicious code had been inserted and the system locked down through a sequence of deep encryption routines, the very style of lockdown I had planned to implement as a security barrier.

"Maybe you should have constructed some back doors into the system," Abdul said while he entered a flurry of keystrokes that resulted in another ACCESS DENIED message.

"Most people consider back doors unethical."

"I am sorry, Matt Decker. I do not mean to say—"

"Don't worry about it. I did, but somebody bolted them shut."

"No one will know from me," he said with a wink.

The telephone networks, even cellular, were holding up pretty well under internal backup power, but everyone was trying to call someone, and the result was a snarled tangle of congestion. "All circuits are busy" was the mantra. It took Tark hours to reach and cancel the incoming crew he had worked so feverishly to line up the night before. Around nine, I volunteered to keep an eye on things while he went home for a shower and a quick nap. He accepted.

No one had seen or heard from Brett Fulton, which was just as well since he was useless for the deep tech mission Abdul and I were working.

"Where can I find James Tarkleton?" a voice behind me said.

"Mr. Tarkleton is away from the complex at the moment," I said as I turned around. "I'm Matt Decker."

The guy stopped in his tracks and stared. "I know who you are. Why are you here?"

"I didn't catch your name."

"Special Agent Bob Rowe, FBI." He flashed his credentials. I guessed him to be about six-four, three inches taller than me. I initiated the handshake. His was perfect, eye contact intense and unwavering—a little too intense, something else was buried there. His face and frame were lean but solid. He looked mid-forties and made an impression.

"Mr. Decker, I'm sure you can appreciate the gravity of the situation we find ourselves in. For security reasons the onsite privileges of all civilians, including government contractors, have been suspended. You'll have to leave now."

"Like hell I will. I was left in charge of this facility and I'll remain so until relieved by Tarkleton."

"It's not optional, Decker. Let's not make more of a scene than exists already."

"Agent Rowe, is it? I assure you I have the authority to be here. In fact, my clearance probably trumps yours."

"I seriously doubt that."

"I'm Restricted Data, about a notch and a half above Top Secret. What are you?"

"Leave this place, Mr. Decker. Now."

"You're wasting your breath. I'm glad the Bureau is here, and I'll be happy to work with you, but if you want me out of here you better start figuring out how you plan to do it. And you better go get some help."

He reached to grab me and instinct took over. Inside two seconds I had his arm twisted behind his back and was prepared to relieve him of his weapon should he be foolhardy enough to touch it.

"You know what the penalty is for assaulting a federal officer, Mr. Decker?"

"Worst case? A slap on the wrist and a fine I can pay and never miss, Rowe. This case? Nothing. I'm not just any contractor. At the risk of sounding arrogant, I'm the man the United States government wants on this problem right now and I suspect you'll find that out soon enough."

I let go of his arm and turned him around to face me in as non-threatening a manner as was possible under the circumstances. I looked him in the eye and said, "There are a grand total of two people here to work on this problem right now, and I'll ask you politely to step aside and let us go to work. If you have investigative questions you'd like to ask, you may ask them while we work. Is that a fair compromise?"

He didn't blink or flinch, but in his eyes I saw that it had been a long time since anyone challenged Special Agent Bob Rowe.

Two more obvious agents walked in and were headed our way in a hurry. A stocky man with a trademark Bureau haircut and an anorexic-looking woman dressed in a navy blue power suit.

"Everything okay here, Bob?" Stocky said to Rowe while he glared at me. Stocky's wardrobe gave me pause. He was the first Bureau man I'd seen wearing twenty-five hundred dollars worth of work clothes. I wanted to see his file for sure.

"Under control," Rowe said. Then he turned back to me. "I'll let you stay, Decker. For now."

"I appreciate that, Agent Rowe."

"You can assist."

"Excuse me?"

I heard a commotion at the door. The second wave of the FBI invasion hit, four scraggly-looking cracker types—hackers are legitimate wizards despite the misuse of the word in the movies—loaded down with computer gear. One of the Bureau's teams of criminal techs performing "rehab" work for the government as a way to avoid jail time. I had no doubt they recognized me.

"My people will be handling the computer problems now," Rowe said. I looked at Stocky, who was staring at me as if I were public enemy number one. Skinny was setting up shop in a corner.

"There will be hell to pay for this stunt, Rowe. These guys know nothing about these systems."

"You're a greedy fascist, dude," one of the hackers said to me. "Information should be free."

"Whatever," I said, then turned back to Rowe. "You can't be serious about turning this bunch loose in here. You could have at least brought genuine Bureau pros."

"They'll learn quickly enough. They may be a bunch of misfits but they're the best of the best, the real experts in this game." The label didn't seem to bother them. They were busy unpacking gear.

"You're a real piece of work, Rowe."

"People in glass houses shouldn't throw rocks, Decker."

"Meaning what?"

"The Bureau has a long memory. We don't think you're so much a technology wizard as a technicality wizard."

"I see."

"I thought you would."

Abdul's brow had scrunched up in a knot, his dark complexion reddening as he rose from his chair. "You are fools. Matt Decker is the—"

"It's okay, Abdul. Let's help them out," I said with a wink only he could see.

"Yes, Matt Decker," he said as he eased back down.

11:51 AM CENTRAL DAYLIGHT TIME

After seeing the crew the FBI sent, I was double-glad I hadn't mentioned the email to them. I shuddered at the thought of the Pierced Nose Gang running roughshod through my laptop. No, keeping that message out of their hands and minds was working just fine, especially when there was nothing to gain from exposing it. For the moment, 69 was a dead end and there were more pressing issues at hand.

"Mr. Decker, Mr. Tarkleton on the blue line for you," the secretary said over the intercom.

I took the call in the lounge, out of earshot of Rowe and his posse. "Decker here."

"Matthew, any headway?"

"No. The FBI showed up with a bunch of cyber-thugs and put them to work. They're giving me a pretty hard time about being here. Still haven't heard from Fulton."

"Are they crazy? Do they know who you are?"

"Yes and yes."

"Why would they not want you on this case?"

"I've made a few enemies in the FBI over the years, Tark. Nothing worth talking about, but law enforcement grudges run long and deep."

"I'm apt to make some enemies myself as soon as I can get back but in the meantime we have another problem. The administrator of the hospital in Tupelo is a friend of mine and he just called me on my cell phone. Their generator is still down and the part to repair it is two days away. They have patients who are going to die soon without surgery. We have to get this grid back up, even if we have to do it manually."

"Tell them to expect power in thirty to forty-five minutes." I hung up the phone. Maybe other hospitals were faring better with their emergency power, but I had to deal with what was in my face.

Back in the control room, the crackers were finding out they weren't quite so sharp when faced with state-of-the-art code instead of the shoddy corporate servers they were accustomed to plundering. I managed a few moments of pride until I remembered I was locked out too.

I leaned over and whispered to Abdul, "Every power plant in our district is still operational, right?"

"Yes. The power is still available but simply cannot pass through the grid switches to be in delivery."

"Let's get ready to manually engage Central Grid One."

A grin tugged at the corners of his mouth. "Yes sir."

"Dude, this is some radical code. You need to clue us in on this stuff," the head cracker said. He had neon green hair and at least a pound of metal in his face.

"I don't have time to baby-sit you. Besides, you're the real experts, right?"

Stocky heard the exchange and plodded over to my station. "Honcho, I'd advise you to start cooperating with our people in a hurry."

"We haven't been introduced yet," I said as I extended my hand. "I'm Matt Decker."

"I don't want to shake your damn hand."

"Suit yourself."

He bent down close enough for me to smell his foul breath. "I can't wait for the day when I slap a pair of cuffs on your arrogant ass. And next time you won't squirm away, you dirty bastard."

He did an about face and left, his face in a blood-red snarl, the tail of his Armani jacket flapping in his wake. Abdul looked at me with a questioning look but I just shrugged and said, "Let's get busy."

It took us twenty-two minutes to make the checks and route all the circuit bypasses needed for a manual override grid engagement. Impressive work. I'd have to speak to Mr. Abidi about a more lucrative future for him when this was over. If he checked out straight, he'd be a bargain at triple his current salary.

It was a risky move but people were in danger and I couldn't sit on my hands. I sounded the countdown: "Five ... four ... three—"

"Exactly what are you two counting down over there, Decker?" Rowe said.

"While your boys were jacking around, we were getting ready to turn the power back on. That okay with you?"

"You got it fixed?"

"In a manner of speaking."

"How'd you pull a bitchrod move like that? We can't get past the first layer," a cracker said.

"Imagine that. Go play solitaire, son. Abdul, let's go. Five ... four ... three ... two ... one—"

The secretary burst through the door waving a piece of paper.

"This better be important," I said.

"I think you'll want to read this, Mr. Decker."

The fax was a printout of an email, forwarded to us by none other than the White House. The sender's email address was all too familiar:

```
FROM: I14_696938@hotmail.com
TO: XEAGLE@WHITEHOUSE.GOV

To the President of the United States:
For too long, the United States'
arrogance has offended the world. Now
you have only begun to pay. Your country
will now be subject to a series of
retributory occurrences as punishment
for your transgressions and your
iniquity. For what you have wrought, you
will tremble mightily.
```

```
I trust the reach of my power has been
aptly demonstrated to all concerned. Any
circumvention of my Decree of Darkness
will result in consequences more harsh
than those you already have in store. Ye
have been duly warned.

By the way, what do you think of your
splendiferous power grid now?
```

Rowe was dialing the phone by the time I stopped reading. He apparently had some priority codes that moved his calls through the phone system. "Bob Rowe onsite at Yellow Creek. What information do we have on that email ... yes ... I see ... come again ... well, there's no need to go looking for him, he's right here ... hold on." He cupped the phone. "Decker, seems you were right. The Director just put out a bulletin for you to be located and brought in on the case. They're patching this call through to him now." He handed me the phone.

"Matt Decker here."

"Hold for the director."

Ten seconds later, he was on the line. "Mr. Decker, this is Keen Brandon, director of the FBI. Have you been briefed on the situation?"

"I haven't been briefed per se, but I've been here at Central since it all began yesterday. I saw the three states drop, I've seen two murder victims, and I've been here nonstop since shortly after the main drop last night. Unless there's something different going on elsewhere, I'm as up to speed as anyone."

"I see. Let me point out the fact that this email was sent to the President's personal emailbox, which has an address that changes daily and is accessible only to a minute number of high-level officials. There's obviously a well-placed agent in the system. Is there anything you can tell me that might help? This sonofabitch is obviously not through with us."

"The sabotage is sophisticated, very pro. Breaking it is doable but it's taking some time. We were just about to manually engage a grid when the fax came in."

"Exactly what does that mean?"

"We're going to bypass the automated systems and manually switch this area back on."

"In other words, you're about to circumvent the Decree of Darkness."

"I suppose we are. In light of this email, I'll defer to your judgment on whether to proceed."

"I want the President to make that call, Mr. Decker. I'll get back to you as soon as I've talked to him."

"Yes sir, Mr. Director. I'll await your call."

"Oh, and Mr. Decker?"

"Yes sir."

"Agent Rowe is one of our best agents. I trust he and his team are being helpful to you?"

"Yes sir." I looked at Rowe before continuing. "Agent Rowe and his team have been extremely helpful to us here."

"Good. I'll talk to you later."

"Goodbye sir." I hung the phone up and Rowe wiped the sweat off his red face with the sleeve of his once-crisp-but-now-soggy white button-down. He had pulled the suit jacket off sometime between eighty-five and ninety degrees on the thermometer at the front of the room.

"Look, Decker—"

"Mr. Decker, Mr. Tarkleton is back on the blue line for you," the secretary said.

Great. "Call me Matt, okay?" There was no need to rub his nose in it, especially since I wanted to stay in their loop as much as possible.

"Yes sir."

"Hello Tark."

"Everybody's ready here. How long before you engage the grid?"

"We've had a complication here."

"Do not tell me that, Matthew. I've told the hospital power is coming."

"We were getting ready to engage when a fax came in from the White House. " I read it to him.

"Sweet Jesus," he said. "I understand the bind you're in, Matthew. Just remember real lives are at stake right now."

"Tark, I'll do what I can."

10

3:36 PM CENTRAL DAYLIGHT TIME (LOCAL)
YELLOW CREEK

Our internal network was working perfectly. It allowed Great American Electric and all four of the control centers to communicate in the absence of external power or networks. Two-way satellite links and a sophisticated private tunnel on the Internet made it work.

"What's your name?" I said to Metal Face.

"Neo, dude. As in The Matrix."

How clever. "Fine. Neo, how about you and your crew work these email headers and see if you can nail down a source?"

"Sorry, dude. I don't take orders from fascists."

"Game over," one of his contemporaries said with a cackle.

"Bitchin' truth," said another.

"Agent Rowe," I said loudly without taking my eyes off Neo. "I seem to be having a bit of trouble with your team. Would you please explain to your flaming friend that I'm about two seconds from pulling his arm off and shoving it up his narrow ass?"

"Decker calls the computer shots. What he says, you do. Is that clear?" Rowe had become oddly cooperative since my chat with his boss.

"Lighten up, dude. Just yanking your chain; no need to get bent," Neo said.

"Work the emails." I slapped the printouts down in front of him. They murmured but went to work. I knew they wouldn't find a source but their depth of penetration would show me what they could do, and the project would also keep them out of my way.

Guys, the Emergency Broadcast System is coming online in a couple of minutes," Rowe said. He headed to the lounge, with me, Stocky, and Skinny close behind. Neo and his gang stood to follow. "Stay on the emails," I said.

Fox had the EBS crisis contract this year and their lead anchor was on the screen as we crowded into the room. "Before we begin our coverage, we have a request to pass on to everyone watching, or listening, since the audio feed is also available via radio. The vast majority of your fellow Americans do not have access to these broadcasts. Please spread the word to your neighbors as best you can. We're all in this together and we appreciate your cooperation.

"We're telling you what we know, as we know it. The United States is at this moment without electrical power. To say the least, this is unprecedented. Power outages in the past, even the worst ones, were confined to cities or occasionally a geographic region, but we've never seen anything of this magnitude. Yesterday, three Southern states lost power at the same time. We have no official confirmation that this national failure is related to what happened down South, but we assume there's a connection.

"We will be covering the situation continuously. Since we are now operating under the auspices of the Emergency Broadcast System, there will be no commercial breaks. FEMA, the Federal Emergency Management Association, has asked us to make it clear that steps are being taken to restore power as quickly as possible—"

The intercom announced a call for me from the FBI Director. "Yes sir ... yes sir, we're still ready to go here ... yes, there is a risk to the system with a manual override, but I think we can make it work ... understood ... goodbye sir ...

"We have permission from the President to proceed with the override of this first grid. If we can make it work without damaging the system, we're to draft detailed instructions and distribute them to the other centers. He wants the power back on and damn the threats of consequences."

I called Tark and gave him the news. Two minutes later we were rolling the countdown yet again. "Abdul, on my mark, five ... four ... three ... two ... one ... mark!" We simultaneously keyed in the final override codes. The command sequence scrolled across the monitors, ordering a series of twenty massive primary switches positioned throughout a seventy-five-mile radius to close their circuits. One by one they reported their status back to the system:

```
PRSW12 COMMAND EXECUTED—CIRCUIT CLOSED
AND READY  PRSW07 COMMAND EXECUTED—
CIRCUIT CLOSED AND READY
PRSW16 COMMAND EXECUTED—CIRCUIT CLOSED
AND READY
```

On the big Sony screen, Mississippi was still dark. Then I saw a flicker of green, followed by another, and another. It was working; the sectors were coming back online. When Yellow Creek's sector went hot I heard the throaty air conditioning units rumble into life and a welcome dose of cool air followed shortly. I found the nearest vent and stood directly under it as a smattering of applause broke out among the crackers. They may not like me but they couldn't help admiring our work.

"Nice job, gentlemen," Rowe said with a smile on his face.

Stocky grunted, walked into an adjacent office he had commandeered, and slammed the door. I looked through the window as he flopped into a chair. He saw me watching and quickly closed the blinds, glaring at me until his beady eyes vanished behind the slats.

11

8:22 PM CENTRAL DAYLIGHT TIME (LOCAL)
HART COMPLEX

Abraham Hart and Dane Christian stood outside the bunker-in-a-barn, gazing west as the orange sun settled into the horizon on a canvas of painted clouds. After all the fine work he and Riff had done for Hart, Dane expected at least a token remark of consolation to acknowledge the loss of his only brother. He did not get one.

Instead, he was again chastised for bringing a witness to the complex. After that, Hart had simply stopped talking and stared at him with those ice-blue eyes as they stood there in the middle of frigging nowhere.

Even though they were supposed to be on the same team, Dane was wondering more and more if there was really anybody at all on the Hart team other than Hart.

When he hired them a couple of years before, Hart had been friendly, charismatic. He understood how Hart attracted his gaggle of brainwashed believers. Over the past months, however, he became more and more distant, obsessed with the most intricate details, increasingly harsh to paid workers. The charm was now shown only to the volunteers. Riff had called them the worker ants.

After staring at the sunset for five minutes or so, Hart closed his eyes and began to speak again, face still turned toward the sun. "You are certain the Central device is ready?"

"I installed it myself."

"You have established communication with it from here?"

"I have. We picked up that grid override in Central the moment it happened. In fact, we knew about it before it happened. I left an audio monitor in place. We're listening to every word that's said in that control room. Trust me, Mr. Hart, everything's ready."

"I should hope so. But I trust no one. In my life, I have found no human being worthy of my trust. Not one." He again stopped talking for several minutes before continuing. "In fact, I have found very few even worthy of salvation from utter destruction. This world cries out for a new era."

Despite the warmth of the summer sun, his voice chilled Dane to the bone. And then for some stupid, bizarre, irritating, nonsensical reason, the image of the teenagers in the truck in Mississippi flashed through his mind, laughing, screaming, full of life. Just like he and Riff did in another lifetime when they were teenagers in an old Ford, circling the town square, revving the engine at every guy they met, Riff always on the lookout for the next girlfriend. Baby brother could always get the babes. Now baby brother was buried in an unmarked Mississippi grave.

Hart turned and headed toward the bunker. He stopped and turned back toward Dane. "Oh, Mr. Christian, I have decided the woman you brought with you will make an excellent concubine. Have her delivered to my quarters by this evening. Be certain that she is dressed in white."

Dane stood gazing into the peaceful sky long after Hart had gone inside, trying to recall the exact point in his life when his humanity totally disappeared. He could not remember, and swallowed four pills of some sort to ease the pain.

He swore he could feel the tumor growing now, pushing his brain out of the way to make more room for its deadly mass. Soon it would push too far. Would there be even one person to remember him as anything other than a monster?

8:36 PM CENTRAL DAYLIGHT TIME (LOCAL)
HART COMPLEX, PRIVATE CHAMBERS

"You are a lovely lady. Always do as I say and you will live comfortably in my service. You will naturally enjoy the time we spend together, but you are never to let that show. You are a servant to deliver pleasure to me and to eventually bear my children. Is that clear?"

Jana's life over the last day or so had been, to put it mildly, unsettling. She had found a dead man in her house, been kidnapped, watched the planting of a bomb near home, hauled across the country to God knows where, and now here she was in this black underground room with this freak laying out what, a job description for resident whore? As revolting as the thought was of actually fulfilling the duties, playing along seemed the safest way to proceed at the moment. If she could figure out what made him tick perhaps she could exploit a weakness. She smiled and nodded in response to his question.

"You know, you remind me of my mother. She was an American woman, blond like you ... " Jana watched Hart as he stopped speaking in mid-sentence and stared into thin air. After five minutes or so, he said, "Yes, I think Mother would like you."

Maybe Mom was the key. "Where is she now?"

"That, my dear, is a fascinating question." He stood up and paced the room several times, finally coming to a stop standing in front of Jana while she sat on a long black sofa, his face alight with enthusiasm. "While I cannot be absolutely certain, there is a better than average chance that at this very moment my naked mother is lying face down on a raft of thorny brambles, floating on a lake of fire within the sulfurous scarps of hell. If that be the case, it naturally follows that she is being sodomized by a horde of beak-faced demons."

Jana swallowed hard and forced herself to act as if it was the most logical thing she had ever heard. "Naturally." Whatever Mom was the key to, needed to stay locked tight.

Hart smiled and sat down next to Jana. She swallowed hard and clasped her hands together.

"What about your father, is he alive?" she said.

"Come." He stood up and extended his hand. She took it, all the while fighting the almost irresistible urge to puke all over the crazy bastard.

"Why, thank you." Jana followed Hart through a maze of dimly lit black corridors and eventually arrived in a room the size of a walk-in closet. He flicked a switch and the room was bathed in the otherworldly glow from black lights hidden behind valances where the walls met the ceiling. He pushed a button and a panel opened up in one of the walls, revealing a cubbyhole about a foot cubed, also lit with black lights. In the center of the cube was a glass display jar filled with clear liquid. In the liquid was a pair of eyeballs. Jana felt a lump well up in her throat as her stomach roiled and her mind spun. "Is that ... I mean, are those ... "

"Yes, my precious. Dear old Dad."

Jana, being a natural conversationalist, instinctively said, "May I ask why you keep his eyes?" The moment the words left her lips, she wondered if she had made a mistake.

Hart looked at Jana, then the eyes, then back to her, his expression betraying nothing. This went on for two or three minutes before he finally said, "Come with me."

After turning off the lights and locking the door, he walked farther down the dim corridor and into another dark room. He flipped a switch and Jana froze in mid-stride.

12

8:39 PM CENTRAL DAYLIGHT TIME (LOCAL) YELLOW CREEK

I looked up from my station and saw Skinny doing battle with a laptop at a corner desk.

"I haven't had the pleasure. I'm Matt Decker."

Unlike Stocky, she did shake my hand. "Julie Reynolds. Pleasure to meet you, Mr. Decker."

"Having trouble with your machine?"

"I can't get it to connect to the Internet, which means I can't file my reports." She blew an exasperated sigh.

"Mind if I take a look?"

"Be my guest."

Her Dell was running the latest incarnation of Windows and I had her online through the Yellow Creek network in two minutes. "There you go." I slid the machine back over to her.

"Wow, that was quick. Thanks."

"No problem. How long have you been with the Bureau?"

"I'm six months out of the academy. This is my first serious case."

"Well, I'm sorry we're all in this mess, but congratulations on the big assignment."

"Thanks. I was excited at first."

"And now?"

She drew a breath as if to answer, then froze for a moment and said, "I better get back to work." She ran her fingers through her hair. Other than being the size of a toothpick, she was attractive enough. And something was wrong.

"You seem frustrated. Anything other than the computer problem?"

"I enjoyed meeting you, Mr. Decker." She smiled politely, spun her chair back around, and started pecking on the laptop. I said goodbye and went back to my station.

By eleven o'clock nine of Central's sixteen states were back online and I had a rough draft of the manual override instructions. I started editing them into something distributable and Abdul kept working our remaining states. Rowe and Stocky, whose name I had learned to be Walter Potella, conferred a lot and said little to anyone else. Julie Reynolds pecked. The crackers were working on the email routes and making little progress. Far too little.

I laid my head down at my station to rest my eyes, but it ended quickly when my phone vibrated in my pocket and simultaneously my laptop said, "You have new mail." After a quick check to be sure no one was nearby I brought up my mailbox. It was from him.

Return-Path: <i14_696938@hotmail.com>
Delivered-To: x7ijljAweRRv
-deckerdigital:com-x7ijljAweRRv@
deckerdigital.com
X-Envelope-To: x7ijljawerrv@
deckerdigital.com
X-Originating-IP: [66.156.171.40]
From: i14_696938@hotmail.com
To: x7ijljAweRRv@deckerdigital.com
Subject: Spam?

I have had a wonderful evening, Mr. Decker. For that reason I will overlook your snide, childish, and insulting little email. But you will learn to treat me with respect. I guarantee it. By the way, your performance thus far has been most disappointing. I expected better of you. Shall I claim tomorrow's victory with equal ease?

Tark tapped me on the shoulder and I lowered the lid on the computer. "Can we talk?" I followed him outside.

"We have to stop this nut," he said, staring at the stars that bloomed in the waning twilight. "This country's in a world of hurt, and believe it or not, we're the front line, you and me."

I was having a tough time paying attention to what he was saying. The new email, with its clear warning of another attack, put me in a quandary with regard to keeping it to myself.

"The government's spinning its wheels," Tark continued. "It runs on bureaucrats and computers. Computers run on electricity. Bureaucrats run on rules and that approach isn't working. The FBI's investigation is running at ten percent of what it should be."

That yanked me back into the conversation. "Where did you get that figure?"

"I heard Rowe and Potella talking in the lounge after Rowe got off the phone with Washington or Quantico or wherever. They can't communicate. They can't research. Everybody's waiting for someone higher up to tell them what to do, and as a result nothing's getting done."

"What did you think of the email to the White House?"

"Had a biblical flavor to it. I still think the guy's some kind of religious nut."

"Most terrorists are."

"No, this one's different. Like I said, it had a biblical feel to it, not the Islamic stuff about infidels we normally hear. 'Transgression' and 'iniquity' are both used heavily in the Bible."

"What does the Bible have to say about power grids?"

"Just telling you what my hunch is, Matthew."

"I appreciate it. Didn't mean to be a smart-ass."

He tried for a smile but didn't quite make it.

"We're going to win this thing, Tark."

"I hope you're right, Matthew."

So did I. "I am."

Tark stood up when Sheriff Johnny Litman unexpectedly walked into the control room with a grim look on his face. "Tark, I'm afraid I've got some more bad news."

"It's not Peggy, is it?"

"No, no, calm down."

Tark exhaled. "What's the news?"

"Brett Fulton was killed in a car wreck last night out on 25."

"Sweet Jesus, that's three of my men in two days, Johnny. How come you're just now telling me?"

"I've been trying to call you all day, but you can't get through to anybody on the dang phone, and we've had our hands full trying to keep things calm."

"Anything fishy about the wreck?"

"Nope, the wreck itself looks like what happens when somebody's driving like a bat out of hell. They said he must've been doing near a hundred when he lost it."

Tark cocked his head. "If the wreck 'itself' doesn't look fishy, what does?"

"Well first, he had a forty-five auto on him. Not in the glove box or under the seat, but tucked in his pants like he might have been expecting trouble. We went to run the numbers on the gun and there weren't any. Serial number filed off smoother than a baby's butt."

"You talked to Jana to see if she knew anything about the gun?"

"I'm getting to that. Say, ya'll got anything to drink around here?"

"Good grief, Johnny. Finish the story." Tark roared for someone to fetch the sheriff a Coke. Abdul volunteered.

"Simmer down, there's a lot to tell. The hospital said Jana got off early last night, and I know she's been staying over at Brett's house a lot so I went on over. Jana's car is there, right? I moseyed on up to the door, knocked on it, and it came open. I hollered for her several times, but the place was quiet as an Indian tiptoeing on snow. Finally I went on in."

I saw Bob Rowe in his corner and it occurred to me

he should probably be hearing what Litman had to say. I walked over and told him that he might want to join the conversation.

"I've heard every word. Local sheriffs usually don't like for the Bureau to invade their turf and I've had enough head-butting for one day, so I'll just sit here and take notes," he said with a wink.

Coke in hand, Litman continued. "The house was a mess. Stuff busted all to hell and back. There was one humdinger of a fight in there. Lot of blood. No body, though."

Rowe had spun his chair around to face us and was listening intently while he took notes on a legal pad. Tark asked the obvious. "I'm almost scared to ask, Johnny, but where's Jana? I sure hope to heavens that's not her blood. That's one sweet gal."

"I don't know whose blood it is, Tark, and I don't know where Jana is. We've sealed off the house as a crime scene, and we're treating it as a homicide even though we don't have a body yet."

Rowe finally approached, hand out to shake with the sheriff. "Bob Rowe, FBI."

"How do." Litman took his hand, and the brief but crucial ritual of males sizing each other up took place. Eye contact. Strong-but-not-too-strong gripping. A contest that wasn't really a contest. "You're welcome to look around the crime scene, Rowe. If you think of something we've missed, let me know."

"Will do, Sheriff. I have a bunch of agents around here busting butt looking for clues and hitting brick walls. If you like, I'll be glad to put a couple of them on this for you. We can get some testing done on the blood pretty quickly."

"Thank you, Rowe. Offer accepted. I'll pass the word along to my people to cooperate with you. For now, I better get back out there on the streets and keep the peace."

I re-joined Abdul and went back to work pounding the keyboard. At five minutes after three, the last grid in Central went hot. We managed to do it without any system damage that we could detect. Fifteen minutes later I emailed the override instructions to headquarters and the other three centers. After a glance to be sure no one was around, I printed both of 69's emails to me and quickly retrieved them from the laser printer.

Tark was in the lounge, napping on a sofa, Rowe likewise in a recliner. I shook Tark and when he stirred I motioned for him to come with me. He unfolded from the couch with a mighty yawn and followed me down the hall, through the control room, and out into the starlit night.

"I need to show you something," I said.

"Go ahead." He yawned again.

"In confidence."

"Go ahead." He rubbed his eyes.

I pulled the printouts from my pocket and unfolded them. "Here. The first one came Monday night, the second a few hours ago."

He read them in the light of a tiny LED flashlight from my keychain, and was suddenly wide awake. "I take it you haven't mentioned this to anyone?"

"Correct."

"Are you going to?"

"I don't see that I have a choice. They need to know he's planning another attack tomorrow."

"What did you say to insult him?"

"I just told him to keep his spam out of my mailbox."

"Sounds like he's making this some kind of game between you two."

"Tell me about it."

"You can't think of who this might be?"

"No clue. Like I said yesterday, I have my share of rivals but this—"

"You know, part of the first one sounds familiar but I can't place it."

"Which part?"

"This." He pointed to the first line in the first email: Never more horror, nor worse of days.

"That's not from the Bible, is it?"

"No, I can't place it right now but it's not that."

"If it's from a well-known source we should be able to find it. The Internet's still crippled but with all the Central states back up, it's hobbling along enough for basic research."

"Dare I ask what the filthy secrets are?"

"I'll explain later."

He didn't argue. We walked inside, turned on the light in the lounge, and roused Rowe. "What?" he said.

"You need to see these," I said, laying the emails on the table.

He got up, stretched, and walked to the table. After reading them he looked up. "When did these come?"

I pointed to the first and said, "Last night, Monday evening," then to the second and said, "tonight."

"Did you reply to these?"

"Only the first one."

"Probably best not to antagonize him any further."

"Agreed."

"It's pretty obvious why you withheld these, Decker, but if you've compromised this investigation I'll have your ass."

"It compromised nothing. Let's worry about finding this guy."

"I'll go along with that," Rowe said. "For now."

13

8:40 PM CENTRAL DAYLIGHT TIME (LOCAL)
HART COMPLEX, PRIVATE CHAMBERS

This is incredible," Jana said, with complete sincerity. It was as if they had walked into a normal family home. A small foyer opened up into a living room complete with sofa, chairs, pictures on the wall, a television, magazines on the coffee table. The curtained windows appeared to be lit by twilight, though that was impossible since they were deep underground. A door in the back of the room led to a kitchen.

Hart smiled with pride. "Do you like it, my dear?"

Jana nodded and walked around the room, taking in more detail now. A few of the magazines were American, but most bore covers in a foreign language. Hebrew? She spotted a copy of Time and picked it up. June 1977. She laid it down and looked for more dates. They were all late seventies, most of them 1977. Even the style of the furnishings projected a retro atmosphere. It was a room frozen in time.

"Was this like the home you grew up in?" she said, hoping to draw him into a conversation where a useful weakness might be found.

"Identical."

"Why did you build it?"

"To memorialize the impact of two pivotal moments in my life ... " His voice faded as he looked around the room, a wistful look on his face, but also the most sane look she had seen yet. "On July fourteenth, nineteen seventy-seven, I came home from school, walked into this room, sat down at this desk, and did my home assignments. It was a day like any other day." He had moved to a corner desk and was gently stroking its surface.

"I was ten years old," he continued. "My father arrived home just as I was finishing my work. He seemed happy, buoyant. As I stood up from the desk to greet him, I accidentally knocked over this cup of writing instruments."

Jana looked at the desk and saw an overturned cup, with five or six assorted pens and pencils strewn around it. Hart stared at them. She said nothing.

"I always held out hope that such a violation might one day be overlooked, but that was a fanciful wish at best, one of many baseless dreams of a naïve child. Such an egregious act could not, of course, go unpunished."

Hart looked toward Jana, and for a moment she saw the eyes of a terrified child. The look faded. He walked to a waist-high table behind the sofa, gazed down at the table, then placed his hands on it. "This is where phase one of my punishment was administered. Father had a razor strap to which he had fitted a two-handed grip for more efficient delivery. I received fifty-three lashes that day."

"For knocking over a cup? Good Lord!"

"'Actions have consequences,' dear Father would say. "After the lashes had been meted out ... " Hart paused and walked across the room to a vertical wardrobe chest about five feet tall. "I would spend from one to five days inside the chest, reflecting on what I had done. This was a seventy-two-hour transgression."

Jana shook her head slowly in disbelief, mouth agape. What kind of monster treated a child in such a way?

"Did this happen often?" she said.

"Certainly."

"What about all the school you missed?"

"Father was one of the community's—in fact, the state's—most generous benefactors. Many knew. None interceded. Whatever academic work I missed, I made up to perfection or I was punished for that, as well."

"That's horrible." Jana's compassion was sincere. Hart was sick, but who wouldn't be. Sick or not, this was not a place in which she wanted to stay. She brought her mind back on track. "Since this happened all the time, what was special about July-whatever?"

"July fourteenth, nineteen seventy-seven, was the day that everything began to change."

"In what way?"

"Mother would often turn the volume up on the television during the lashing phase, especially if an interesting program was playing. I never cried, for that doubled the number of lashes, but the sound of leather on flesh could be rather distracting, you see. Anyway, pardon my rambling.

"The salient point is that I learned to escape into the world of the television. I believe psychologists would call that a coping mechanism. This day, the evening news broadcast was on, and they told a most fascinating story."

"What was it?"

"The night before, a rogue electrical storm near New York produced a number of lightning strikes that eventually caused a blackout across the city. It was really a quite extraordinary chain of events, a domino effect of breakers tripping and distribution components failing."

Hart's melancholy mood was gone now. His eyes shone with excitement. "ITV was broadcasting an American account of the story, including a remarkable clip that showed this massive swath of the city going dark in an instant. I thrust myself into that world and roamed those dark streets in my mind. I embraced the darkness, even looked forward to my time alone in here after that day." He had moved to the wardrobe cabinet and stood caressing its wooden surface.

"Darkness became my friend, my protector, my safe haven. That day also marked the end of my wasting time uttering prayers that were never answered."

"You stopped believing in God?"

Hart chortled. "Ah, my poor precious," he said, clucking his tongue the way a kindergarten teacher might do with a student. "Of course I did not stop believing in God. I simply saw the old man for what he was: obsolete."

"I see."

"No, I sincerely doubt that you do, because you have not yet heard the entire sequence of events. Shall I continue?"

"By all means."

"Life went on as normal until I finished my studies in Israel, after which I went away for my time of service in Zahal, what you would call being drafted into the army. It was there that I became enlightened on a few other matters. For example, I learned that my father did not really have remote eyes that could see me no matter where I was. I also came to believe that it was my responsibility to rescue my mother.

"After months of careful planning, I returned home for the first time and told her of my plan; once my time of service was complete, we could both move to another country, perhaps England, where I planned to attend university. Unfortunately, she did not share my enthusiasm. She slapped me for daring to impugn Father. At that moment I realized I was not only sired by a monster, but born of one, as well." Hart sighed.

"I'm sorry," Jana said.

"Thank you, but I dealt with the situation quite well."

"Oh?"

He started toward the facsimile kitchen that lay through the door at the back of the living room. "Come."

Hart continued to talk but as soon as Jana stepped into the room his voice faded to a distant chatter. She looked around in disbelief at another room locked in the jaws of time. While the living room had held its own horror stories, they were concealed behind a veneer of normalcy. Nothing was concealed here.

What looked like blood was smeared everywhere. Grisly chunks of meat and bone littered the floor and the counters, and on an island bar in the center of the room was the most macabre sight Jana had ever seen. The eyes in a woman's severed head stared at her, so very real-looking. Beside that was a man's head, but it did not stare. The eyes were missing.

She felt faint and backed up against the wall to steady herself. Hart kept talking but she didn't understand what he was saying. Finally he shook her. "There's nothing to be frightened of, dear. They can't hurt you. Just like they can't hurt me anymore. And this is, after all, a re-creation."

Jana willed herself back into a lucid state. She had to remain in control if she ever hoped to leave this hell alive. She looked at Hart. He was smiling.

"This," he said as he gestured to the room with a grandiose flourish, "represents the happiest moment of my life, for it was then that I realized that I was the master of my fate. Not only did I not need God. I *was* God."

DAY TWO
WEDNESDAY

And there went out another horse that was red:
and power was given to him that sat thereon
to take peace from the earth,
and that they should kill one another:
and there was given unto him a great sword.
Revelation 6:4

14

11:13 AM PACIFIC DAYLIGHT TIME (LOCAL)
LAPD HELICOPTER #4
LOS ANGELES, CALIFORNIA

Sure am glad they got the power back on," Captain Rusty Boskin said to his co-pilot, Lieutenant Hank Starling.

"Amen to that."

"I can't believe how quiet it is today after last night. You know, thugs remind me of cockroaches, living it up and raising hell in the dark, then scattering as soon as the lights come on."

"Never thought of it that way, Rusty, but I guess you got a point. Hey, you want me to take the stick for a while?"

"Yeah, thanks."

Starling took the cyclic control and banked the little Huey west, flying the grids, criss-crossing the city at fifteen hundred feet above ground level while Boskin watched the ground for signs of traffic trouble and monitored the radio for calls from dispatch. Neither man saw the Beech Bonanza single-engine airplane at their six-o'clock high position.

On the bottom of the chopper, attached with two strong magnets to the fuselage just aft of the cabin, was a stainless steel cylinder, eighteen inches long and four inches in diameter. A black box was fitted on the forward end with a short cellular-style antenna angled downward from it. A one-millisecond signal hit the antenna as the Bonanza made a tight right turn and departed the area to the northeast. Inside the black box, a circuit switched modes from receive to transmit, now broadcasting on several frequencies within the 100MHz and 900MHz bands, blocking both police and standard aircraft radio traffic to and from the chopper.

At the same time, another circuit sent a five-volt signal along a red wire that ran from the black box to the rear end of the canister. The current hit an actuator, opening a tiny valve in the tail of the tube. The pressurized aerosol contents sprayed out from the valve in an ultra-fine mist, the wash of the helicopter's rotor blades blasting it down and out in a reddish plume that spread thinner and thinner as it fell to the ground. Above and for'ard, Rusty Boskin and Hank Starling continued to enjoy an unusually quiet day as they canvassed the skies of Los Angeles, covering the city in the same thorough and conscientious manner that they always did.

On the ground, businesses were again open and Los Angeles was returning to normal. Donna Madsen waited in line at a gas station with Zack and Michelle in the rear of the Dodge Caravan.

"Mommy, Michelle won't give me back my red crayon."

"It's my crayon."

"Is not!"

"Is too!"

Donna turned around to face them. "If you two can't play nicely, we're not going to Disneyland." The bickering stopped and Donna turned back around. She looked in the rearview mirror and saw four-year-old Zack stuck his tongue out at his sister, a year older. Someone at the front of the line finished fueling and the line moved forward one car space. Donna cranked the air conditioning a notch higher and wished her husband Steve could have gotten the day off to go with them.

"Mommy, look at the helicopter," Michelle said.

"That's nice, honey." Donna had seen a million helicopters and had no desire to see another one right now. She just wanted out of this line.

"It's smoking," Michelle said.

"That's not smoke," Zack said. "Smoke ain't red."

"Zack Madsen, don't let me hear you say 'ain't' again. You're supposed to say smoke is not red."

"See, Michelle? Mommy says smoke is not red too. Told you so."

"Well it looks like smoke. Doesn't it, Mommy?"

Donna finally looked out the window to see what they were talking about and saw the helicopter flying in a line parallel to the street they were on, about a hundred yards to the left and by now a quarter-mile in front of them. It was leaving what looked like a cloud of red dust in its path that drifted down. The dust was just reaching the ground across the street, where there was a park filled with people enjoying a mild day of Southern California sun.

As the dust settled into the park, people began grabbing their throats. Not just some of the people. All of them. She rolled down her window to get a better view and heard screams. People were rolling on the ground, clawing at their faces, thrashing about in violent spasms. At the front edge of the park, a man on the ground rolled into the street right in front of a car. Kerthump-kerthump. She gasped in horror. Now other people were running out into the street. Cars were shrieking to a stop and the sounds of vehicles hitting each other filled the air along with the screams.

It finally dawned on her that the red dust was causing this. She frantically rolled up her window, turned the air conditioning off, and pulled the minivan out of the gas line. The helicopter was far ahead of them now, but it was turning around and would soon be coming back toward them. She pulled out into the street and weaved a u-turn through the wrecked cars and people who were obviously dying. As she swung into a lane on the far side of the street, a woman ran toward them screaming, "Help me! Oh God, somebody help me!" Her face was covered in grotesque bubbles and blood poured from her eyes, nose, and mouth.

"Mommy, I'm scared!" Zack said. Michelle started crying.

"I need you both to be brave and quiet," Donna said as she tried to work her way through the horror on the street. "Can you do that?"

"Okay, Mommy."

"Yes ma'am."

Donna finally cleared the worst of the congestion and floored the accelerator. They were going to make it. She fished her cell phone out of her purse and dialed 911. "There's a helicopter spraying some kind of poison over Santa Monica!" she screamed when someone answered.

"Ma'am, I need you to calm down. What did you say?"

In the back, as she had done a hundred times before when they were hot, Michelle reached up and turned the switch for the rear air conditioning in the van.

"A helicopter, it's spraying some kind of red substance that's killing people! Do something!"

"Ma'am, you're breaking up. I can't understand you."

Donna's eyes started stinging. Michelle and Zack screamed. "Oh God, no!" Donna said.

"Ma'am, are you there? Ma'am?"

After that, the emergency operator heard nothing except blood-curdling shrieks. Other operators were taking similar calls nonstop. One caller had the presence of mind to note the number painted across the bottom of the chopper. Dispatch tried frantically to reach LAPD Helicopter #4 via radio but got only silence in return.

The department had a number of other choppers, but the crews couldn't get to them without walking through the outside air. One valiant crew tried and failed. Forty-one minutes after the canister activated, Lieutenant Brian Hallow of the United States Navy arrived in Los Angeles airspace in his F-18A Hornet after being scrambled out of San Diego. Unable to fly at the chopper's much lower airspeed, the Naval Aviator made three passes across the front of the Huey and tried to get the crew to understand that they needed to follow him.

"What the hell is that showboat pilot trying to do?"

Hank Starling said as the Hornet passed in front of them in a blur.

Rusty Boskin shook his head. “Damn Navy jocks.”

Lieutenant Brian Hallow had his orders. He swung hard around and came up on the Huey’s six-o’clock, bit his lip, and blew the chopper out of the sky with a brief burst from his 20mm cannon. “Returning to base.”

LAPD Helicopter #4 had covered an immense amount of ground before the F-18A arrived.

15

2:15 PM CENTRAL DAYLIGHT TIME (LOCAL)
YELLOW CREEK

We stood huddled around the television as a stunned anchorman delivered the news. "The unthinkable has happened. About an hour ago, at eleven-sixteen Pacific Time, a weapon of mass destruction was loosed on Los Angeles, California. The details we have so far are sketchy at best, but the reports we're getting say that a highly toxic chemical gas, known in military circles as 'Red Death,' was somehow discharged into the atmosphere." He stopped talking and listened to his earpiece for about ten seconds.

"These numbers are certain to increase, but we're told that as of this moment, based on the population of the areas most affected, officials are estimating that two million Americans have died in the Los Angeles area. That's two million of our fellow citizens, dead. The number of seriously injured people that were exposed just slightly is estimated to be in the millions, as well. We now have a crew on the ground in Los Angeles, and we'll go there live."

The picture on the screen cut to the interior of a broadcast van, its four occupants clad in yellow HAZMAT suits. One of the network regulars was inside one of the suits and began to report. "To say the very least, we've never seen anything like this. The streets of Los Angeles are literally filled with dead bodies and wrecked cars. The gas apparently acts so fast that drivers simply died at the wheel of their cars. We're not going to go outside this van, obviously, but we do have a camera set up to shoot through the windshield so the viewers can get a glimpse of what we're looking at here. Parents, we strongly advise that you do not let your children watch this footage. Again, we strongly advise that all children be kept away from the television for the next couple of minutes. We'll start a thirty-second countdown now before cutting to the live camera, to give you time to move your children out of sight of your television sets."

Thirty seconds later, the picture cut to a shaky view looking out through the windshield of the van. The scene was like something from a disaster movie. As the reporter had warned, dead bodies were everywhere. The sidewalks were filled with them. Wrecked cars filled the streets, most smashed, many sitting at odd angles that they had come to rest at as they stopped, most obviously having stopped only when hitting another car or wall or telephone pole. The reporter kept talking, unnecessarily explaining what we were seeing on the tube. The close-up shots showed the gruesome effects of the Red Death gas;

horrendous red sores, each about a half-inch in diameter, totally covered the face of the poor soul whose dead face was being broadcast around the world. His eyes were wide open, the whites replaced by blood red.

The anchor kept a dialogue going with the reporter, getting explanations of how the crew had survived the calamity, what emergency procedures were in place in the city, and so on.

I watched a few minutes more of the broadcast, then followed Abdul back to the control room. Tark and the entire FBI gang stayed in the lounge.

"Abdul, take a break," I said when we got back to the console.

"I am fine and will continue to work."

I admire a tireless work ethic but I also needed a few minutes alone to do some snooping. "Seriously, go take a walk, clear your head."

"If you are insisting, Matt Decker."

"I am," I said with a pat on the back. He reluctantly walked outside. Now that Rowe had the emails, and had probably shared them with the others, dealing with them could get dicey and I wanted to know who they were. I was inside the FBI's internal database within three minutes and had Bob Rowe's file on screen. Twenty-two years with no complaints, not to mention commendations for meritorious service. Steady track toward major management. Unmarried and no ties. He was a textbook career agent without a blemish.

Potella's record did not have the same new-penny sheen. Walter Potella had a temper that had resulted in three complaints and one suspension during his fifteen years with the Bureau. Pay grade GS 12, which put his salary in the fifties. He came from a middle-class family, no ties to money, which meant he spent over two weeks' salary on one suit of clothes.

Fifty-two-year-old Walt lived with twenty-eight-year-old wife Tiffany--no, I'm not kidding--in Falls Church, so I tapped into the Virginia Department of Motor Vehicles. His DMV file showed two entries, a Range Rover and a Mercedes, both bought within the past few months at a combined cost of nearly two hundred thousand dollars. If data files had a scent, Potella's would surely reek with the malodorous stench of rotten fish.

I heard Tark and Potella coming down the hall and made a brisk exit from the world of covert research. The email came about five minutes later:

```
Return-Path: <i14_696938@hotmail.com>
Delivered-To: x7ijljAweRRv
-deckerdigital:com-x7ijljAweRRv@
deckerdigital.com
X-Envelope-To: x7ijljawerrv@
deckerdigital.com
X-Originating-IP: [66.156.171.40]
From: i14_696938@hotmail.com
To: x7ijljAweRRv@deckerdigital.com
Subject: Consequences

My Dearest Mr. Decker:

It is quite apparent that you chose to
ignore my earlier warning regarding
circumvention of the Decree of Darkness.
Reinstate the Decree within one hour
and meddle no more, or suffer more
consequences.
```

Underneath the text was a picture that looked like a frame from the video we had just seen on television. It was a ghastly shot of a man's ravaged face, his blood-red eyes open and staring right out of the screen. Across the picture in big stencil-looking letters was one word:

CONSEQUENCES

Rowe wasn't in the room so I showed the email to Potella and Julie Reynolds. "Nice of you to share this one with us," Potella said.

"You people didn't exactly ride in on a wave of cooperation, Potella, so why don't you knock off the hostile badass routine and let's work together for a change?"

"I'm just getting started."

Julie Reynolds, standing behind him, rolled her eyes.

Potella called some deputy director at FBI headquarters, who called the Director, who called the President, who called me. The process took four minutes.

"Mr. Decker, this is the President. I want you to shut everything back down immediately. All of it."

"Yes, Mr. President." He hung up without saying goodbye. "Abdul, what's it looking like in the other regions?"

"I am saying rough twenty-four states up plus our own sixteen," he said.

"Start bringing all our grids down, right now. I'll get a message out to the others to do the same," I said.

I noticed that Potella was staring at me, holding a file folder in one hand, slowly tapping the edge of it on the palm of his other hand. "Decker, I've got our people doing everything possible to trace that email," he said. Looks like he's turned this into a personal issue between you and him."

"I noticed."

"Any insights you care to share with us?"

"What's that supposed to mean, Potella?"

"It means that whatever you know, I want to know. And if you don't come clean, I'll bust your ass this damn minute for obstruction of justice."

"You've lost it, Potella. And considering the fact that we're all supposed to be working on issues of national security here, you're about a vindictive prick who can't put petty issues aside."

His fleshy face knotted into a swirl of angry red jowls and fierce eyes, and he started toward me. Rowe had obviously heard the commotion and ran into the room. "Potella, back off."

He kept coming and Rowe stepped in front of him. "Walt, back off right now or I'll have you removed from this case. I'm ASAC here and this is not a request. It's an order."

Potella spun and stomped out of the room, blasting a series of obscenities over his shoulder as he slammed open the front door and stepped outside. Julie Reynolds had stood up in the corner and had a look on her face that suggested a mix of amazement and embarrassment. Rowe slowly shook his head. "Decker, I'm really sorry about this."

"I appreciate you calling Potella off, but this is getting old. I do not have time to deal with this crap."

"I'll have a talk with him. The Director has seen both emails, and while he wasn't happy, he concurs that we don't have time for bickering."

"Maybe I need to have the talk with him instead, see if he'll agree to a truce until we can get this case under control."

"Suit yourself, but you won't get anywhere. Potella came to the Bureau from an old school police department. He thinks you embarrassed the agents that were after you, and by extension, in his mind you've embarrassed every law enforcement agent in the country. He's a good man but he's also a dinosaur. The cloak of secrecy around your case has done nothing but ferment the angry mentality. You obviously pulled big powerful strings and the agents who actually worked your case won't even say what it was all about. Although the brass obviously don't have a problem with you, you're like some phantom enemy among rank-and-file agents. And now these emails pop up. Potella won't change his mind."

"Just the same, for the good of all involved, I'm going to try."

"Good luck." Rowe left the room. At least he had come around. Far better to deal with one case of vengeance lust than two.

I turned to head outside and felt a hand on my shoulder. It was Julie Reynolds. "Mr. Decker," she said as she looked around to be sure no one could hear her, "I'm sorry, too."

"Thanks. You ready to tell me what else is troubling you, Agent Reynolds?"

"I'm new and I can't afford to lose my job, Mr. Decker. I'd be black-balled."

"I won't break your confidence, Julie. You have my word."

She glanced around the room again, then walked back to her desk in the corner. I followed. "Let me show you something I ran across while I was filing case reports," she said as she tapped the keys of her notebook. A document soon appeared onscreen:

FBI CASE NO. 6298-5534
LOCALE: YELLOW CREEK (MS) FACILITY
RE: PERSONNEL ASSIGNMENT

As per ASAC request, the following personnel are assigned to the above referenced case until further notice.

Barry Pearson - Technical Specialist
Marcus Givens - Technical Specialist
Margaret Drummer - Technical Specialist
Daniel Roper - Technical Specialist

APPROVED BY HUMAN RESOURCES, WASHINGTON DIVISION

"There's a problem here," I said. "The team that's here is all male. What happened to Margaret Drummer?"

"The problem is bigger than that."

"How so?"

"None of the people on that list are here."

"Are you serious?"

"Every person listed above is a legitimate full-time Bureau technician, not hackers pulled out of their bedrooms. It caught my eye because I personally know Daniel Roper. I managed to get an email through to him, and he hasn't heard anything about being assigned to this case."

"Then who are these people?"

"I took the liberty of finding out," she said. "Earlier today, while everyone else was out of the room, I asked their names, told them I had to do some benefits paperwork."

"And?"

"They're nobodies, Mr. Decker. All of them. Low-level hackers busted for a variety of minor cyber-offenses, non-destructive for the most part. All on mild federal probation."

I thought about it for a moment and said, "Now I understand why they were getting nowhere on the work assigned to them. They're—"

"—not experts at all," Julie said.

"Exactly. They were put here to fail. You realize what that means?"

"There's a mole in the FBI."

"No doubt about it."

"What are you going to do?"

"I'm not sure yet but I'll be careful that it doesn't lead back to you, Julie."

"Thank you. When it all comes out, I don't mind cooperating but right now I'm at the bottom of the food chain and I don't want to be booted out of here."

"Understood."

I walked casually over to the line of workstations where Neo and his merry band of incompetents were still getting exactly nothing done. After watching for a couple of minutes, I said, "How goes it?"

"Not, dude. This stuff is bitchrod hard, man."

"Keep at it." I hung around the area until I was sure Rowe was back in the room, then shook my head as if I didn't understand. As planned, he saw it and walked over.

"Problem, Decker?"

"Yeah, I need a word with you."

"Shoot."

"Let's go to the lounge." I headed that way. He followed. Tark was there, looking over system logs and glancing up at the television occasionally. "I'm concerned about the tech team, Rowe."

"How so?"

"They're not making any progress."

"These things take time, right? Not everyone has your level of expertise."

"I appreciate that, but let me be honest. This team is bad weak, not up to Bureau caliber at all." Never hurts to blow a little sunshine, especially when it's based in truth.

"I don't know what to say, Decker. Keep an eye on them and if they don't start making progress maybe we can get another team assigned."

"Fair enough." Rowe turned to leave and just before he stepped out the door I said, "Oh, one more question?"

"What?"

"Just wondering how this particular team got assigned. Have you worked with them before?"

"No, I don't know anything about them. I signed off on the paperwork and turned it all over to Potella."

"Okay, thanks."

"No problem."

He was wrong, of course. There was indeed a problem, and it reeked of the malodorous stench of rotten fish.

Agent Reynolds, what were you talking to Decker about?" Rowe said.

"Nothing much, small talk. Why?"

"I don't need to remind you he's a civilian, do I?"

"No, you don't."

"Good. If you can get something useful out of him, so much the better. Just remember that the flow of information is a one-way street. Are we clear?"

"I don't think—"

"Are we clear, Agent Reynolds?" Rowe's face had hardened, his eyes locked onto hers like a laser.

"Clear."

"Always remember that the Bureau is a team, Julie."

"I got it, Bob."

"Good."

16

9:38 PM CENTRAL DAYLIGHT TIME (LOCAL)
HENRY ROBERTS'S LAND

Henry, why you want to come walking out here every night?" Missy said as they strolled along the only clean-cut area on their six acres of weeds and briars, the strip maintained by Great Central Electric because of the fiber optic line buried across the property.

"I like to look at the lights flashing in this little box up here. When I was a kid my mama bought me a toy called a Lite-Brite for Christmas one year. It had all these little things that you poked in holes and they lit up real pretty."

"Yeah, I remember them things too. I didn't never have one, though. What the hell's that got to do with this box on a pole out here?"

"It reminds me of my Lite-Brite. That's about the best

Christmas I ever had. Daddy run off that next spring and it was harder than all get-out after that."

"Hmmph," Missy said, as she tucked a pinch of Copenhagen in her bottom lip.

Henry stopped at a square metal pole with a metal box fitted on top. A bright yellow label on the outside of the box that said GREAT CENTRAL ELECTRIC COMM CHECKPOINT C47. TAMPERING WITH THIS EQUIPMENT IS A FEDERAL OFFENSE PUNISHABLE BY A MAXIMUM PENALTY OF ONE YEAR IN JAIL AND/OR A $10,000 FINE.

He opened the cover on the box and pointed inside. "See what I mean, ain't that pretty?"

"If you say so."

"Lot of blinking lights tonight. Usually ain't that many."

"What happened to the lock that used to be on that box?

"I tore the damn thing off so I could see inside."

"I'll swanee, Henry, you're gonna get yourself thrown back in the lockup if the light company finds you out here messing with their stuff."

"Aw, to hell with them bastards. They ain't even got enough sense to keep the lights on."

"Wonder why them little lights is still blinking when the lights in the house or nowhere else ain't working."

Henry cocked his head to the side and pondered the question for a few. "Hell, I think I'll go over there tomorrow and ask them sumbitches about that."

11:00 PM CENTRAL DAYLIGHT TIME (LOCAL) HART COMPLEX

After spending the day locked in a spacious suite, Jana was once again taken by Dane Christian to Hart's living quarters. Three hours had passed without him saying a word to her. He walked the room, talking on a headset telephone, and made dozens of calls.

He spoke in various foreign languages during some of the calls, but on the ones in which he used English, she gathered enough information to know what he was doing. Jana had a Roth IRA that she managed herself, and in so doing she had learned the basics of the stock market. Hart was executing stock transactions, many of them. She recognized many of the company names as global blue chips, and also took note of the fact that every transaction he made was either a sell or a short sell. He was unloading in a huge way, hundreds of millions of dollars worth, if not more.

The calls finally stopped and he sat down in front of a computer. "Do you live here all the time?" Jana said.

"This is but one of many homes I own, my dear."

"I see. Where are the others?"

"You will see them all in due time. I am too busy to converse this evening."

"Sorry I bothered you."

"You are forgiven."

At precisely eleven o'clock, Hart looked away from his computer long enough to say, "You may go." Dane Christian met her outside the door and escorted her to an elevator.

When the elevator door closed, she said, "I'd really

love to know how much you're getting paid to work for this maniac."

"A hundred million dollars."

"I see. And is that money going to make you happy when you lie awake at night thinking about what you've done?"

The elevator door slid open with an airy hiss and Dane led her down the corridor toward her room without answering.

"Please help me get out of here. Please."

Dane stopped and turned to her. "I'm sorry I brought you here, but what's done is done. Nothing I can do."

"You mean nothing you will do."

He continued to her room and unlocked the door. "Have a good night."

"Yeah, it'll be a blast. Thanks a lot." She slammed the door, walked to her bed, and fell onto it.

Just as Dane locked Jana's door, Hart's voice came over his radio. "Return to my chambers, Mr. Christian."

"Yes sir."

Hart was working at his computer when Dane arrived. "You wanted me?"

"Status update, please."

Dane felt detached from himself, as if he were hearing someone else speak. "D-E-two exceed—"

"I am not a soldier and I loathe soldieresque abbreviations that butcher language. Do not use them in my presence again."

"Excuse me," Dane said, dramatically enunciating. "Distraction Event Two exceeded expectations. Over two million dead in Los Angeles proper, and we got lucky with wind distribution. Several million more were affected. The medical system is completely ineffectual. To put it bluntly, the entire region is in chaos."

"Outstanding," Hart said through a brilliant smile. "And the upcoming events?"

"I assume you handled Number Three tonight yourself?"

"That is correct. Continue."

"Number Four is on schedule, as is Six."

"And the Premier Event?" Hart stood up and leaned forward in anticipation.

"I received the updated data today. The professor says it will be accurate for at least a week, so we can start programming the target packages."

Hart's eyes lit up like a child at Christmas. "Wonderful. Where is the data now?"

Dane pulled a thumbdrive from his pocket. "I have a copy of the entire package here. Would you like to see it?"

"Indeed." Hart eagerly took the key and plugged it into a USB port on his computer. A high-resolution map of Israel filled the screen. A few keystrokes later, the image appeared on a large flat panel display mounted in the wall beside the computer. On the eastern edge of the tiny country, a jagged blue line running north-south marked the Jordan River, and underneath that, the bulging Dead Sea. Running roughly parallel to this border was another line, this one a transparent, glowing red. At the bottom of the screen, with an arrow that pointed to the red line, was a label: Jordan Fault.

Hart walked to the display and slowly traced—to call it a caress would not have been inaccurate—his finger from top to bottom along the red line on the display. He closed his eyes, inhaled deeply, then opened them. "You are confident the data is accurate?"

"Absolutely. This data was intercepted directly from

the satellite downstream and interpreted by Doctor Hilton."

Hart smiled. "And what of the good professor?"

"He won't be teaching anymore."

17

11:12 PM CENTRAL DAYLIGHT TIME (LOCAL)
YELLOW CREEK

"Decker, we both know your past isn't quite the All-American story it's made out to be. You've made a ton of money legitimately, but I know about the other business you ran on the side for years."

It took me much of the day to get Potella cornered for a talk, but we were finally having it. I would've normally spent the time and energy to deny what he was saying, but I didn't have any of either to spare, so I shrugged and said, "I'll tell you what else we both know, Potella: You don't have one thing that will stick. If you tried to do anything, it'd be for pure spite."

"Oh you were slick with it, I'll give you that. But don't get cocky. The people you dealt with have the loyalty of snakes. They'd turn on you in a heartbeat if it benefited them, and while I might not be able to get a conviction, I could damn sure end your days as a high-paid government contractor."

"That's a reach, but let's get to it, Potella. What do you want from me?"

"Three things. First, I want to know if there's anything to suggest this psycho is someone you've dealt with before. Second, I want to know what 'filthy secrets' he referred to in that message."

"And the third?"

"I want to know why you dealt with those bastards in the first place."

"If I answer your questions, what then?"

"Answer them honestly, and unless I find out you've done something totally treasonous, your case will be closed as far as I'm concerned. Forever. You have my word."

We walked the sidewalk around the control building, neither of us saying anything for the next several minutes. Mississippi in August is a miserable place to be. It was almost midnight and the air was still so hot and heavy that it clung to me. I wiped a film of sweat from my forehead and thought about Potella's offer. I could put myself in a precarious position by talking to him without the benefit of a written guarantee of immunity, but things like contracts and legalities seemed so unimportant at the time, almost surreal. What mattered was survival, and not just my own. I needed this guy off my back and on the same team. There was also the insurance of my growing cache of information on Mr. Potella. If he got carried away, it could probably be used to rein him back in.

"Well," I said, "first let me say that I can't imagine any connection between this situation and my work history.

My competitors are ruthless but they're not killers and I have positively no idea who this guy is.

"As for filthy secrets, he can only be talking about the things you tried to bust me on and—"

"This is a waste of time. Didn't take you long to start lying."

"What?"

"I know what the secrets are, Decker, and they don't have squat to do with what we tried to bust you on. We were after you for hacking into databases and cleaning up things for politicians and anyone else who had the green to buy your time."

"I know damn well what you were after me for, Potella, and I hate to disappoint you, but that's all there is." That wasn't quite accurate but there was no way he could know about any of the things I cleared from my own record.

"You make me sick. Did it ever occur to you that you were not just breaking export regulations but also betraying your country?"

"I've never betrayed my country, and I have no idea what you're talking about when you say 'export regulations.'"

Potella stopped walking and whirled angrily to face me. "You developed, among other things, an arms-trading network for terrorist groups, so secure that the C-I-frigging-A couldn't track it. Before your little exercise, we knew what they were buying and a lot of the time how they planned to use it. Once your little project became operational, we were blind as bats. That didn't create a problem with your patriotism?"

"Whoa, chief! You have some seriously bad information. I've never written a line of code for any arms-trading network. I think you and I are on entirely different pages here. In fact, I know we are."

"I have a strong trail of evidence that says I'm right and you're wrong."

"Like what?"

He opened the file folder and handed me a sheet of paper. It was a copy of a bank statement from Suisse Banc Geneve, dated a week earlier. The account number was redacted but the account was in my name. With multiple large deposits posted in it. "Potella, I know nothing about that bank account." I spoke truth. Switzerland doesn't come close to the Caymans in the no-questions-asked genre of banking.

"This came straight from the bank."

"I don't care where it came from, it's not my account; I am not and have never been involved in anything like this. Like I said, you have bad information. How long have you had this?"

"It was faxed to me today," he said.

"Look, I agreed to be honest with you and that's what I'm doing. Can't you see that somebody's trying to set me up?"

"I see you backpedaling, Decker, and I don't like it. It's obvious from the way you were talking two minutes ago that you're guilty of something. Now this song and dance—"

"Do what you want, Potella," I said as I walked away. I sized up the situation, deciding whether to drop a hint about the information I had on him. I decided to keep my cards close.

11:48 PM CENTRAL DAYIGHT TIME (LOCAL)

Tark tracked down someone he knew at a nearby bedding factory and talked them into bringing over several mattresses. They were spread across the floor in the lounge so we could catch naps without leaving. He was sound asleep on one of them. Abdul Abidi was a machine that needed neither food nor sleep.

I lay down on one of the mattresses, but even exhausted, sleep was slow to come. My mind wouldn't shut down. I knew intellectually that I made the right move by bringing the power back online, that there's no way I could have known a lunatic would barbarically murder a multitude as a result. But knowing it intellectually didn't assuage the guilt. I had been a party to the deaths of two million innocent people. Hitler killed six million and is held by history—rightfully so—as one of the worst monsters to have ever lived.

Innocent intentions or not, what conclusion would the world draw about Matt Decker? Should I have considered the consequences more carefully before being so gung-ho to prove what a genius I was? Did I want the power back on to help other people, or was it just one more battle for me to fight and win for the thrill of it?

In addition to the guilt, it had been a frustrating day. Between digesting the horror of the news from Los Angeles, then having to bring all the grids back down, and dealing with Potella, the day had been consumed. That meant 69 was still out there, and I was no closer to knowing who or where he was.

DAY THREE THURSDAY

And I beheld, and lo a black horse;
and he that sat on him had a pair of balances
in his hand. And I heard a voice in the midst
of the four beasts say, A measure of wheat for a penny,
and three measures of barley for a penny;
and see thou hurt not the oil and the wine.
Revelation 6:5-6

18

8:23 AM EASTERN DAYLIGHT TIME (LOCAL)
SITUATION ROOM
THE WHITE HOUSE

President Stanson was not known for early-morning meetings, but these were not normal times. He sat at the head of the long mahogany table, flanked on both sides by the upper echelon of American government. On the right side was his national security advisor, Rich Henning. Beyond Henning were the joint chiefs of staff, the top military officers from the Army, Navy, Air Force, and Marine Corps. Jonathan Golden, the chairman of the Federal Reserve, sat in the number one chair on the left. Past him were Keen Brandon, the director of the FBI, the FEMA director, and the secretaries of defense and state. White House Chief of Staff Arnessy paced and took notes as he listened.

Golden was speaking. "Mr. President, as you're well aware, the U.S. stock markets have naturally been closed for the past two days. Foreign markets, however, have remained in operation in an attempt to make things appear as normal as possible under the circumstances. The dollar has taken a hell of a beating against the Yen and the Euro, but nothing that couldn't be overcome once things return to normal.

"The foreign markets themselves have suffered some pretty heavy losses, with stocks of American companies that trade on those exchanges getting hit the hardest."

"Of course," the president said with more than a hint of impatience. "Move on."

"Sir, last night, about halfway through the afternoon session of the Nikkei, massive sell orders started hitting the desks for a number of major companies."

"American companies?" the national security advisor asked.

"No. These were all Japanese giants. Matsushita, JVC, Sony, and several others. Their stock prices had already fallen an average of around twenty percent over the past couple of days as a result of our troubles. We expected another round of heavy selling last night and I personally asked the director of the Nikkei to suspend trading until we could get a handle on this thing."

"And did he?" asked the president.

"No, sir, he did not. He said his obligation was to let the traders of Japan buy and sell stocks as they see fit, period. The trading started and, as expected, the American companies got slammed. What we did not anticipate–and rest assured they didn't either–were the enormous sell orders that started piling up on the Japanese companies."

"Get to it, John. We have a lot of ground to cover here

and most of it is probably more important than the stock markets."

"With all due respect sir, we'll find that the markets are incredibly important. You see, once those big sell orders started, others followed, and others, and others. Sir, the Nikkei crashed last night. Hard. It lost eighty-four percent of its value before they got it shut down."

"Dear God," the president muttered. "Give me the nutshell version of the immediate ramifications, John."

"I'm afraid there's more. The eastern markets like the Nikkei are the first ones open on any given trading day. If this had happened early in their session, the European markets probably never would have opened. But it didn't. The sells that started the slide didn't start executing until Europe had opened. And the panic spread, sir."

The President was on the edge of his seat. "For Christ's sake, Golden, tell me what happened!"

"Sir, the bottom line is that most of the world's stock markets crashed last night. We're looking at a worldwide economic meltdown and I believe it was orchestrated."

"If it was, can't we track down the source?"

"We're already looking into it, but remember that everything is now moving at a snail's pace. We're crippled."

"I don't give a happy damn if you're crippled. The people don't want to hear that their government can't protect them and I won't accept it. It's our job to protect and we will by God do just that by whatever means necessary. Now finish your explanation as to what we can expect next with regard to economic fallout."

Golden cleared his throat and continued. "It'll hit the more advanced areas first and hardest, but it will eventually hit everywhere. Our own system was already on the edge of a cliff. As soon as the news of this filters out, it'll fall off that cliff. There's not much commerce taking place as it is, but what goods are being sold will quadruple in price. We're talking twenty dollars for a loaf of bread, if you can find one left at all. And it can only get worse.

"Manufacturing is at a standstill. Food and perishables were already in bad shape and now they're going to be worse. Ironically, the population will for the most part deem traditionally expensive items like cars, appliances, and electronics to be meaningless and those values will deflate. It will quickly deteriorate into economic chaos. Mr. Henning can probably give you a pretty good prediction of where things will go from there." Golden closed his folder and leaned back in his chair.

"Rich?" the president said.

"Mr. President, economic chaos will turn into social chaos and it will happen almost immediately. People will sense that things are out of control and do almost anything for them and their families to survive," Rich Henning said.

President Stanson turned his attention to Bill Fremont, the director of FEMA. "Bill, how are operations holding up?"

Fremont looked down at his notes and spoke quietly, "It's not going very well, sir."

Stanson slammed his fist down on the table, rattling water glasses. "The entire reason for FEMA's existence is to be prepared for something like this. Explain to me why the hell your agency isn't doing its damn job!"

"Nothing of this scale was ever considered a possibility. We're woefully short on resources. We had five thousand gas-powered generators. We need a hundred thousand to effectively provide services. We're commandeering more, but that's not going well. People aren't keen on turning over their private property to the government."

"Commandeering? Are you telling me that you're going around this country taking generators away from the citizens who own them?"

"Yes sir. We have no choice. Hospitals and law enforcement must take priority."

Stanson shook his head and rested his forehead on his hand, speaking into the table. "God help us. We sound like communists."

No one said anything. "I want specific recommendations right now. The floor is open to you all," President Stanson said.

The chairman of the joint chiefs of staff spoke next. Admiral Bradley Stockton looked as lean and crisp as his heavily decorated dress blue Navy uniform as he snapped up out of his chair and looked directly at the president. "Mr. President, sir, I believe we must declare martial law immediately."

"Brad, how did I know you might say that?" The president attempted a smile and most of the others followed suit with half-hearted attempts to do the same. The moment of forced levity faded quickly.

"I'm a military man, sir. My colleagues and I are in unanimous agreement. Looting is rampant. Police departments are outmanned ten to one by thugs and formerly decent people who are being turned into criminals by fear. If we could flip a switch right now and return everything to normal, it would still take months to repair the property damage that's already been done. Who knows how long it will take to rebuild the confidence in our infrastructure and our ability to provide the 'domestic tranquility' we're so fond of."

Henning was rapping a pencil on his knuckles, head tilted to one side. The president read him. "Rich, what's on your mind?"

Henning turned to Admiral Stockton. "Admiral, you know I'm an ex-military man myself, and you and I agree more often than not. With that said, though, are we at a state of military readiness to accommodate martial law?"

"Of course we are, Rich. We've been looking at the possibility for days. Our forces are more than up to the job." The general in Army green was nodding.

"How much of the Army would it take?"

"It'll take all of it. Keeping two hundred fifty million people in line will take a lot of manpower and a lot of logistical resources."

"And if we do that," Henning said, "how prepared will our borders be to resist compromise? There exists the possibility that we're being set up, distracted as a matter of strategy."

The president looked to the Defense Secretary, Jonathan North, and arched his eyebrows. "I've seen no intelligence to indicate possibility of invasion," North said, to the agreement of the admiral and three generals.

Henning glanced from man to man, and finally to the president. "Sir, with all due respect to these men in whom I have a staggering amount of confidence, not a single one of our intel sources had the first blip on their screens to suggest that we would be sitting in the mess we're in right now."

"Good point, Rich," Stanson said. "Gentlemen," he said, turning to the joint chiefs, "I'm definitely not ruling out the possibility of martial law, but I need a few hours to think this over. This nation has never had tanks rumbling through the streets. I want to be sure there are no alternatives left."

"I understand, Mr. President," Admiral Stockton said.

The president turned his attention to Brandon. "Keen, what's the progress on finding this lunatic?"

A Navy steward walked in with a tray of fine china cups and a steaming pot of Navy-made White House coffee, purported by many to be the best there is. The young man went about his duty quietly with obvious pride, and all those at the table welcomed the coffee. Sleep was in short supply in Washington and caffeine was becoming even more of a staple than normal.

Brandon inhaled the aromatic steam and took a sip. "Sir, we have an incredible amount of manpower on it. At this point, we're working these emails, the one sent to us and the one sent to Matt Decker."

"And what progress have you made?"

"Not much but we've narrowed the origin of the emails down to either New York or Los Angeles."

"Well how very helpful that is," the president said.

"It's all we have, sir. I'm sorry—"

"I do not want to hear that you're sorry. For God's sake, man, our nation is in a state of catastrophe and the whole damn world is right behind. Do not tell me you're sorry. I'm going to start making calls to my contemporaries in Europe and Asia, and assure them that we are going to find and stop this bastard. And I want exactly that to happen. Is that clear?"

"Yes sir," the room answered in near unison.

Chief of Staff Arnessy stayed behind when the others left. "Hate to bother you but there are a couple of housekeeping issues to tend to, sir."

"Make it quick."

"The press are clamoring for a conference."

"For what? They're all shut down."

Arnessy shrugged.

"Denied. Have them pick a representative and I'll give fifteen minutes of face time. What else?"

"Do you remember Doctor Chaim Hilton?"

"The Israeli professor who helped us with our earthquake readiness research in California?"

"Right."

"Yes, I remember him. Delightful old fellow. What of him?"

"He was kidnapped about a month ago, and his body was found this morning in the Negev desert. I think it would be a good idea for you to make time to call his family."

"Of course. Any idea why he was kidnapped?"

Arnessy shook his head.

"What a shame. Anything else?"

"No sir, that's it."

19

8:45 AM CENTRAL DAYLIGHT TIME (LOCAL) YELLOW CREEK

Tark and I were the first ones awake. Even Abdul had finally given in and was sprawled across one of the mattresses on the floor in the lounge. We quietly brewed a pot of coffee and headed to the Control Room.

"Matthew, something's been bothering me and I can't get it off my mind. Why don't you believe in God?"

I was still on my first cup of coffee and he caught me off guard. What the hell. "For what it's worth, I used to believe. I finally saw the evidence that he's not that different from an imaginary friend that a seven-year-old might conjure up to keep from being lonely. I saw the light, as you Christians might say." I sat back and waited for the sermon.

"What kind of evidence?"

"My father was a preacher, Tark. He stormed around his pulpit and scared everybody half to death talking about hellfire and brimstone. Then he'd talk about the wonders of God, how he'd never let you down. Jesus was love, he'd never forsake you, nosirree. Just like most people in that little church, I believed what my father said.

"My mother died giving birth to me, so I never knew her. My father explained that while it was painful, the Lord works in mysterious ways. Being an organ donor, her death gave life not only to me but to others, as well. It was a stretch, but it was plausible coming from my father, as everything always was. Dad really was a great father, everything a boy could want, and he was all I had.

Tark was listening to every word, and as much as I hated this subject, for some reason it felt good to be setting him straight on the matter. Who knows, maybe he'd wise up in the process and reconsider the fairy tale, so I continued. "Dad preached Jesus and I believed. I sang in the youth choir. I talked less fortunate friends—ones who got the hell beat out of 'em by their fathers, ones who were lucky to get a decent meal a day—into coming to church with me. There they learned from my father that they weren't alone. Jesus was with them. He'd always be with them. It never did quite make sense to me why Jesus would stand by and watch some asshole beat up a kid, but Dad always found a way to twist it around so it made sense.

"When I was thirteen, my father was on his way home from visiting a local nursing home when a drunk in an eighteen-wheeler hit him head on. It was then that it became evident to me that there is no God. If he did exist, then why the hell would he let that happen to my father, one of his own, a man wholly devoted to the cause? The answer of course is that there is no God. There's only this right here, and we're in control. Good people, bad people, drunks in eighteen-wheelers. It is what we make it, nothing more. Last I heard, the drunk got religious and became a preacher, if you can believe that one."

"I assume your father was killed?"

"No, he's lying in a long-term-care ward in a nursing home, in a coma. As soon as my finances permitted, I had him moved from a state-run hellhole to Alpine Village, the finest facility in the Northwest. I've spent hundreds of thousands of dollars on every kind of treatment available from the best neurologists in the world. All for nothing."

"I wouldn't call it nothing. You've tried. What happened to you after your father got hurt?"

"Uncle Seth, my father's brother, took me in. He didn't have a pot to piss in, but he took care of me, and we got along pretty well. He didn't go to church, didn't judge people, and didn't sit around waiting on things that were never going to happen. He taught me that we're responsible for ourselves, period."

"How'd you get involved in computers?"

"That's an odd story. Uncle Seth liked to hang out at this local gym where a few wannabe boxers trained. He loved to bet the fights and thought he could get a better insight into who to put his money on by watching them up close. Well, I naturally hung out there with him quite a bit, and wound up taking some martial arts classes over on the other end of the gym. Turns out I had a knack for it, and I moved through the belts pretty quickly; I was pretty advanced by the time I was fifteen."

He smiled and patted his belly. "Unlike me, looks like you keep yourself in good shape. You still do it?"

"Just enough to stay loose. Anyway, I fell in with a

couple of other guys in the class who were pretty rough. The ethic of never using our skills for anything other than sport or self-defense didn't appeal to them. They were dirt poor and didn't want to stay that way, and I'd gotten pretty tired of it myself. We started our own little gang, called ourselves Trinity. Pop would've loved that if he had ever awakened."

"We started out small, doing a little shoplifting here and there, selling our wares on the street. We were afraid the merchants were getting wise to us, though, so we changed our approach. There were quite a few gangs roaming the streets, so we'd intentionally invade their turf and start a ruckus. They'd jump us, we'd kick their asses, then take every dime they had right out of their pockets while they laid there. The beauty of it was that we knew they'd never say a word about getting creamed by three guys because their respect would be crap."

"Good grief, Matthew, didn't they have guns?"

"Yeah, some did. Guns, knives, knucks, you name it. Youth knows no fear, and none of us ever got shot or stabbed. We took many a gun and knife, sold them on the streets. We were doing pretty well, knocking down a lot of cash. We also had a great time with the girls of the conquered gangs. Not forced, mind you, we weren't like that. Girls that hang out with gangs are turned on by power, and to the victors go the spoils, including those of the flesh."

"This is all interesting, Matthew, but I'm still waiting for the computer connection."

"Bear with me," I said, "I'm almost there. We picked out a new gang on the other side of town for our next conquest and strolled into their neighborhood. Started talking trash like we always did, but they never would make the first move. So we made it for them. It felt weird the whole time, because they didn't fight much at all. As soon as I reached in the first leather jacket and pulled out the guy's wallet, cops poured out of the woodwork. That new gang was a gang of cops. We fell right into the sting, like criminals always will if they push the envelope long enough.

"So there I was, sixteen years old, in jail, charged with strong-arm robbery among other things. I agreed to plead guilty in exchange for them treating me as a juvenile. I got sentenced to three years suspended, but I had to go to a rehabilitation center three times a week. Part of the rehab was learning a skill, and I chose some computer courses. I picked it up pretty quickly, and seventeen years later, here I am."

"Good to hear you turned your life around, and no one can deny that you've made something of yourself, Matthew. That's quite a story. Does Potella know about your arrest record? That might be part of what's in his craw, too."

"Nope, he has it in his head that I'm working with arms-traders, which is pure bunk, but he knows nothing about the travails of my youth."

Tark shook his head and smiled. "You made your record go away, didn't you? Don't worry," he said, "we'll let this be our little secret, okay?"

"I'd appreciate that, Tark."

"Not a problem," he said as he left the room to refill his coffee cup.

I sat there by myself in the Control Room, already hot and soon to be hotter as the merciless sun made its morning climb. I hadn't planned to blab my background to anyone, much less a Bible-thumper like Jimmy Lee

Tarkleton, but it felt good. I had spent my entire adult life fighting to conceal that past, to maintain my entrepreneurial image. Letting go and telling someone the truth felt good, like a dark cloud lifted that I didn't know was there. And I wasn't worried about it going any further. Tark said it would be our secret and I believed him. He stuck his head back into the room and said, "Come to the lounge, Matthew. I think you need to hear this."

The Fox anchor was on the screen, looking haggard and sounding spent. "Fox financial correspondent Bart Brann is here with me now. Bart, with the U.S. already in a state of crisis, how will these foreign market crashes affect us?"

"I finally managed to get a friend in London on the phone a few minutes ago. He's describing the situation over there as chaotic. The only thing we really have to compare something like this to is the twenty-nine crash, and our current situation is far worse than that."

"How so?"

"The first infamous Black Thursday crash took place on October 24, 1929, when the New York Stock Exchange went through a selling frenzy that shaved four billion dollars off the value of the exchange. Despite this colossal selloff, news spread much more slowly in those days, and so did the effect of the crash. In more rural areas of the country, where people's livelihoods were more dependent on their own food and livestock than on external factors, it took as much as a year for the effect of the crash to trickle down and make an impact.

"That's not the case now as we deal with a brand new Black Thursday. When something happens in the twenty-first century, the world knows about it instantly and people react quickly. Major financial events start feeding on themselves, spiraling into a vicious downward cycle within hours or even minutes. That's what's happening. The Nikkei crash began and instantly carried over into the European markets. The news was immediately disseminated to the people in those countries, and panic buying of food and other essential items set in. Sellers knew what was going on and began raising prices, some out of sheer greed, some because they had already gotten word from their suppliers that replenishment goods would come at substantially higher costs. In the same way that the downward spiral of stock prices took place, prices for basic goods were accelerating upward within hours. What we have in the end is hyperinflation on a worldwide scale."

"Can you give us any examples?"

"Gasoline in England is going for the equivalent of thirty U.S. dollars per gallon. A loaf of bread is fifteen dollars, a gallon of milk nine dollars. And all these prices continue to rise as people pay the prices and sap the dwindling supplies of these goods."

"What can we expect here at home?"

"It's going to be worse here because the United States was already in dire straits. Manufacturing is shut down. Deliveries are all but impossible because refueling of trucks can't take place. Planes have of course been long since grounded. Los Angeles, a major hub of American commerce, is in shambles as they struggle to deal with the horrendous loss of human life. And finally, let's remember that the power is still off and we don't know when it will be back on. Parts of the country were back in operation for a brief period, but the power went back off without warning. It's rough out there."

"Okay, thanks Bart. We appreciate the update and

we'll no doubt be calling on you again as this crisis continues to develop—"

I turned the volume down on the television set. "There's a pattern to all this," I said. "Black Thursday nineteen twenty-nine. Black Thursday now. History repeating itself. There's something here we're not catching, hidden clues we aren't seeing, a method to the madness."

"Nothing new under the sun," Tark mumbled.

"What?" I said.

"It's from Ecclesiastes chapter one, verse nine."

"What's the whole verse?" He had triggered a new line of thought. It was vague at the moment, but it was a beginning.

"That which has been is what will be, that which is done is what will be done, and there is nothing new under the sun. What are you thinking?"

"It's a book full of patterns and recurring themes. And you already think the guy is a religious nut. Abdul, I need your help." I was already on my way out of the lounge, headed to the Control Room.

"Matt Decker, I am pleasing to help you but my Holy Bible knowledge is most poor."

"Don't worry about it, just come with me."

"Yes, Matt Decker."

20

9:32 AM CENTRAL DAYLIGHT TIME (LOCAL)
HART COMPLEX

A myriad of cleverly concealed satellite dishes around the grounds of the complex collected and routed information from around the world into the bunker and down to Hart's private quarters. He sat in the darkened room, scanning through screen after screen of financial data that poured in from Europe, Asia, and Africa.

He planned the events of the previous night for years and it worked to perfection. Plan the trade and trade the plan. Through the use of dozens of cash-laden shell institutions scattered around the world, he had single-handedly triggered a worldwide state of financial meltdown. His sale of hundreds of thousands of shares each of different key corporations started a slide in stock prices that would live in infamy.

He didn't actually own the shares before selling them, instead using a common trading technique known as selling short. A seller relies on his financial strength to borrow shares to sell, then waits for the price to fall and buys shares on the open market at a lower price. Those shares are then used to pay back the borrowed shares and he reaps the difference between the price he sold at and the lower price at which he bought the shares to cover his obligation.

Through the use of this technique, Abraham Hart had booked just north of thirty billion dollars in profits the night before. More importantly, his crisis, and thereby the scope of his power, had surged beyond the borders of the United States. Others had spent years babbling about a New World Order. He had just installed one, and he was only getting started.

He smiled as he thought about how powerless the mighty United States was against him. His sources–he had them everywhere–were certain that those in charge of the investigation were essentially clueless as to who he was or what lay ahead. The plan was proceeding. Nothing could stop it. No one could stop it. They were in a frenzy, playing catch-up while the clock ticked ever closer to the most awesome display of power in the history of this pathetic world.

9:35 AM CENTRAL DAYLIGHT TIME (LOCAL) YELLOW CREEK

"Abdul, I need you to pull the system logs from Monday afternoon, the first grid failures," I said.

I fired up my laptop and went online through the Yellow Creek network. From a commercial standpoint the Internet was dead but the Fox News site was operational and I hoped that they'd have the information I needed. Even though they had gone to a bare-bones text format for the sake of speed, the site was still slow.

Tark, Rowe, and Stocky Potella had followed us into the control room. "What are you looking for?" Rowe said.

"I have a hunch about a pattern. I need a few minutes online to verify it."

Abdul rattled away on his keyboard and I heard the printer start cranking out logs. Four clicks and six minutes into the surf, I hit pay dirt. They had a simple time line of the crisis events—

"You have urgent mail," my laptop blared. I clicked into my email program and saw a lone message in the inbox. Its subject line paralyzed me: YOUR FATHER IS NOT LOOKING WELL.

"Sweet Jesus," Tark said. Rowe and Potella came over and looked on over my shoulder. After about ten seconds I started breathing again and opened the email:

```
Return-Path: <i14_696938@hotmail.com>
Delivered-To: x7ijljAweRRv
-deckerdigital:com-x7ijljAweRRv@
deckerdigital.com
X-Envelope-To: x7ijljawerrv@
deckerdigital.com
X-Originating-IP: [66.156.171.40]
From: i14_696938@hotmail.com
To: x7ijljAweRRv@deckerdigital.com
Subject: Change
```

```
My Dearest Mr. Decker,

I too have a father who is but a relic
of what he once was, much the same as
the unfortunate soul who lies in Alpine
Village Suite 321 day after silent day.
Maybe it would be best for all concerned
should he be released from the tentacles
of vegetative captivity in which you
keep him bound.

I have decided to implement a new
rule for our ongoing challenge. You
will no longer be allowed to conduct
investigation via the Internet. I have
provided you with more clues than you
deserve. Use them.
```

I spun my chair around to face Rowe and Potella. "I want protection for my father."

"Exactly where is Alpine Village?" Rowe said after reading the email.

"Gold Coast, Oregon. Your people won't have any trouble finding it."

"I'll take care of it." He picked up a telephone and punched in a series of numbers. Moments later he was barking instructions at someone.

Julie Reynolds mouthed a silent "sorry" from her perch in the corner of the room. Even Potella had an unnatural look on his face that could have been construed as at least a pretense of compassion. I rubbed my temples in a vain attempt to chase away the vision of someone holding a pillow over Dad's face as he lay in his bed, unable to fight or even scream. I finally turned back around to my notebook and started typing.

"What are you doing there, Decker?" Potella said. I kept typing.

Rowe hung up the phone. "San Francisco field office is contacting the local authorities in Gold Coast."

"I appreciate it. Let me know the moment you've heard back from them." I shut the notebook and walked outside.

I thought it couldn't be any hotter outside than it was in the control room. I was wrong. It had to be over a hundred degrees with not the slightest whiff of a breeze, the humidity so thick you could literally feel the air. There was a walking track along the edge of the waterway, and I made my way toward it, trying to clear my head and come up with a plan.

I smelled the pipe before I heard him. "Matthew, wait up." I stopped and waited for Tark to catch up with me.

"Potella's raising Cain in there. Wanted to look at your computer to see what you were typing but Rowe backed him down."

"It's nice of Rowe to look out for me, but it's not necessary. My machine will ask for a twelve-character password when the lid is raised. But I'll tell you this," I said, emphasizing each word with a stab of my finger in the air, "I have had about enough of Potella."

"I want you to know I'm praying for you."

"You know something, Tark? When I showed up here, I thought you were an asshole. I was wrong. I've really come to like you over the past few days, which is something I don't do very often. With that said, I'll ask you again to lay off the preaching. If you think you're going to win me over and bring me back into the fold, you're mistaken. I can't stop you from wasting your time, but use it on somebody else. I have enough going on in the real world right now."

"You need God's help, Matthew. Right now. I feel it, really strong. The forces of evil are lining up against you and nobody, I mean nobody, but God will be able to save you."

I rolled my eyes and regretted it when they squarely caught the sun. I had no time for this. Just as I drew a breath to lay into him, he reached over and squeezed me on the shoulder—the way my father used to do when I was having a hard time—and I lost the urge. The stress was piling up but there was no point in taking it out on someone trying to help, no matter how misguided they were. "Thanks for your concern. I just need to clear my head."

"What do you plan to do about Potella?"

"I think he's dirty and before long I'm going to turn the tables on him.

"What makes you think that?"

"He dresses like he makes a half-million a year, while he really makes fifty grand. He and his young wife drive two hundred thousand dollars worth of vehicles. The man reeks."

"How'd you find all that out?"

"I tapped his Bureau file. He's also the one who brought that gang of snot-nosed hoodlums in as supposed experts. Between all that and this arms-trading nonsense he's trying to hold over my head, I've had it."

"What are you going to do?"

"I desperately want to take him down but I need to watch him a little longer and see where he might lead us. It's like 69 knew the moment I went online."

"You think Potella's feeding information to him?"

"He has a laptop set up in that side office, and it only takes a minute to send an email."

Tark thought it through. "Possible, but how can you know for sure?"

"I just installed a packet sniffer on the network. I'll be able to analyze any traffic going in or out of here now."

"Good idea. Keep me posted and let me know if I can help."

"Will do."

Rowe approached me as soon as we walked back inside. "Gold Coast P.D. confirms that one Nathaniel Decker is safe and sound in room three-twenty-one. There's been no suspicious activity around the nursing home, but they're keeping an eye on the place until we can get a pair of agents up there from Frisco."

I closed my eyes. "I appreciate that more than you know."

"Not a problem," he said as he patted me on the back. "We're all in this together."

Back at my station, I forwarded the latest email to FBI headquarters in Washington and their academy at Quantico, then re-read each of the emails. 69 claimed to have provided clues. Where were they?

21

11:11 AM CENTRAL DAYLIGHT TIME (LOCAL) YELLOW CREEK

I coded a modification to the packet sniffer, dropped it into a hidden folder, and activated it. It would monitor network traffic and discreetly forward all emails into or out of Potella's machine to me.

He was hunkered down in the side office, pecking at the computer, so I took advantage of his absence from the control room and went online. Although I was confident my machine was secure, I still found myself half-expecting another chastising email to come sliding in. Outside the United States, the Internet was fully functional, so I found a solid UUNET international backbone and tiptoed my way into Geneva's registry of banks, looking for more information on my alleged clandestine Swiss bank account.

Suisse Banc Geneve was a major conglomerate, headquartered quite naturally in Geneva, with branches all over Europe. I went to their web site and searched for an account under my Social Security number. YOUR SEARCH RETURNED 0 RESULTS. SEARCH BY ACCOUNT NUMBER? I had no account number. Deeper access was needed. I cracked my knuckles and went to work.

Their security was impressive, but eighteen minutes later I was roaming the cyber-corridors of the financial giant. There were ninety-eight accountholders named Decker, three with a first initial of M. First up was Madeline, then Martin, then ... Matthew? I assured myself that the world had plenty Matthew Decker's but my pulse ignored that assertion, racing ahead of my fingers and hammering my temples as I worked my way into the account.

The first account screen showed the current balance, $1,243,552.23, and a list of the last five transactions. Five deposits, the most recent one being three months old, the oldest about a year. I was almost certain the amounts and dates matched those on the document Potella had shown me. It still meant nothing. There was obviously another Matthew Decker making out okay financially.

One level deeper I found the option I was looking for: VIEW/EDIT PERSONAL DETAILS. I selected it and hit the ENTER key. As the screen came into view, my pulse stopped hammering the inside of my skull because my heart stopped beating. The room around me receded. Abdul's supersonic typing was a distant clacking in an otherwise silent world. I was looking at the impossible, a picture of myself. It couldn't be, but it was. I had no Suisse Banc Geneve account, yet there it was.

A rapidly blinking line of text at the top of my screen yanked me back into reality with a jolt. WARNING. INTRUSION DETECTED. EXIT IMMEDIATELY. Damn! How long had that been there? My machine was cloaked but the protective countermeasures in place on this system were a far cry from Hotmail. I reached for the F12 key, which was programmed to lay down a trail of electronic chaff to cover my tracks, then sever the network connection, but my finger froze. I desperately needed more information but once I left, re-entry would be far too risky. My fingers blurred as I slammed the keys, printing screens as I went.

The warning text was blinking faster, a signal that the trace was closing in. As soon as the last critical screen loaded and before I had a chance to view it, I hit the print command and immediately followed up with an F12. The warning text changed. ANALYZING RISK. After blinking for what seemed like a month, it changed again. LIKELIHOOD OF IDENTIFICATION BY REMOTE SYSTEM: 51%. I cleared the message and rubbed my eyes. I could see that room full of reporters. Mr. Decker, is it true that you have been charged with a felony violation of the International Cyber-Protection Treaty? Mr. Decker, how will you spend your days in prison? Mr. Decker, have you ever been someone's bitch? Mr. Decker?

"Matt Decker?" I jumped as Abdul tapped me on the shoulder.

"What?" I shook my head, trying to clear the fog.

"I am not knowing what you have printed but Potella is coming this way at us."

I sprang from the chair and jogged to the laser printer at the end of the console, scooping up the sheaf of papers from its output tray a half-second before Potella ambled past. He glared at me and craned his tree trunk neck trying to see the papers but I folded the stack over on itself before his beady eyes could get a lock.

"One day, Decker. One day," he said through a crooked expression that was half smile and half sneer.

Sooner than he thought.

3:48 PM CENTRAL DAYLIGHT TIME (LOCAL)

I walked to the lounge for a stretch and found Tark there. After leaning out the door to verify no one was within earshot, he said, "Anything else on Potella?"

I shook my head. "I'm going to draw him out soon, though. Stay sharp."

"You're talking to a tack, Matthew." He flashed a foot-wide smile and winked.

A BREAKING NEWS logo flashed across the television screen and I turned the volume up.

A fresh newscaster: "We're about to go live to the Oval Office, where the President will make a brief statement. Stand by," he said.

Moments later the screen cut to President Stanson. "My fellow Americans, I come to you with a heavy heart as we all mourn the grievous loss of life that our nation has suffered. I want to assure each of you that we are working around the clock to end this crisis, and we will succeed.

"Until that time, however, we must maintain order and calm. For that reason, I have regrettably decided to declare a state of martial law. The brave men and women of our military are already preparing to keep the peace, and it is likely that you will soon see them arriving in your area. I urge each American to give them your full cooperation, as they are there for the good of all, not to rule over you but to protect you.

"To the cowards responsible, let me say to you that we will chase you to the ends of the earth and deliver justice unto you. You have wounded us, but the United States of America will not be defeated.

"Finally, I want to ask those of you who are able to see or hear this message to pass it on to your nearby friends and neighbors who don't have access to television or radio. By working together we will be stronger. May God bless each of you, and may God bless America."

The television went back to the newscaster, who started rattling off a list of rules that were to be followed under martial law, including sunset curfews and rationing of food and medical supplies. I walked back to the control room, wondering how Norman was making out.

The printouts from the Suisse Banc Geneve account were damning, especially the screen detailing the origin of the deposits. All came from overseas shell corporations, all acting as covers for a variety of terrorist organizations that the United States government would not deem acceptable business partners. The front companies were so poorly disguised that a competent college student could have connected the dots. It was an obvious frame but on its face the evidence was enough to make me look like a traitor and even if I was exonerated in court, my days as a government contractor—or as a contractor for any major entity—would be finished. The situation needed to be debunked and defused in the worst way.

Within the space of two hours the Potella email sniffer triggered five hits, all correspondence between him and Tiffany, aka his "Snuggle Queen." He loved her, missed her, worshiped her, would die for her, would kill for her, would walk ten miles barefoot in a snowstorm for her, and couldn't wait to get home and ravish her in all her buxom beauty. That was the first message. Numbers two, three, and four were more of the same. Snuggle Queen managed one brief reply to his four messages, in which she opined that the Internet was broken and somebody should damn well fix it. She also asked if he knew when the next payment would arrive because she needed a new iPad.

22

4:15 PM CENTRAL DAYLIGHT TIME (LOCAL)
HART COMPLEX

Hart watched Stanson's hollow threat with amusement, then switched the television off and turned back to his computer. Three clicks later, clandestinely collected audio from the control room at Great Central Electric again streamed from a pair of Harman/Kardon speakers. The eavesdropping device had been a pleasant surprise, a nice and thoughtful gift from Dane Christian. So had Jana Fulton, who sat on the nearby sofa. Dressed in a simple white gown with black trim, she took the definition of beauty to a new and unexplored height. Her eyes were so blue as to appear electric, not unlike his own. Silken blond hair that approached her shoulders before turning up at the ends in a teasing flip. Medium breasts rising and falling in slow waves against the satin fabric of the gown.

She was consumed with raw desire for him; she said nothing but he could see the blue-hot flames of passion burning in her eyes. Such was to be expected, but she would simply have to wait until the time was right for him to grace her with his stunning man-talents.

"I still want to hear about this pattern you thought you found." Hart recognized the voice as that of the FBI agent, Robert Rowe.

"Checking on it now if this site will ever load. Geez, this reminds me of the fifty-six-k days, for crying out loud."

Hart's lips tightened into a thin line and his nostrils flared. This Decker was entirely too stubborn. After ample warning to stay off the Internet, he dared to defy Abraham Hart. Was he insane? Perhaps so, but that did not mitigate the risk of Decker stumbling onto information that could jeopardize the operation.

He typed and sent another warning to Decker, one that should keep him busy for a while, then leaned back in his chair and rested his chin on steepled fingers. Fewer than four days remained, and for the first time, Hart began to think that continuing the game with Decker might be a bad idea. Taunting him was great fun, but too much was at risk. Decker was already ruined, and for now, that was enough. Time for him to make an exit.

He picked up a secure satphone that was linked to an up-top antenna and dialed a number.

4:21 PM CENTRAL DAYLIGHT TIME (LOCAL) YELLOW CREEK

Potella had been off the grounds for several hours with Sheriff Litman, so I set the trap and waited for his return. He had been back for about five minutes when Rowe walked up and said, "I still want to hear about this pattern you thought you found."

"Checking on it now if this site will ever load. Geez, this reminds me of the fifty-six-k days, for crying out loud." I had throttled back my bandwidth in order to slow down the surfing. I wanted to be online, but I didn't want Potella to see me do any genuine fact-finding and a molasses mission was the best way to accomplish that.

He watched over one shoulder and Rowe over the other. Within two minutes Potella said to Rowe, "I have things to do. Let me know if this asshole finds anything."

"Give it a rest, Walt. We're on the same team," Rowe said as Potella was walking away.

"Yeah, right," he said as he walked into the side office and shut the door. Bingo.

I busied myself plunking around on the FNC site, all the while complaining about the snailesque speed for the sake of authenticity, and waited. Rowe pulled up a nearby chair. Less than five minutes after Potella's exit, I heard: "You have new mail."

```
Return-Path: <i14_696938@hotmail.com>
Delivered-To: x7ijljAweRRv
-deckerdigital:com-x7ijljAweRRv@
deckerdigital.com
X-Envelope-To: x7ijljawerrv@
```

deckerdigital.com
X-Originating-IP: [66.156.171.40]
From: i14_696938@hotmail.com
To: x7ijljAweRRv@deckerdigital.com
Subject: Thy Clock Doth Run

Mr. Decker:

You have apparently chosen to willfully defy my instructions by going online again. You are beginning to anger me. I am quite certain your little Persian lapdog has been trying to break the encryption of the DECREE OF DARKNESS code within CEPOCS, so inform him that we are now playing a game of very high stakes, Mr. Decker.

If you have not produced the password within eighteen hours, I will impose another harsh penalty upon this nation, I will make you pay a dear personal price, and I will dispose of your friend's family in Iran. If you do obtain the password, you may not use it. Do so and Los Angeles will pale it comparison to the consequences I will invoke. Since you seem so fond of the Fox news web site, should you discover the password you are to place it prominently on their front page in unwritten form. The game clock is ticking, Mr. Decker.

Rowe read the message and started to say something but his cell phone rang. Make that a satphone; when did the Bureau start issuing fifteen-hundred-dollar phones to field agents? Rowe walked outside to take the call. Two minutes later, he was back, reading over my shoulder. I read it again and shook my head, drawing Julie's attention. She walked over and read it.

"Has it occurred to you that the subject is monitoring your Internet connection? Seems to me he knows every time you go online," she said.

Julie was leading the conversation exactly where it needed to go but I wanted them to have a handle on the tech basics before I dropped the Potella bomb in their laps. "Not possible. He could have a packet sniffer out there watching for my machine, but it would draw a blank because of the routing I'm using to log on."

"Can you put that in English?" Rowe said. "We're cops, not nerds."

"Geeks," I said.

"Whatever. Give us an abbreviated explanation of how someone might monitor a certain computer, and why it can't be happening to you."

"Data sent and received on the Internet is handled in little chunks called packets. Each packet also has an electronic ID tag attached to it, providing information about the origin and destination machines, which each have a unique identifying number for Internet purposes, called an IP address. Devices called routers interpret these ID tags and direct the packets to their destination, sort of like a traffic cop. So when I request information from the Fox site, for example, the request packet is labeled as coming from my machine with an intended destination of whatever Fox machine has the information I need.

The routers direct it to that Fox machine, it assembles the data I requested, and sends out a stream of packets containing that data, this time flagged with a destination of my machine. Am I making sense so far?"

"Yeah, I'm with you. So a packet sniffer is like the online equivalent of an eavesdropping device?"

"Exactly. Given all that's happened, it's safe to assume this guy has access to the IP of just about any machine he wants, meaning he's hooked into our two-way satellite feed. So he could instruct his packet sniffer to watch for any traffic coming from or going to the computers here at GCE."

"Then why did you say it's not possible that he's monitoring your activity? Sure sounds possible to me."

"He may be monitoring GCE's machines, but I didn't log on through a GCE machine. I tied in through my laptop, and you won't find a more secure machine. Right now it may be disguised as a public computer in a Barcelona cyber-café. Five minutes from now, a library in London, and so on. It constantly changes and takes on the appearance of some innocuous machine far away that can't be linked to any individual. Like I said, he's not monitoring me."

"Maybe it's just coincidence," Julie said.

It was time. "No, I think this latest one," I tapped the email on the screen, "rules out coincidence. He knew when I went online." I let the hook take hold. "And I think I know how."

"Oh?" Rowe said. Something akin to surprise flashed across his face at the speed of light, present only for a flicker. Julie's eyes grew in anticipation and she gave a "come on" gesture with both hands.

"We have a mole among us." This time the look of

surprise on Rowe's face didn't flicker. It appeared and stayed. Julie's eyes darted at Rowe and back at me.

"There's no way it's coincidence, and as I just explained, my machine is not being monitored. That means someone is keeping the subject informed on our activities here."

Julie cleared her throat. "Someone here, you mean, at this facility?"

"I think it's Potella," I said. You could've parked a bus in either of their mouths.

"Decker, what the hell do you base an accusation like that on?" Rowe said. Julie's face was frozen in time, a pretty spire decorated with a gaping cave.

I focused on Rowe. "First, he—"

"On second thought, hold up a minute. I won't be a party to discussing this behind an agent's back. I'll go get him."

I grabbed his arm and said, "He can defend himself later. Let me finish explaining to the both of you first. There's value in keeping this quiet. He could—"

"Nope." He wrenched his arm loose and headed toward Potella in the side office.

So much for the idea of discreetly following the mole to see where he might take us. "Julie, we already discussed this possibility. Now you seem blown away. Why?"

"I had no idea you suspected my partner, Decker. Someone in the chain of command, maybe. Walt? No way."

"You're wrong."

"Tell it to him."

Rowe was on his way back, with Potella lumbering close behind.

"What is it?" Potella said when they arrived.

"Tell him, Decker," Rowe said.

I leaned in close to Rowe and quietly said, "This is a bad idea and a very unprofessional way to handle it." He stepped away from me.

"Potella, Decker thinks you're dirty."

"The hell you talking about?"

"Says you're keeping the UNSUB enlightened on our investigation."

Potella's beady eyes burned. "That so, Decker?"

"Yes," I said. "There's no doubt 69, my code name for the subject, is being tipped off as to what we're doing. Take this last incident. Shortly after I went online, you retired to your office. Minutes later, in comes the latest threat."

"You ever hear of coincidence, big shot?"

"There's more. Your finances don't add up. You make fifty grand and spend like you make ten times that."

Rowe chuckled. "Everyone in our office knows Walt won over a half-million dollars in a lottery about a year ago," Julie Reynolds said.

"Why wouldn't something like that be in his fi—" I stopped myself too late. This was coming unraveled in an ugly way.

"You been snooping around in my files?" Potella lunged at me and Rowe grabbed him.

"Let him finish, Potella. If he's made unauthorized entry into federal files, he'll pay."

"You brought in that team of incompetents on one of the most important cases in Bureau history. Explain that," I said.

Potella looked puzzled. Reynolds explained. "The hacker team. They're not the technicians assigned by Quantico."

"I had nothing to do with that. I showed up here like I was told to and they were here."

I stared at Rowe and he looked away. "Agent Rowe, surely you don't deny what you told me earlier?" Rowe said nothing. Why wasn't he backing me up on at least this point?

Potella continued, "You know what I think? I think we got a rat here all right, and I think it's you, Decker."

"You've lost your mind," I said.

"Oh yeah? Remember that Swiss bank account you denied earlier?"

"What account?" Rowe said.

"Seems our pretty boy here has quite a little sideline going. He made computer programs to help terrorists buy and sell arms that we couldn't trace. This sonofabitch is a damned traitor and I have proof." Potella stomped back to his office and returned with a piece of paper. "What the two of you don't know," he said to Rowe and Reynolds, "is that this information came to me yesterday. I confronted him about it and he denied it. I actually wanted to give him the benefit of the doubt, so I decided to verify it some more before mentioning it to either one of you. I've done that now."

"Let me see that," Reynolds said, and Potella gave her the paper. She studied it for a minute, then shoved it at me. "I'd like to hear your explanation for this myself, Decker."

It was a faxed copy of the same bank statement had shown me earlier. "I've already seen this and it's bogus."

"That's not exactly what you saw before, Decker. Look closer."

Potella was right. The top of the page was a reduced-size photocopy of the bank statement, but the bottom held new information.

To the United States Federal Bureau of Investigation:

We have examined the above document and the related SBG account. It is a true and accurate copy, and the banking officer who handles this account has verified that Matthew Decker, widely known as a technology magnate, is indeed the accountholder.

As you are aware, we oppose divulging information such as this and do so now only because certain transactions within the account meet the criteria for mandatory disclosure as specified in the recently adopted International Anti-Terror Treaty.

Pirmin Heinz
President, Suisse Banc Geneve

"I don't give a rip what this says. It's wrong." All three of them stared at me and said nothing. I turned to Rowe and Reynolds. "Potella obviously forged this and faxed it himself."

"I don't think so," Rowe said. "In fact, that's impossible."

"And why is that?"

"Look at the time on the fax, Decker. At the time that fax came in, Potella was off the grounds with Sheriff Litman."

I looked at the fax timestamp. He was right. I replayed the sequence in my mind. Potella came back with the document and said that he hadn't mentioned anything about it to either of the other agents before. Reynolds asked to see the document, read it, then handed it to me. Rowe never saw it. But he knew the timestamp.

My mind spun and my stomach roiled as I processed the information. It was all Rowe, not Potella. Rowe was the one who signed off on the crackers. Rowe was the one who came in with an attitude on day one, then shifted gears when his boss talked to me about the case. And Rowe was the one who had set me up for a hard fall.

There was zero chance Potella would side with me if I tried to explain it now. A quick glance at Julie Reynolds confirmed that my guilt was a done deal in her mind, as well. "Look, people, I'm no traitor and when this is all over I'll prove that. For now, I'm going back to work."

"Not for long," Rowe said as they walked away. Julie burned a hole in me with a stare that shone with disappointment.

I sat down at my workstation and turned to Abdul, who had heard everything. "I'm innocent, Abdul."

"Yes, I believe you, Matt Decker."

"I appreciate that, my friend."

"What did the last email say?"

I turned my laptop around and pushed it over to him. "Matt Decker, he is going to hurt my family?" he said, a look of sheer panic on his face.

"I know it's tough, but what you need to do right now is keep working on that password, Abdul," I said.

He started crying. "My family knows nothing of anything like this! My father is taxicab driver. My family are good people. I will work faster on password, Matt Decker." He wiped his eyes and went back to pounding keys.

Seeing and hearing the news on television is one

thing. Witnessing the pain up close is another. Other than my comatose father, I didn't have a family anymore but I remembered the pain of losing him all too well. This psychopath had to be stopped.

The big grid display screen was sitting idle, so I hacked together a kludge—a small, quickly written program–to turn it into a giant computer screen for us to work from. Within three minutes I had every communication we had gotten from him displayed.

"Abdul, you see anything unusual in this last email?"

He studied the screen and said, "I don't speak English very well, but I understand it perfectly in writing. There are mistakes in this one."

"Exactly." I highlighted them on the screen. "He said 'pale it comparison' and he had a couple of sentence fragments.

"What do you think they might mean?"

"Small errors aren't uncommon in emails, but his first three messages were grammatically perfect. Stilted, very formal, but technically correct in every regard. Maybe he's becoming agitated."

"I hope he gets no more crazy than he already is."

"Agreed. Something else I find interesting is the subject, 'thy clock doth run.' Tark may be right. This does have a biblical ring to it."

"Yes, it is sounding to me like the King James."

"You have those system logs handy?" He handed them to me; I took them and the printouts of all the emails and made for the lounge.

"Do you think you know something?" Abdul said as I was leaving.

I looked back over my shoulder and held up the printouts. "There's a pattern here, and if I can manage some time without emails or catastrophic news or phone calls from the President, I intend to find it."

23

6:18 PM CENTRAL DAYLIGHT TIME (LOCAL)
HART COMPLEX

Jana's suite didn't have a clock but this new age dungeon did and she used these visits to mark the time. This was Thursday, her third day, and not even the briefest possibility of escape had come her way. She spent most of the day locked in the suite, then got hauled down here late afternoon or early evening, and stayed until around midnight, when she was escorted back to her cage.

At the moment, Hart was eavesdropping through his computer. Her heart quickened when she heard Abdul Abidi's voice. She was across the room from the speakers and had to strain to hear, but she didn't recognize any of the other voices or names: Roe, Becker, Reynolds, Marcella? She was sure it was Great Central, but where was Brett? Or Mr. Tarkleton? And who were these other people? Hearing a voice from home was both comforting and exasperating, so close, so impossibly far.

Hart abruptly switched the speakers off, stood, and walked into a restroom off the main room. Jana saw an opportunity. If caught she might be killed, but she deemed it worth the risk. She strode quickly across the carpeted floor to the computer and scanned the screen for a way to send a message. There it was, a window already opened to Hotmail. She listened carefully for sounds coming from the restroom. Nothing. She clicked COMPOSE, then filled in the recipient. She heard the toilet flush as she was typing the message: KIDNAPPED, SOMEWHERE IN NEBRASKA. ABRAHAM HART. HELP. DON'T REPLY TO THIS! JANA. The faucet in the lavatory was running now. She clicked SEND and stepped away from the computer just as the restroom door began to open. She stopped in place halfway between the computer and the sofa, and was stretching when Hart stepped out. He stopped, a brief moment of curiosity registered on his face, and then he smiled back.

"Got kind of stiff sitting there," she said, her pulse pounding her eardrums, sweat covering her palms. She took the remaining steps to the sofa and sat back down.

Hart walked over and stood in front of her. "I apologize for neglecting you today, my lovely. An evil man taunts me, causing me much tribulation."

"I'm sorry to hear that." Oh, how she'd love to cause the freak some tribulation.

"Thank you, but that is quite enough of that for now. I have some exhilarating news to share with you."

Maybe some more eyeballs in a jar. "Oh?"

"Yes, I have decided to make you my queen. We will

marry tomorrow, consummate our holy union, and you will reign at my side."

She drew a deep breath. "Wow."

"I knew you would be pleased."

She smiled at him and fought back the lump in her throat. "May I ask a question?"

"Certainly, my dear."

"What exactly are you, I mean we, going to reign over?"

"The world, of course."

"How?"

"Strictly. Fairly, of course, but strictly."

"But how are we going to, you know, do that? What about the leaders who are already in place?"

His face darkened. "Ah, you fear resistance?"

"Yes."

"After Monday next, there will be no resistance, only compliance."

"What happens Monday?"

"Si fort de terre trembler," he said, his head tilted back like a king issuing a proclamation.

"I don't understand that."

"It is French, my dear. Very old French. It means 'the earth will tremble very mightily.'

"Who wrote it?"

"It is from Quatrain nine by Nostradamus, a prophecy."

"About what?"

He took Jana's hands in his, gently kissed her on the cheek, and said, "About me."

She prayed that Brett would check his email soon.

6:30 PM CENTRAL DAYLIGHT TIME (LOCAL)
YELLOW CREEK

"Decker," Rowe said, motioning with the telephone handset. "The director wants to talk to you."

"This is Decker."

We had a bad connection, making his voice sound weird. "Mr. Decker, given the information Agent Rowe has just relayed to me, I'm ordering you to withdraw yourself from any involvement in this situation. Your security clearance has been immediately revoked and as soon as all this is over, I'm certain formal charges will be filed. This—"

"You can't be serious. I designed these systems. You have no shot at getting to the bottom of this without me!"

"Oh, I'm serious, Decker. You designed the systems all right, and look where they've gotten us. Considering what's come to light about you, for all I know you may be involved in this whole thing. You could've easily tampered with the system yourself and no one would be the wiser."

"That's ludicrous, Brandon. We're facing a deadline a few hours away to break a password or this guy is going to kill more people. Don't you understand that for whatever reason he's turned part of this into a personal game between me and him?"

"I think I understand the situation perfectly. Leave the facility at once and consider yourself fortunate that I'm not having you arrested right now. Oh, and don't leave the country, Mr. Decker."

"And what if I refuse to go? What if I say that I'm not going to leave and let this guy win?"

"Then I'll issue orders for Agent Rowe to forcibly remove you."

"Agent Rowe will need help," I said as I shot a steely look toward the low-life.

"Rest assured help is available if needed, Decker."

I slammed the phone down and bagged up my laptop. Rowe watched me like a smirking hawk. Potella outright laughed and Julie Reynolds looked at me with disgust. "Where are you going, Matt Decker?" Abdul said with even wider eyes than normal.

"I've been ordered off the grounds. The world's falling apart and we've got a crew of crooks and pinheads running the show. You find that password. I'll be in touch." Abdul nodded and turned back to his machine.

I stepped outside, fifteen miles from my motel, without a car. Tark's wife was feeling ill and he'd gone to check on her. He probably wouldn't be back for a couple of hours. I suppose Abdul could have given me a ride, but the game clock was ticking and he needed to be working on that password. I had no intention of asking Rowe or the others for anything and doubt they would have agreed anyway.

The sun beat down on me from a late-afternoon angle as I walked along the shoulder of the road, while the black asphalt blasted me from below with heat it had saved up all for my torture. It was so hot my shoes stuck to it as I walked. The roadsides were a foot tall in weeds, no doubt teeming with all manner of biting insects and who knows what else, so I stayed on the hot road, step-peel, step-peel, step-peel.

My shirt was drenched and stuck to me within five minutes. By the time I'd covered a mile I could feel my underwear bunching up in a hot, wet, mess. The laptop weighed four pounds and felt like forty as I shifted it from shoulder to shoulder. After four nights of very little sleep, I had been exhausted when this day began. The adrenaline produced by my anger at Rowe helped me cope with the first couple of miles, but it faded quickly after that.

I was probably into the fifth mile when I saw a truck coming. Walking in the sweaty socks had rubbed blisters on the bottoms of my toes, making each step painful. I stopped walking and for the first time in my life, stuck my thumb out for a ride. The truck slowed and pulled over, and it was a beauty. Late seventies Ford F150 in a lovely shade of rust. He was heading away from the Iuka Country Inn, but I didn't care. I wanted off the road and into something with a motor. I had no doubt that wherever he took me would be an improvement.

"What's your name?" he said as he eased back onto the road. The truck had no muffler and the sound was deafening. "Matt Decker," I shouted. The truck reeked of beer and my feet rested on an aluminum mountain of Milwaukee's Best empties.

"Henry Roberts here," he said. I couldn't swear to it, but I'm pretty sure either Henry or a twin brother was in the movie Deliverance. A bag of bones with a week of stubble and a stench to match.

"Where you heading, Henry?"

"I'm going to the light plant."

"Great Central?" Surely I hadn't crawled into this rolling hunk of rust only to be taken back there.

"Yup. And you know what? If they get smart with me, I'm just liable to whoop some ass."

Great. I'd just been thrown out by the director of the FBI and now I was about to drive back up with an incestuous hick with three teeth in his head who was "just liable to whoop some ass." My day kept getting better.

"What'd you say your name was?" he said.

"Decker."

"Well Dicker, I'll tell you right now that it ain't nothing for me to whoop a man's ass. You might've heard of me."

"Could be, Henry. Why'd you say you're going to the electric company?"

He spit a hefty stream of snuff juice out the window. "They got some lines run across my land. Only reason I let 'em stay there is because of the lights in the box that I like to go out there at night and look at."

"Lights in a box?" It was becoming more obvious by the moment that Henry was an intellectual giant.

"Yup. There's a box on a pole, got a running ton of lights in it that flash. I like to go out there at night and watch the lights while I drink beer. Say, you want a beer, Dicker? I got some left." He popped the top on a hot can of beer from the floorboard.

"No thanks."

"Anyways, them lights ain't blinking right no more and I aim to tell somebody about it. Bad enough that I got to drink damn hot beer all week long. Now my blinking lights ain't right. They either ain't blinking at all or they're flashing like a bat out of hell. It's pissing me off, Dicker. You know what I'm talking about."

"How big is this box on the pole?"

"She's about two foot square, black on the outside with lights inside ... "

He was describing a field-accessible diagnostic checkpoint. Power was of course transmitted through high tension wires like it had been for a century, some underground and some on poles. The circuitry that made it all run, though, was pure fiber optics. These bundles of glass lines fanned out from the control center in every direction, providing communication links from the control computers to the grid switches at substations and other distribution points throughout the region. It never occurred to me that there were people on this earth who spent their nights watching the lights blink inside a junction box in what I presume was the middle of nowhere, as was often the case with this particular type of module.

" ... and that's what I'm talking about, Dicker. You sure you don't want a beer?" he said as he tossed one can out the window and promptly popped the top on another. He'd been babbling nonstop and I'd stopped listening.

"I'm sure. Say Henry, I don't suppose I could hire you to run me back up to Iuka before you go whooping ass, could I?"

"What you paying?"

"Twenty bucks."

He nearly slung me out the window as he spun the truck around and headed back toward Iuka. Fifteen minutes later, we pulled up to the Iuka Country Inn, where I paid Henry and said goodbye amid the thunder of his departure.

24

7:45 PM CENTRAL DAYLIGHT TIME (LOCAL)
YELLOW CREEK

You did what?" Tarkleton screamed.

"To be accurate, the director ordered him out of here, not me. He sure got no argument from me on it, though. I think Decker is bad news. Even if he's not involved in it himself, all he does is piss this guy off. For all we know he's responsible for what happened in Los Angeles," Rowe said.

"You're as full of crap as a Christmas turkey, Rowe. You know dang good and well that what happened in Los Angeles had to have been planned long ago. It most certainly didn't happen because Decker was here, no matter what the guy is saying. He's just yanking chains, trying to distract us, and it looks to me like it's working. You people need your heads examined if you're so simple-minded that you can't see that."

"Thanks for sharing your opinion, Mr. Tarkleton. It's of much value to us."

"Abdul," Tarkleton said, turning his back to Rowe, "what's wrong with you? You look bothered."

"You do not know of the final email to Matt Decker. We are having until 10:22 tomorrow morning to find the CEPOCS password or my family is going to be killed and maybe Matt Decker's father and many more Americans."

"Rowe, you idiot! You sent Decker off with this going on? And why didn't you mention this email to me just now?"

"I have no obligation to tell you anything, Tarkleton. You're a plant manager, nothing more. You have no role in this investigation other than to follow my orders. The Bureau is in charge of this investigation and I'm in charge of this facility until further notice. In case you haven't heard, we're under martial law and that means we have a bit more latitude in setting the rules."

Rowe never saw it coming as Tarkleton walked calmly toward him. Tarkleton hit Rowe square in the mouth with enough force to loosen three front teeth and send blood pouring. "And in case you haven't heard," Tarkleton said, "this is the United States of America, not some piss-ant third world hellhole where people like you decide to take over and everybody falls in line just because you said to!"

Rowe slowly picked himself up from the floor, using his forearm to wipe the blood streaming down his chin. Abdul watched the fracas for about thirty seconds and returned to the task at hand, his fingers flying over the keys as his eyes scanned the screen for signs of success. Tarkleton stuck a big finger right in Rowe's face. "You're out of control, Rowe."

"I swear to God, you'll pay for that, Tarkleton."

"Maybe so, Rowe. Or maybe not," Tarkleton said as he stormed out of the room and slammed the door behind him.

8:13 PM CENTRAL DAYLIGHT TIME (LOCAL)
IUKA COUNTRY INN

I almost left my skin when I stepped out of the dark shower and saw Jimmy Lee Tarkleton sitting in the chair beside the bed. "Good grief, man, ever heard of knocking?"

"I did. Guess you were in the shower, so I got the manager to let me in. He's a friend of mine. How'd you get here, Matthew?"

"Hitched a ride with a real winner, some guy named Henry. You heard what happened at the plant?"

"Agent Rowe and I had a discussion about it."

"I was wrong about Potella. Rowe's the mole."

"Do tell?"

"I'll explain later. Right now we have to figure out how I can get back on this thing. We have a new deadline."

"So I heard. I'm with you, but how do you propose we get you back in?"

"How many agents do they have on site?"

"Rowe, Potella, and Reynolds were the only ones there when I left. They have two more in the area, but they've been out working the Fulton investigation with Litman's boys."

"Speaking of the High Sheriff, whose side will he come down on?"

"Johnny and I go way back, but asking a county sheriff to go head to head against another law enforcement agency, especially the FBI, is a tall order. I used to pull a few shifts as a reserve policeman and I can tell you the blue wall of solidarity is a real thing."

"I thought it was the blue wall of silence."

"Same thing, trust me. They stick together."

"We'll have to tear that wall down this time. We don't have a choice."

"I'm with you come hell or high water, Matthew, and I'll do what I can with Johnny Litman, but I can't make you any promises where he's concerned."

"Fair enough. Let's go."

Hell, Tark, I could wind up in jail. Not a good place for a sheriff to be."

"Johnny, you remember Billy Sneed?"

Litman wagged a finger in Tark's face. "This ain't going to work, Jimmy Lee."

"Do you remember him?"

"You know dang well I do."

Tark turned to me. "Billy was the class bully from the first grade on. Always had it in for this scrawny little buddy of mine named Johnny Litman." He looked back at the Sheriff. "How many times you reckon I saved you from him?"

"Plenty, but—"

"No buts, Johnny. I was always there for you. Always. Didn't matter if it was Billy or somebody else, first grade or summer camp or tenth grade or whatever. Until you got where you could take care of yourself, I was there for you and I've never asked you for one thing. Now I'm asking. This nut's liable to kill a million more people if he's not stopped, and Matthew here is the one with the best shot at that."

"Why don't ya'll call Rowe's boss and let him handle it?"

"The people in Washington and Quantico aren't getting anywhere," I said, "and we can't sit around waiting for them to get their act together. And besides, how do we know who we can even trust up there? We know there's at least one other turncoat and there could be a dozen more," I said.

"Dang it, Johnny, why don't you reach down in your britches and be sure you even got a pair left," Tark said. Litman's nostrils flared and red splotches appeared on his face.

"Sheriff, I'm going back in there," I said. "Maybe we can avoid anyone getting hurt if you're with us, but I'm going in with our without you."

"That goes for me, too," Tark said.

Litman rolled his eyes. "Decker, if this backfires I'll be knocking on your door for a job." He keyed the mike on his shoulder and turned his head toward it to speak. "Dispatch, S.O. One."

"S.O. One, Dispatch. Go ahead."

"Find Ray Johnson and patch him through to me, ASAP."

"Ten-four, Sheriff."

Litman had been slow to come on board, but once he did he fully engaged and had the clout to bring plenty of high quality guests to the party. I learned that Ray Johnson was Lieutenant Ray Johnson, brother-in-law of Johnny Litman and somewhat of a local hero as a result of his service in Afghanistan, during which he led a charge into al-Qaida's Tora Bora cave complex.

Of current interest was the fact that he was the Army Reserve officer in charge of the local e-brigade, Itawamba County's National Guard component of Mississippi's 3rd Brigade, 87th Division, which rolled under the moniker Dixie Thunder.

The Humvee was loud and hot. "Matthew, way back in 1787 Thomas Jefferson said something that we might be put in jail for saying today. He basically said a rebellion was needed at least every twenty years, that the tree of liberty must be refreshed from time to time with the blood of both patriots and tyrants. Those were telling words." Tark was shouting to be heard over the roar of the hefty engine and the whine of the mammoth tires on the behemoth.

"I'd rather not water the tree tonight if we can avoid it," I said.

"Do I strike you as a violent man?"

"You could."

He grinned and slapped me on the back. "I'm just a big old teddy bear, son."

Our Humvee was the number two vehicle in the convoy, right behind Sheriff Litman's cruiser as we made our way into the GCE complex. Behind us were three more Humvees, two of them topless and bristling with mounted M-60 .50 caliber machine guns. And rumbling along way back at the back of the pack, unbelievably, was an M1A1 Abrams tank.

Abdul is a codeslinger extraordinaire. He was one with his machine, barely looking up when we burst into the room like a team of vigilante commandos at midnight. I did see him crack the faintest smile, though. He knew the cavalry had come.

Potella and Reynolds spared no time getting their hands airborne when the swarm of armed men hit the room. For about a thousandth of a second, Rowe looked like he wanted to reach for his gun, but common sense took over and he too raised his hands. Litman relieved Rowe's shoulder holster of the .40 caliber Glock, along with a .32 revolver tucked away in a nylon ankle holster. He cuffed him and a pair of deputies escorted him to the side of the room. "Hold him right there for the time being," Litman said.

I noticed earlier that the knuckles on Tark's right hand looked bruised. I saw Rowe's swollen lip and understood. Someone stripped Potella and Reynolds of their weapons and escorted them from the control room.

"What do you want me to do with this bunch?" Litman said, pointing at Neo and his band of merry misfits.

"Got any work for them over at your jail?"

"My computers work fine, thank you very much."

"Who said anything about computers? Any floors need mopping?"

Litman grinned. "Now you're talking." He motioned for a deputy to round them up and usher them out.

"Tark," I said, "let's get the Bureau on the line and break the news about who's in charge down here. Maybe Brandon will come to his senses and work with us."

"Rowe, give me the director's phone number," Tark said. Rowe broke loose from the two deputies and hit the door running, his arms shackled securely behind his back thanks to a regulation pair of Smith & Wesson handcuffs. The deputies gave chase and we fell in behind. Ten yards down the hallway I stepped on something that clanked. The handcuffs. He used his own key to release the locks while we were talking.

He flew through the outer door and hit the parking lot in a sprint. The man could run. I was in good shape, normally running four to six miles a day depending on how busy I was, and I was getting winded after a hundred yards. He was going toward the waterway, showing no sign of slowing down as adrenaline pushed him forward. I heard the splash as he hit the water, then another as one of the deputies plowed in after him. The second deputy wanted no part of the water, manning the flashlight from the bank instead.

He swept the beam of the Mag-Lite across the surface of the water, looking for Rowe but finding only the other deputy. Rowe was nowhere to be seen. He had dove underwater and surfaced elsewhere. The black water of the unlit night made it tough to see anything. Lots of talking and pointing flashlights and speculating went on, but Special Agent Bob Rowe was gone.

"Abdul, any progress?"

He shook his head but his fingers never stopped. Tark was still dialing the phone. He covered the handset and said, "You see what I mean about a biblical flavor on that last email?"

"Yeah, let's brainstorm that as soon as we get it quietened down around here."

DAY FOUR FRIDAY

And I looked, and behold a pale horse:
and his name that sat on him was Death,
and Hell followed with him. And power was given
unto them over the fourth part of the earth,
to kill with sword, and with hunger, and with death,
and with the beasts of the earth.
Revelation 6:8

25

1:02 AM CENTRAL DAYLIGHT TIME (LOCAL) YELLOW CREEK

It took forty-five minutes but Tark finally had FBI Director Keen Brandon on the phone, explaining the newly established Yellow Creek command structure to him. I was talking to Abdul when Sheriff Litman walked back into the room. "Of all the times for Henry Roberts to pull one of his routines, he sure picked a doozy."

Litman turned to one of the deputies. "Bobby, go out there and get his drunk self and see if you can find a place around here to lock him up. Make it as far away from here as you can so we ain't got to listen to him."

"I had the good luck to hitch a ride with Henry today. He's a piece of work," I said.

"He's been like that his whole life. Hell, his daddy was like that. Always drinking and picking fights. Thank the

Lord he and Missy didn't have kids. Maybe that line will finally die off."

I was wondering why any human woman would want to marry Henry, when an avalanche of realization fell over me. "Take me to Henry right now," I said.

"Why on Earth—"

"Sheriff, I'll explain later, just take me to him."

"Bobby, take him on," Litman said while he shook his head.

They had him locked in the guard shack at the main gate. Another deputy stood outside the diminutive structure while Henry threatened to whoop all kind of ass from inside. "Open the door," I told Bobby. He nodded to his colleague and seconds later Henry came charging out.

He stopped in his tracks when he saw me with the deputies and just stood there trying to figure it out. "Dicker!" he finally said. "You come to help me whoop these candy ass sumbitches?"

"Henry, I need you to calm down for just a minute. I have a question for you."

"I like you, Dicker," he slurred as he threw an arm around me.

"I like you too, Henry. Now please pay attention." He half-stood, half-leaned on me, bobbling from side to side, but he appeared to be listening. "When was the last time you saw the blinking lights in the box?"

"Last night," he said. "They were acting stranger'n hell."

"You're sure it was last night?"

"Why hell yeah, Dicker. You want me to whoop your ass too?"

I crouched and stepped out from under his arm. "Maybe later," I said back over my shoulder as I jumped into the driver's seat of the deputy's cruiser and headed back to the main building with the deputy standing beside Henry looking confused.

Abdul, we're almost to the switch. Have you confirmed there are no active communication links from GCE into the fiber?"

"Yes," his voice crackled quietly on the handheld radio.

"Matthew, when are you going to tell me what's on your mind?" Tark said.

"I think I know how 69 is staying informed on our investigation." We were making our way through the narrow clear-cut on the Robertses' land, coming up on the switch from the rear.

We were about ten yards out when I heard a faint zip of a whistling sound overhead, followed a quarter-second later by the report of a small caliber weapon up ahead. I hit the ground, dragging Tark down with me. Another shot fired. And another. I could hear the bullets ripping through blades of Johnson grass beside the narrow path. It sounded like a .22 rifle.

Tark raised his head up and I tried to pull him back down. "Missy, is that you?" he bellowed. Geez, is there anybody around here he doesn't know?

"This is Wildcat Roberts! Who the hell's out there on my land?"

"Missy, it's Jimmy Lee Tarkleton. Quit shooting at us, for crying out loud!"

"Okay, I'll quit." I heard her coming through the weeds, and soon enough she came into view in the moonlight. I saw her and wished I hadn't. No longer did I wonder how Henry had managed to find a wife. I wondered how she managed to land a prize like Henry.

Wildcat and Tark slid into a conversation and I walked around them to the front of the switch. Just like Henry had said, there were lights. On the very left was an LED labeled LINK. It was a bright, steady green. Immediately to the right was a vertical row of ten blue LEDs that worked like a graph to show activity passing through the switch. The very bottom light was intermittently blinking. I keyed up my radio, watching the blue LEDs carefully. "Abdul?"

"Yes." LEDs two and three blinked, then died.

"Talk about the weather or food or something and move slowly around the room."

He walked and talked and I watched as the lights grew stronger and weaker and stronger as I guided him. After five minutes of the back and forth I had the sweet spot nailed. "Abdul, remember your current location. We're heading back."

"Yes."

I was right; no one had been monitoring my laptop. The control room was bugged, and 69 had been listening to every word we said.

"Well I'll be a jack-in-the-box. What are you planning to do with the bug?" Tark said as we began our hike back to the car.

"For now, we'll leave it in place and let him hear what we want him to."

"Sounds like a plan. Oh, you were in such a fit to get out here, I didn't get to tell you what Brandon said on the phone."

"How belligerent was he?"

"Keen Brandon said he hadn't talked to you or Bob Rowe this afternoon. You were ordered off the case by an imposter."

That put a stutter in my stride. "Interesting. How'd Brandon act?"

"I wouldn't call him happy about our taking over his crew with a homegrown posse, but he was way more upset about his crooked agent."

"Make that plural. Someone called me."

"What about Potella?"

"No, he and Reynolds were in view while I was on the phone."

"How do we know who to trust in the FBI, then?"

"We don't."

"So what do we do, Matthew?"

"We get back to Yellow Creek and figure this thing out ourselves. We'll stay in touch with the Bureau and as long as their input passes the smell test we go with it. And our people stay on hand just in case Brandon attempts a coup. Bottom line, they can't slow us down if we're one step ahead."

26

1:42 AM CENTRAL DAYLIGHT TIME (LOCAL)
HART COMPLEX

Jana slid into a shallow sleep in her suite. Soft knocks on the door jolted her out of it. She couldn't believe she was about to be dragged back down to the dungeon again so soon. Hadn't she just left there? Or was it the next day? Her heart started pounding; if it was the next day, it could be time for the royal wedding.

She opened the door and saw Dane Christian there. "May I come in?"

"As if I have a choice."

"You do. I'm not here to take you to him."

Relief flooded over her, followed quickly by apprehension. "Then what are you here for?"

"I'd like to talk to you."

"What time is it?"

He looked at his watch. "Around one-forty."

"AM or PM?"

"AM. Why?"

"I just like to know. Come on in, I guess. After all, how often does a girl get a chance to chat with her kidnapper in the middle of the night? Lucky me."

Dane eased into the room like a shy boy picking up his first prom date, and Jana saw the chink in the armor. He was there with something personal to say, a fish out of water. Conversely, when it came to one on one, Jana was very much in her element.

"For what it's worth," he said, staring at his feet, "I'm sorry all this happened."

"So you've said, but I'm still here, aren't I?"

"I'd like to help you get out, but it's not possible."

"I don't buy 'impossible,' but first, why don't you tell me what in heaven's name is going on."

He pulled a bottle from his pocket and swallowed a handful of pills from it. Jana took the bottle and looked at the label.

"You just took a handful of Percocets. Why?"

"Tumor. My brother didn't even know."

"I see. How bad?"

"It's been there for several years but it's growing like crazy now. I have a couple of years, maybe less."

"Despite what you've done to me, I hate to hear that. Is this how you want to wrap up your life, kidnapping and murder?"

"I said I'm sorry. I meant it."

"I appreciate the fact that you didn't want to leave me at home where the bomb is, and of course that you didn't kill me, but it's hard to see how you did me a favor by bringing me out here and handing me over to that monster downstairs."

"I had no idea he was going to pull that."

"He's certifiably crazy, Dane. You do know that, right?"

"You have no idea," Dane said, still staring at his feet. "And you have no idea what horrible things I've done for him."

Jana knew he was a hardened criminal but he suddenly looked like nothing more than a sad and broken human being. She took his hand in hers. "What kind of things? What is this all about? Please tell me."

He shook his head and Jana saw the wet eyes. "I'm so sorry ... so many people dead ... so many more to die ... so sorry ... "

Jana walked him to the bed and sat him down. She took his face in her hands and looked him in the eye. "Dane, you can't help what you've already done, but can't you stop more people from dying?"

He took his fatigue jacket off and used it to wipe his face as the tears flowed. "No, it's too far gone. His people are everywhere. People I hired and trained to set everything up out in the field. It's already in motion and he won't let anybody stop it. Aside from the professionals that had to be bought, he has hundreds of people out there who worship him. They think he's some kind of savior or something. This has been in the works for years, and they'll die for him."

"What's in the works, Dane? What is he going to do?"

"He's had all communications cut off and any exit from the grounds is barred unless he gives express approval. He'll never let us out of here. Even though I've been the operational head all along, he'd have me shot if I tried to drive off the compound right now. And while we're inside, he can sit down in that room and seal us all in here forever. He can cut off our air. But I'm going to try to—"

A small radio on his belt chirped. "Mr. Christian. I require your presence in my chambers immediately," Hart's voice said.

"We can get out of here together. I'll help you stop him," Jana said.

"I'll be back as soon as I can," Dane said on his way out, "and I'll tell you more about what's going on."

27

1:45 AM CENTRAL DAYLIGHT TIME (LOCAL)
YELLOW CREEK

Show me where the last spot was," I whispered in Abdul's ear. He moved like a cat—quick, limber, silent—to the end of one of the console cabinets in the middle of the room and stopped. I nodded, he stepped back, and I got down on my knees for a closer look. The cabinet had a vented metal panel on the side. That would be X on this treasure map.

Tark held a flashlight while I gingerly removed four retaining screws and eased the panel off. And there it was, the microphone itself about half the size of a thimble. It was wired to a bare circuit board that was in turn patched into a fiber communication junction. 69 had enjoyed a streaming audio feed, unfettered access to everything we said. Who knows how long it had been there, but one thing was for sure: his entertainment package was about to change.

I powered up my laptop and routed a message to the big display. *Back to work on the password, Abdul.* Act naturally. I'm splitting this screen so we can work together. A duplicate of your monitor will show up on the left side, mine on the right. Tark, I need you outside.

"I know this is your plant, Tark, and I'm not trying to bust your turf. Right now we're in the tech end of things and I need operational control. You got a problem with that?"

"You just let me know how to help."

Seems as though I'd pegged the guy wrong on the pissing contest thing. Maybe I was the one with a penchant for the game. Maybe I'd need to rethink parts of Decker Philosophy 101 when this mess was fixed.

"I appreciate it. I need you to get hold of the Bureau. It's hard to figure Rowe's angle on this thing, but maybe they can shed some light on it. And we really need to know what their profilers have to say about this guy based on what we have from him."

"All right, what else?"

"Be sure Litman has people on Rowe's trail. His car's still in the lot and transportation and other resources will be hard to come by. He expected to remain in charge here and he's out there unprepared."

"I can handle that. What are you going to focus on?"

"We have a nasty deadline coming up in eight hours. I intend to find that password. I don't know what he'll do if we do find it, but I sure don't doubt that he'll make good on his threats if we don't."

Ask me out loud if I think it's safe to go online. The big screen was coming in very handy for non-verbal communication.

"Will you go online again?" Abdul said.

"No, can't take the chance. He's tapped into my laptop somehow and I don't want to risk it. I'll follow his rules and keep trying to break the code here."

"Okay," Abdul said with a wink as I was logging on through the satellite link.

I grabbed the stack of system logs Abdul had run for me when I first started trying to check out my pattern theory and striped the key events with a highlighter. The Fox site was way perkier at two in the morning, and within three minutes I had their timeline downloaded and printed. I took the hard copies and headed to the lounge, where I spread them out across a table and started scanning for the pattern I was sure existed.

I didn't have to look long. It was so obvious that I felt like an idiot for not having seen it far sooner. I ran—not walked—back to the control room and slid into my workstation. *Abdul, I need the text files of the system logs that you printed. ASAP.*

The man was good at ASAP. The file icons appeared on my laptop within fifteen seconds. I opened them and went to work merging the list of internal GCE system events into the Fox list, cutting, pasting, pulling it all together in a spreadsheet file. As soon as I was done I printed the results and motioned for Tark and Abdul to follow me as I headed to the break room.

"You guys see anything odd about this list?"

"Yes," Abdul said. "Everything happened at sixteen minutes after the hour."

"Sure did," Tark said. "First failure here was at one-sixteen. National drop was exactly twelve hours later, and the chemical weapon attack in Los Angeles was at eleven-sixteen. I guess it could be coincidence, but it sure would be a stretch."

"It's no coincidence. The pattern is stronger than that. Take another look," I said. They looked but I could tell they didn't see it. "These events didn't just happen at sixteen minutes past the hour. They all happened at sixteen past the same hour." I handed them another version with all the times transposed to U.S. Eastern Daylight Time.

"Oh my gosh," Tark said. "You're right. Everything on here happened at two-sixteen Eastern!"

"Exactly," I said. "And there's no way that happened by chance. This, my friends, is a hard pattern. The guy has a thing for two-sixteen."

"How did everybody miss this? It seems so obvious now," Tark said.

"It's easy to see why we missed it," I said. "Since I got here on Monday afternoon, we've been putting out a steady stream of fires."

"What about all everyone else, however?"

"Strong question, Abdul. Knowing Washington has its stables of investigative geniuses all over this case, why hasn't someone else picked up on it? CIA, FBI, National Security Council, they all miss it while our little ragtag crew down here in Mississippi spots it first."

"There are plenty of smart people up there, but our government got caught with its britches down and they're scrambling to keep their heads above water too," Tark said.

"I guess so. All right, let's keep our forward progress going. What does the pattern mean and how does knowing it help us?"

The speculative brainstorming began. A February sixteenth birthday? Something special about the two-hundred-sixteenth day of the year? A latitude or longitude? We had our pattern but we seriously needed to get something out of it because the deadline was bearing down on us and the trial-and-error code breaking was going nowhere.

"One-oh-eight times two ... " Abdul was pacing, thinking out loud. "Fifty-four times four ... "

"Does that number mean anything special in computers?" Tark said.

"Nothing jumps out at me," I said. "We do of course want to try it and every variation we can think of as the password."

"It divides by two so it is not a prime number ... twenty-seven times eight ... "

"One-one-oh-one-one-oh-oh-oh ... "

"That's binary for two hundred sixteen," I explained to Tark, who had a puzzled look on his face.

"D-eight ... "

"You boys can stop guessing," Tark said slowly, a strange look spreading across his face. "I know exactly what it is."

He walked over to a whiteboard on the wall and wrote out *216 = 6 x 6 x 6,* then turned to us and said, "It's six-six-six, the mark of the beast."

28

2:02 AM CENTRAL DAYLIGHT TIME (LOCAL)
HART COMPLEX

"Are you absolutely certain the audio monitor is functioning properly?" Hart said.

"It's working. We heard them talking just a few minutes ago," Dane said.

"But they're not talking as much. I want to know why."

"Mr. Hart, it's two o'clock in the morning. They're probably worn out. I know I am."

"Sleep at a time like this is for fools and simpletons. This is a time of destiny." Hart had not slept in three days and night. He was wild-eyed, circling the room.

"How the hell could a simpleton like me have a sense of destiny? Have you ever shared the whole story with that crew of robots upstairs? Does anybody on this whole damned earth know what's going on other than you? Destiny, my ass."

"How dare you speak to me like that. I won't hesitate to order you executed for insubordination."

"I want my money and I want out of this. I've had enough."

"You are thoroughly delusional, Mr. Christian. You're not going anywhere."

"You're wrong, you sick asshole. And you know what? I don't even want your money. I'm out of here."

Dane stood up and headed for the door. He heard the hammer going back on Hart's Walther PPK and hit the floor as a .380 hollow point bullet punched into the concrete wall in front of him. He instinctively rolled and reached for the small .38 revolver he always kept in the right cargo pocket of his fatigue jacket. Only then did he realize the jacket was lying on the bed in Jana's room.

Several more shots rang out and he sprang into a low running crouch, heading for the cover of Hart's most prized possession, the glass-encased ancient copy of the Torah in the middle of the room. It worked. Hart froze, his face locked in a look of panic at the thought of harm befalling the treasure. The smell and haze of gunpowder hung in the air. Dane stayed in a crouch behind the pedestal—also made of glass—of the display, circling to keep it between them as Hart resumed his advance.

Hart circled and closed, and Dane knew he was running out of time. In thirty seconds Hart would be close enough to shoot him pointblank without fear of hitting his precious book. His only option was a few seconds of distraction. Without warning he gave the heavy pedestal a shove. It hit the floor and shattered into a hundred pieces but the case holding the Torah itself must have been

Plexiglas because it didn't break. Hart shrieked like an animal and Dane sprinted toward the door.

He felt the searing heat of the bullet between his shoulder blades just before he heard the report of the shot. He reached for the doorknob and heard the SNAP of a dry fire. Hart was empty. He hobbled through the door and made it to the tube-shaped elevator, which raised him quickly to the uppermost subterranean level where Jana was being held. Leaving a trail of blood, he half walked half crawled to her door and swiped his magnetic key through the lock before collapsing onto the floor.

Jana heard a noise and saw the green light flash on the door lock. She opened the door to find Christian sprawled face down on the floor, the top of his back bleeding profusely. "Dane! Dane! Wake up, we have to get you inside. He rolled over and muttered something unintelligible and she saw blood pouring from his mouth and nose. She pulled him inside and propped him against a wall, leaving his arm between the door and frame until she could stick a towel in the doorjamb to prevent it from closing and locking her inside.

"My ... jacket ... " he said in an awful gurgling voice, pointing toward the bed. Jana looked and saw he had left his fatigue jacket on the bed when he was there earlier. She started to pick it up, then saw the bottle of pills that had fallen out of the pocket and onto the bed. That's what he wanted from the jacket.

Jana's nursing experience made reality plain enough. Dane Christian, her one best—if not only—hope would be dead within minutes. She shook a whole handful of the powerful painkillers out of the bottle and gave them to him along with a glass of water.

He forced the pills down through a mouth and throat full of blood and again pointed toward his jacket. "More pills aren't going to help, Dane. Give those a few minutes to take hold." He tried again to say something else but couldn't get the words out and finally gave up. Jana held his hand until the narcotics started to work. His shallow breathing slowed and his eyes glazed over, his lips barely moving as he slipped into a twilight sleep. Then he died.

Jana knew the trail of blood would quickly lead Dane's erstwhile foe—most likely Hart himself—to her door, and she needed to make an immediate exit. She gently closed Dane's eyes and laid him down on the floor. He may have been a terrible man but he seemed repentant at the end and she couldn't bear to leave him there propped up against the wall like a stuffed animal. She thought about how ironic it was that his brother had died in exactly the same position, in her brother's house, probably at his hand.

She went to get Dane's jacket to drape over him and was surprised by its weight. Something heavy was in the pocket. A revolver, .38 caliber. That could come in handy. She popped the cylinder out to check her ammunition, suddenly grateful to her farmer father who had insisted she learn how to handle weapons as a teenager. "Just in case," he always said. She had rolled her eyes at the time, but she was rolling the cylinder now and snapping it back in place, ready for action if need be. The time for passivity was over.

Feeling around in the other pockets of the jacket yielded two full Speed-Loaders, bringing her total store to fifteen rounds. Maybe the gun was what Dane was really pointing her to, not the pills. She checked the last pocket and found a thumbdrive. She needed the fatigue jacket's cargo pockets, so she pulled the towel from the doorjamb, laid it over Dane's face, put the jacket on, and hit the door running.

Outside the door she headed left down the long hallway that led to the elevator. If she could get up top she might have a fighting chance. The people she'd seen working in that computer room when she first got here looked like a gaggle of nerds and she liked her chances against nerds with a .38 Special. She had the elevator in sight fifty feet ahead when the heard a soft electronic tone and a whoosh of air. Someone was about to disembark the elevator.

She had just passed a crossing hallway and quickly retreated and ducked into it before the doors on the elevator opened. She flattened herself against the wall, the gun in her right hand with her finger on the trigger. The steps were coming quickly down the hall, echoing off the hard tile floor and cinder-block walls. Her body was frozen as Hart walked by the intersection of the hallways, his eyes on the blood trail that would lead him to her former cage.

She heard him open the door, waited five seconds, then hit the main hallway and headed back toward the elevator as quickly and quietly as she could.

29

2:27 AM CENTRAL DAYLIGHT TIME (LOCAL)
YELLOW CREEK

"As embarrassing as it is to the Bureau, you do have our gratitude for identifying Rowe as a mole, Mr. Decker."

"I didn't figure him out soon enough, Director. I thought Potella was the dirty one."

Brandon snorted into the phone. "Walter Potella is an oaf and a disgrace who we keep confined to a desk. If it weren't so damned hard to fire a government employee he would've been pounding a beat in some one-cruiser town years ago."

"What about Julie Reynolds?"

"I don't know Agent Reynolds. I'm told she has potential but she's green as grass. I'll have to say Rowe obviously did his best to assemble the sorriest team imaginable."

"Any progress analyzing the emails on your end?"

"The task force at Quantico is working around the clock. They've just completed a profile on the UNSUB. White male between forty and forty-nine years of age. English probably not native language, well educated, most likely in Europe. Very little else."

"So he could be any of a few hundred million people."

"Afraid so."

"What are your plans going forward, Mr. Brandon?"

"We'll be dispatching a new team to your location. I'll pick and vet the members myself this time, so it's going to take a little longer. Expect them in around twenty-four hours."

"So long as they don't interfere with what we're doing."

"We are grateful to you, Mr. Decker, but do realize when all is said and done we're running this investigation, not you. You can participate but we will be calling the shots, both overall and at Yellow Creek."

"Let's discuss it later. Right now I need to get to work. Goodbye, Director." I hung up the phone, shook my head at the obtuse nature of career bureaucrats, and went back to the lounge.

"Tark, to be sure we're on the same page, you're not thinking this fruitcake is really the antichrist, are you?" I of course didn't believe in the notion of some supernatural evil devil-man at all, but I needed to know where he stood. I needed his biblical knowledge from an investigative standpoint but there was no room, no time, for religious emotionalism to further fog the situation.

"No, Matthew. This world may be approaching the end of days, but I plan to be raptured before antichrist is revealed. Besides, antichrist will almost certainly enter the world stage disguised as some sort of wonderful, kind savior. I think this guy's shot any chance he had at being perceived that way."

"Agreed. Now let's figure out who he is and how to stop him. Abdul, try every permutation of six-six-six you can think of on the password. Tark, you got a Bible around here?"

He came back from his office with a Bible the size of a small car. "Giant print edition," he explained. "They gave me one of those over-the-hill birthday parties here last year when I turned fifty."

"Let me know if you need a Geritol break," I said with a smile. He laughed and slapped me on the back. When I got my breath back I opened the behemoth to its final book, Revelation. "Okay, let's get inside this guy's head. He thinks he's the antichrist. What—"

Abdul burst into the room. "Matt Decker, you must see this. Come now."

We went to his station in the control room. The monitor was filled with a graphic that looked like an ancient parchment scroll with this inscription:

Here is wisdom. Let him that hath understanding count the number of the beast: for it is the number of a man; and his number is six hundred threescore and six.

We may not have hit the password but we were on the right track. "What'd you do to trigger this?" I asked after we walked back out of the control room and away from the bug.

"I was trying six-six-six for the password."

I turned to Tark. "I assume this is from Revelation. Do you recognize it?"

"I don't remember chapter and verse but it won't take me long to find it."

"Did anything else happen when you entered it?" I asked Abdul.

"Yes, there were sounds playing. Do not worry, for I had my volume low so it could not be heard by bug."

"Something spoken?"

"No, they were horns blowing."

"Like musical horns?" Tark said.

"Yes, they were like trumpets blowing."

"That makes sense," Tark said.

"How's that?"

"Revelation's got more trumpets than a marching band."

Abdul went back to work on the password, and Tark and I moved back to the lounge. He was all worked up, giving me a nutshell explanation of end-times prophecy as he saw it. John, the guy who wrote Revelation, had one hell of an imagination. In our particular situation it didn't matter one bit if it was true or not. Our psycho obviously believed it and had written himself into a starring role.

In *The End According to Tark*, there would be one main antichrist, the beast, and he'd have a helper, the false prophet. The beast would rise to world power right about the time all the good saved Christians were magically sucked up in the air to meet Jesus. The false prophet would be the beast's right-hand man, taking care of the details of setting up the much-feared One World Government.

Right about the time they got started, God would begin pouring out his wrath on an evil world in a series of judgments. There were to be several different groups of judgments, including the trumpet judgments. Some of these terms were vaguely familiar from my father's old sermons, but that was a long time ago and the main things I got out of those sermons were terror and a seizing fear that some of these creatures might be under my bed.

"Those sounds weren't in that code by accident. What's the first trumpet judgment?"

"You're jumping the gun. We need to cover the seven seals first."

Seals. Trumpets. It all started running together. It was the middle of the night and still at least eighty-five degrees in the building. I couldn't remember how long it had been since I'd eaten, much less showered. Reality started piling up and I felt overwhelmed. How could we fight this guy? We didn't even know who he was. A feeling of hopelessness settled over me like a dark, pungent mist, choking me, blinding me. I suddenly realized that I was choking on it. Something was in the room, smothering me with a wet stench of death—

"Matthew ... Matthew! Wake up!"

I opened my eyes and shook my head.

"You dozed off," Tark said. "We were talking about the seven seals."

"Sorry, run through it again if you don't mind. I'm spent."

He reached over and gave me a one-armed hug. "You have a right to be worn out. Don't worry about it."

"Okay, seven seals."

He went to the whiteboard and made a list numbered one through seven, writing more information as he talked. "These judgments get a lot of attention in the movies, but Hollywood usually doesn't worry about being biblically accurate. In the movies, it's always up to someone to do something to stop the judgments from taking place and postponing the end of the world as we know it.

"That's hogwash. Once all this starts, it will go forward and no power in the universe will be able to stop it."

"Okay, who's supposed to be opening these seals?"

"Jesus. A lot of Revelation is symbolic, but a lot of scholars agree with some uniformity on the underlying meaning of the symbolisms."

The clock on the wall said three o'clock. Seven hours and change until the deadline. "What's number one?"

"Seals one through four will unleash the four horsemen," he said, writing WHITE HORSE on the board beside seal number one as he lectured. "You may've heard these supernatural cowboys referred to as the four horsemen of the apocalypse. The first rider will be on a white horse with a bow and a crown, generally thought to symbolize antichrist getting ready to conquer the world."

"What kind of horse for our second cowboy?"

"A fiery red one, its rider equipped with a sword to symbolize bloodshed." He wrote in RED HORSE. "Number three is a black horse." BLACK HORSE. "Its rider appears to have some power over the buying and selling of goods."

"And number four?"

PALE HORSE. "The pale horse is the sickly color of death, like bloodless corpses, which its rider is scheduled to dispense through a combination of warfare, famine, and pestilence. In fact, this rider is specifically called Death."

He kept talking, but I'd tuned him out a bit and was focusing on the whiteboard. Something was there, beginning to come together, a vaporous outline I needed to cajole into an understandable structure. Sheriff Litman, who was hanging out in the control room with Abdul, walked into the room. "FBI on the horn for you, Decker."

"Tark, you mind talking to them?" I said. "I want to stay on this."

"I'll take it in my office," he said.

He and Litman left and I stared at the board. WHITE HORSE. RED HORSE. BLACK HORSE. PALE HORSE. Four horses. Four horsemen. WHITE HORSE. RED HORSE. BLACK HORSE. PALE HORSE. My mind was racing, processing, looking for the embedded clues. In four days and nights I had barely had enough real sleep for one night, but I was on fire now, the fatigue gone, my mind screaming for answers.

I stood at the board, closed my eyes, and tried to envision those horses and their riders, thundering across an open field side by side. No, that wouldn't work. They weren't a gang of bandits. Each man-and-beast team worked alone. One horse. One rider. One mission. And one distinct meaning to this psycho.

The white horse would go first, the warrior-rider sitting high in the saddle, wearing his crown and wielding his bow, conquering all in his path. How long would that take? A week? A month? A day? My mind stopped and I opened my eyes. Yes, a day! I headed down the hall to get Tark.

30

3:18 AM CENTRAL DAYLIGHT TIME (LOCAL)
HART COMPLEX

Jana wondered how long her luck would hold. She had made it to the elevator, which shot her up to ground level. Only when she stepped out did she realize that amid the excitement she had left the room without shoes. Her bare feet made for quiet movement on the balcony that wound around the perimeter of the main floor where all the computers were, but if she did happen to make it outside the building the lack of shoes would quickly shift from advantage to handicap.

She crouched behind the balcony wall and peeked down at the floor. She counted only four people, each of them working at a computer. Three were men, all working side by side on the same console. The fourth was a woman and she was alone and nearest the exit door.

Jana stayed in a half-crouch and worked her way around the balcony. A metal spiral staircase wound down to the floor, and she slowly eased down it, keeping her eye on the woman. A support pillar blocked her view of the men in the center of the room.

The sound of rushing air startled her. She turned around and realized the sound was the elevator going back down. If it was going down it would no doubt rise shortly, probably bearing Hart. The elevator and the staircase were the only two ways off the balcony and one of the men from the center of the room below had moved to a console no more than ten feet from the foot of the stairs. The whoosh of the elevator whined to a stop, then restarted with a different sound. It was on the way up.

Each step of the steel staircase felt like ice to the soles of her naked feet. Five steps to go. Four. The third one from the bottom creaked ever so slightly under her weight. She froze but it was too late. The man at the bottom turned toward the sound.

She had never hurt a living thing but she had no qualms about starting now. *THWUMP* went the man's skull as Jana dove on him and landed a solid blow with the pistol butt. He slid to the carpeted floor and Jana felt his blood, warm and sticky like thin pancake syrup, on the butt of the gun as she withdrew it.

Above her on the balcony, the elevator's pneumatic mechanism faded to a stop a moment before the door opened. She dropped to her hands and knees and peeked around the corner of the console. The two men in the middle of the room were still working, talking to each other. Their conversation must have masked the sound of her cracking their friend's skull. Crawling at an impossible pace, she worked her way across the room to within six feet of the woman working nearest the exit, then rose and closed the gap before bringing the pistol down on the crown of the woman's head. She was quickly making up for her prior lack of inflicting bodily harm.

The door that led outside was twenty feet away. She eased the unconscious woman out of her chair and dragged her across the floor into the small entranceway, where she quickly stripped her of her sneakers and access card. The shoes were too big but they would have to do.

She stepped to the door, swiped the card, and said a quiet yes! when a green light pulsed and the massive doors began to slide open.

"Hey, what's going on over there? You know we can't exit without authorization," one of the men said, his voice getting closer. The doors opened slowly and Jana turned sideways and pushed through as soon as the opening was wide enough.

The air was cool, the moon hanging brightly in a star-speckled sky as she ran in a dead sprint away from the building and toward an open-walled tractor shed about two hundred yards away. The shoes flopped on her feet and the sound of them slapping the damp grass was as loud as an eraser being banged on a chalkboard. Inside the shed, she leaned on the far side of a tractor to catch her breath. Ten seconds later an alarm started wailing back at the main building and the area lit up with floodlights. Looking back over the top of the tractor, she counted six men coming out of the building and fanning out. Two were headed directly toward her and she had nowhere to go. Looking away from the building, there was nothing but flat land spread out to infinity. She was trapped.

Hart walked at a brisk clip from the elevator to the stairwell, stunned that the woman had dared to leave her room without permission. There would be a price to pay for her insolence, beginning with a reduction in status. Her tenure as queen was over before it started, a royal candle snuffed dark through her own wanton treachery.

She didn't even deserve the title of concubine. She would henceforth be referred to by the unadorned moniker of whore. And there would be no more waiting. As soon as he found her, she would accompany him to his chambers and be immediately initiated into her new role. The bitch would undoubtedly enjoy that—as had every woman he had ever graced—but she would do well to keep that pleasure concealed if she had any thoughts of ever regaining a more elevated role within the structure. Queen was out, but reassuming the position of concubine was within the realm of possibility.

He stepped from the elevator and shouted from the balcony, "Where is the lady who just came down?"

"We think she made it outside the building, sir," one of the three men said from the floor below. "Security has been deployed."

Hart made his way briskly along the balcony. "How did this happen, my son?"

The man came to meet him, bowing slightly as he waited near the foot of the stairs. "She hit a female technician in the head and took her shoes and key card, sir."

The staircase shook as Hart pounded down the steps, growing more inflamed inside as he thought about the sheer incompetence around him. Fools. He was utterly surrounded by fools, and yet he was forced to pretend that all was well. "I see. Where is this technician?"

"She's over here by the door. We called the doctor down to look at her head. It's bleeding pretty badly."

Hart walked to the woman and looked at the doctor. The trash was not worth the price of a bandage, but speaking with candor at this juncture could be problematic.

The doctor backed away as Hart approached and the woman—sitting barefoot on the floor, holding her hand to the back of her head—looked up through watery eyes. "I'm so sorry, sir. She snuck up behind—"

Hart kneeled and spoke with the reassuring voice of a father. "Fear not, child. All will be well." Tears formed in her eyes as she looked into his.

"Thank you, sir."

He nodded and turned to the doctor as he rose back to his feet. "See that this dear servant is healed."

"Yes sir."

Hart swiped his own card and stepped through the exit door into the night. As soon as the door closed behind him he raised his arms and wailed, "Security! Come unto me!" Two of the men arrived in a jog from behind the building, followed by two more, then two more. His voice returned to a soft calm. "Gentlemen, where is my whore?"

One of the security officers, a thick-faced bull of a man, said, "We haven't found her yet, sir, but we will. We're trying to locate Chief Christian, as well."

"Mr. Christian will not be responding to your pathetic cries for assistance, you moronic slug. He has been terminated."

"You fired Chief Christian?" the bull said, his face crinkled in disbelief.

"I said nothing about fired. He has been permanently

term-i-na-ted, a fate you may well share if you do not produce my whore within the next sixty minutes. Is that clear?"

"Yes sir. Perfectly clear, sir."

"When you locate her, deliver her to my quarters. I am holding you personally responsible for that delivery."

"I know it's unlikely, but what if she makes it off the grounds. Should we—"

"You are authorized to pursue her into the pits of hell if need be. Bring her back." Hart turned on his heel and walked back inside.

"Let's go find the girl," the bull said.

31

3:42 AM CENTRAL DAYLIGHT TIME (LOCAL)
YELLOW CREEK

I waited as long as I could for Tark to get off the phone, but he was still talking. Mostly listening, actually, and taking lots of notes. I went back to the control room, sat down at my laptop, and sent a message to the big screen:

Abdul, I have a password for you to try. And put your main display on screen so I can see what happens from here. You ready?

YES.

Okay, try the password WHITE HORSE.

He entered the phrase and the action began. Another graphic appeared, this one far more elaborate than the one from the 666 entry. From a cobalt blue background came an animated white horse, its rider wearing a golden crown and holding a bow. As he drew nearer on the screen he raised and pulled the bow, then let loose a flaming arrow that grew larger and larger until the flames filled the screen. The flames died down, revealing the unencrypted module of CEPOCS code. We were in.

Tark bounded in with his notebook, motioning for me to follow him back into the hall. "Matthew," he said, "the FBI is making some progress. I need to fill you in right away."

"We got the password," I said.

"What?"

"We got it. We're into CEPOCS."

"Well praise the Lord! What was it?" he said as we walked back toward the lounge.

"White horse. And I think I have a basic idea of what our guy is up to."

"I'm all ears," Tark said as we made it back to the lounge.

"Okay, you say that the antichrist is supposed to be the rider on the white horse; I think this sick puppy sees himself as the rider."

"How so?"

"First of all, the chunk of malicious code is what we call a Trojan horse in the business. It was hidden inside our normal program, just waiting to come pouring out and causing grief. That's what turned me on to trying the password. I kept looking at all those Revelation horses and it suddenly occurred to me that what we were looking for in the code was a Trojan horse."

"But why a white horse?"

"Because this twisted bastard thinks he is the mighty warrior. He's cooked up this apocalyptic bullshit and thinks he's bouncing in the saddle of his precious white horse."

Tark stroked his chin. "Yeah, I can see that. Maybe he sees himself as a bright shining light in the darkness. Darkness he created, of course."

"That's not all he created, Tark." I walked to the whiteboard, grabbed a marker, and beside WHITE HORSE I wrote TUESDAY. "The white horse was the first step, his triumphant entrance amid the so-called Decree of Darkness."

"Go on."

"All right, what happened Wednesday?" I asked.

"The Los Angeles catastrophe."

"Exactly. Catastrophe by a chemical weapon called—"

Tark figured it out before I could finish. "Red death," he said, his mouth hung open. I wrote WEDNESDAY on the board beside RED HORSE.

"Red death, red horse, massive bloodshed, which fits the prediction," I said.

"And then comes the black horse," he said. "A measure of wheat for a penny, and three measures of barley for a penny. Economic chaos. Black Thursday." I wrote it in, THURSDAY.

"The pattern is unmistakable," I said.

"It dang sure is, Matthew. He's trying to enact the seven seal judgments."

"You got it. One seal per day. We're into day four now, the pale horse day."

Tark leaned over the car-sized Bible and read aloud. "And I looked, and behold a pale horse: and his name that sat on him was Death, and Hell followed with him. And power was given unto them over the fourth part of the earth, to kill with sword, and with hunger, and with death, and with the beasts of the earth. That's chapter six, verse eight."

"Sword, hunger, death, and beasts, all wrapped up in one. Wonder how he plans to pull that one off?" I said.

"Let's hope he doesn't."

"He hasn't failed yet. Oh, what did the FBI want?"

"They said your finding the bug was a huge break, and not just in the sense of watching what we say. According to their technical people he has to be somewhere near New York or Los Angeles, so they're concentrating the investigation on those two areas."

"Say again?"

"They had a communications expert explaining that to me, and he said that the fact that our bad guy was able to monitor a ... hang on, let me get my notebook." He flipped pages for a moment, then continued. "He was monitoring a live sound feed on fiber, so he must be within twenty miles of a class five fiber switch, the type that's only found where the big transoceanic cables are."

"Coms aren't my specialty, but I find it hard to believe that there are only two top-level switches in the whole country."

"Just telling you what he told me."

"Let them proceed under that premise, but let's you and I assume the guy could be anywhere."

"I'm with you, Matthew."

I liked Tark more all the time. He was straightforward, a human embodiment of the WYSIWYG design model. What you see is what you get. Very refreshing, and it felt good to have him on my side. He stood in front of the Bible, hands on the desk as he peered down through his reading glasses. Then he flipped back into the Old Testament.

"Why are you moving out of Revelation?" I said.

"John's not the only one who had an apocalyptic vision. Way back when, a fellow named Daniel had quite a dream himself. Listen to this: And in the latter time of their kingdom, when the transgressors are come to the full, a king of fierce countenance, and understanding dark sentences, shall stand up."

I leaned over and kept reading:

```
24  And his power shall be mighty, but
not by his own power: and he shall
destroy wonderfully, and shall prosper,
and practice, and shall destroy the
mighty and the holy people.

25  And through his policy also he shall
cause craft to prosper in his hand; and
he shall magnify himself in his heart,
and by peace shall destroy many: he
shall also stand up against the Prince
of princes, but he shall be broken
without hand.
```

"That does sound like our boy," I said, "but how does it help us?"

"Next time you swap emails with him, maybe you can use some of this to get under his skin a little bit."

32

4:25 AM CENTRAL DAYLIGHT TIME (LOCAL)
HART COMPLEX

Jana knew daylight would soon come and destroy any chance of escape from the complex. She estimated twenty minutes since she heard the men searching the shed as she lay motionless underneath the big tractor's cowling, on top of the six-cylinder diesel engine. Now she was easing her way out of the cramped quarters as quietly as possible. She dropped to the ground and stretched her aching muscles.

Peeking around the corner of the shed, she saw the play of flashlight beams behind the main building. The area between her shed and the building was clear. She made her way to the end of the shed farthest from the building, stepped outside, and set out in a dead run toward a barn about two hundred yards away. The oversized shoes flopped up and down on her heels as she ran, slowing her down.

Her thigh muscles were on fire by the time she reached the barn, her breath coming in short, hard gasps. It was the farthest and fastest she had run since winding up her track career in high school. In fact, despite being ten years older, she felt sure she had just run faster than she ever did on the asphalt oval at Itawamba High. Probably had something to do with motivation. There was a heck of a difference between running for Coach Gruber and running from Abraham Hart.

She pulled the barn door open just enough to slip inside and collapsed on the dirt floor. A rustling noise deeper inside the dark barn pumped the adrenaline again and she stood up quietly and flattened herself against a wall, listening. There it was again, only more of a shuffling sound this time. Her breathing began to slow and the smell of the barn registered. It was a stable. She moved closer to the shuffling sound and saw that it came from a horse. A big, beautiful white horse that shone in the moonlight streaming through the high vent windows in the barn.

Perhaps her luck was turning. All the tack needed to fit the horse for riding was right there in the barn. Jana had no trouble saddling and bridling him, having grown up on a farm where riding a horse was as common as riding a bicycle. The barn sat at an angle to the main building and its rear door offered an exit that was out of sight to the searchers.

She eased the horse away from the barn in a light trot for the first hundred yards before kicking him into a full gallop. The grassy field was open and flat and she could feel the fine spray of dew against her bare ankles as the mighty hooves ate up the distance. After about a mile she slowed down, afraid to push the horse any farther at full speed. Looking back, she saw no one in pursuit.

Her eyes had adjusted to the moonlight and she could clearly see a white pasture fence a few hundred yards ahead. After listening for a moment to be sure the horse's breathing didn't sound distressed she kicked him again and rode hard. When she was close enough she started looking for a gate in the fence and saw none. "Boy, can you jump?" she asked. "Sure hope so."

She kept going, not slowing up, waiting to see what he would do. He gracefully cleared the fence as if he had done it a thousand times. Immediately past the fence was a road. Jana stopped and patted the horse, his coat wet with sweat, his big nostrils flared and sucking hard. She checked behind her and still saw no one coming, then looked left and right on the road, trying to spot any sign of civilization nearby. Nothing. She pulled the reins to the right, then reconsidered. Once they figured out she was on the horse she would be an easy target if she stayed out in the open. Across the road was a stand of woods. She clucked her tongue, gave him a gentle nudge in the ribs, and said, "Let's go there, boy. We need to find our way back to civilization."

33

6:20 AM EASTERN DAYLIGHT TIME
SOUTH LAWN, THE WHITE HOUSE
WASHINGTON, D.C.

The manicured lawn was painted in the long shadows of early morning as the man walked with a tiny sat-phone held close to his ear.

"You are an insurance policy, one for which I am paying lofty premiums. Can you assure me that my benefits are being properly administered?" Hart said from over a thousand miles away.

"I have everything under control, but it's time for you to wire the second installment. My risks are incredible."

"Do not whine to me about risks. You knew them when you agreed to take my money. And there is no need to remind me when payment is due. I meet my obligations. Be certain that you meet yours. Is that clear?"

The man pursed his lips in a tight line, unaccustomed to being talked down to by anyone other than the President. "Is that clear?" Hart repeated.

"Yes."

"Very well. Have a good day. Your funds will be wired shortly."

He punched the phone off and dropped it in an inside pocket of his suit coat as he walked toward the service entrance of the White House. He still seethed, but he was dealing with it. No matter one's station, a lot of pride could be swallowed when the price was right, and this one was so right. Today his Grand Cayman account would have a balance of twenty million dollars. Three days later, the final payment would push it to thirty.

"Beautiful day, isn't it, George?" he said as the doorman opened the door for him.

"Yes sir, Mr. Brandon, it certainly is."

5:38 AM CENTRAL DAYLIGHT TIME (LOCAL)
YELLOW CREEK

The sun was coming up and I was spent. My mind was a mush of determination sprinkled with random thoughts of exhaustion, and the whole mix was something approaching delirium. I was suddenly very sick of it all. This mess. The world. My pitiful excuse of a life. I was slipping into middle age and couldn't name five people in the world who I was sure really cared about me. Not my money. Not my company or my business. Just me, Matt Decker. Five? Get real. There was one. Norman. Then the list went flat when I remembered Norman was a dog. He was a great dog and I missed him and wished I was home with him, but he was still a dog.

I sat at the table in the lounge, straining every muscle in my face to keep my eyes open. I was so alone. My work was all I had and look what that work had done to the world. I was the one who dreamt up the system that broke down all to hell and back and put the world in a state of disaster. The whole world. Despite the fatigue—my eyelids felt like lead weights—a crystal memory surfaced, one I hadn't thought of in ages.

On July 14, 1977, my father and I were sitting in the living room of our home, a modest three-bedroom job furnished by the church, watching the evening news. I was six years old, and the lead story transfixed me. The night before, multiple lightning strikes had started a chain reaction that eventually knocked out the power to New York City. They were playing a homemade film shot by a tourist from the top of the World Trade Center, and it captured these huge blocks of the city going from a lighted spectacle to eerie darkness. It was the most fascinating and terrifying thing I had ever seen, all those lights going off at once.

"Matty, I think I see a sermon in this," Dad said.

"Where?" I squinted at the screen.

He laughed and whisked me from beside him onto his lap with one big strong hand. "I mean there's a message for us in this."

"I'm just six, Dad. I don't know what you're talking about." Dad had a habit of getting over my head and sometimes I had to bring him back down to where I was.

"It's like this. All those buildings and streets are still there, right?"

"Yes sir." They were still there all right, with gosh

knows what other kind of creatures of the dark running around in and between them.

"And we could still walk down those streets if we were there. It would just be harder. Right?"

I nodded.

"God is like everybody's light, son. We can still stumble our way through life, but it sure is easier when we have the light to help us."

"Ohhhh, I get it." He just smiled, glad that I got it. Then he went to work on his sermon. And I kept thinking about how it looked when all those lights went off, and how all those people—Dad said there were millions of them in that one town—must be so scared without the lights. I thought about it long after the lights in New York came back on.

I still missed Dad so much. It wasn't fair. Nor was it fair to all the people who were now in the dark because my system failed. It was my fault. All my fault. I was sorry, so very sorry.

"Matthew, wake up, son."

"Dad?" I said, opening my eyes and finding Tark towering over me instead.

"You were moaning 'I'm sorry' over and over. This isn't your fault."

I shook my head and processed what he said. "Tark, that's nice of you to say, but when all is said and done this is my system and my responsibility."

"That's horse hockey and you know it. If you hadn't built the system, someone else would have. What was that company that fought you so hard for the contract?"

"Hardier. Big Israeli outfit that threw together a North American shell to try to undercut me."

"Right, I remember now. The head honcho never

showed at the hearings, kept sending busloads of lawyers."

"That's the one. I was outmanned but I called in a lot of chits and pulled it out. Maybe I should've let them have it."

"And the same thing would have happened. And remember, the power grid is just one little piece of this puzzle."

"Yeah, but it's the power grid that brought everything grinding to a halt. You said yourself that the Bureau can't even run a proper investigation. The fate of the world is at stake and everything is so crippled that they can't even put up a decent fight."

"There are supposed to be contingency plans in place for everything, including something like this, but the fact is our government let us down by not being ready, not you. That's how it really is, Matthew."

He leaned over and got right down in my face, eyeball to eyeball. "Do you hear me?"

What he was saying started making sense. My mind started clearing, my eyelids growing lighter as my fighting spirit gathered steam. "I do."

"Good, let's nail this son-of-a-buck."

"Agreed."

I stood and stretched, and Tark said, "You think we should bring the FBI up to speed on what we've found?"

"We better. They need the information. I'll play it safe and send it directly to Brandon."

34

6:35 AM CENTRAL DAYLIGHT TIME (LOCAL)
EARTH, TEXAS

Mayor Charlie Raymond was a strapping bulk of a man, six feet four and two hundred sixty pounds of zero body fat topped with a Texas jaw. He stepped out of his house and shut the door quietly, trying not to wake his wife and kids. Charlie was still going to the office every morning before seven, just like he always had. There was little for him to do there, but he had been mayor for years and he was determined to do all he could to maintain at least the appearance of normalcy for the thousand-plus citizens of Earth, Texas.

Before the crisis began, his routine had been to stay in the mayor's office from seven to nine, then walk down the street and open his hardware store for business. The mayoral position was part time, to say the least. But the hardware store was now closed, so he spent most of his time at City Hall, hoping an encouraging word would crackle in on the old two-way radio that kept them linked to the state police.

An ancient diesel generator rattled noisily from the basement as he made his way in through the front door. The exhaust was vented through a pipe that led to the roof, but a hefty dose of diesel fumes still made their way up the stairs and into the offices. Bruce Thurman, Earth's Chief of Police, was waiting.

"Charlie, there's some fellows from the federal government in your office. Said they need you to call a town meeting right away."

Raymond cocked an eyebrow and headed that way. Both men stood up when he walked in, one tall, one short, both awfully sturdy looking for government weenies.

"Mayor Raymond, we're from the Federal Emergency Management Agency," the taller of the two said. "We're here to explain to the town what the government is going to be doing to help out, and we need you to gather up all the people you can for a meeting this afternoon at twelve-thirty."

"Well that'll be a little tough for me to pull off. It's not a big town by any stretch, but all we have for city officials right now are me and Bruce, and the only way to spread word around here right now is door to door. So how about you fellows just fill us in, and then we'll start passing it on to the people." Raymond said.

"I'm afraid that won't work, Mayor. We have a certain protocol to follow, and it requires us to hold the meeting ourselves," Tall Man said. Short Man still said nothing.

"I don't believe ya'll told me your names," Raymond said, a hint of irritation creeping into his voice.

Short Man, who despite being a solid looking specimen only came to Charlie Raymond's shoulder, finally spoke with a hard deep voice. "I'm Luther Ross, Mr. Mayor. My partner here is Paul Prather. We are just doing our jobs and you have nothing to worry about."

"All right, gentlemen," the mayor said. "You win. We'll start spreading the word right now. Good enough?"

"Yes sir, thank –"

Chief Thurman spoke up. "Charlie, there ain't no way in hell we can get around to everybody in so short a time."

"We'll manage, Bruce. Let's go get started." Raymond turned back to the visitors. "Fellows, ya'll just make yourselves at home. We'll start working the town and see you back here in a few hours."

"Ain't no dang way," Thurman muttered under his breath as Raymond steered him out of the office by the elbow.

Once outside, Raymond walked briskly to the town's lone patrol car with his Chief of Police in tow, mumbling all the way. Raymond got in the passenger side and as soon as Thurman was in he said, "Drive, Bruce. Right now."

As soon as the cruiser left City Hall, Raymond said, "Bruce, I don't know what's going on with those two, but I guarantee you it's not good."

"What you mean?" Bruce Thurman wasn't a dumb man, but despite twenty-two years as Earth Chief of Police, he could hardly be called a brilliant investigator, either. It just hadn't been necessary. Earth was a lazy little hole in the road where the locals got along and outsiders didn't stay long.

Mayor Charlie Raymond was a different story. He had spent fifteen years as a Texas Ranger working out of

Houston, and he could for a fact be called a brilliant investigator. One of the best ever of the famed Rangers, to be accurate. He was a criminal's worst nightmare, with an uncanny ability to be in the right place at the right time. Until one night when it turned into the wrong place at the wrong time for Ranger Raymond. He took four well-aimed .44 Magnum slugs from a drug dealer's revolver to the chest. The Kevlar vest stopped the monster rounds but the sheer impact nearly killed him.

He spent two weeks in the hospital and, after much pleading from his wife, turned in his badge and moved the family back to his boyhood home in Earth. His father was thrilled to turn over the keys of the family hardware store to him and Charlie Raymond settled right into the quiet life of Earth, Texas, eventually running unopposed for mayor when old Hank Buford retired from office the hard way, in a pine box.

Until four days ago it had been a great life. Then the power died and people started turning into morons who fought and bickered and griped and whined and usually wound up blaming it on the Mayor when all was said and done. After all, he did get paid $250 a month to take care of things.

Now it was time to really earn his keep. "Bruce," he said, "first of all, why the heck would FEMA send two officials to Earth? I know we love it, but let's be honest; we're just a hole in the road, a thousand people and change. If they sent two here, how many did they send to Houston, two thousand? It makes no sense."

It seemed to be sinking in with Chief Thurman. "I guess that is pretty odd, ain't it?" Slowly sinking.

Raymond looked the other way and rolled his eyes. "Second, those guys don't look like any government weenies I ever saw. They're built like tanks. Both of 'em." Thurman nodded. "Third, the tall one smelled like diesel, and my guess is he picked that lovely smell up from our basement, where he had no business being. And last but not least," Charlie said, "the short one is packing a weapon."

"Good Lord!" Thurman said, nearly running off the road in the process. "You saw it?"

"I saw the bulge in his jacket. Large frame automatic is my guess. There are always low-lifes waiting to take advantage of a bad situation, and I think it's safe to assume that's what we're dealing with in these two."

"Look Charlie, I don't mind telling you that I don't have the training to handle something like this. What are we gonna do?"

"I know, Bruce. I don't want to step on your toes, but with your permission I'll sort of take over on this thing."

"You got my permission and my blessing and any dang other thing you want, Charlie. Just name it."

"Good deal. I have a plan. Let's run by my house for just a minute and then we'll get started on it."

"Ten-four, Mr. Mayor," Thurman said as he hung a right onto Raymond's street.

Please keep your mouth shut and let me do the talking from now on," Tall Man said. "You sounded like a bad actor, 'we are just doing our job.'"

"I was just trying to help."

"Help quietly next time."

"It's not my fault I'm not smart like you."

"Nobody said it was. Just be quiet, okay?"

"Okay. Is everything ready here?"

"Both canisters are loaded, the primary remote's in my pocket, and the failsafe timer is set on the secondary unit," Tall Man replied as he consulted a small notebook from his pocket. "We'll need at least a hundred and twenty-five in here, so as soon as we start the meeting in the Civic Center, we'll count out enough and you'll bring them over here."

"You sure that many are just going to follow me because we say so?"

"Sure, we'll tell them that the crowd is too big for us to handle in a single meeting. They have no reason to doubt us."

"If you say so."

"Be sure to lock the doors, then come back over where I am and I'll activate the canister with the remote. I calculate a hundred and forty for over there, to be on the safe side."

Short Man stared vacantly into space for a moment, then said, "Can we really do this, man? This is way out there."

"We have to do it. It's all part of the Messiah's plan. These people are of no consequence. We're tools of destiny, my friend. Besides, this is nothing compared to what the L.A. team did."

"I know, I know. I believe in the cause, but it feels different than I expected. I don't mind combat, but these folks ain't much of an enemy."

"It's not about enemies. We're not really killing them anyway. We're setting their souls free where they'll be in his presence all the time, just like we'll be someday. If they could only understand the truth they would line up willingly."

"I wonder."

"Don't. Let's get busy. We want to be ready when the rest of the crew arrives," Tall Man said as he walked toward the door with Short Man close behind.

"That big dude, the mayor, did he look familiar to you?"

"Nope."

"I swear I've seen him somewhere before."

"What does it matter?"

"Don't suppose it does, just making conversation."

"We can talk later, after we've taken care of our duties to the Messiah."

"I still don't feel good about it."

"Jesus G. Christ, would you please get a grip?"

"I thought we weren't supposed to say that name."

"It was a slip of the tongue. Your yapping is getting to me."

"What do you think the Messiah would do if he heard you say the 'JC' word?"

"He'd probably have me killed so I hope you'll keep your mouth shut."

"You ain't got to worry about me."

"I wonder."

Mayor Charlie Raymond slipped in through the back door of City Hall and stood rock still, listening. After hearing nothing he eased down the stairway to the basement. The generator clamored, reeking with the pungent smell of diesel. Raymond moved slowly around the old chamber with his flashlight, looking for anything out of place. And then he saw it, a contraption taped to the side of the air conditioning ductwork on the output side that branched out into the old building. He moved in for a closer look and saw that it was a stainless steel canister about the size of a can of spray paint. A hose came out of the nozzle end and fed through a hole that had been punched into the main duct that branched out and routed air to the whole building. Next to the canister was a small black box the size of a matchbox, with a thin black wire hanging down from it and a yellow wire running to what looked like a small valve on the canister. A radio-controlled receiver was Raymond's guess.

Disarming such devices was well outside the realm of his expertise, but the gadget looked fairly straightforward and didn't appear to be booby-trapped. The small rubber hose pulled easily off the nozzle. He pulled the duct tape loose and gently set the thing on an old table nearby. He examined it carefully but there were no markings of any kind. He held his breath and pulled the yellow wire loose from the connector on the canister. Nothing happened. He breathed again.

News was hard to come by but they had been able to listen in to the Emergency Broadcast System on the radio and knew full well what horror a chemical weapon had wrought in Los Angeles. Charlie Raymond was determined not to see a repeat in Earth, Texas. He stepped carefully back up the stairs, taking the deadly device with him.

At the top of the stairs he opened the door and checked the hall in both directions, then walked with amazing lightness for a man of his bulk toward the rear exit. He passed by the old grate in the wall at the end of the corridor, not noticing the tiny marks on the heads of the rusty screws that held the grate in place.

Behind the grate, which served as the air conditioning intake duct for the ground floor, was a $2.96 disposable filter from Wal-Mart. The slots that held the filter in place on the backside of the grate were designed such that the grate did not have to be removed in order for the filter to be changed out. For this reason, there had been no reason to remove the rusty screws holding the grate assembly to the wall, for the past twenty-two years. Until today. Directly behind the filter, inside the intake duct, sat a device identical to the one Charlie held so carefully as he opened the back door and stepped outside City Hall and into the merciless Texas sun.

35

7:15 AM CENTRAL DAYLIGHT TIME (LOCAL) NEAR THE HART COMPLEX

Jana left White Thunder—the name she'd given the horse—tied to a small tree about fifty feet inside the woods and eased toward an open field that joined them. She had ridden slowly through the low density stand of mostly oak and walnut trees for nearly three hours. The riding was easy, with very little ground vegetation to hinder progress other than occasional runs of scrub brush. She eased out of the woods on her hands and knees, concealed by the tall prairie grass in the bordering field. The early morning sun was hot, having already burnt off most of the dew.

Once in the edge of the field, she raised up just enough to scan the surrounding area, hoping to see some sign of nearby civilization in a direction other than the one from which she had come. She saw nothing but the grassy field laid out to the horizon. No houses. No barns. Not even fences. Just lush green desolation to infinity. She made her way back to White Thunder, sat down, and leaned back against a large maple tree.

The shade of the forest would eventually yield to the searing heat of the sun, but for now it was cool and pleasant. Jana looked at White Thunder, tied several trees away. He would have looked like a statue if not for the occasional swish of his tail. A red-headed woodpecker hammered relentlessly in the tree above him, until the horse gave a soft snort. The woodpecker left, leaving nothing behind but a soothing amalgam of bird and insect song.

She needed to keep moving, needed to find a town, a house, a church, a sane human being, a phone, anything. She had to warn the people back home about the bomb. What if she was too late? Maybe Great Central Electric was nothing more than a smoldering heap of charred concrete and metal by now. Perhaps the whole town was. Would anyone believe her story of being kidnapped and imprisoned as future queen to a maniac? It sounded like something from a movie. Time to stop thinking and start riding. Find help. After a few minutes sleep she would do just that.

7:24 AM CENTRAL DAYLIGHT TIME (LOCAL)
HART COMPLEX

"*Kostia, druzhishe.*" *Kostia, my old friend.* Hart greeted the General on the other end of the secure connection in Russian before continuing in English. "It has become necessary to accelerate certain portions of the schedule. I will be leaving the country this evening en route to you. I shall expect to see you on Sunday instead of Monday. Will the package be ready for delivery?"

"Ah, that will be difficult, Abraham. It takes a great deal of precise cooperation to effect the transfer of this type of merchandise. Expensive cooperation."

"Expense is of no concern to me, Kostia, only results. Do you understand?"

"I do indeed. I shall make it so."

"Very well then. May you have a pleasant weekend," Hart said as he gently laid the phone in its cradle.

He moved back to the desk with the big Bible, opened it to the seventh chapter of Revelation, and began to read, softly speaking the words aloud:

7:3 Saying, Hurt not the earth, neither the sea, nor the trees, till we have sealed the servants of our God in their foreheads.

7:4 And I heard the number of them which were sealed: and there were sealed an hundred and forty and four thousand of all the tribes of the children of Israel.

7:5 Of the tribe of Juda were sealed twelve thousand. Of the tribe of Reuben were sealed twelve thousand. Of the tribe of Gad were sealed twelve thousand.

7:6 Of the tribe of Aser were sealed twelve thousand. Of the tribe of

Nephthalim were sealed twelve thousand. Of the tribe of Manasses were sealed twelve thousand.

7:7 Of the tribe of Simeon were sealed twelve thousand. Of the tribe of Levi were sealed twelve thousand. Of the tribe of Issachar were sealed twelve thousand.

7:8 Of the tribe of Zabulon were sealed twelve thousand. Of the tribe of Joseph were sealed twelve thousand. Of the tribe of Benjamin were sealed twelve thousand.

He then closed the old book slowly, closed his eyes, and said, "We shall soon test the protective value of these pathetic Zionist seals, and I shall do what Ishmael and Esau should have done in millennia gone by. I shall complete what Hitler began but was too weak to finish."

36

10:05 AM CENTRAL DAYLIGHT TIME (LOCAL) YELLOW CREEK

With the deadline minutes away, we were gearing up to post the password on the Fox site as ordered. Working the control room without talking was inefficient so I removed the audio bug from its hiding place and flushed it down the toilet, hoping he was listening. Before busting the code we were a bit perplexed by the instruction to post the password in "unwritten form," but once we uncovered it as WHITE HORSE we were confident on how to handle it. Fox was cooperative and managed to produce a picture of a stunning white stallion. I inserted the graphic, saved the page file, and uploaded it back onto the web site's server. And there it was for all to see, including one particular unknown lunatic, whom we had now dubbed AC.

We waited for a response, Tark staring over my left shoulder, Abdul looking over the right. 10:21 came and went, and still we waited.

"Wonder what's keeping the old boy?" Tark said.

I stood thinking for a couple of minutes, when suddenly it dawned on me. "I think he's had us chasing our own tail."

"What are you speaking of, Matt Decker?"

"I mean this was all just a ruse to keep us busy, and it worked to perfection. Instead of trying to track this idiot down, we spent all night cracking a password."

"Yeah, but we can at least get back into the CEPOCS code to restore power, so it's not a bust," Tark said.

"Stanson won't allow us to turn it back on for fear of another retaliatory strike."

"I must say that I was very afraid for my family," Abdul said.

"Of course you were. He counted on it. But I guarantee you he's not going to waste the resources to hunt down a family somewhere in the middle of Iran whether we had the password or not. Your family's fine and I'm sure my father ... " The realization hit me. Bob Rowe was the only person who had—allegedly—checked on my father's safety, and it was Bob Rowe who supposedly arranged for an increased police presence around the facility where he lay.

My heart hammered against my rib cage as I grabbed the phone and dialed. "All circuits are busy," said the infernal synthetic voice.

I stepped with big strides into the receptionist area outside the control room and scribbled the number on a Post-It note. "Andrea, keep trying until you get through. Come get me as soon as you get them on the line." I walked back into the control room, then stuck my head back around the corner and mouthed a silent "thank you" to her. She was already dialing and gave me a smile and a nod.

Back on station, Abdul rubbed the swollen red rims around his eyes. Tark looked a little ragged, but better than Abdul. "You think something is wrong with your father?" Abdul said.

"No, I'm sure it's fine." Abdul wasn't convinced. I dropped to a knee next to his chair. "Have you tried calling your folks?"

He shook his head. "I have not left here since Tuesday morning and I do not want to make international long distance on company phone."

"You don't worry about that," Tark said. "Call right now. If you can't get through, give it to Andrea and she'll keep trying."

"Thank you." He started dialing and I levered myself up and back into my chair, something that took way more effort than it should have.

"What now?" Tark said.

"Email travels in both directions. Let's send him a reminder."

"Do we run it by the FBI first?"

"I say no."

Tark shrugged. I typed.

```
FROM: x7ijljAweRRv@deckerdigital.com
TO: I14_696938@hotmail.com
SUBJECT: Check the FNC home page

You assumed victory. I've handed you
defeat. If this is to be a fair game, to
this victor go what spoils?
M. Decker, He of Fierce Countenance
```

10:44 AM CENTRAL DAYLIGHT TIME (LOCAL)
EARTH, TEXAS

Mayor Charlie Raymond had spent the last few hours quietly knocking on doors. He knew virtually every soul in town, and he knew the best candidates for the job ahead. The plan called for men who were armed and prepared to fight if need be. Such men are readily available in the Lone Star state and little Earth had its share.

The group of twenty-four was gathered in the band hall at Springlake-Earth High School, a safe distance from City Hall and the intruders. Bruce Thurman was at the downtown area to keep a loose watch on the two and was staying in touch with Charlie with a set of walkie-talkies on a different frequency from the two-way base station back in the P.D. He reported that the two thugs unloaded some sort of equipment from a van and put it in the Civic Center where they thought their town meeting was going to take place.

Charlie asked for quiet and the men turned their attention to him. "Fellows, I appreciate every one of you being here and I thank you for doing it quietly like I asked. We have a situation brewing and I'll need your help to take care of it."

"You just tell us what you need, Charlie," someone said.

"Dang straight!" another chimed in.

"I got to tell you right up front that it may very well involve breaking the law," he said. The room went quiet. "It's entirely possible that there will be shooting—"

"You gonna tell us what's going on or not, Mayor?"

"There are a couple of fellows downtown who I believe came here to kill a bunch of us, maybe all of us for all I know. They claim to be government agents, but I don't believe it. Most of you know my background and I can tell you that I've been around enough crooks in my time to know what they smell like."

"Just two of 'em? Hell, they ain't got a chance against all of us!"

"I want you to end that thinking right now. Given everything that's gone on this week, it's obvious a lot of well-trained people are behind it. We're going to assume these men are competent and deadly. I'm very serious about this. Do you understand?"

The room murmured in agreement and big Charlie Raymond walked to the chalkboard and started drawing. Within two minutes he had a respectable rendition of City Hall and the Civic Center for all to see. "Okay, listen up. They're expecting a bunch of folks to show up for their meeting at twelve-thirty. We don't want to put anyone at risk, so our first order of business is to spread the word that nobody—and I do mean not one Texas soul outside this group—is to go anywhere near downtown this afternoon."

He divided his chalk town into eight sections. "There are twenty-four of you, not counting Bruce and me. Three-man teams is how it'll work, so get into those groups now."

After five minutes of shuffling and arranging that reminded Charlie of teams being chosen on a schoolyard playground, the groups were formed and he divvied up the assigned areas.

"Let's get moving, and remember, not one word about what's going on. You tell the people to stay away and you make sure they get the message, but nothing more. Don't tell your wife, don't tell your girlfriend, your mama, or your Aunt Rosie. If you do, all you're doing is putting innocent people in danger."

* * *

I'm not supposed to be telling nobody about this, so you keep your mouth shut about it, you hear?" Bert Cole said to his wife Susie.

"Well, I don't understand why you got to go down there and get all mixed up in it. Let the law take care of it, Bertie."

"I gotta do my part. You just remember to keep in the house and don't say nothing to nobody about it."

* * *

Gladys, only reason I'm telling you is because I know you won't let it go no further and I want to be sure you keep all your young'uns away from down there. I got to go now. Bertie would get all in a tizzy if he knew I was talking to you."

* * *

That's right, Eunice! A whole gang of killers. It's awful, I tell you, just awful!"

37

11:33 AM CENTRAL DAYLIGHT TIME (LOCAL)
NEAR THE HART COMPLEX

A hot blast of air on Jana's face woke her up. She opened her eyes to see White Thunder leaning down looking at her, as if he had intended to wake her up. She had no idea if she had been asleep for ten minutes or two hours. After standing up and stretching she noticed the temperature had risen considerably and the sun was near mid-sky. Her nap had been more than the few minutes she intended.

The woods buzzed faintly with the sounds of nature, insects, birds, and squirrels scurrying about as if everything was normal. Jana walked around, trying to limber up sore muscles, thinking about what to do next. She heard water running, and found a small clear stream about thirty yards from the tree where she had slept while White Thunder kept watch. She untied him from the tree and led him to the stream, where he wasted no time refreshing himself. Nor did she. The water was cool—a pleasant surprise—and it felt good to drink and wash her face. When White Thunder finished drinking, she mounted up.

Staying in the woods made for slower progress, but she was afraid to leave their cover. The stream ran straight through the woods in a path that headed directly away from Hart's property. It was shallow with a bed of fine rocks worn smooth by years of flow, so she rode down the middle of the stream, hoping it would make her harder to track as she put distance between her and that psychopath and his band of nuts. She guessed it had been about two hours when the saddle started feeling like a slab of rock but she rode on, stopping occasionally for a cool drink of water from the stream for her and the horse. The stream made a gentle curve and the end of the woods came into view ahead. Just beyond that was a house. She gave a gentle kick and clucked her tongue and they were on their way.

Jana tied him to a small maple about ten yards inside the edge of the woods and jogged across a manicured lawn toward the house ahead. The back of the large modern home faced the woods, surrounded by a sprawling redwood deck around a swimming pool filled with chlorine-deprived green water. She made her way through a small gate and around the pool to a set of sliding glass patio doors and peeked inside.

"Can I help you, young lady?"

Jana shrieked and spun around to see a distinguished looking man of about sixty years standing behind her.

"I was in the garage and saw you make your way out

of the woods. Don't take this wrong, honey, but I don't see many beautiful ladies popping out of the woods in my back yard."

She had her hand over her heart, trying to catch her breath, tears of relief running down her face. The man put an arm around her shoulder and she fell sobbing against him.

"Let's go inside and you can tell me what's going on, okay?"

"I have to use your phone immediately," Jana said as soon as they walked inside.

"You can try, but I haven't had any luck getting through to anybody for the past couple of days. I'm Hank Harrington. You got a name?"

"Jana. Where's the phone?"

He pointed toward the kitchen, where Jana found a wall phone with no dial tone. She went back to the den where Hank was and said, "Do you have a car? We have to get out of here."

"Hold on there, sweetheart. I'm not going anywhere, and neither is my car, until you give me some idea about what's going on with you."

"Mister, let's talk on the road. It's a matter of life and death. Please!"

"You really should calm down, Ms. Fulton," he said.

Jana froze for a moment, then slipped her hand into the pocket of the fatigue jacket and curled her hand around the butt of the revolver. "I haven't told you my last name, Hank." She turned to him as she pulled the gun and leveled it at him. His eyes expanded to the size of small moons.

"Look, I know you have troubles, honey—"

"Do not call me 'honey' again. Do, however, tell me

right this moment how you knew my last name. I've had a bad week and I will indeed blow your head off."

Hank was shaking. Hank peed in his khakis, a big dark spot swelling from his crotch and trailing down his leg. "They called from the circle-six and said you broke into the stable and stole their prize stallion. Said you were some kind of animal rights wacko. That's all I know, lady. Now please put the gun down."

"For the record, I was kidnapped in Mississippi and brought to this God-forsaken place, you idiot. And that's no ranch. There's a seriously deranged man over there. He's the one behind the power outages and everything else that's going on and there's no telling what else he's going to do if I can't find somebody to stop him."

"Fine, whatever you say, Ms. Fulton. Just don't hurt me, please."

"Hank, has anyone ever told you what a wuss you are? Don't bother answering that; just get your car keys and get ready to drive. Now!"

Hank retrieved the keys from a soggy pocket.

"One thing before we go," Jana said, "do you have a computer here?"

"No, I've never owned one."

"That figures. Let's roll, Hank."

38

12:50 PM CENTRAL DAYLIGHT TIME (LOCAL)
EARTH, TEXAS

Short Man and Tall Man waited in the empty Civic Center, wondering where the townspeople were. Everything was ready; as soon as the right number of people were in both the Civic Center and City Hall, they'd hit the switches and immediately grab their gas masks from underneath the table. The switch would throw the magnetic locks they had installed on the door and simultaneously open valves on the three tanks of military-grade EZ-4 knockout gas in the Civic Center, along with the infinitely more evil canister—at least that was the plan as far as they knew—in the basement of City Hall. Within seconds the room would be filled with unconscious bodies and the grisly but necessary work would begin.

Suddenly a siren whooped a couple of cycles from the street outside the building. Both men bolted to the door and stepped outside to find themselves greeted by what looked a great deal like a Texas posse from an old western movie. Lots of blue jeans. At least a baker's dozen of cowboy hats. And worst of all, a multitude of gun barrels pointed their way.

Hello, gentlemen," Mayor Charlie Raymond said as he stepped out of the group and walked up to the pair. "Get your hands in the air. If you so much as twitch a finger toward your guns you'll be cut in half." Short and Tall did as they were told. Charlie first drew a semi-automatic from a shoulder holster on each of them, then had them lean on the wall of the building for a more thorough search. That search produced what looked to be an electronic remote control with two toggle switches underneath a protective cover, two more handguns—both snub-nosed revolvers—and a total of three knives.

Charlie motioned for Bruce Thurman and whispered something in his ear when he got there. Bruce scurried off in the direction of City Hall. "Now let's ease back inside here and see if we can't figure out what you boys had planned for us Earthlings," Charlie said with a half-grin.

The two men sat tied to chairs in the middle of the Civic Center, looking at a semi-circle of unhappy but well-armed Texans. Charlie snugged up the final knot on the back of Short Man's chair and walked around to face them. "Who are you?"

"I told you we're from FEMA, you lunatic. Have you any idea what kind of trouble you're going to be in for assaulting federal officials like this?" Tall Man said.

Charlie Raymond extended his hand toward the man nearest him, and the man laid a 12-gauge Remington 870 riot style shotgun in the mayor's big hand. He shucked the pump, chambering a 3" Magnum load of 00 buckshot. "One more time. Who are you?" he asked without raising his voice.

"How many times do we have to say it, heathen?" Short Man said, angry veins bulging from his stocky neck.

Charlie pulled the trigger. The roar inside the room was deafening, but it didn't come close to covering up the animal shriek coming from Short Man as the buckshot took off the toes his right foot. Some eyes grew wide in the posse but no one said a word.

"Wrong answer," Charlie said. The man kept screaming, blood pouring from the mangled stump. Charlie turned to his men and said, "Would somebody shut this lady up, please?" A man stepped forward with a roll of duct tape and wound three good rounds around Short Man's head, muffling the screams that were now turning into groans.

Tall Man's eyes had gone wide at first, but quickly narrowed into a steely gaze of defiance. "Shoot me too if you like, but we won't tell you anything. You're wasting lead."

Chief Thurman opened the door and walked lightly to the center of the room, holding the canister apparatus that Charlie had found in the basement of City Hall. Charlie took it from him in one hand, still wielding the Remington in the other. He casually set the device on the floor between the two and pulled the remote control from his pocket. He was turning back around to face Short and Tall when he felt Thurman pulling at his elbow.

"What?" Charlie said.

"Thurman leaned in close and whispered, "Somebody talked. There's a slew of folks coming up Main, headed this way."

"Chrissakes, why won't people listen?" Charlie motioned to several men in the crowd and walked to the side of the room. The designated followed. "We got people coming. I want you boys to head them off. They'll put up a fight if you tell them to go home, so put them in City Hall for now where they'll be safe. Tell them they can look out the windows and they won't miss anything."

"But they can't see in here from the windows—" one of the men said with a puzzled look on his face.

Charlie closed his eyes for a moment, rubbed his forehead, and prayed the Patience Prayer he had just invented. "Then lie to them."

"Okay, can do."

The men scurried out the door of the Civic Center, and Charlie returned to his captives in the middle of the room.

Short had passed out from the pain. Tall's eyes had lost any trace of defiance, now filled with terror as they darted back and forth between the canister and the remote in Charlie's hand. "Please don't touch that switch. You have no idea what that is," he said, his voice trembling.

"I'm sure it's something you planned to use on us," Charlie said. "Didn't work out that way, though. So in a few minutes, we're all gonna take a little stroll outside and leave it right there with you FEMA boys while I start flipping switches. What do you think about that?"

"Please mister, I'm begging you! I'll tell you what you want to know, I swear. Just get that thing away from me." Tears streamed down the hard face.

"I have a better idea. You start talking. If I hear one thing that strikes me as a lie, so help me God I'll walk right out that door and unleash this on you. I dealt with pieces of crap like you for years, so believe me, I know what a lie sounds like. Sing, Pedro."

Tall Man drew a deep breath and started talking.

1:12 PM CENTRAL DAYLIGHT TIME (LOCAL)
CITY HALL
EARTH, TEXAS

"It ain't right! We got a right to see what's going on over there. I heard a gunshot!"

"Yeah!"

"Damn straight!"

Bruce Thurman was among the makeshift containment crew sent by Charlie Raymond, and he took admirable charge of a situation that was quickly growing out of control. "I'm telling you right now that you're not going over there and that's that. You are to stay right here in City Hall and if you don't, I will personally arrest you and see that you do some time in the lockup for interfering with an investigation. It's not up for discussion. Shut your traps and look out the window if you want to, but that's as close as you're getting."

The crowd of thirty to forty Earth citizens grumbled and groused but backed down. Charlie left the rest of his little team in place to maintain order, and locked both the front and rear doors of City Hall before leaving.

1:14 PM CENTRAL DAYLIGHT TIME (LOCAL)
CIVIC CENTER
EARTH, TEXAS

Tall Man explained to Charlie Raymond that, no, they weren't really FEMA agents. And yes, they had intended to pull some shenanigans in Earth, Texas today. By using knockout gas to put a couple hundred of them to sleep, he and his accomplice would have been able to easily relieve the good townspeople of their valuables. Not a good thing to do for sure, but also not worthy of blowing a foot off if you asked him.

"Sounds like a crock of crap to me," Charlie said. "When you saw that canister you freaked out. I think there's more in them than knockout gas. But it's easy enough to find out, isn't it?" Charlie said with a one-sided smile.

Unlike before, Tall Man didn't react. No fear in his eyes. Nothing. Maybe he was telling the truth, Charlie thought. Short had regained consciousness and was making a valiant effort to say something through the duct tape. Charlie sighed and ripped the tape off.

"What time is it?" Short Man said.

"One-fifteen. Why?" Charlie Raymond said.

"Shut up, you dumb-ass," Tall said, glaring at Short.

"You have to tell him, man. Hurry up!"

"Tell me what?" Charlie's eyes darted back and forth between the two.

"It's too late," Tall Man said. "Praise the Messiah."

"There's a timer that'll go off at one-sixteen," Short Man said. "I been trying to tell you, honest I have."

Charlie glanced at his watch. One-seventeen. Nothing was happening in the Civic Center. That left City Hall. He broke in a run out the door and across the street, with several men following him.

Charlie and company heard the screams before they were halfway across the street. "Dear God, no ... " he said as his run turned into a wide open sprint.

One of the younger men passed Charlie and had his hand on the door handle, thumb pressing the button down to open it when Charlie arrived. He looked in through the small pane of reinforced glass in the door and knocked the man back. Just as Tall Man had said, it was too late.

Of all the situations Charlie Raymond had faced over the years, the gunfights, investigating the scenes of hideous crimes, watching killers go free on technicalities, and a thousand other heartbreaking scenarios dealt with during his tenure as a Texas Ranger, not one incident came close to the horror of what he was forced to watch unfold through a pane of glass in a door that he had ordered locked. He may as well have lined up his fellow citizens, his constituents he swore to protect, his friends—against a brick wall and shot them himself, for he had just as surely sent them all to this grotesque poison-gas death.

He turned and walked away from the building, away from the screams, back toward the Civic Center.

"Jesus, Charlie, aren't we going to help them?" someone said.

Charlie kept walking, his eyes as lifeless as puddles of stagnant water in a field of mud. "There's nothing we can do. They're dead already and if we go in there we'll be dead too."

When he walked back into the Civic Center, one of the few men who had stayed behind was holding the shotgun on the men in the chairs. Without saying a word, Charlie Raymond took the shotgun from him, held it a foot from Tall Man's face, and pulled the trigger, covering himself in a grisly spray of blood, brain, and bone.

He leveled the gun at Short Man. "Is there anything else you'd like to tell me, Hoss?"

"Please don't shoot me, mister." Tears rolled off his blockish face.

"More people coming?"

Short nodded.

"How many?"

"Not sure, a few."

"When?"

"Two o'clock."

"Somebody find something to bandage his foot with. And let's get ready for the rest of our guests."

39

1:58 PM CENTRAL DAYLIGHT TIME (LOCAL)
CIVIC CENTER
EARTH, TEXAS

Charlie and what remained of his crew—many lost family members in the carnage at City Hall and were hardly in a state of mind to do battle—were positioned on both sides of Main Street. He had reached the state police by radio and they were en route, but they would not make it in time. Crouched behind a garbage truck on one side and a row of hedges on the other, they waited.

His radio squawked, "White Suburban just turned onto Main."

"Roger that." He stood and yelled, "Heads up! Show-time in sixty."

As the Suburban drew near and slowed to a stop in the middle of the street, Charlie jutted his neck around the corner of the garbage truck. His view was at an angle, but predominantly from the passenger side. The windows were tinted to a deep charcoal and he couldn't see how many men were inside. He clenched a chrome whistle in his teeth, drew a deep breath, and waited.

The passenger door opened and a black-booted foot touched down on the pavement. Then another, followed by a man so tall he unfolded more than he stepped from the vehicle. A dirt devil danced its way down the street, kicking a Pepsi can in circles of sand and grit and died out when it hit the front end of the Suburban. The man was dressed in black assault coveralls, blond hair cut so close that he looked bald at first glance. He scanned toward City Hall on his right, then checked out the Civic Center to his left, looking across the top of the vehicle.

Charlie realized he was holding his breath and slowly exhaled. The man reached inside the truck with a "come on" gesture and then stepped away from the truck as the other three doors opened in near unison. Charlie appraised the situation as they exited; a four-man fire team, each of whom moved with a fluid style that screamed professional. They also outgunned the Texans from a firepower perspective, each holding Uzi 9mm assault weapons, most likely full auto. The two on the passenger side moved toward City Hall, the others toward the Civic Center. Charlie drew one more deep breath, closed his lips around the mouthpiece, and loosed a banshee shriek from the whistle. He was the first to fire. Charlie Raymond was a marksman, his aim true as the 30-30 round found purchase directly on the first man's heart.

The impact drove the man back against the right front fender of the Suburban, where he slid to the ground like a cartoon character as Charlie levered another round into the chamber of his old Winchester. The man from the rear passenger side immediately fell back behind the door he had exited and returned fire with the Uzi, a rapid-fire barrage of rounds hitting the garbage truck like a dozen sledgehammers.

Charlie's men were now firing and all being fired upon as the three remaining attackers retreated into the Suburban. It lasted less than thirty seconds, claimed the lives of all four attackers and two of the hometown boys, and left several more injured. He screamed for them to hold fire and stepped into the street. An acrid haze of burnt gunpowder hung in the air, the silence so abrupt it was deafening. Big Charlie Raymond cried.

40

3:53 PM CENTRAL DAYLIGHT TIME (LOCAL)
NEAR OMAHA, NEBRASKA

Hank Harrington drove. Jana pointed the gun. "Can you please put that handgun down? Those things make me nervous. I don't believe in them."

"You're a fool if this one doesn't scare you. Shut up and drive."

"Can you at least tell me where we're going?"

"You're taking me to civilization. We're going to find someone who has a working telephone and hopefully a computer. You're going to tag along with your stinky self and act like we're big pals so I don't have to shoot you. There are some houses up ahead. Slow down." Hank slowed the car and Jana said, "Turn into the second house on the right, the one with the blue car."

They knocked on the front door and an attractive lady

who looked to be in her mid-forties answered. "Could I help you?"

"We desperately need to use a phone. Is yours working?"

The lady looked skeptically at Jana in the fatigue jacket and sniffed the air trying to figure out what the odd odor was, but finally said, "Yes, it's working. Come on in. It's over there on the end table."

"Thanks so much," Jana said. She turned to Hank and said, "Come on, dear." She went to the phone, picked it up, and dialed.

"Great Central Electric," came the answer, the most beautiful words Jana had ever heard.

"Is Brett Fulton there?" she asked.

"No, I'm sorry ma'am. Mr. Fulton was killed in an automobile accident."

Jana stood there, stunned, but no tears fell. Her brother lived hard and fast, and news of his death was something the whole family had come to expect. She could cry later, if she could manage to stay alive herself—

"Ma'am, are you still there?"

"Yes, who's in the control room right now?"

"I'm not allowed to give out that information."

"Who are you?"

"Ma'am, security has been stepped up a lot around here in the past few days. I'm not allowed to say much of anything about what's going on here. In fact, I probably shouldn't have released the information about Mr. Fulton. May I ask who's calling?"

"Jana Fulton, Brett's sister."

"Oh dear, I'm so sorry! My name is Andrea. I used to work in accounting but they moved me to the switchboard to help out with all the calls—"

Jana felt something cold on the back of her neck and turned around to see the bull-of-a-man guard from Hart's place, holding a gun. She scanned the area and saw the lady who owned the house standing across the room with a terrified look on her face. Hank looked even worse. The situation didn't look good, but she decided she plain would not go back to the hellhole she had just escaped. She swung at the bull and he grabbed her wrist. Her strength was no match for his, but it didn't have to be. While he was occupied with her left hand, her right slipped into the pocket of the jacket. She pointed the gun and pulled the trigger.

The bullet entered his lower abdomen and tore through his intestines before hitting and shattering two lumbar vertebrae and severing his spinal cord. His newly-paralyzed legs collapsed under him and he crumpled to the floor moaning as black blood gushed from the hole in his stomach. It was the last thing Jana saw before everything went black.

Hank Harrington dropped the vase he had clubbed her on the back of the head with and said, "This woman is crazy. Let's get the police over here."

The lady who owned the house disconnected Jana's call and dialed 911, shaking all the while.

4:00 PM CENTRAL DAYLIGHT TIME (LOCAL)
YELLOW CREEK

I was talking to Tark when Andrea ran into the room. "Mr. Tarkleton, I didn't know you were back! Jana Fulton called!"

"Come again?" Tark said.

"Jana Fulton, that's Brett's sister!"

"I know who she is, Andrea. When did she call? Where from?"

"I don't know. That's the weird part. She didn't even know about Brett and then she just stopped talking, and ... " Her eyes started tearing up and she was gasping for breath.

"Calm down, Andrea. We need the details," Tark said.

"She's hyperventilating," I said. Abdul sprinted out of the room and returned in what seemed like two seconds with a paper bag. We sat her down and had her breathe into it for a couple of minutes.

"I'm sorry," she said.

"It's okay, just tell us the rest of it if you can," I said.

"I answered the phone and she asked for Brett. Before I even thought about the rules, I blurted out what had happened to him. She went real quiet, didn't say anything for a while. Then she wanted to know who else was here. I wouldn't tell her anything and asked who she was. She told me she was Brett's sister. Then I told her who I was, but she didn't answer me and I thought she was just upset ... "

Her eyes started tearing up again. Tark gently put his arm around her and whispered something in her ear. She dried her eyes.

"I heard someone else talking in the background, and then I heard a bunch of scuffling and a loud bang. I'm sure it was a gunshot. It scared me to death. I kept screaming for her over and over but no one answered and then someone hung the phone up on that end."

"Thanks, Andrea. Tark, please tell me you have caller ID or some sort of call logging on the switchboard," I said.

"Not locally. All of our calls get routed through a switch at headquarters. I'll call them and see if they can track it for us."

42

4:40 PM CENTRAL DAYLIGHT TIME (LOCAL)
DOUGLAS COUNTY JAIL
OMAHA, NEBRASKA

Jana's eyes fluttered open to the sight of a dingy ceiling. She rose up and the back of her head exploded in pain, quickly bringing her back down. Rolling her head to the left, she saw the bars of the jail cell door. At first she thought she was dreaming but as the fog cleared it was evident it was all too real. Her heart started racing, which increased the pounding in her head, and she forced herself to stand up and walk to the door. "Hello, is anyone there?" she said, softly at first, then in a scream. After the fifth time, a female guard clanked her way through an outer cell door and made her way down the hall.

"You need to be quiet, missy. I'm not about to listen to a bunch of this."

"Where am I?"

"You're in the Douglas County jail, little lady, after being arrested for murder. I suspect you'll be arraigned in the morning."

"Murder? Have you lost your mind? I shot that guy in self defense! And I have important information about what's going on with the electricity!"

"Uh-huh. Half the guests this week have had 'important information' about what's going on. Everybody's looking for a deal, sugar, but we ain't dealing."

"Would you please listen to me? There's a bomb at Great Central Electric back in Mississippi!"

"Well that's one I haven't heard yet. Still not dealing, though. Save your stories and your innocence for your lawyer."

"I don't have a lawyer! I haven't been offered one. I haven't been read my rights. I need my phone call."

"Well let me take care of that. You not only have the right to remain silent, I insist on it. You'll get a public defender lawyer as soon as we can round one up. Things are working a little more slowly these days. As for a phone call, ours don't work, so it looks like you're up that creek without a paddle. Now go to sleep or something."

The guard walked away and Jana heard the outer door open, then clank shut, its metallic tones reverberating through the halls of bare concrete and cold steel. She walked back to the bunk and sat down. Things weren't exactly going her way, but at least she was safe here. When her lawyer arrived, maybe she could get a message to Great Central.

5:03 PM CENTRAL DAYLIGHT TIME (LOCAL)
HART COMPLEX

Hart bounced along the narrow farm road in the Hummer, headed for the airstrip on the backside of his sprawling property. The pilot was staying in the small apartment inside the Gulfstream's hangar, ready to leave with little notice. Without telling anyone, Hart had radioed ahead and the engines were at a low hum when he arrived. He hated to leave without his whore, but such was the unfairness of life.

"Where to, sir?" the pilot asked when Hart stepped on board.

"Moscow."

"Russia?"

"Yes."

"It'll take me a little while to plan the flight, get clearances, find a qualified co-pilot—"

"There will be no co-pilot and no flight plan."

"Sir, I'm not happy about a transoceanic solo flight, but I'll do it. Doing it without a flight plan is another matter altogether. With no commercial traffic to clutter the skies, an unauthorized private flight will draw a lot of attention. If we don't file a flight plan, we'll pick up an Air Force escort within a hundred miles."

Hart closed his eyes and breathed deeply, summoning control. The pilot deserved to be shot in the groin and fed through one of the turbine engines, but Hart could not fly the aircraft himself. "Plan your flight, and have me out of here in fifteen minutes."

"Yes sir."

5:05 PM CENTRAL DAYLIGHT TIME (LOCAL) YELLOW CREEK

Andrea was working the phones hard. In addition to trying to reach Alpine Village for me and Abdul's family for him, Tark had her trying to reach someone at headquarters to get the info on the call from Jana. I had also sent an email requesting the trace, but there had been no response. Tark was in the lounge going over all the communications that had come in from AC during the week. "You have new mail," my laptop said.

```
Mr. Decker:

My name is Larry Bond and I have been
instructed by the director to liaison
with you. I will keep you posted on all
significant developments and of course
ask that you do likewise. For the sake
of expediency, my communications will be
informal as opposed to official reports
which take too long to prepare.

We just received a bizarre report
from a town in Texas called Earth. A
number of men showed up in this small
town (pop. ~1000) and had plans to
“exterminate” one fourth of the town’s
official population, half with VX nerve
gas and half with swords. Several dozen
townspeople were killed, along with all
but one of the intruders.
```

```
Will forward more details when I have
them. Please let me know if you and your
people can make any sense out of this.

Best ...
Larry
```

I printed the message and headed for the lounge. "Tark, take a look at this," I said.

He read the message and shook his head. "Lord help us. He figured he couldn't kill a fourth of planet Earth, so he went for Earth, Texas instead. He was cutting some corners in another way too, though."

"Explain."

He peered at the big Bible. "Verse eight calls for a fourth of the Earth to be killed through sword, hunger, and the beasts of the earth. Looks like they had the sword part covered. The beasts of the earth passage is theorized to be some kind of plague or pestilence."

"The poison gas could be pestilence."

"Yep, but he missed the famine altogether. Hard to figure why he's so meticulous on some things and sloppy on others."

Andrea ran into the room. "I finally got hold of headquarters. They're having generator problems and can't access the phone computers until morning."

"Any luck reaching the other places?" I said.

She shook her head. I suddenly couldn't keep my eyes open and laid my head down on the table. "Just keeps getting better," I said into the table.

"Andrea, it's five o'clock but we need you to stay if you can." Tark said.

"I'm here as long as you need me."

He thanked her and I pushed myself upright. He was readying the pipe for another session, tamping tobacco with furious purpose.

"Tark, you're onto something. What is it?"

He flicked his lighter and sucked the flame into the bowl. "I've figured something out, but I don't know that it's any help to us now."

"I'm listening."

He puffed and studied a sheet of paper. "We've already spotted the antichrist theme, so this part is sort of irrelevant."

"Come on, out with it."

"Hold those ponies, Matthew, I'm getting there. You remember your first email, when I said the first line sounded familiar?"

"Sure, the 'Never more horror' line."

"That came from one of Nostradamus' quatrains."

"Meaning?"

"Generally thought to be part of an end-of-days prophecy, which fits right in with the antichrist stuff."

"I agree, that's irrelevant. We already—"

"I'm not through." He was power-puffing now, sweet billowing clouds. "Once I figured that out, I looked at the rest of the emails. Here, take a look at the one he sent to the White House." He shoved it in my face.

"What am I looking for in this one?"

"'You will tremble mightily.'"

"I see it."

"Guess who else used that line?"

"Nostradamus?"

"Bingo." He picked up an open book from the table. "I swung by the house on my last trip back from the hospital and brought back anything I thought might help. Peggy bought this thing at a yard sale years ago."

I took it from him and looked at the spine. *Nostradamus Complete.* It was open to a page with a heading of Century Nine, Quatrain 83. Underneath was the verse itself, first in French:

Sol vingt de Taurus si fort de terre trembler,
Le grand theatre remply ruinera:
L'air, ciel & terre obscurcir & troubler,
Lors l'infidelle Dieu & saincts voguera.

Then in English:

Sun twentieth of Taurus the earth will tremble very mightily,
It will ruin the great theater filled:
To darken and trouble air, sky and land,
Then the infidel will call upon God and saints.

"So, AC uses a line from Nostradamus," I said as I continued to read, "predicting an earthquake."

"And the sixth seal involves a massive earthquake."

"So the question is ... "

"How do you fake an earthquake?"

DAY FIVE
SATURDAY

I saw under the altar the souls of them that were slain for the word of God, and for the testimony which they held: And they cried with a loud voice, saying, How long, O Lord, holy and true, dost thou not judge and avenge our blood on them that dwell on the earth?
Revelation 6:9-10

43

MIDNIGHT DAYLIGHT CENTRAL TIME
0500 GREENWICH MEAN TIME
80 NAUTICAL MILES SOUTH-SOUTHWEST OF REYKJAVIK, ICELAND

Hart burst into the cockpit and heard the pilot talking into his headset. "Roger that, Approach. Descending through ten thousand to three thousand. Expecting left base for runway zero-two."

"Affirmative, two-one-six. Contact tower at outer marker on one-eighteen-point-three. Good day, sir."

"What are you doing?" Hart said.

"I'm landing at Keflavik International to top off the tanks, sir."

"You will do nothing of the kind. I know full well that this aircraft has the fuel necessary for the trip without stopping and you will fly it directly to Moscow."

"No sir. I will not. After we land, you're welcome to hire another pilot if you like, but I will not start across the North Atlantic with anything less than topped-off tanks."

Hart wailed like a wild animal and scurried back to the cabin. The pilot made a mental note to seek other employment at the earliest possible opportunity, and checked the weather again. Conditions between Iceland and Europe looked good at the moment, but the North Atlantic tracks were notorious for changing their minds for the worse. He wasn't a particularly religious man but he said a prayer anyway, and started working the pre-landing checklist.

4:30 AM CENTRAL DAYLIGHT TIME (LOCAL) YELLOW CREEK

I woke from a fitful sleep and a torrent of bad dreams to find myself on one of the mattresses, not remembering how I got there. The room was dark. So was the hallway outside other than the scant light that spilled into it from the control room at the other end. I couldn't remember what I had dreamed, but its melancholy ambiance carried over into my conscious state. As I lay there in the quiet, hot dark, a dreadful realization settled over me so strongly that I said it out loud. "I have no life."

I had no family beyond distant relatives whom I didn't know. There were women I dated, but none I loved and to my knowledge none who loved me. My address book was filled with business acquaintances. I lived in a spectacular and absurdly large house on top of a mountain that overlooked the Pacific on one side and lush green valleys on the others. I had every toy money could buy and more money than I could possibly spend. My adulthood had been spent in the relentless pursuit of more. More money. More stuff. More "success" at what I did. I had it all. And I shared it with a dog. Something was wrong.

After washing my face in the bathroom I plodded and stretched my way into the control room. Abdul was at his station but sound asleep, head flopped back and snoring. I checked my laptop for email and found none, then slipped outside for a little air.

The night was crystal clear and the temperature had dropped enough to call it pleasant. I could hear the diesel emergency generator on the backside of the facility, clattering over the insect life of the summer night. The generator didn't power the outside lights and the absence of light pollution made for a dazzling overhead show. A shooting star slashed across Orion and faded at Pleiades. The moon was a small crescent settling into the western horizon. I sat on the edge of a little pier on the waterway and gazed at the majesty of it all, feeling even more insignificant. After a few minutes I caught an aromatic whiff behind me. Tark and his pipe.

"Morning, Matthew. Hope you rested well."

"I'm feeling much better, thanks." Physically, that was true.

"Any contact from AC?"

"Not a word."

"FBI?"

"I talked to Brandon himself last night, gave him the skinny on the earthquake prediction. He said they'd work on it, that he'd personally task the right people on it. Nothing since."

"I think we should turn the power back on."

"We're into CEPOCS and I can fix it outright within a few hours, but that's the President's call."

"Maybe he'll have the courage to order it. Whoever we're fighting is moving according to a plan that's been in place a long time, not in response to what you or anyone else is doing. He'll go for the fifth seal today, no matter what."

"Refresh me."

"Martyrs, slain for the Word of God."

44

11:10 AM GREENWICH MEAN TIME (6:10 AM CENTRAL DAYLIGHT TIME) 1500 MILES EAST OF REYKJAVIK, ICELAND

Hart had taken up residence in the co-pilot's seat. "Why do you not go around this weather?"

"Too late for that, sir. All we can do is ride it out and hope we make it through."

Hart's voice had lost its earlier edge; the pilot was now his best friend. "What do you mean, you hope we make it through?"

The Gulfstream pitched violently into a sixty-degree left bank. No sooner had the autopilot leveled the wings than the altimeter spun counter-clockwise as the aircraft hit a radical area of low pressure and started a dive as lift deteriorated. It hit the bottom of the air pocket like concrete, shuddering hard enough to flex the wingtips several inches.

“Flying the North Atlantic in summer is a two-man affair. It’s a full-time job keeping up with the weather on radio and radar. You wanted a solo flight. You got it. Warmer air from the south hits cold northern air and creates mammoth disturbances in weather patterns. On top of that, we’re right on the axis of the jet stream.”

“What does that mean?”

“We have a wind blowing right up our tailpipe at three hundred knots. That kind of tailwind pushing us into this thunderstorm is not a good mix. I’ve never been in anything like this and I’m not sure the airframe can—”

A lightning bolt slashed diagonally in front of the small jet, accompanied by a thunder bumper that shook it so violently that oxygen masks dropped in the cabin. Then they hit the path of the lightning bolt, essentially a vacuum. The right engine sucked for air, and for a half-second, found none. The result was a flameout. Lights flashed and the plane’s computer spoke. “Engine failure. Engine failure. Engine failure.”

The pilot silenced the alarm, killed the autopilot, and stomped the left rudder pedal in an attempt to compensate for the tremendous yaw to the right caused by having only the left engine operational. He looked over and saw that Hart’s dark complexion was now alabaster.

“What now?” Hart screamed, sweat dripping off his nose.

“We keep trying to ride it out.”

“Are we going to make it?”

“I don’t know, sir. I really don’t.”

10:10 AM CENTRAL DAYLIGHT TIME (LOCAL)
YELLOW CREEK

Matt Decker, I think you should see this," Abdul said. I walked to his station and he had two identical pictures of the white horse we'd put on the Fox web site, displayed side by side on his monitor.

"I set an alarm to let me know if this web page changed and the alarm did sound. When I looked at the page, I could not see a difference. I still had the copy of the page on my own hard drive from when we created it and inserted our horse picture, so I compared it to the current version online."

"And?"

"The difference is in the picture."

I looked it over for a half-minute and said, "I don't see it, Abdul."

"There is no difference to see, but there has been a change. Our picture was a JPEG format. Now it is BMP."

That was curious. JPEG picture files are widely used because it's an excellent compression algorithm that produces good quality with reasonable file sizes. BMP files, usually called bitmaps, consume a lot more disk space and thus more bandwidth when used online.

"Have you checked with Fox to be sure they didn't make the change?"

"I have emailed them and they said they did not do anything since we uploaded our page."

"Are you thinking what I'm thinking, Abdul?"

"If you are thinking steganography."

Steganography involves hiding files within files. The

technology got its first big public exposure after 9/11, when the government found out the terrorists were sending coordination messages to each other via pictures on the Internet. The secret file is embedded inside another carrier file—typically a picture or sound file—and the unlock mechanism that separates the single file back into its individual components is encrypted for security.

"It's exactly what I'm thinking," I said. "You got a decryption app handy?"

"I have Steganos."

"Let's try to bust it up and see what happens."

He started clicking and after a few seconds said, "We were right. It is a steg file! It's encrypted, but the password prompt looks like a clue."

I leaned over his shoulder and studied the screen. The password prompt said:

```
VERY GOOD WITH THE FIRST. NUMBER THREE
WILL LEAD YOU HOME. YOU HAVE THREE
TRIES.
```

The cursor was blinking. Waiting.

Tark burst into the room. "I just got an email from headquarters. They traced the call from Jana. It came from a house outside Omaha, Nebraska."

"Nebraska? You sure about that?" I said.

"Yep, they've called the FBI and passed everything on to them. You get a chance to check out your new contact yet?"

"Yeah, he looks clean."

"Reckon you should contact him or Brandon on this Nebraska lead?"

"I'll take a chance and trust Bond for now. Brandon doesn't check his email regularly and it's a monumental pain to get him on the phone."

"You're the boss."

"Abdul, print that screen, please," I said. He did and I gave it to Tark. "We've found a hidden file he posted on the Internet. We need to figure out the password to get inside it. Here's what we have to go on. You mind taking a look at this problem while I work on something else for a little bit?"

"Not a bit, my boy. I'm on it." He reached for the pipe pouch and left the room in big pounding strides.

I fired off an email to Larry Bond, telling him what we had and asking if he had anything else for us. I'd saved a picture of Jana Fulton to my hard drive the night I researched her and everyone else, and I pulled that picture up and wondered if she was okay. I also wondered if a woman could possibly be as beautiful in the flesh as she was in that picture. Nebraska. Last I heard, the Feds were still confining their search to New York and Los Angeles.

I hit the Internet and tried to research the issue a bit more, but everything other than a few government and news sites yielded "server cannot be reached" errors. I went back to the Fox site and checked for updates. There were none. A banner ad for a site selling "As Seen on TV" products was blinking at the top of the screen. I sat staring at the obnoxious rectangle and it hit me. The Feds were wrong. Bad wrong.

My FBI liaison Larry Bond wasted no time replying to my email:

Matt,

Cryptos examining password issue now. Will advise of progress or suggestions. Field agents in Omaha presently investigating source of Fulton call. Suspect captured in Earth, Texas is cooperating but of surprisingly little help. He is part of a religious movement loyal to a "messiah" who is supposed to usher in a new era. Movement operates in classic compartmentalized cells, so individuals and smaller teams have no idea about the activities of others. They do know some major part of the plan is supposed to happen TODAY, however. They claim no knowledge of what the event is and special interrogation team reports confidence in veracity is Delta level. I'm told you will understand what that means.

Larry

I printed the message and took it to Tark. "What's Delta level veracity?" he said.

"It means the interrogators are positive the suspects are telling the truth."

"How can they be positive? Lie detectors?"

"Not the kind you're thinking about. After the World Trade Center, some laws were quietly passed and a few executive orders issued that gave the Feds enormous latitude when dealing with suspected terrorists. Special interrogation teams were formed and these guys were given carte blanche to get the answers they needed. All in the name of national security, of course."

"You telling me they made it okay to beat people and such?"

"Torture," I said. "They legalized torture. Beating isn't the half of it, although that's certainly a part. Electrical shock. Chemicals. No holds barred, get the answers."

"Good heavens, I had no idea."

"Pretty amazing, huh?"

"Obama tried to do away with it while he was in office, but sometimes what a president doesn't know can't hurt him."

Tark shook his head and returned to his Bible. "You still got that time line handy?"

"Sure. What's on your mind?"

"Just a hunch." I got the printout from the control room and handed it to him. He relit the pipe and puffed and squinted, slow at first, then it shifted into high gear.

"You see something, don't you?"

"Yep, Matthew. I believe I do."

45

11:12 AM CENTRAL DAYLIGHT TIME (LOCAL)
YELLOW CREEK

Everything this guy does," Tark said, "means something to him. If we overlook anything we run the risk of missing important clues."

"We've established that. What's your point?"

"And two-sixteen is the pattern, right?"

"Yes."

"But not the whole pattern, you see. We missed something."

I sighed and motioned for him to get on with it.

"My point is this. It didn't begin at precisely two-sixteen. Fact is, it began at two-sixteen and thirty-seven seconds. Since he does nothing by accident, why not two-sixteen on the mark?"

"Good find, Tark. Any idea on the significance of thirty-seven?"

"Hold your horses, there's more. Now that we're thinking in hours, minutes, and seconds, take a look at the times between the three states blacking out on Monday."

I picked up the printout and looked. "I'll be damned."

"That may well be, but you can change that with a quick prayer," Tark said.

I started to ask what he was talking about but it clicked and I moved on. "Mississippi went down at two-sixteen, thirty-seven seconds, then Alabama at two-eighteen-twenty-one, and finally Tennessee at two-twenty-one-nine. All two minutes sixteen seconds apart. Amazing that we've missed this, but other than reinforcing two-sixteen, and by extension six-six-six, what's the meaning?"

"Let's move back to the importance of thirty-seven seconds. What was the first computer password you finally figured out after looking all night for it?"

"White horse."

"Now take a look at this." He shoved the Bible across the table to me and pointed to the top of the sixth chapter of Revelation. "Count the words," he said. I counted, and then looked at him and shook my head. Word number thirty-seven was the "white" in "white horse."

1 And I saw when the Lamb opened one of the seals, and I heard, as it were the noise of thunder, one of the four beasts saying, Come and see.

2 And I saw, and behold a white horse: and he that sat on him had a bow; and a crown was given unto him: and he went forth conquering, and to conquer.

"Good work, Tark." I had jotted the current clue on a scrap of paper and read it out loud: "Very good with the first. Number three will lead you home. You have three tries."

"The white horse was the first horse and also the first password."

I looked to the whiteboard that was still filled with our earlier scribbling about horses. "And the black horse was the third one, number three." I started counting words.

"I've already counted it. The 'black' in 'black horse' is the hundred-forty-third word in chapter six, assuming he sticks to King James." I headed to the control room with him in tight tow.

"Abdul, let's try a password on that steg file," I said. His fingertips hovered at the ready. "One four three."

We held our breath as he slowly keyed it in and pressed ENTER. "That's it!" Abdul said. An elaborate animation ran that showed four horses, one white, one red, one black, and one a creamy color. The horses came in from the corner of the screen, met in the middle, and dissolved into what looked like a digital clock set at 00:00. Underneath the clock a scroll opened up that said PRESS ENTER TO CONTINUE. Abdul looked to me for confirmation. I nodded and he hit the key.

An unearthly voice boomed from the computer speakers, "Thank you for your participation." Then I noticed that the digits on the clock were no longer zeros. It now showed 00:53:14 and was counting down. I glanced at my watch and did the math, as if it was even necessary.

"It's counting down to one-sixteen our time. Eastern time, that's two-sixteen," I said.

"But counting down to what?" Abdul said.

"The fifth seal," I said.

46

12:18 PM CENTRAL DAYLIGHT TIME (LOCAL)
YELLOW CREEK

I fired another email to Larry Bond:

Larry, a couple of things to report here. First, call off the cryptos. We solved the password. Turned out to be a numerical reference to a passage in Revelation. I'm attaching a file showing the breakdown so your people have all the knowledge we have. Bottom line is another event should be expected at 2:16 PM Eastern time.

Also recommend immediate, large scale follow-up on the issue of Jana Fulton's possible presence in Nebraska. I was told earlier that the Bureau and other agencies are concentrating their search for AC (our code name for the suspect) in NYC and LA, presumably because comm techs determined that only those two areas had access to a fiber backbone large enough to facilitate the communications that have taken place on the other side. That info is faulty. Research shows that Omaha, Nebraska is a site of massive fiber junctions. Most of the nation's largest telemarketing (as seen on TV infomercial crap) fulfillment centers are located near Omaha. They started locating there because of low overhead and access to the comm lines that ran through the area due to its fairly central location. After a while, it became a major industry and accelerated the growth of fiber-comms in the area even more. Omaha has essentially the comms capability of NYC and LA.

This would likely be an attractive area for any clandestine operation, plus you must consider the fact that we now have a direct link (Jana Fulton) to the locale.

Will advise on further developments here.

Matt Decker

With less than an hour remaining on the countdown, I walked outside to limber up. A big bank of dark clouds was rolling in from the west and bringing a cool breeze with it. It was the first time since getting there on Monday I had felt anything outdoors other than suffocating heat. I wound down the little asphalt path to the waterfront and sat on the edge of a concrete pier. It was a far cry from the water view I had back home, but it still soothed my ragged nerves.

I sat very still, feeling the wind on the back of my head, watching the water in the canal move slowly downstream. Other than the generator several hundred yards away, the world was void of man-made sounds. Grasshoppers chirped. The flowing water made the soft sound that flowing water makes. No trucks whined on the highway, no contrails sliced the sky. I looked around and for the first time noticed that Mississippi was a beautiful place. Gently rolling hills stretched as far as the eye could see, lush green pastures competing for space with thick forests. It was majestic, and I felt small again.

The life I had made for myself, the importance I had accorded to my own existence just five days earlier, seemed small and petty. For years, computers were my friends. Machines. Boxes of silicon and copper and steel and plastic. Money, money, and more money. People meant nothing to me beyond their ability to somehow enhance my own world. I remembered being a child and feeling very different. I closed my eyes and I could see Dad, standing proudly in his pulpit. A cantankerous old cat named Bernie who would purr in my lap and then bite me for no reason. Random bits and pieces ebbed and flowed through my mind. My life.

I laid back on the pier and looked up at the clouds roiling past, their churning, seething underbellies thick with shades of blue and almost-black, the wind growing stronger. And then the magnitude of what had happened that week began to sink in. Two million dead. Two million intricate worlds of hopes and dreams and loves and disappointments and victories and defeats. Gone. Why? It was the same question I asked when my father became a vegetable. A good man who loved and cared for others, yanked from this earth for no reason at all.

I was angry as hell. I pulled myself up, stretched my arms out and screamed to the sky, "What kind of sick God are you? What kind of God would take both my parents from me? What kind of God would let some sick bastard kill all these people? How can you call yourself God at all?"

12:45 PM CENTRAL DAYLIGHT TIME (LOCAL)
DOUGLAS COUNTY JAIL
OMAHA, NEBRASKA

"Ms. Fulton?" The voice at the cell door startled her and she hit her head on the frame of the bunk above her as she jumped up.

"Yes?"

"I'm with the Federal Bureau of Investigation. We're going to get you out of here and into our custody."

A voice approached from the hall, reverberating as it drew nearer. "You're not taking this prisoner anywhere. She's being held on a variety of state charges."

"Sheriff, we're in a national state of emergency and

I guarantee you my power supersedes yours concerning any person in this jail. We don't have time for a turf war, and if you stand in the way of what I'm doing I'll have my men come in here and put you in one of your own cells."

"I'd like to see you try," the sheriff said. He was right beside the agent now, towering a good six inches above the Federal man.

The agent yanked a radio from his belt, keyed it up, and spoke quickly. "All units inside immediately. We have a situation."

"Don't let them in here," the sheriff shouted down the hall.

"Sir, that'll be hard to pull off," came a reply.

"Why is that, Deputy?"

"Because there are two of us and six of them and they have much bigger guns, sir."

"Like I said, Sheriff, we don't have time for this," the FBI agent said. "This will be the last time I ask you politely. Open this door."

The big man muttered but he unlocked the door, and Jana wasted no time moving through it. The agent took her by the arm and escorted her briskly down the hall and out of the cellblock into the lobby area of the jail. They were headed toward the outer door when Jana said, "Do we have time to get my things?"

The agent looked at the sheriff and the sheriff nodded to a deputy. Two minutes later Jana had her personal effects, which consisted of the late Dane Christian's fatigue jacket, sans revolver.

As soon as they stepped outside Jana saw what the deputy had meant by "bigger guns." There were four men and two women, all dressed in black tactical uniforms emblazoned with FBI in ten-inch yellow letters, and each armed with what looked like an assault rifle. They made their way to an unmarked car and the agent motioned for Jana to get in on the passenger side, front seat.

The agent left the parking lot with tires squealing, the rest of the crew in close formation behind the car in a black Suburban. "I'm glad to be out of there," Jana said, "but I'd really like to know where we're going."

"No problem," the man said with a smile as he hit the door locks. "We're taking you back where you belong, whore."

47

1:10 PM CENTRAL DAYLIGHT TIME (LOCAL)
YELLOW CREEK

After recovering from my encounter with insanity on the pier I came back into the control room and found Tark gone. Abdul said he ran home to check on Peggy, who was still sick.

"Matt Decker, you know something else?" Abdul said.

"Yeah?"

"I think there is more hidden in the file."

"What makes you think that?"

"The entire file was nearly five megabytes. At first that didn't seem unusual, because the animation is extensive and should be expected to be quite large, yes?"

"Sure," I said. "And since it was in bitmap format, that made it even less efficient from a size perspective."

"But it is not in bitmap. The original picture of the

horse was altered from JPEG to bitmap. That is what first aroused our interest. But the movie animation of the horses and the clock is a Flash file."

He had my interest. Flash animations are very efficient with regard to file size. Very doubtful that animation would go five meg. "Go on."

"Since I have nothing else to do except sit here and worry about my family, I have been trying to make my mind busy. So I started breaking down the encrypted file into its individual components. The original bitmap of the horse is around five-hundred-k. The Flash animation of the four horses and the clock is a little over three megabytes. That makes a total of about three-point-five megabytes. The encryption overhead itself might be another five-hundred-k at most, which means the total file size should be maybe four megabytes. Yet you can see here that the file is five megabytes. So my question is—"

"What's that other meg," I said. "Great eye, Abdul."

"Thank you. Your nice words make me very proud."

"No problem, my friend. Have you made any progress getting deeper into the file?"

"Not yet, but I have only just begun."

"Okay, let me know the moment you find anything."

"Yes, Matt Decker."

I walked into the outer office and found Andrea still dialing. "No luck reaching Alpine Village yet?" I said. She shook her head.

1:15:00 PM CENTRAL DAYLIGHT TIME (LOCAL) HART COMPLEX

The moment finally arrived. All around the control room, where so many had worked so hard for so long carrying out the orders of their Messiah, anticipation charged the air. All eyes were on the large monitor in the middle of the room as it counted down to the big event. No one in the room knew what the big event was; the details of this, like the premier event, had been closely guarded from virtually everyone, but the Messiah promised to reveal this one in time for them to understand what they would witness on the screen when the countdown was complete.

1:15:18—Abraham Hart faded into view. The video was recorded in his chambers, him sitting at a desk with a large Bible laid open in front of him. The lighting was carefully orchestrated to feature him in his white suit as a shining light in the dark surroundings. He looked into the camera, smiled briefly, then looked down to the Bible.

1:15:24—He began to read: "And when he had opened the fifth seal, I saw under the altar the souls of them that were slain for the word of God, and for the testimony which they held." Hart closed the Bible and looked back into the camera.

1:15:35—"My dearest friends, thank you for your faithful service. Today thou shalt be in paradise, and after a little while, I shall join you there."

1:15:42—The screen faded to black and then back to a large rendering of the countdown. *15 ... 14 ...*

1:15:47—All around the room, confused faces looked

to one another to see if anyone understood what they had just seen and heard from their master.

1:15:50—One man understood perfectly and left his desk in a run for the door. "Where are you going?" someone shouted.

1:15:55—The man frantically entered his code into the keypad beside the door, and its screen scrolled the message, "Access Denied. Rest yet for a little season."

1:15:59—"Oh Jesus Christ," the man said as he hung his head.

1:16 PM CENTRAL DAYLIGHT TIME (LOCAL)
HART COMPLEX

The Suburban passed them and led the way to the main building of the complex. It was within twenty yards of the main building when a fireball billowed from every side of the building. Flames shot out far enough to engulf the big SUV and it left the road and overturned in a fiery heap. The explosion's shock wave hit the windshield of the car Jana was in head on, shattering it into a thousand shards of safety glass. Jana ducked just in time for the glass bullets to go over her head but the driver's reflexes weren't quick enough. His hands left the wheel and grabbed his face as dozens of the projectiles hit. The car careened off the narrow asphalt road and came to a stop when Jana yanked the emergency brake handle between the seats.

She left the car and assessed the situation. No one made it out of the Suburban, which was by then fully involved in orange flames. The driver of the car was shrieking in pain, blinded by glass in his eyes. The closest intact building was the storage shed she had hidden in earlier, fifty yards away. She sprinted to it and climbed up into the driver's seat of the John Deere tractor inside. The key was in the ignition and moments later she was on the road with the tractor throttled wide open. She thanked her lucky stars for having been raised on a farm. The tractor was fitted with a front-end loader that was blocking her view. She stopped long enough to figure out how to lower its bucket and was again underway at full speed. She was off the grounds and back on the main road within two minutes.

With the benefit of daylight she could see that a narrow paved road intersected with the main road and paralleled the stretch of woods she had escaped through last night, or was it night before last? She turned onto the paved road, figuring that it would lead her to Hank Harrington's house at the end of the woods. Fifteen minutes later, his house came into view. Without slowing she wheeled right and rumbled through the yard on the side of Hank's house, pulling the lever to lower the bucket on the front of the tractor as she approached. The tractor didn't have a speedometer, but she guessed her speed at about twenty miles per hour and braced herself for the impact as she plowed right through the wall and into his master bedroom.

Hank was still in bed when the John Deere hit, and she figured he peed the bed just like he peed his pants. He scrambled off the bed in boxer shorts, eyes the size of full moons as she shut the tractor down and made her way down and toward him. He backed up against the wall and Jana caught him square in the jaw with a roundhouse. She smelled ammonia and knew she'd been right. Hank slid down the wall and cowered his head with his hands.

"Hank, I don't like you anymore," Jana said. "And if you ever cross me again in any way whatsoever, I will kill you with my bare hands. Are you with me?"

"Yes ma'am," Hank whimpered. "I'm afraid I can't help you this time, though."

"And just why is that?"

"Because my car is out of gas about a mile up the road. It made it that far back and I walked the rest of the way."

"Hank, you're just about worthless, you know that?"

"Yes ma'am."

Thunder was still tied to the tree in the edge of the woods, waiting patiently. Jana unhitched him and walked him up to Hank's house and right inside. "Hank, meet Thunder. He's hungry. He can have cereal. Make sure he gets it."

"I'm scared of large animals like that. Terrified!"

"Be more scared of me. When I come back, if Thunder ain't happy, I ain't happy. Got it?"

"Yes, ma'am."

She backed her tractor out of the wreckage of Hank's bedroom and rumbled off, bound for Omaha once more.

Thank goodness I reached you," Hank said to the 911 operator. "Listen, you won't believe who's headed back to Omaha."

48

3:05 PM EASTERN DAYLIGHT TIME (LOCAL)
SITUATION ROOM
THE WHITE HOUSE

No." President Stanson held his hand up for silence. "I don't want to hear any more of it, Keen. This nation is crippled. Our economy is in total collapse and the damage may be irrecoverable. Your people have had free reign in this whole affair and the job is not getting done. Nearly every single thing in this case that has been solved has happened as a direct result of the work of those 'unqualified personnel' in Mississippi. You told me this nutcase had to be in New York or Los Angeles. Decker claimed you were wrong, and shortly thereafter we start getting reports of some kind of command center having blown up in the middle of a Nebraska cornfield. I know you and your people are working with tied hands because of the communications problems we're having, but we're past the point of desperation here."

"Yes, Mr. President."

"Admiral Stockton," the President said to the Chairman of the Joint Chiefs of Staff, "here's how we're going to play it."

A White House aid handed out navy blue folders embossed with the presidential seal to everyone seated around the big conference table that had been the centerpiece for so many monumental decisions in the history of the country.

Stockton took his copy and paced the room as he read it. "I understand, Mr. President. Our forces are ready." His colleagues from the Army, Air Force, and Marine Corps all voiced confirmation.

"How are things going out there with martial law?" National Security Advisor Rich Henning said.

"As expected. The citizens as a whole are cooperating, with the exception of a few groups we're keeping close tabs on. Order has been restored," Stockton said.

"Very well," the president said. "So there's no misunderstanding, let's recap. From this point forward, NSA Henning has full coordinating control of the entire operation. He will answer directly to me. The Bureau continues to head the investigation, but Decker and whoever's helping him will be given full cooperation and deference. We still have the capability to set up the full-time live videoconferencing link with Mississippi, right?"

"We do," Brandon said.

Stanson nodded and continued, "The military will continue at DEFCON four. Admiral Stockton and his designates have the authority to act as needed at any given moment, without prior clearance from me if the situation is such that it is not feasible to contact me before taking action. This is a 'by any necessary means' operational authority, including the use of weapons of mass destruction. I do not want the person responsible for these attacks put on trial. I want this person dead. If anyone here has a problem with that position, you are free to resign your post immediately, but that is the position of this administration."

He looked around the room for any negative reaction. Chief of Staff Arnessy said, "Sir, do you realize the political fallout if just that statement were to ever leave this room?"

"Dick, the next person to use the p-word is fired, including you. Do you realize that?"

"Yes sir."

"Are there any more comments?" There were none. "Good. That is all."

Only Arnessy stayed behind as the others filed out. When the room was empty, he said, "Good show, Mr. President. Everyone in here saw you put the country ahead of politics. Just remember that politics is reality, even now."

"I just want what's best for the country, Dick."

"Of course, so do I. And what's best for the country is a strong leader in the White House, someone who can lead us back. But there's something else to consider. The last thing the people will want is a year of finger-pointing between agencies."

"Your point?"

"Right now Decker has the hot hand, but as soon as the time is right, we can drop the blame for this thing right in his lap. You'll come out stronger than you were going into this thing and we'll have a nice clean finish."

"I don't like screwing people, Dick, but you're right, the country will have enough to deal with."

"My point exactly, sir."

49

2:20 PM CENTRAL DAYLIGHT TIME (LOCAL)
YELLOW CREEK

How's Peggy?" I said when Tark walked back into the control room.

"Pretty good, thanks for asking. Some kind of bad female cramps."

"You missed quite a bit while you were gone."

"Very true," Abdul said. He was in high gear on the steg file. The more I watched this guy the more impressed I became. It's one thing to type plain text at a hundred-forty words per minute. It's a different world to write code at that speed, but he did. There was no way to break the strong encryption, but if he was right about this layer's existence, just getting to the password prompt itself could prove to be a clinic in hacking. Decker Digital could use that kind of talent.

I was bringing Tark up to speed when mail arrived on the notebook. It was from Larry Bond and it was worth routing to the big screen for all to see.

Dear Matt,

It would appear you were on target with your Nebraska thoughts. There's a lot going on and this will be a long mail, but first let me summarize the Jana Fulton situation.

She was arrested yesterday in Omaha on SOM (suspicion of murder) and kidnapping charges. She had abducted an older man at gunpoint and made him drive her to Omaha, where she entered a woman's home to make a phone call. This was apparently the phone call to your people at Yellow Creek. While there, a security guard of some sort showed up, a scuffle ensued, and she shot and killed him. The police were able to take her into custody and she was subdued and jailed. Earlier today the sheriff released her to a contingent of heavily armed "FBI agents." Our Omaha field office knows nothing of this. The agents were imposters and we have no idea where she is.

Now we have received reports of a large explosion at a farm, apparently near the man who was abducted. We have agents on the scene but no further information at this time.

Finally, there has been a meeting concerning you at what was described to me as “highest level.” I have been instructed to facilitate the following:

1. A live videoconferencing feed is to be established between our office and your location. A satellite is being tasked to handle the relay and I should have setup details to you within a half-hour.

2. Until now, I was required to get clearance before passing on any information to you. You will now be fully “in the loop.” In fact, my orders are to essentially take orders from you and the director himself expects to consult with you on all matters pertaining to the investigation.

3. A team of U.S. Marshals from Memphis is being dispatched to YC to assist you.

I am honored to be working with you and I am at your service. As you can tell from these developments, your investigative work has not gone unnoticed. I am officially at your service and will be back in touch soon.

Larry Bond

I was dumbfounded. My relationship with the FBI had certainly progressed to a different level since my first encounter with Bob Rowe a few days earlier. That was the first time I had thought of him in a full day and the fact that he was still unaccounted for stirred the acid in my stomach.

"Wow, Matt Decker, maybe when marshals arrive you can be like Matt Dillon," Abdul said.

"Only if Tark agrees to be my Festus." That brought the first round of laughter I'd heard in five days. When it faded, I said, "Guys, what do you think about bringing the grids back up?"

"I say throw the switch. He's going to do what he's going to do," Tark said.

"I cannot say," Abdul said. "I want power but still I am worried about my people."

"Guess I'm the tiebreaker," I said.

"Not really, Matthew," Tark said. "This isn't a democracy; you're calling the shots. What you say, we'll do."

Abdul nodded but his face was creased in angst. I put a hand on his shoulder. "Remember, he threatened my father, too." His mouth moved but he pulled up short of saying it, that my father was all but dead already. He hung his head as if to apologize for thinking it. I remembered my Dad bowing his head to give thanks for one of the million meals he and I shared alone at a table always set for three. My eyes burned.

"Let's do it," I said.

As promised, the satellite coordinates, encryption passwords, and other details for the videoconferencing link arrived within a half-hour. Fourteen minutes to be exact. Ten minutes later, we were live and I got my first look at Larry Bond.

I envisioned a prep office assistant in his late twenties. The real Larry Bond was balding, fortyish, and anything but prep. One glance told me he worked in the bowels of the Hoover building, the secretive basement that housed a labyrinth of computers and the computeresque people who ran them. It was the only place in the building where Bureau people wore anything other than business suits and got away with it.

Larry sported a casual pullover shirt painted onto a muscular frame underneath a square jaw and several days of dark stubble. He sipped coffee while he talked and I could see a nicotine patch on the outer side of a large left bicep. He was a high strung smoker and quite possibly a geek. Surprises abound.

He looked square into the lens. "Matt, Larry Bond here." The audio and video quality was excellent. I had it on the big screen and a workstation, and could drop the big display and go private with one click.

"Nice to see you, Larry. Are you alone?"

"Pretty much. Why?"

"Just wondering how I managed to move this far up the chain of command."

"Hang on a sec." He turned off camera and said, "Red Bull, please," waited a few seconds, then turned back into the camera and lowered his voice. I clicked down to workstation display only. "I heard the director talking to one of the deppy-dudes—"

"Deppy—?"

"Sorry, slang for deputy director. Anyhow, word is he took a reaming straight from POTUS. Got chewed not getting the job done and was told to bring you in on everything since you guys look to be a step ahead."

"I see. Larry, I think we need to consider a move."

"Tell me more, Mr. Decker."

"It's Matt. You're a tech guy, right?"

"Yeah, I'm head rat down here in the maze."

"Good. Listen, we've got the fix for the CEPOCS code. We can have Central's power back on in two minutes flat. Within an hour I can have it on everywhere."

"The whole freaking country?"

"Right."

"Man oh man, that'd be sweet. We're in a world of big hurt chasing this puppy without a spark."

"Shoot me straight, Larry. How much clout do I really have up there?"

"Plenty." He reached out and took a Red Bull from someone's hand, then leaned closer to the camera and spoke quietly. "I'm telling you, Matt, whatever you want, you can get. The top is sold on you. If you want to go for it, I'll go get the director and you tell him you have a recommendation. Then lay it out for him. If he bucks you, tell him you'd like to speak directly to the president. He won't want that. He's a good guy but he's in over his head. Throw him a rope and he'll grab it."

"How long will it take you to get the director down there?"

"Twelve minutes. They're making us use the stairs now to save the backup power."

"Go get him."

Director, I've talked it over with the other people here who are consulting with me, including a specialist in the apocalyptic mindset that we believe the suspect is in." Tark rolled his eyes. "He concurs that nothing we do is likely to have any causal effect with this guy. He's on his own timetable and is just playing games with us. He's counting on us crippling ourselves out of fear of retaliation."

"Look, Decker, I want the power back on myself, desperately. But can we be sure it won't trigger another catastrophe like Los Angeles?"

"We're dealing with a maniac and what we can be sure of is that he will attempt to act out the rest of these seven seals. Our position, however, is that he'll do it no matter what, and we can put up a much better fight with the power on."

Brandon leaned his chin on his fist and drummed the table with the fingers of his free hand. "All right Decker. You may proceed."

"Do we need presidential authority?"

"No. He's issued a written mandate of power. You're authorized."

"Very well. We'll bring Central back up first. We'll get the sanitized CEPOCS program out to the others, and with a bit of luck this nation will have the lights on well before sundown."

"Good luck, Decker."

"Thank you. I need to speak to Larry for a moment before we proceed."

"Be my guest," he said and stepped out of the picture.

"Larry, your people made any progress on this earthquake issue?"

Larry's face went blank. "I'm afraid you lost me."

"Is the director still there?"

He looked around. "No, he's gone. You need me to get him back?"

"No, we'll talk about it later." I put our feed on stand-by, the equivalent of hitting the MUTE button on a telephone. They couldn't hear or see us, though they could signal us to go active in the event they needed us back online.

"Strange they wouldn't keep Bond in the loop on that," Tark said.

"Let's turn the air conditioning back on, and then I'll find out what's going on."

50

3:15 PM CENTRAL DAYLIGHT TIME (LOCAL)
YELLOW CREEK

Abdul held his finger above the ENTER key, waiting for me to give him a GO. I gave it. We had the display back monitoring the systems with its big map and it was a cool thing to watch those fifteen states fade back up to the beauty of glowing green. The air that almost immediately started pouring from the air conditioning vents was even cooler. Celebration and back-slapping broke out, but it didn't last long.

"Problem," Abdul said, pointing at his monitor. I was headed to his station to check it out when I saw Larry's call signal flashing in the corner of the big display. I brought the videoconferencing feed back online and saw the smiling faces of Larry Bond. Keen Brandon was back, as well.

"We told our field offices in the Central region to let us know the instant they got power. Three emails have already come in," Brandon said. "Nice job, Decker!"

"Ditto!" Larry said.

"Thanks, guys. Might want to hold up on the champagne, though," I said.

"Meaning what?" Brandon said. Rather than try to explain it, I grabbed the little video camera and aimed it at Abdul's monitor. The smile slid from Brandon's face and I was sure I heard it hit the floor in Washington. On Abdul's monitor was this:

```
I WARNED THEE NOT TO TAMPER
BUT THOU DIDST SPURN MY PLEA
BY THINE OWN HAND IS FOSTERED
THY TIME NOW CUT BY THREE
```

"I knew it, I knew it, I knew it. I told you this was a bad idea!" Brandon said.

"Give me a break, Brandon. Thirty seconds ago you were ready to dance a jig."

"God only knows what this psychopath will do now. And it's on your head, Decker!" Brandon stormed off and left Larry sitting there.

"Larry, I need to start studying this. Back in a few."

"No problem."

I put the riddle on the big display and turned to Tark. "Is this from Revelation?"

"No, it may have a King James flavor but that's not from the Bible."

"Abdul, is there any way the CEPOCS code you just loaded was vulnerable?"

"It was loaded from the virgin archive."

If this was in the archive code, the pool of potential saboteurs had just narrowed way down. "This code has been stored in an ultra-secure data vault for months, accessed only for bug squashing, then meticulously examined by a verification program that checked it line by line before restoring the archive. The only people with access to that code at any level are you and the console person in each region. Abdul, that leaves you and your three counterparts around in the other regions." I put it out there and let it hang. I didn't want it to come across as pointing a finger at him specifically, because I liked the guy and I thought he was straight. Being a Middle Easterner, he had no doubt endured his share of dirty looks over the past few years, and it of course could have been one of the other three. Then again, Yellow Creek seemed to be an epicenter for trouble.

He turned slowly and looked at me. "Don't forget, Matt Decker, that you too have always had access to the code at all levels. You did write it, no?"

"Yeah, I had access. But I guarantee you I didn't do it."

"And I know I did not."

"I believe you, Abdul." I really did. I think. It could have also been someone within my own company, but the chances of that were nil. My organization was small and tight, and I personally vetted each and every person and security process. Stringent was an understatement. "Tark, let's go to the lounge and see what we can come up with."

"You heard back on that email you sent him?" Tark said.

"No, looks like AC is too busy to talk to me."

3:42 PM CENTRAL DAYLIGHT TIME (LOCAL)

Andrea was so excited she was out of breath. "Jana Fulton's back on the phone!" I ran from the lounge to the control room and grabbed the first phone I came to.

"Jana, are you there?"

"Yes, who is this?"

"My name is Matt Decker. I'm here at Yellow Creek trying to help sort out the mess. Where are you?"

"Matt Decker, the famous computer guy?"

"Yes, tell us where you are."

"I'm on a pay phone in Omaha. Just spent a week in hell capped off by a three-hour tractor ride. I can fill you in on all that later, but first you need to know that there's—"

I heard scuffling and loud voices, then she was gone. I screamed her name over and over, but there was no answer.

"Damn!" I slammed the phone back into its cradle.

"Mr. Decker," Andrea said, an uneasy look creeping across her face, "just before she called, I finally got through to Alpine Village."

"And?"

She looked down, shifting her weight back and forth between feet. "Your father's bed was found empty about an hour ago."

Larry, we have to find Jana Fulton right now," I shouted into the camera. "She has information we have to have, not to mention the fact that her life may still be in danger. We have our hands full here. I need you to get with Great American and get a trace on her call, and find her."

"I'm on it, Matt."

"Now, on my father—"

"I'll also personally take care of getting agents dispatched on that. Work the riddle. I'll work this, buddy."

"Jesus Christ, will this nightmare never end," I said as I clicked off.

"Sure it will, son. And you're asking just the right person for help, too," Tark said, puffing away on his pipe, some goofy look of satisfaction on his face. Bible-thumpers never quit. Just when you think they have, they pop back up in their little pulpits. Christians like Tarkleton are relentless, bloodhounds on a scented trail, going after their prey, chasing and chasing, wearing you down. "Tark, what's your take on the riddle? Give me something."

"I'm stumped, Matthew. I don't suppose I could interest you in praying for guidance?"

It's the same approach my father would've taken back in the day. "No, you cannot."

"Okay, you work it your way. I'm going to the lounge to do just that." Off he went.

"Abdul, how do you stand it, living in the Bible Belt?"

"It is no problem for me, Matt Decker. I too am a believer of Jesus the Christ."

"You don't say?"

"I have seen the light and it is good."

I closed my eyes and took a deep breath. I was surrounded.

3:44 PM CENTRAL DAYLIGHT TIME (LOCAL)
OMAHA, NEBRASKA

"Oh please, why won't you people leave me alone?" Jana said as the shining young policeman held her upper arm. "I have important information! There's a bomb!"

"I don't know about that, lady, but what I do know is that your face is all over the place as a murder suspect and all-around bad girl. You're under arrest. You have the right to remain silent. Anything you say—"

"Save it, I've heard it all before. Don't suppose you'll let me finish my phone call before we go?"

"Don't think so, ma'am. Let's go."

"Oh all right, whatever you say," Jana said with a resigned smile and a bat of the eyes. She saw his shoulders drop ever so slightly as he took the bait and relaxed, even smiled back. He reached behind his back to retrieve his handcuffs, still looking into her eyes. She thrust her hands forward in gentle surrender, tilted her head and turned the smile up a notch. His brightened, too.

In the space of a second, Jana had his gun out of its holster and pointed at him. Both smiles were gone. "I hate to do this, but I don't have time for more games with the Omaha Police Department. Do you know where the FBI office is?"

"If you'll give my gun back and cooperate, lady, I won't mention this."

"Don't confuse reluctance with a lack of resolve, officer. I will shoot you. Do you understand?"

He nodded.

"Where is the FBI?"

"Over on Burt Street."

"Now we're getting somewhere. Let's go."

The officer got into the cruiser and Jana slipped into the passenger seat. "Can you make a phone call through your radio?"

He started the engine and put the car into gear. "No."

"Cell phone?"

"Not allowed on patrol."

"Then drive like hell to Burt Street."

4:04 PM CENTRAL DAYLIGHT TIME (LOCAL)
FEDERAL BUREAU OF INVESTIGATION
OMAHA DIVISION

Mercifully, the phone was working and the other end was ringing. The same woman she had talked to the day before answered. "This is Jana Fulton, put me back through to Mr. Decker. It's urgent."

"He walked outside a few minutes ago. Let me go see if I can find him."

Jana closed her eyes and quietly pounded the desk while she waited. "Please hurry up," she said over and over. She opened her eyes and looked around. The FBI office was a testimony to utilitarianism with its artless walls, flat gray carpet, and fluorescent lighting. Two minutes passed.

"Jana, are you still there?" the woman—Andrea, she believed—said.

"Yes, what's taking so long? This is an emergency to say the least. If you can't find Mr. Decker, just put someone on the line who has some authority around there."

"I found him. He's on the way back in now."

"Good." Jana looked at the computer on the desk she was sitting at and noticed it had a thumbdrive plugged in the side, which made her remember the one in the pocket of Dane's jacket. She reached for her pocket and remembered taking the camouflage jacket off. She left it draped over the back of the tractor seat, across town by the phone booth.

"Jana?" Decker's voice on the phone startled her.

"Yes, thank heavens you're there. Ya'll need to get out of the building. There's a bomb in there."

"What makes you say that?"

"I saw it. Get out of there!"

"Can you tell me where it is?"

"Yes, it's in the bottom of that big TV map thing in the main control room; it's really fancy looking, like something out of a movie."

"Okay, we'll evacuate the building. Are you safe now?"

"Yes, I'm at the FBI office in Omaha."

"Good. I'm sorry about Brett."

"I appreciate it. Shouldn't you be getting out of the building?"

"Very soon, but it's past 2:16 so we're probably safe and I have some important questions to ask you."

"What's 2:16 got to do with it?"

"I'll explain later. How did you wind up in Nebraska?"

"I was kidnapped by a man named Dane Christian. I'm a little out of touch but his boss is behind the power outages and I think some other things."

My heart pounded. "Who's the boss?"

"His name is Abraham Hart, and he's crazy as a betsy-bug."

I was stunned. The "game" turned out to be a competitor with a grudge after all. "Can you tell us where he is now?"

"Don't know. I escaped and haven't seen him since and hope I never do again. Do you know about his place blowing up?"

"I've heard. Do you think he might have been inside?"

"Even if he was he probably wasn't hurt. He has a spread way underground, calls it his 'chambers.'"

"I see. Did you hear anything that might help us know what he's planning next?"

"No, sorry."

"Okay, thanks much, Jana. We're going to evacuate this facility now but I'll be in touch."

Jana gave Decker the FBI office's telephone number and hung up the phone. She had a feeling she was forgetting something, but fatigue won out. She laid her head on the desk and was sound asleep within sixty seconds.

51

5:12 PM CENTRAL DAYLIGHT TIME (LOCAL)
YELLOW CREEK

I briefed Tark, Abdul, and Larry on Jana's information and we bailed out of the complex and gathered at the front gate. The U.S. Marshals from Memphis showed up around five o'clock. I brought them up to speed, after which a debate ensued. "The witness says the bomb is very high-tech looking. Other than the explosives proper, a modern bomb is pure electronics and that happens to be something I know about," I said to the leader of the three marshals.

"Decker, we need to get a bomb squad in here on this. You're not qualified—"

"I'm not waiting. We have to get that thing out of there so we can get back to work. We just got the power back on to fifteen states. If this facility is destroyed, those states will go back down and be down for an extended period. I can't let that happen."

"According to our information, you're the only one who's making any headway at tracking down the UNSUB. We can't afford to lose you, Decker. I've been ordered to guarantee your safety and that's hard to do if you're playing with bombs."

"I'm going in. Who's going with me?"

The lead marshal sighed. "I'll go with you. No one else. Period."

"Good enough."

Once we were back inside, the first thing I did was move our videoconferencing camera to a spot that had a clear shot of what we were doing. I turned around and faced it. "Larry, how's the view?"

He raised a thumb and said, "Our top EOD specialist is on the way here from Quantico. They're choppering him in so he'll be here any minute. He says to remove just the door to the cabinet it's in, but don't touch the bomb until he's here."

"Fair enough." I wasn't keen on getting involved with the bomb at all, but I was concerned it would take too long for Explosive Ordnance Disposal troops to get there and something had to be done. I also had a feeling the bomb was Hart's version of an earthquake, the sixth seal. It would be set for two-sixteen, but that could be AM or PM.

The marshal stood a good fifteen feet away, content to watch me remove the cabinet panel from a distance. Who could blame him. With every turn of the screwdriver I questioned my own sanity a bit more. The air conditioning was working but a thin film of sweat formed on my forehead. I wiped it off after the last screw was out.

I carefully set the panel aside, and there it was. It looked to be fashioned from aircraft aluminum and was about four feet long, two feet tall, and a foot and a half or so deep. "Larry, you getting this?"

"Yeah, I got it, Matt. I also just got word that the EOD officer is in the building. Hold what you got."

"Can do." Two minutes later a man with a classic military look showed up on screen. Crisp uniform, upright posture, a face that looked to have been forged from steel. "Mr. Decker, Major Todd Thompson here."

"Hello, Major. Tell me what to do."

"The intelligent move is to stand down until I can get a contingent of EOD troops to your location."

"Where's the closest base?"

"There's a Local EOD Control Center in Huntsville, Alabama."

"How far is that?"

"Just over a hundred miles."

"Only two hours by road. That might—"

"Actually, Mr. Decker, it will take them considerably longer to be on location."

"Why?"

"A broken arrow was reported this afternoon and—"

"A nuclear accident?"

"Correct. A PNAF bird, that's Primary Nuclear Air—"

"My company's done a lot of work with the military so I'm somewhat familiar with the jargon. What happened?"

"We received a mayday transmission from a C-17 transporting B83's to the Nuclear Underground Storage Complex at Kirtland. The locally assigned EOD team was overtasked on an unrelated exercise, so we deployed the Huntsville team."

"And?"

"There was no C-17 and no mayday."

"A decoy designed to get the Huntsville team away from this area. We've been had."

"It would seem so."

"Where are they now?"

"Washington."

"How long to chopper them here from D.C.?"

"Not D.C., Mr. Decker. McChord in Washington state."

"We can't wait that long, Todd. We have work to do. I guarantee you that timer is set for two-sixteen Eastern time, but that could be AM, just seven hours away. You can't get your team here in time."

"True."

"We're wasting time. What do I do?"

"First I need you to light the area. Do you have a light source you can place inside the cabinet?" A light source. He couldn't just ask for a lamp.

"Yeah, hold on a sec." I commandeered a little fluorescent banker's lamp from Tark's desk. After getting it into position I said, "Better?"

"Much. Thank you, Mr. Decker."

"Todd, let's drop the formality. Call me Matt. If I'm about to get blown up I'd rather it happen while I carried on a normal conversation."

"No problem, sir. What I need you to do now is get the camera and move it slowly all around the case." I did that while he directed, part of which involved me actually crawling up inside the cabinet with the contraption. Sweat poured.

"Great," the major said. "I don't see any evidence of the device being booby-trapped with regard to placement. Before we proceed, though, I want you to forget the camera and look very closely all around for any evidence of a wire connecting the device to the cabinet." I did and didn't see any. After I reported that to him he continued, "Now, inspect the bottom of the unit as closely as you can without actually touching it and certainly without moving it. What we're trying to determine here is if the bottom of the casing itself might have some sort of pressure-sensing capability that would trigger the device if moved."

Again, I did as I was told. "I don't think so. The bottom of the unit looks to be one piece of extruded aluminum. No seams. No joints," I said.

"Okay, do you have anyone there who can help you?"

"Help me do what?"

"Help you move the bomb outside the cabinet."

I took a deep breath and looked up at the marshal. He didn't look brave like Matt Dillon or even cocky like Tommy Lee Jones. He looked scared out of his mind, but he did nod. "Yeah, I have help."

"Very gently, slide the device out."

We each grabbed an end of the casing, slid it out, and ever so tenderly picked it up and set it on the floor. "Excellent," the major said. "Can you estimate its weight for me?"

"Forty to fifty pounds."

"That's outstanding."

"How so?"

"If it were a thermonuclear device it would probably weigh more than that."

"I see, Todd. It's probably not a nuke, which means it'll still blow the hell out of me and the Marshal here, but at least it won't take out a fourth of Mississippi if it goes."

"Oh, even if it was it wouldn't be large enough to do damage beyond a mile or so, and I understand you're in a fairly rural area."

"Thanks, Todd. You're very comforting. What now?"

"There's not much we can do until we open it up. Standard protocol before doing that is to—"

Call it fatigue or insanity or whatever, but I had no interest in protocol. There were three latches on the front of the case and one on each side. I flipped the first one and saw the marshal's legs start trembling ever so slightly in my peripheral vision. "Mr. Decker, don't do that!" the major's unflappable demeanor was flapping. I flipped the other four latches and raised the lid. Four or five big beads of sweat dropped down from my face onto the electronics inside. I couldn't see Larry Bond but he was grinning. I knew it.

From my gadget-freak perspective, the unit's interior was a thing of beauty. An apparatus took up two thirds of the space from left to right. It consisted of a sphere about half the size of a basketball. Its surface looked like sort of like polished aluminum, the type you'd see handrails made from in a chic, contemporary opera house. In the center of the ball was a three-inch tunnel that went all the way through from left to right. Immediately to the right was a cylinder that looked like the core of the tunnel. On the right end of the cylinder was a black box that had a bundle of wires running into the electronic control section that took up the right side of the box.

"Can you get the camera closer, please" Major Johnson said.

"Sure, Todd." I grabbed the camera and moved it all around for him.

"From here, Mr. Decker, it looks like the sphere definitely goes almost to the bottom of the case. Is that your perception by eye?"

"Yep, it does. In fact, it's resting on a little foam cradle right in the bottom."

"On the control mechanism, underneath its panel, is the left side closed off or is it open where you can see the wires running into it?"

"It's open."

"Roger. Can you describe what you see underneath that control panel?"

"Couple of circuit boards. That's it. I can see right to the bottom of the case."

"Very, very odd."

"Explain."

"We can see everything inside the case, and something crucial is missing."

"Please tell me what it is, Major. We're sort of edgy around here these days."

"There are no explosives."

"Come again?"

"You're looking right at the contents, Mr. Decker. There are no explosives in it."

"But what about the ball?"

"Does the sphere look to be attached to anything?"

"Not really."

"Pick it up."

"You sure about that?"

"Quite sure, sir. Pick it up." I grabbed it and it came right out of the case. I guessed it to weigh around thirty pounds.

"This device was made to look like a nuclear device, but it's not one. "

"So it's not really a bomb at all."

"Exactly, sir."

"Then what the hell is it?"

"I can't immediately answer that, sir."

"Todd?"

"Yes, Mr. Decker."

"You've noticed it has a countdown timer here on the control panel, right?"

"Yes sir. I see it."

"Have you noticed what's rather strange about it?"

"Yes sir, I've noticed that and I'm sorry to say I cannot immediately—"

"Okay, Todd. Over and out from Yellow Creek."

"Good day, sir."

I said goodbye to Larry and shut down the video feed. Then I looked at the countdown timer. It was six digits, arrayed in what could be seen as an hour-minute-second format, and counting down. But the odd thing is that it was moving too fast for a standard time countdown. I compared it to my watch. The digits on the right side of the countdown were moving exactly three times faster than my TAG was clicking off the seconds. Triple time. I stared at it for a moment, trying to figure out the significance of that. The riddle. Thy time now cut by three. I turned to the marshal. "Go get the others right now, please."

52

5:45 PM CENTRAL DAYLIGHT TIME (LOCAL)
YELLOW CREEK

I thought I knew what was going on with the speedy countdown but needed to be sure. "Abdul, what time did we reload the virgin CEPOCS code and bring Central back online?"

He made a few clicks, squinted at his screen, and said, "One minute after three o'clock."

"That's local time, right?"

"Correct."

I did the math in my head. A two-sixteen AM event didn't tally, but PM did. "At that point, two-sixteen Eastern time tomorrow afternoon, which is one-sixteen our time, was twenty-two hours fifteen minutes away." Abdul nodded. Tark motioned for me to hurry up, puffing frantically. I sat down at a station and routed its signal to the big display. "Okay, here's the riddle." I put it up on screen. "Pay close attention to the last line, thy time now cut by three."

"What's twenty-two hours fifteen minutes divided by three?" I asked.

"Seven hours twenty-five minutes," Abdul said.

"Exactly. Now figure seven hours twenty-five minutes from the time we brought the grids back up."

"Ten twenty-six tonight."

"And how much time is left between right now and ten twenty-six tonight?" I said.

The room had a big digital clock on the wall that was synchronized with the national atomic clock in the Naval Observatory. Tark looked at it and said, "Five fifty-two right now, so ten twenty-six is four hours and thirty-four minutes away."

"Okay, everybody gather round and take a look at this." I led them to the device at the front of the room and pointed at the countdown just as it whizzed through 13:42:03 on its downward spiral, exactly three times 4:34:01.

"Matthew, that's some impressive detective work but what's it counting down to? The bomb is fake," Tark said.

"That's the big question. Let's remember that Hart had no way to know we'd find the device in the bottom of the cabinet. That means its countdown would have expired and we would have known nothing about it. It makes no sense."

"I also do not understand something. Why would they go to all the trouble to make the false bomb at all, especially one that looks like an atomic bomb?" Abdul said.

"There's another question," I said. "That device was not connected to anything. How the heck did it know that we had defied Hart's 'decree' and brought the power back online? The speed increase in the countdown had to happen at that exact time or the math would never have worked out the way we just broke it down. Switching the grids was definitely a trigger, but how?"

"If there are no wires," Abdul said, "then the trigger must be wireless."

"That has to be it. It has a receiver in it that picked up the event," I said.

"If it has a receiver in it, who's to say it doesn't have a transmitter too, one that could trigger something else when the time is up?" Tark said.

"Whatever it is, we'll have to figure it out on our own. The experts are too far away. We need to talk to Jana. She may have information," I said.

Several attempts to call the FBI office in Omaha failed to go through.

I brought the videoconferencing back online and buzzed Larry when our screen showed an empty chair. He was back in twenty seconds. "Sorry about that, Matt. Nature called. What's up?" I filled him in. "We don't have a video feed out there but I'll get her patched through to you on our internal landlines."

"Good enough."

We watched him work and within minutes her voice came over the speakers. She sounded groggy. "This is Jana."

"Jana, Matt Decker here. Thank you for the tip on the bomb. It turned out to be a fake, but we think the device may have some other function that we don't know about. Is there anything else you can tell us?"

"I was there when he put the thing in," she said. Our earlier conversations had been under more frantic circumstances and I'd failed to notice that she sounded as beautiful as her picture looked. A deep but very sweet voice, with a healthy dose of Southern Belle built in.

"Where is the guy who planted the bomb?"

"Dead, killed by Hart."

"Did you actually see this man?" I asked.

"Oh yes, I saw way too much of him. He's certifiably insane and getting worse."

"We definitely want to hear about what you've been through, but for now we need to focus on this device. Did he plant anything else? Did you see him tamper with any of the equipment in the room?"

"All I saw was him doing something to one of the computers and planting that bomb, or what I thought was a bomb, but he left me locked in a closet for a while. He had some kind of big box, old looking, on this dolly when he left me there, and when he came back he didn't have it. That's all I know about what went on there, but I have quite a bit I can tell you about Hart."

"Ms. Fulton, my name is Larry Bond. We understand you were pretty tired when you got back to our field office, but if you're up to it our people there need to start debriefing you."

"No problem. Get me some food and I'll sing for my supper."

"That's a deal," Larry said.

"Oh, there's one more thing," she said. "I left a horse in a man's living room. Someone needs to go get him."

"Uh, I'll see what I can do on that but I don't know if we have anyone qualified to take care of a horse."

"I've had a rough week, Mr. Bond, and this point is not negotiable."

"All right, Ms. Fulton. You have my word," Larry said.

"I get the impression that Mr. Decker's running this show. I want his word," she said.

"They'll take care of the horse, Jana." I like horses and I like helping stunning women who like horses.

"Good enough," she said.

"No problem," I said, "and Jana?"

"Yes?"

"I'm very sorry about the crummy week you've had."

"Thank you, Mr. Decker."

"Call me Matt."

"Thank you, Matt."

The line clicked and I looked to Larry. "Did you catch what she said about an old box?"

"For sure. I'll pass that on to Major Thompson."

I assume you have the full investigative resources of the Bureau looking for information on one Abraham Hart?"

"The Bureau, the CIA, the NSA," he said. "Phones are ringing and hard drives spinning."

"Good deal. Ten twenty-six is bearing down on us, so we're back to work on our immediate problem. Stay in touch, Larry, and please stay on top of the situation with my father. I know the fate of one man pales in comparison to the stakes at hand, but it's a hell of an issue to me."

"I understand, and you have my word."

I killed the feed, glanced at the clock, and turned to my crew. "Gentlemen, we have three hours fifty minutes. I suggest we start finding some answers."

53

SUNDAY, 3:50 AM MOSCOW SUMMER TIME (LOCAL)
(SATURDAY, 6:50 PM CENTRAL DAYLIGHT TIME)
METROPOL HOTEL
MOSCOW, RUSSIA

My Dearest Children:

Prior to this momentous time, this world has existed in a state of chaos and confusion. It gives my heart and soul untold pleasure to announce that the end of this misery is at hand. Hear me explain!

Each human being craves to know that he or she exists for a reason. This longing drives people to search for meaning in their everyday lives, meaning in the world about them, and meaning in the universe. For many millennia, untold numbers have clung to a plethora of religions and arcane belief systems, because the human mind and spirit is generally incapable of deciphering the real meaning of life. I lived for years in just such a yearning existence myself. That has changed.

Throughout and during the past years I have discovered that I am not really human. I am immortal, the quintessential embodiment of life and all that it entails. There have been many false teachings purveyed by scores of false teachers and prophets. Some of these were well-meaning souls. Others were utter frauds. I will not call names for it would be a pure waste of time within this brief missive, but the Truth I shall soon share with you encompasses, supersedes, and nullifies all iconic religious personalities who have preceded me.

Regarding the current situation, as you are no doubt aware, aeons have foretold the significant events have taken place over the past few days, primarily in the United States of America. Fear not! These happenings are the fulfillment of prophecy. A twisted version, a Program of Events so to speak, can be found seeded all throughout the Book of Revelation in the Holy Bible. I encourage you to read the book, but please my children, bear in mind that the Bible was written long ago by many different MORTALS who were inspired by my lingering cosmic presence over a period of hundreds of years, but their regrettably weak minds and numerous imbecilic translations have skewed the true meaning which I desired to impart.

Alas, the portions of the Bible that speak of the teacher known as Jesus have been hopelessly butchered. They lead to believe that this man was the Christ. Is it not extravagantly exciting to know that the real Christ is among you right now? I am Christ. I realize that all those who are reading this are likely beside themselves with spewing joy, but there are yet more good tidings. Tales concerning the so-called AntiChrist are also mangled groupings of incoherent thought. There is no separate AntiChrist. I am the Christ and I am the AntiChrist. There is no distinct personality known as Satan, beyond certain necessary elements of my immortal being. I am Satan. There is none other but me. I created the universe and all that exists within it, and have subsequently lain dormant with regard to my reverential being until now. I shall reveal myself fully unto you in the near future for you to worship me! You are henceforth warned that things are often not what they seem. Rely on my Word for your sustenance and survival. To that end, you may expect a series of further communications over the coming days. Until then, I bid you fond adieu.

God

Hart had written and perfected his manifesto over a period of months, then painstakingly edited it once more. After the years of preparation, he had been disappointed to find the actual unfolding of the plan's elements somewhat anti-climactic. He had fantasized so long and so often that reality had lost some of its edge. The game with Decker—while frustrating at times—had rekindled the excitement. And what was a game without clues? A victory that provided no interaction with the adversary would ring hollow. After a final reading, he pasted it into the email and clicked SEND. The message would be routed through a series of four online services providing anonymity as to its origin. Laws enacted in the United States in the wake of terror attacks meant two of the cloaking companies would readily run traces at the government's request, but the other two were based in small European countries who weren't bound by or beholden to the world's only "superpower." Despite the safeguards they might be able to eventually trace the message back to this room in Moscow's lavish Metropol Hotel, but it would do them no good. He would be long gone. The document would be delivered to all major media outlets, as well as the adversary himself.

Having slept for a few hours, his first rest in days, he was invigorated, refreshed and ready for what lay ahead. He picked up the phone and punched in a number. "Kostia? It is loaded on my aircraft? Excellent. I shall depart at once. The transfer of funds will be executed within the hour. You have done well, Kostia. Eternity will look kindly upon you, my old friend."

He hung up the phone and reflected on the past several days. To be certain, there had been a few glitches, but they had been overcome. The magnificent train of destiny chugged inexorably forward on its fateful track, leaving the past behind as it rumbled into the future, a future in which the world would bow before him. Even his old nemesis Decker.

General Konstantin Nikonorovich Zheleznyakov laid the handset back in its cradle, leaned backed in his tufted leather office chair, and bit the end off a Cuban cigar as he gazed out the window at the gray Moscow river from his office at Genshtab Military Headquarters. With a smile on his face he said, "*Nyet, spasibo, druzhische.*" *No, thank you, my old friend.* Thanks to the millions the insane man would soon wire into a Grand Cayman bank account, Kostia's days of slaving away in a vain attempt to restore a vanished grandeur were almost over. Grandeur would be had, not by his beloved Motherland, God rest her mighty spirit, but most definitely by Kostia as he left the brutal winters of Moscow behind forever.

54

7:19 PM CENTRAL DAYLIGHT TIME (LOCAL)
YELLOW CREEK

Intel is starting to pour in on Hart now," Larry said. "Matt, this is one bizarre bird. Here's the skinny. Birth name is Abraham Hardier, son of Bernard Hardier. Daddy happened to be, now get this, one of the largest defense contractors in the state of Israel. They now buy most of their hardware from us, but thirty or forty years ago Hardier Enterprises built a lot of it for them using our specs ... why are you shaking your head?"

"No wonder he made it personal."

"You saying you know this creep?"

"Never met him, but we've done battle before. Remember the fight for the CEPOCS contract?"

"Oh cripes! This guy is the Israeli that scrapped tooth and nail, isn't he?"

"One and the same. The clock is ticking. Let's get to the here and now."

"Hang tight, bro. It all fits in, believe me. When little Abe was around nineteen or twenty years old, Mommy and Daddy met a grisly death. Chopped into itty bitty pieces in the kitchen at their house. So guess who got the family dough?

"Was he a suspect?"

"Numero uno for a month, at which time his team of lawyers managed to produce an airtight alibi. The gardener was eventually convicted."

"How much money did he inherit?

"Billions, and that was a lot of cash back then."

"It's still a lot of cash."

"You ought to know, boss."

"Move on, Larry. No time to get chatty."

"Okay, okay. Junior ran the company for around three years himself, but it started losing money hand over fist and he turned management back over to the guys who had been there for years, and then disappeared off the face of the earth. Five years later, he Americanizes his name from Hardier to Hart, moves over here, and starts gobbling up real estate. Matt, this sucker owns the equivalent of city blocks in New York and L.A."

"Where else?"

"Where do you think?"

"Nebraska."

"Bingo. Ten years ago he bought almost twenty thousand acres of prime farm land in a bunch of different parcels, scattered around Omaha. The place where the explosion took place was one of them. He started building on that land three or four years ago. There aren't many neighbors out there, but the ones we've talked to said that he set a record for the longest time consumed building a barn and a few other structures."

"Anything else?"

"That's about it right now, but we're still working. If there's more on him, we'll find it."

"Have the investigators on the scene gotten inside the building yet?"

"They're in, but there's nothing up top to do us any good. Whatever detonated in there melted everything, and I do mean everything, including bodies. The underground area Ms. Fulton mentioned is sealed off but they're working to clear it. You guys making any progress on the ten-twenty-six predicament?"

"Not yet. We're about to disassemble the device and see if we can find a transmitter in it. No choice, we're running out of time."

"Good luck, bud. I'm here if you need me."

"Thanks, Larry." I switched the screen back to systems mode and stared at the fifteen states still running green. The President axed the plan to bring the other states back online after our little incident with the speedy countdown. I had spoken to him directly and it wasn't pleasant. I don't care how rich you are, how successful you are, how independent you are, getting reamed by POTUS is a unique experience.

Abdul was at his station, still convinced there was another layer to the encrypted file, something we hadn't seen yet. Tark was in the lounge researching, or praying, or maybe he was outside howling at the moon, who knows. His theory was that the people who were killed in the explosion were the martyrs of the fifth seal. If true, the bastard had killed his own people. What a guy. I was sick and tired of seals and judgments, exhausted to a point that I had never experienced despite the few hours of sleep I got the night before. I wanted more, but I had a fake nuclear bomb to dissect and figure out in three hours.

Major Todd Thompson was back on screen. I had the electronic components of the device laid out on a table and was moving the camera over them for him. "Hold right there, Mr. Decker." I had just about given up on getting him to ease up with the formality. Some military men are just built that way and the major was obviously one of them.

"I need you to turn the countdown timer over and move the camera in close on the backside." I held the camera right on it for thirty seconds, and looked up at the screen. His eyes were locked and tiny beads of sweat broke out on his upper lip. Men like him don't often sweat.

"Talk to me, Todd."

"Mr. Decker, this is not good. You see that next component to your left, that is indeed a transmitter. It's disconnected from any power source now, so it obviously can't transmit."

"Exactly. We're a step ahead of him for once. What's the problem?"

"The problem, sir, is that I'm afraid it's already transmitted its signal. It probably did so when the trigger occurred to increase the countdown speed."

"How on earth could you know that?"

"The countdown timer is still running."

"Yes, it still has a battery pack attached to it, but we can pull that and stop it."

"It won't do any good."

"Why?"

"You see that little coil apparatus on the back of the countdown timer?"

"I do." 22.3 was stamped on it.

"Mr. Decker, that's a frequency. Twenty-two-point-three Megahertz. And that countdown timer? I'm afraid it's a receiver."

"You're telling me it's receiving this countdown from somewhere else?"

"Yes sir."

The understanding fell on me like a pallet of bricks. "Todd, are you saying this same exact countdown is already running on some unknown something sitting out there, that this is just a remote display of it?"

"That is correct, sir."

I laid the camera down, took a deep breath, and rubbed my eyes. I aimed it at myself and looked into the lens. "Major Thompson, what now?"

Thompson leaned over and whispered for about thirty seconds to Larry, who then said, "Oh my God." And it wasn't just what he said, it was how he said it. Three distinct, widely spaced words: Oh. My. God.

"Matt, we need to get some more experts in on this," Larry said.

"No, you people need to tell me what's going on. We're the ones sitting here and whatever you think you see here, I need to know. Right now."

"Tell him, Major," Larry said.

The major brought his arm up and wiped the sweat off his face with the sleeve of his uniform. That crisp, starched uniform that could stand at attention by itself. The dressy kind that a man like Thompson would never defile in such a manner. "I believe that countdown is taking place on a nuclear device, Mr. Decker."

Abdul's clattering keys went quiet. I swallowed hard and felt my heart swell against my ribcage. "Go on."

"That frequency, twenty-two-point-three Megahertz, is an old frequency we've seen before."

"On what?"

"Russian portable nuclear device."

"How big?"

"They come in different sizes, but since the terror attacks started in '01, we've done a great job of tracking down most of the previously unaccounted-for devices. We believe the only ones remaining are the smaller one-kiloton units."

"I mean physically what size, Todd, so we'll know what to look for."

"They're about the size of a golf bag."

"Great. There won't be over a couple of thousand hiding places around here for something like that. What exactly will it look like if that's what this is?"

"Assuming it's in its original casing, probably a flat military green color, rectangular in shape. My guess is this is the old box that Ms. Fulton mentioned."

"I see. Earlier, when we were first found this device, you said a small one couldn't do damage beyond a few hundred yards. How certain is that?"

"That assessment has changed considerably, Mr. Decker."

"Todd, if you call me Mr. Decker one more time, or say 'sir' to me one more time, I'm going to explode myself! Got it?"

"Yes—uh, yes. Roger that, Matt."

"Good. Tell me why the damage assessment changed."

"I hadn't had an opportunity to study your locale at that point."

I thought for a moment and realized what the problem was. "You didn't know about the waterway."

"Correct. A nuclear detonation at the Yellow Creek facility, even a device of relatively small kilotonnage, would cause massive radioactive contamination of the Tennessee-Tombigbee canal. The contamination would instantly spread south to the Gulf of Mexico and there's nothing, I repeat, nothing, that we could do to stop or even contain it. The results will be catastrophic."

"How do we find it? Will Geiger counters pick it up?"

"That's old technology, not suitable. What's called for here are AD-PDR43 RADIAC's, portable survey monitors designed to detect beta and gamma."

"How soon can you have some here?"

"We'll need a number of them in order to cover the space of the complex in time, so—"

"Quick question, Todd. How do we know it's even here at the complex? Why couldn't this receiver be picking up the signal from miles away?" I asked.

"The tuning apparatus is a low-sensitivity unit. I'm confident the source is within a few hundred yards."

"Okay, back to the original question, how long until you can get them here?"

"The Oak Ridge nuclear research facility in Tennessee is fairly close. I can get a chopper full of monitors, and people to run them, out of there within a half-hour, and have them to you in another forty-five minutes."

"By the time they're on the ground, we'll have under two hours. If they find it, what then?"

"Let me work on that."

"Work fast, Todd. Larry, any word on my father?"

"A team is in place at Alpine Village. No leads yet, but I'll keep you apprised."

55

9:03 PM CENTRAL DAYLIGHT TIME (LOCAL)
YELLOW CREEK

Damn Murphy. The helicopter on hand at Oak Ridge was too small to carry the entourage and another had to be brought in from Chattanooga. The teams were finally in place and searching but with less than an hour and a half to go. Even worse, Major Thompson had no answers as to what to do with the thing once we found it. Finding an expert on disarming Soviet suitcase nukes and getting him in visual communication with us in a couple of hours was looking like an impossible task.

"Matthew," Tark said, "take a look at this." He had a stack of blueprints and mechanical diagrams for the Yellow Creek facility laid out on the table in the lounge.

"I'm a programmer, Tark. Mechanical engineering

plans are as meaningless to me as Chinese. If you have a suggestion, let me have it in plain English."

"Okay, before this place was Great Central, it was meant to be a lot of other things. At one point they were going to build solid rocket boosters for the space shuttle, and then Boeing tried to set it up as an aircraft factory. None of it ever worked out. In the beginning, though, it was built by the government to be a nuclear power plant. They spent billions on it before the funding dried up. Now here's the good part. Look right here."

He was pointing to a drawing of an object I did recognize, the massive concrete housing for a nuclear reactor. It was a cutaway depiction that showed the cylindrical housing for what was supposed to be a new, safer design. Tark ran his finger down the page. "This tunnel you see going down from the reactor, as well as the housing, was completed. All that was left was to drop the actual apparatus in place and tie it in to the labyrinth of pipes and valves and steam generators that magically turn a little fissionable material into lots of electricity."

I tapped my watch. "How's it supposed to help us right now, Tark?"

"This tunnel is six feet across and goes straight down into the ground for nearly half a mile. At the bottom it opens up into a huge cavern that was blasted with high explosives dropped down through the tunnel. After the cavern had been created, they started at the bottom and built a reinforced concrete wall for the shaft all the way up. The opening in the finished shaft is just over three feet wide."

"This is all very interesting but—"

"Don't you see? We can drop the bomb down the shaft."

I looked at my watch again. Six minutes wasted hearing a plan to drop a nuclear bomb down a hole and then hang around while it blows up. "Tark, have you lost your mind? The blast will come right back up the shaft and—"

"Oh no it won't. The sole purpose for this shaft was to evacuate the nuclear core and contain any radioactivity in an emergency. This will work."

I shook my head and walked out. In the control room, I got Larry and the major back on screen and shared it with them. To my shock, Major Thompson said, "Very resourceful. I've seen the plans for these shaft-evac units before but I didn't realize one had ever been built. Let me see if I can find some hard data on the system. Give me ten minutes."

"With all due respect, Todd, what's to keep the blast from coming right up the shaft and vaporizing this whole place?"

"I need to review the data, s—, I mean, let me go find the data, Matt. Ten minutes."

Larry shrugged and I clicked off.

"Abdul, any progress on that file?"

He was typing so fast and so hard I could feel the counter shaking. "I am almost in."

"No way! You've busted strong encryption without a password?"

"No. For some reason this last layer of the file wasn't protected as strongly as the rest. It's almost like he wants us to see this last part, Matt Decker."

That made very little sense, but then again, what you can expect from a card-carrying psychopath? "Let me know when you get it."

"You didn't let me finish," Tark said. He pulled out another drawing. This one was a more artistic rendering of the system. Above the reactor housing was a large telescopic pole that went from the top of the concrete cylinder all the way to the roof of the cavernous building, a good two hundred feet. "This thing drops down into the shaft in sections and winds up going a thousand feet deep. Once it's locked in place, fifty butterfly valves inside it close off. In theory it has a baffling effect that subdues any energy coming back up the shaft, with the result being that most of any blast is directed into the cave at the bottom."

"Let's go see what Thompson has to say about it," I said. Tark and I made our way back to the control room. On my orders, Sheriff Litman had moved everyone else out of the building and a quarter mile away from the complex. The three of us, plus Abdul and the RADIAC teams, were the only people still there.

"Matt, I found the documentation on the system. It was designed to contain radioactivity from a problematic core, not a nuclear detonation. I don't have a good feeling about it at all," Thompson said.

"That makes two of us, but the key question is do you have anything better?"

"I don't have anything else, period."

"Then this is our plan." I glanced at Tark to see if I'd spot a smug 'I told you so' look on his face. I did not. In fact, he was a trifle pale.

"Our plan is worth exactly squat," he said, "if we don't find the bomb."

56

10:10 PM CENTRAL DAYLIGHT TIME (LOCAL)
YELLOW CREEK

A RADIAC technician named Bert hit the mother lode in Building C. The device looked like an oversized ammo can, drab olive green with a clunky utilitarian design the Russians are famous for. As Major Thompson had predicted, it was a long rectangular box about the size of a golf bag. Building C was as far you could get from Building F, home of the reactor housing and our only hope for salvation. We had it on a squeaky dolly and were wheeling with much haste.

The people who had manned the RADIAC's were ordered to evacuate and move behind Sheriff Litman's wide perimeter. No resistance was offered. The only people left in the whole complex were Tark, Abdul, and me. Larry and the growing entourage of viewers at his end tried to get me to leave the premises, to no avail. I was determined to see this thing through for better or worse. Abdul stayed in the control room, hammering away on his keyboard, committed to busting that last layer of encryption. Tark had to be on hand for the big event, since he was the one who had been studying the operating procedures for the shaft-evac system. He was in place and had the system ready when we squeaked in. I pulled the countdown timer from my pocket and laid it on the floor beside the housing. We had just over eight minutes.

Tark had the top of the housing open. I leaned over the edge of the concrete structure and peered down into what looked like a bottomless hole. Despite Major Thompson's assurances that impact could not detonate the bomb, I still had serious misgivings about dropping a nuclear bomb thousands of feet down a hole to a very hard landing. He had shown me diagrams of the construction, and what it took to effect a detonation. Theory is one thing. Being there with the nuke is another. Six and a half minutes. It would take the telescopic apparatus five minutes to extend itself down into the shaft and activate its dozens of containment valves.

I looked at Tark and grabbed one end of the bomb. He grabbed the other, and we eased it into position over the top of the shaft. "Three, then drop," I said. "One ... two ... three ... *NOW*!" We nosed it over into the shaft and let go. The cavernous room sounded eerie echoes as the metal casing bounced off the shaft walls on the way down. We listened carefully and finally heard a faint thud, then nothing.

"Starting sequence," Tark said as he turned a keyswitch on the system control panel. The big rod slid down from the tall ceiling with a gentle hum and penetrated the shaft like a plunger in a gargantuan syringe. The fit of the outer sleeve of the telescopic rod to the shaft was perfect. 4:03 remained in real time.

I grabbed the timer and said, "The farther away we can get now, the better. Let's roll." The countdown whizzed through the 00:03:00 mark at triple speed. One minute to go. We were almost back to Building A, which housed the control room. I stepped inside and shouted for Abdul to get out.

"I must stay, Matt Decker. I am only seconds away from the bottom of the file!"

"You'll never break it if you're dead, Abdul. Have you made offsite backups of everything?"

"Yes. I sent everything to the CEPOCS cloud."

"Great, then get out of there. We're out of time!"

He typed a blur of keystrokes as he was getting up and said, "I'm in!"

"Let's go, Abdul!"

He headed for the door but didn't make it before the timer in my hand squealed. A fraction of a second later, a massive concussion shook the ground so hard it knocked both of us down. I looked over at Tark. He was still on his feet but swaying as the ground shook. I felt the ground under our feet drop several inches. Pavement cracked and the metal siding on the building creaked and groaned. Windows shattered as the whole building warped, showering us with shards of safety glass.

The rumbling continued, the noise deafening. Building F, the epicenter of our man-made earthquake, was collapsing. Glass broke and metal shrieked as the huge structure came down. Something caught fire and smoke started pouring out of the wreckage before it stopped falling. The vibration of the ground finally stopped.

"Tark, I guess we should've thought of this before, but do we have any kind of working fire control?"

"Yeah, plenty of hydrants and hoses."

"Good deal. Are you fit to man a hose?"

"I'm fine, Matthew."

I yanked a walkie-talkie out of my back pocket and keyed it up. "Sheriff, we need help in here, fast!"

"On my way," he said.

"Let's grab some hoses and try to set up a perimeter around F," I said. "We don't want to put the water right on the wreckage unless we have to. We don't know what kind of radioactive fallout is in there and the last thing we want to do is start spreading it around with water."

"Understood," Tark said. The big man was in a dead run. I saw a fire hydrant ahead, around fifty yards from the heap of mangled metal that used to be Building F and sprinted toward it. I passed him and seconds later Abdul sped by me. He was fast. Really fast. He beat me to the hydrant and broke the glass out of the housing next to it that contained the four-inch diameter hose and hydrant valve wrench. He threw the wrench on the ground, grabbed the nozzle, and started unspooling the hose.

"Just a perimeter around it, Abdul. We just want to keep it from spreading to the other buildings," I said as I slipped the wrench onto the valve and cranked it open.

"Got it, I'll work on wetting down the other buildings," he said. Something about the way he said it spooked me and I froze, trying to decipher the goose bumps that rippled down the back of my neck there in the searing heat of the flames now engulfing Building F. Then it clicked. For five days I had listened to his thickly flavored, broken English that sounded like something out of a comedy flick. Now he had just rattled off a perfect sentence without the slightest trace of an accent.

57

6:51 AM SUNDAY EASTERN EUROPE SUMMER TIME (LOCAL)
10:51 PM SATURDAY CENTRAL DAYLIGHT TIME
ANCIENT CITY OF PETRA, JORDAN

Hart watched as the sun climbed high enough in the eastern sky to start erasing the shadows in the old city. Other than still being featured in a movie from time to time or explored on occasion by adventurous tourists, mysterious Petra lay untouched and unseen. Sitting at the crossroads of ancient trade routes, the buildings of Petra had been carved right out of the pink sandstone walls of the canyon. This unique architecture, along with a narrow alley-like entrance, made for a superb defensive position in times of old, strong enough for its original inhabitants to ward off would-be conquerors for hundreds of years.

The defense finally came to an end in 106 A.D., when the Romans under Trajan took the city. Many surviving inhabitants fled and the busy Petra became a forlorn and eventually deserted place. Westerners wouldn't even learn of Petra's existence until 1812, when local Bedouins shared its story with a Swiss explorer named J.L. Burckhardt.

Hart intimately knew all the history of Petra that there was to know, but as he watched the sunlight spread across the striking stone facade of the treasury, his mind was on the future, not the past. This time, Petra's defense would endure. No Roman invaders would capture her. Where the Nabataeans had failed, his people would succeed. His adversaries would be led here like a moth to a flame, while he kept a date with destiny.

During the '90s and '00s, Petra turned into a popular tourist stop, complete with five-star hotels on a mountain overlooking the picturesque canyon scene. A series of terrorist suicide bombs while the area was full of American college students on an archaeology study trip ended that era. Without tourism and without a climate and environment suited for any other enterprise, Petra died again. Property owners gladly parted with parcel after parcel when a shell corporation backed by Hardier Enterprises started buying. Money changed hands and no questions were asked. It was the way things worked in that corner of the world.

For two years, Jordanian laborers and imported construction workers—who were paid well and understood to keep their mouths shut or die—worked to turn Petra into a modern fortress. Reinforced concrete lined the sandstone walls inside rooms that had been hollowed out of the canyon walls thousands of years before. New tunnels were bored deep into the ground, leading to a self-contained power plant with enough diesel to power the complex for years, as well as freshwater and air conditioning systems that belied the harsh desert surroundings outside. To anyone who happened along, Petra would appear as she had for almost two thousand years. And they would not be allowed to look beyond the facade.

A small army of several dozen mercenaries guarded the area, vigilant for signs of intruders from the desert. Dressed in local garb and mounted on camels, the perimeter guards patrolled a 500-meter circle around Petra. Inside the canyon walls, another line of defense was made up of more heavily armed soldiers in desert camouflage gear with a cadre of advanced weaponry at their disposal, including shoulder-fired surface-to-air missiles and a variety of ground-to-ground armaments. The inner sanctum could be sealed with steel doors on a moment's notice but there was no need. All was quiet in Petra.

Hart stooped to walk through the entrance of a small cave that opened into a larger cavern housing his private quarters. He sat in front of a computer—connected to the Internet via a satellite uplink/downlink concealed in a natural rock trough on top of the canyon rim—and opened his web-based Hotmail inbox. There waited the most recent email from the impertinent and irrelevant Decker, to which he typed a brief reply:

To: x7ijljAweRRv@deckerdigital.com
Subject: Spoils

Mr. Decker:

You proved to be an amusing and
surprisingly resourceful adversary. With

that in mind (although I find a reference to fair play laughable coming from a corrupt little weasel like yourself) I have elected to reward your meaningless victory by leaving be both your father and the Persian's family.

GAME OVER.

After sending the email, Hart opened a file containing a document he had read many times. This would be the final reading, the one to cherish.

CONFIDENTIAL ANALYSIS OF JORDAN FAULT
BY: DR. CHAIM HILTON, Ph.D.

* * *

HISTORY: In the early twenty-first century, a pattern of unprecedented seismic activity was observed in the state of Israel. The activity comprised numerous minor tremors in the 1.5 – 3.0 range. Of more significance was the sudden commencement of activity where none had been previously observed. Subsequent measurement and analysis confirmed the existence of a paleo tectonic fault system, one that lay dormant for millennia and has now gone active. The system is exacerbated by the proximity of the vertical component of the fault to a known high pressure hydraulic vent. On the surface, the fault line extends from the northern Sinai region in Egypt, roughly north along the Israeli-Jordanian border to Lake Kinneret, at which point it extends diagonally across Lebanon in a north-northwesterly trajectory. The fault is listric in nature, extending vertically along the fault line to an unusually shallow depth, then extending westward at a downward angle. The land mass of Israel is in essence an angular slab resting precariously upon what could be viewed as a giant underground hillside. The fault system was given the name JORDAN FAULT.

POST-DISCOVERY ANALYSIS: A dense system of remote electronic monitoring devices was installed along the fault line and augmented by a series of space-based seismic surveillance units. To oversee and coordinate study of the fault system, the Negev Academic College of Engineering established a research program under my guidance. Activity in the Jordan Fault continued to accelerate in both frequency and magnitude.

FINDINGS: Due to the speed at which the fault activity was developing, we moved quickly to form a panel of leading scientists from the United States, Great

Britain, Russia, and other nations, in order to insure the highest confidence in our findings. Rarely has consensus among differing scientific camps been so thorough. Without significant dissent, it was agreed that the Jordan Fault is the most unstable seismic system on the planet.

STATUS: Stability continues to deteriorate at an alarming rate, but the seriousness of the situation remains largely masked by the low magnitude of continuing events. It is the vehement and unanimous opinion of this panel that adequate resources are not being allocated to this problem. And although this panel has complied with the confidentiality dictums imposed upon it by the state of Israel, we strenuously object to the continued concealment from the public of the facts contained herein.

OUTLOOK: It is possible that this system will eventually stabilize and return to dormancy. Such stabilization could take years, decades, or centuries. In the Jordan Fault's current state of flux, however, the risk of a seismic event of cataclysmic proportion is high. The area immediately surrounding the primary fault line should be evacuated and

```
protected. Any external stimulus could
trigger the event. Possible stimuli
include construction, military activity,
or even normal motor vehicle traffic.

RAMIFICATIONS: A seismic event of
magnitude 7.0 or greater is likely
to start a chain reaction. The
angular placement of the land mass,
aidd by the release of fluid from
the nearby hydraulic vent, creates
the potential for separation and
lubricated gravitational slip. Bluntly
stated, Israel could slide into the
Mediterranean Sea. In addition to the
near-total loss of human life and
property on the land mass, this would
in turn precipitate an oceanic event of
severe proportions.
```

Hart smiled and closed the file, then left his quarters and went to the command center. “Status report,” he said to the man in charge of the local operation.

“All conditions nominal, sir.”

“And the corridor to the actual location?”

“Clear, sir.”

“Splendid. Come with me for a moment. I have a new slate of diversionary intelligence that needs to be distributed post-haste.”

58

11:12 PM CENTRAL DAYLIGHT TIME (LOCAL) YELLOW CREEK

The damage was extensive. Every building in the complex had broken windows and cracked walls. Roofs had caved in on several. Fortunately the control building was one of the least damaged. The main power was out but the emergency generator had kicked in and systems were coming back online. Abdul's disappearing accent was very much on my mind but I decided to act as if I hadn't noticed and keep a close eye on him.

With the help of a deputy outside adjusting the satellite dish, he had just gotten the videoconferencing feed to Larry operational. When our picture came into view on their end we heard several cheers. "You made it!" Larry said.

"Yeah, we picked up some battle scars down here but we came through, Larry. Is Major Thompson around?"

“I think he’s still in the building. You need him?”

“No, just pass along my thanks for his help.”

“Will do. We’re showing power still on all across the Central region. What’s the status of the facility?”

“Heavy damage. We’re on auxiliary power here. The RADIAC teams are sweeping for levels. Trace amounts of radioactivity right on top of the explosion, but other than that everything is looking negative. You got any updates for me?”

“You bet. Media outlets all over received a communiqué from our boy Hart several hours ago. We knew you had your hands full so we didn’t mention it.”

“Any new clues?”

“Nothing obvious. This dude’s a whack job from the word go. Signed it as God. Our analysts are studying it.”

“Trace?”

“Nope, thoroughly cloaked.”

“Send it over as soon as you can. What else?”

“The Omaha office is hot to talk to you. Turns out the Fulton lady brought a flash drive out with her when she escaped. Has the beginning of a letter on it from the guy she says planted the device down there. He’s dead and gave the key to her just before he expired.”

“What’s in the letter?”

“I haven’t seen it yet. They’re supposed to email it directly to you. I gave them your addy.”

“Can you put me through to the office?”

“Sure thing. Hold.” He spun in his chair and worked a phone like a seasoned operator. “Patch is live. Go.”

“Mr. Decker?” It was the blissful voice of Jana Fulton.

“Call me Matt, Jana. How’s the horse?”

“Happy and well fed, I’m told. Was anyone hurt in the explosion?”

"Nothing serious. I believe you've said it was Dane Christian who planted the device here. Is he the one you got the flash drive from?"

"Flash? Oh, the thumbdrive. Yes, it was in his jacket. It has part of a letter on it, I think it was a confession. There was goodness in that man way down deep."

"What about the rest of the letter?"

"It changes to gobbledy-gook after a couple of paragraphs. Hold on a second." I heard her talking to someone in the background. "Matt, they said to tell you the file is corrupt but they're sending it anyway."

I got lost in her voice, which seemed pretty silly given the seriousness of the situation, but it captivated—"

"Did you hear me?" Jana said.

"Sorry, no."

"They're sending the file."

My phone buzzed in my pocket. "I shut my laptop down before the explosion and haven't booted back up yet. Ask them to send it to Abdul's address. I'd like to see it right away on something other than my phone."

"Give me the address and I'll tell them."

"A-B-D-U-L dot A-B-I-D-I at G-C-E dot D-O-P-U dot G-O-V," Abdul said.

"Got it. Is there anything else I can help with?" she said.

"Not right now. Thanks, Jana."

"Goodbye, Matt." I nodded to Larry and he killed the patch to Omaha.

Abdul's machine chimed.

"Larry, I'll get back to you after we look this over. Did you say there was something from Hart too?"

"Yeah, already sent that to you."

"Okay, back to you in a few."

"Roger that, bud."

Abdul opened the Christian attachment:

MY NAME IS DANE RUDOLPH CHRISTIAN. IN THE EVENT OF MY DEATH THIS MESSAGE MUST BE DELIVERED TO THE UNITED STATES GOVERNMENT. I HAVE BEEN INVOLVED FOR SEVERAL YEARS IN A PLOT TO CARRY OUT VARIOUS OPERATIONS FOR A MAN NAMED ABRAHAM HART. HE CLAIMS TO BE A MESSIAH AND HAS A HUGE NUMBER OF FOLLOWERS IN HIS CULT. THEY ARE EVERYWHERE, MORE THAN YOU CAN IMAGINE.

HART PAID ME AND MY LATE BROTHER, RIFFERT JAMES CHRISTIAN, TO ORGANIZE AND CARRY OUT CERTAIN ACTIONS. FOUR OPS ARE COMPLETE. I DO NOT KNOW NATURE OF FIFTH. SIXTH IS THERMONUCLEAR DEVICE HIDDEN BUILDING C YC COMPLEX. DISARM CODE 46656. I AM ATTACHING FILE FOR SEVENTH. SEVENTH IS DEVASTATING TO THE WHOLE WORLD AND MUST BE AT STOPPED AT ALL

Then garbled text went on for what would amount to thousands of pages.

"A corrupt file. Frigging unbelievable," I said. "Now we know something 'devastating to the whole world' is in the works and we haven't a clue."

"I am afraid I do know what it is," Abdul said. I turned to look at him and could've sworn that just for an instant I saw a flicker of a smile. Or maybe not.

"Talk to me," I said.

"Look." He tapped his display onto the big screen. "This is what was to be found in the final layer of the white horse steg file."

There on the screen was a high-res image of a missile. Without any point of reference there was no way for us to know whether it was three feet long or thirty. The Russian writing on its side, however, was clear, as was the yellow international nuclear symbol near its business end. In light of my new leeriness of Abdul, I checked the file myself to be sure there were no more layers. There were not.

"Send this to Thompson, Abdul." I gave him the major's email address and he sent it.

"No riddles this time?" Tark said.

Abdul shook his head. "Only the one picture and nothing more."

"Behold the seventh seal," Tark said.

"Let's look at the Hart document. Maybe it will give us a clue as to where this thing is headed." Larry had already sent it to my mailbox so I reached for my laptop; it wasn't there.

The vibration from the explosion had jarred it off the console. It was lying on the floor, the bottom casing cracked. I picked it up, plugged the AC adapter into the jack on the back, and hit the power button. Nothing. I looked closer and saw the crack wasn't confined to the case; the power supply circuit board was split. The machine was trashed. "Just keeps getting better," I said, then I found the email on my phone and forwarded it to Abdul.

I moved back into position at my workstation and soon had Larry back on screen. "You need to track Thompson down with all possible dispatch and tell him to check his email," I said.

"Consider it done."

"Later, Larry."

"Okay, bud."

I was just about to click into standby when I remembered an issue that had been lost in the chaos. "Larry, you still there?"

"Yo."

"Are we private?"

"Nobody close. What's on your mind?"

"You remember me asking you about an earthquake issue this afternoon?"

"Sure thing. Didn't know what you were talking about then."

"But you do now?"

"You bet. That nuke was a simulated quake, the sixth seal. Right?"

"Exactly. Who mentioned the earthquake angle to you?"

He took a sip of Red Bull. "Nobody mentioned it. I read it."

"Someone sent you a memo?"

"Hell, no, I looked up the seals in Revelation, all by my lonesome."

"You're telling me that there was no one in the Bureau officially working the idea of a simulated earthquake today?"

"I'm all over this case, Matt. When I'm not talking to you, I'm making calls, sending emails, doing everything I can to stay up to speed so I can keep you informed as to what we're doing. The word 'earthquake' has not been uttered in an official Bureau sense. Not here. Not Quantico. Not anywhere."

I thanked him and clicked out. "Tark, you hear that?"

"Yep. Doesn't sound good, Matthew."

"It explains a lot, though, like why the Bureau's making so little progress."

"You got that right. How do we handle this?"

"We hand him a rope."

"I like it," Tark said, pulling out his pipe.

DAY SIX
SUNDAY

... lo, there was a great earthquake; and the sun became
black as sackcloth of hair, and the moon became as blood;
And the stars of heaven fell unto the earth,
even as a fig tree casteth her untimely figs,
when she is shaken of a mighty wind. And the heaven
departed as a scroll when it is rolled together; and every
mountain and island were moved out of their places.
Revelation 6:12-14

59

3:55 AM CENTRAL DAYLIGHT TIME (LOCAL)
YELLOW CREEK

I woke up in the lounge after four hours of sporadic sleep and lay there in the dark trying to clear my head. There were no distinct days anymore, just one big nightmare that refused to end. The details of the current situation started coming back into focus.

After we read the Hart manifesto/gibberish, Tark went to the lounge and crashed on a mattress.

I soon followed, and dreamed I was back in my childhood church. I was grown, but everything around me was as it was back then. My Sunday School teacher, Mrs. Dixon, sat to my right on the very front pew, listening with rapt attention to every word my father rumbled from his pulpit, turning to me with a sweet smile and patting me on the knee every now and then. To my left was

Jimmy Lee Tarkleton, eyes wide, soaking up the sermon like it was the grandest thing he'd ever heard. Mrs. Dixon would pat me on the knee, and Tark would reach up and squeeze my shoulder and whisper, "Now that man can preach!"

Time came for the offering, and there to pass the plate was none other than Abdul, except he had a thick shock of jet black hair swept back into a pony tail. Ha! For sure there would've been no pony-tailed ushers in my father's church back in the day.

While Abdul passed the plate, the choir rose to sing. There was Mrs. Edelbrock, the first-grade teacher who used to whack me on the hand with her ruler for talking in class, singing her heart out. And Mr. Denton, and all the other fixtures of the town I grew up in. And right in the middle of the choir, with an angelic voice that lofted beautifully above the others, was Jana Fulton. She even looked like an angel. Her face radiated in a beautiful glow and her eyes looked right at me while she sang Love Lifted Me. Somewhere in the sanctuary, someone snored loudly.

I found myself drifting back into the same dream and shook my head to wake up again. Abdul was snoring on the other sofa so I got up and eased out of the room and down the hall to the control room. There was a coffee pot in the corner and I started a pot brewing, then fired up the link to Larry. He was dozing at his desk. When the coffee pot stopped gurgling, I poured a cup and tapped on the microphone on the front of the video camera. Larry jumped up, rubbed his eyes, and said, "Morning, Matt."

"Hi, Larry. Got an I.D. on that missile yet?"

"Uh, hang on. Let me see ... " He rubbed his eyes some more and fumbled through a stack of papers on his desk. "Yeah, the major knew exactly what it was. It's Russian, but you already knew that. Let's see, the model is—"

"The model won't mean jack to me. How big is it?"

The look on his face said it before his mouth did. "Big enough, Matt. It's one of the new-generation Scud-E jobs, GPS guidance, pinpoint accuracy. "

"How many could it kill?"

"In a populated area, millions. You want me to put you through to Major Thompson? He's at the White House."

"No, tell me what else you know about it. How can it be launched?"

He dug through more papers. "It can be fired from a silo."

"Well, that's a relief. There's no way he's built a friggin' nuclear missile silo on the sly in this country."

"It can be fired from a silo. It can also be fired from something called a Topol-M, which is a truck-mounted launcher."

"Geez, surely he hasn't been able to smuggle in something like that."

"I understand they're in a serious pow-wow over at the big house, Matt. Military, NSA, CIA, the works. I heard the President has been up all night."

I suddenly felt like an idiot for sleeping. "Any other developments in the past few hours?"

"This has pretty much taken top priority. A few more sketchy pieces of intel on Hart have dribbled in, but nothing useful."

"Do we have a picture of this guy? I want to see what he looks like."

"Not a one. Nothing. It's like he hasn't been near a camera in his life," Larry said.

"Okay, thanks for the update. I'll be in touch. Let me know the second anything breaks," I said.

"You bet, bud."

5:06 AM CENTRAL DAYLIGHT TIME (LOCAL)
YELLOW CREEK

Tark was awake and we were examining the Hart document. "Blasphemous lunatic," he said.

"How does the missile square with the seventh seal?"

"Hmmm." He fetched his pipe and Bible and sat down on the sofa, the world's first pair of eyeglasses riding the tip of his nose.

"Are you sentimentally attached to those glasses or something?" I said.

"Belonged to my grandpa, why?"

"Just wondering."

"Remember," he said, "we're actually a little bit ahead of him now. Before the countdown was accelerated, the bomb at the plant wasn't supposed to go off until two-six-teen Eastern time this afternoon. That's seal number six."

"How does a nuclear missile mesh with number seven?"

"The seventh seal gets some pretty special treatment, Matthew." Puffing hard now. "You see, chapter six ends after the sixth seal. It talks of people being in a terrible state of fear after the earthquake, running here and there, trying to hide from the wrath of God. Take a look."

He handed me the Bible and I read the last few verses:

```
15  And the kings of the earth, and the
great men, and the rich men, and the
```

```
chief captains, and the mighty men, and
every bondman, and every free man, hid
themselves in the dens and in the rocks
of the mountains;

16  And said to the mountains and rocks,
Fall on us, and hide us from the face of
him that sitteth on the throne, and from
the wrath of the Lamb:

17  For the great day of his wrath is
come; and who shall be able to stand?
```

"Now read on into chapter seven a little bit," he said. I did. "Tell me what you see there."

"I don't see anything about the seventh seal. It's all about 'sealing' the foreheads of different tribes of Israel."

"Exactly. Now look at chapter eight."

I read the first verse out loud, "'And when he had opened the seventh seal, there was silence in heaven about the space of half an hour.' What kind of attack could silence be?"

"To understand it, we have to consider the whole picture of what happens between the sixth and seventh seals. Remember, this is all the same story, not a bunch of isolated incidents. The sixth seal, the earthquake, takes place first. We've already seen his version of that. Then the people of God are sealed, issued protection from the wrath still to come."

"According to that brilliant document he sent out, he himself is God. So in that mindset, who are the people of God and how are they protected?"

"Who indeed. He thinks he's the Father, Son, Holy

Spirit, and antichrist all rolled up into one big ball. He's made it pretty clear he considers us all his children, so to get any meaning at all out of this part we have to assume he's talking about the same chosen people the Bible is. And that would be the tribes of Israel. In the real tribulation, most Biblical scholars believe these people will be set aside and protected."

I sensed a long-winded derailment coming and steered him back on course. "What about this; he says the Bible has been skewed, right?"

"Yup, that's what he says. He's wrong, but that's his position."

"And in his schizoid world, he's also the antichrist, correct?"

"You got it, Matthew. What's your point?"

"As far as people go, who will be the antichrist's least favorite group?"

"The chosen people of God. The descendants of the ancient Israelites."

"Jews, right?"

"It's a little more complex than just saying 'Jews' but generally speaking, yes."

"Then I think we have to consider Jews to be his next most likely target."

"I concur."

"But what could he do targeting Jews that would be devastating to the whole world?"

"Maybe that was a bit of exaggeration by a twisted mind, like his substituting Earth, Texas, for the planet Earth."

I shook my head. "No, if it were something from him, I'd buy that. This description came from Dane Christian, and he was warning us to stop it. There would be no reason for him to aggrandize the event."

"Sure would be nice if we could see the rest of his letter."

"Not just nice. Crucial."

60

8:17 AM CENTRAL DAYLIGHT TIME (LOCAL)
YELLOW CREEK

Tark managed to round up some workers to start cleaning up around the complex in the aftermath of the explosion. Abdul found and fixed the glitch that had us on emergency power, and as soon as Tark and I gave the okay he patched us back into the grids. If I had believed in God I would have issued a word of thanks for allowing me to be born in the post-Freon era. Before this week, I didn't realize what an air conditioning junkie I was.

I mulled over the Abdul situation some more and almost confronted him but decided to give it a while. It was possible, even likely, that he wasn't aware of his faux pas. I didn't want to believe he was a traitor—he had definitely been responsible for real breakthroughs during the week that only helped us—but it was possible it was an elaborate cover and I wanted to keep the upper hand.

Restoring the Christian file was top priority. I had a hunch about how it got corrupted, and I made a call to check the theory.

"Jana, when you went through the main door at Hart's place, do you recall an unusual tingling sensation, like static electricity?"

"No, why?"

"I thought there might have been a data security field, an anti-espionage device that destroys data passing through it."

"Sorry, Matt, no tingling."

"Thanks, I'll talk to you later."

"Bye bye," she said in that sweet drawl.

I hung up the phone, but I could still hear her voice. Lost in it again. What difference did the means of corruption make? None, I admitted, which made me a pretty sorry excuse for a hero, calling a girl while I was supposed to be saving the country, or maybe the world. I suddenly felt like an ass and went back to work.

The file reported a size of just over twelve megabytes, which might be accurate. Or just as easily, not. The attached file was what we needed, not the rest of Christian's letter. An hour into the hack session, I located the marker that delineated the two components. It was a major step but it was going far too slowly. At this rate I'd still be hammering the keys while Hart did his thing on Monday.

The videoconferencing chime sounded and I pulled up the feed expecting to see Larry. What I got was something altogether different.

"Mr. Decker?"

"Yes, Mr. President." I quietly asked if someone would grab me a glass of water.

"I want to personally thank you for your heroic efforts on this matter."

"Thank you, sir, but—"

"Is this conversation private on your end, Mr. Decker?"

I made a few clicks. "Yes sir."

"Do you mind if I call you Matt?"

"Of course not, sir."

"Good. Matt, I need not tell you that we're gravely concerned about this possible missile threat. We've spent the whole night assessing possible target areas for such an attack, and quite frankly we're coming up with goose eggs. Do you have anything else that may help us, anything at all?"

"I have a theory, sir, but I'm not sure how much help it will be."

"By all means, let's have it."

"After conferring with my prophecy consultant, I believe Hart is planning to target Jews."

"Why in the hell would he do that? Oh, never mind. Who cares why the crazy bastard is doing anything. The question is where and when."

"We can almost certainly narrow the 'when' down to two-sixteen Eastern time tomorrow, most likely PM since he adhered to that pattern in four of the six events thus far. I have no idea where at this point."

"I see. Matt, you've become our go-to man on this operation. I'm counting on you to come through on this. The moment you have any relevant information I want you to contact us. Your feed has been switched here to the situation room instead of the FBI, and I intend for it to remain here for the duration."

"I'll do my best, Mr. President."

"I know you will. That is all."

"Mr. President, before you go, is Director Brandon with you?"

"Yes. Why?"

"I just want him to know how grateful I am for the assistance he gave on the simulated earthquake issue."

Stanton's face registered confusion. "Simulated earthquake?"

"Yes, sir. I'll let the director fill you in."

"Very well. Goodbye for now, Mr. Decker."

"Goodbye, sir."

The screen went blank and I chugged the glass of water someone had fetched.

If Abdul was on the other side, he was doing a great job of working to maintain his cover. Shortly after I briefed Tark and him on the conversation, he said, "I know you are working on the file from the Mr. Christian, but have you been thinking to look at the original file of the Abraham Hart document that was sent to the press people?"

It took about ten seconds to soak into my brain in its depleted state. "Of course! There could easily be an encrypted layer to that file, just like the White Horse file."

"That is what I am thinking, Matt Decker."

The phones were reasonably operational but I couldn't get a soul on the line at Fox News who had a technical clue. I couldn't get a human on the line at any of the other major media centers at all. Working a step or two away from the President has its benefits. I raised Larry, who had moved his liaison operation to the White House, and explained our need for the original file. It arrived four minutes later. The Presidential little black book obviously has a different set of phone numbers.

I held my breath as I pulled the file up on my notebook, then deflated like a balloon at the sharp end of a pin. "Good idea, Abdul. But the file is only twenty-seven K. Nothing there but a dot-doc file." I opened it and read through the babble one more time. It was still just babble.

"Maybe there's a code in the text itself," Tark said.

"Worth checking out," I said. I asked Abdul to run it through a cryptology scan. He started working it and hitting dead ends, which wasn't surprising. Looking for a needle in a haystack is easy compared to trying to uncover a code in five paragraphs of text without any reference point. Nonetheless, he tried. And tried. And tried some more. I paced and pondered, keeping a watchful eye on his efforts to be sure they were genuine. I saw nothing to indicate otherwise.

Tark paced the room with a copy of the document in his hand, leaving a trail of sweet smoke in his wake.

"I am having no luck," Abdul said.

"Why don't you try running the Bible code on it?" Tark said.

"Bible code? You want to start praying for an answer?"

"That wouldn't hurt, but that's not what I'm talking about. I'm talking about the Bible code. Surely you've heard of it?"

"Surely I haven't, but I'm all ears now."

"Back in the nineties, an Israeli mathematician found a bunch of hidden messages in the first five books of the Bible. There were a bunch of books out on it. A bunch of high-brow intellectuals tried for years to debunk it but couldn't. It's amazing stuff, Matthew."

I had gargantuan doubts regarding the existence of hidden Bible messages, but we were getting nowhere with our shotgun approach and a Bible-related code would seem to fit the bill with our man. "You know anything about the methodology?"

"I remember that now," Abdul said. "It was based on skipping letters. By skipping a certain number of letters ... "

Abdul kept talking but it occurred to me that with the power back on I might have some luck finding some working Internet sites. I was right. My buddy Jeff Bezos over at Amazon.com had wasted no time getting his shop back online; even though the power at their main facility was still down, they had mirror data centers dotting the world.

My first search hit a book creatively titled The Bible Code. I read the reviews and a few excerpted pages, then started digging for more detailed information. Even with servers and backbones operational in only one region, there was still plenty of information to be found on the topic.

Abdul was right; the methodology was simple. Pick a starting point, then skip every other letter and see if you come up with a readable sequence. If not, try using a letter, skipping two, using a letter, skipping two more, and so on. Then skip three, then four, and so on. The so-called messages in the Bible were often found by skip sequences of up to thousands of letters. The resulting information was interesting, but that was brain candy for another day.

I brought Abdul up to speed and asked him if he thought he could come up with a quick kludge to apply the search to the Hart document. He grinned, rubbed his fingertips together, and went to work. The program was ready to go in minutes.

"Start with the first letter and let's see if we get lucky," I said. "And don't count any spaces or punctuation, just the actual letters like they did when they were searching the Bible."

"What skip sequence?"

"That's easy. Skip two hundred fifteen; that'll have us using every two hundred sixteenth letter. If he happened to use a code like this, I have no doubt that he used his magic number."

We watched closely while the little program ran. Nothing. "Try starting with letter number two-sixteen," I said. Again, nothing. Then starting with number four thirty-two. And six forty-eight. No matter where we started, the resulting sequence of letters was nothing but gibberish. I started pacing again.

On my third trip around the room I heard Abdul say, "Oh my goodness graciousness!"

"Got something?"

"I'll put it on the big screen!"

I looked in disbelief and said, "How'd you get that?"

"I included punctuation marks in the last search."

And there it was, plain as day and bigger than life. Using every two hundred sixteenth character, including punctuation marks, yielded a definite sequence:

My Dearest Children:

Prior to this momentous time, this world has existed in a state of chaos and confusion. It gives my heart and soul untold pleasure to announce that the end of this misery is at hand. Hear me explain!

Each human being craves to know that he or she exⒾsts for a reason. This longing drives people to search for meaning in their everyday lives, meaning in the world about them, and meaning in the universe. For many millennia, untold numbers have clung to a plethora of religions and arcane belief systems, becauⓈe the human mind and spirit is generally incapable of deciphering the real meaning of life. I lived for years in just such a yearning existence myself. That has changed.

Throughout and during the past years I have discovered that I am not really human. I am immoⓇtal, the quintessential embodiment of life and all that it entails. There have been many false teachings purveyed by scores of false teachers and prophets. Some of these were well-meaning souls. Others were utter frauds. I will not call names for it would be Ⓐ pure waste of time within this brief missive, but the Truth I shall soon share with you encompasses, supersedes, and nullifies all iconic religious personalities who have preceded me.

Regarding the current situation, as you are no doubt aware, aⒺons have foretold the significant events have taken place over the past few days, primarily in the United States of America. Fear not! These happenings are the fulfillment of prophecy. A twisted version, a Program of Events so to speak, can be found seeded alⓁ throughout the Book of Revelation in the Holy Bible. I encourage you to read the book, but please my children, bear in mind that the Bible was written long ago by many different MORTALS who were inspired by my lingering cosmic presence over a period of hundreds Ⓞf years, but their regrettably weak minds and numerous imbecilic translations have skewed the true meaning which I desired to impart.

Alas, the portions of the Bible that speak of the teacher known as Jesus have been hopelessly butchered. They lead to belieⓋe that this man was the Christ. Is it not extravagantly exciting to know that the real Christ is among you right now? I am Christ. I realize that all those who are reading this are likely beside themselves with spewing joy, but there are yet more good tidings. TalⒺs concerning the so-called AntiChrist are also mangled groupings of incoherent thought. There is no separate AntiChrist. I am the Christ and I am the AntiChrist. There is no distinct personality known as Satan, beyond certain necessary elements of my immoⓇtal being. I am Satan. There is none other but me. I created the

universe and all that exists within
it, and have subsequently lain dormant
with regard to my reverential being
until now. I shall reveal myself fully
unto you in the near future for you
to worship me! You are henceforth
warned that things are often not what
they seem. Rely on my Word for your
sustenance and survival. To that end,
you may expect a series of further
communications over the coming days.
Until then, I bid you fond adieu.

God

The message was clear: ISRAEL OVER! It was time for a conversation with the White House.

61

10:18 AM CENTRAL DAYLIGHT TIME (LOCAL)
SITUATION ROOM
WHITE HOUSE

The news that Israel was the likely target for Hart's finale cast a long shadow of quiet over the room and its assembly of powerful men.

"Everything on this planet always seem to wind up back in the Middle East," the President said when he finally broke the silence. He turned to the Chairman of the Joint Chiefs of Staff, Admiral Bradley Stockton. "Brad, what's the most likely origin over there for a missile strike on Israel?"

"Christ, sir. It could come from anywhere. They're surrounded on every side by people who hate them and would love to see them vaporized. Any nation-state in the region is a potential conspirator who might aid and abet this maniac."

"We've spent a fortune on increasing intel there for more than a decade. How could this have happened? How do we know he's not bluffing?"

Major Todd Thompson spoke up. "With all due respect, sir, he hasn't bluffed yet. And given his known acquisition of the one Russian nuke, we have researched and confirmed that a number of other Russian nuclear assets are unaccounted for."

"A number? Are you saying that he could have more than one missile?"

"I'm afraid so, sir. The delivery vehicles, the missiles, are plentiful in a number of nations we would consider hostile to Israel. For years, the Russians have been willing to sell them to anyone with the cash. The warheads are the real problem and there are presently three missing. This isn't the first time it's happened, but we do believe it's the first time it has happened in Moscow right under the noses of the top brass. Prior incidents have all taken place in the outlying provinces that used to be under Soviet control. There's also a chance he could get something from the Iranians, but the Russian scenario is far more likely."

"I see. What size are these warheads, and how long have they been gone?"

"Eighty kilotons, devastating. Our sources indicate they were smuggled out within the past thirty days by substituting dummy warheads so they wouldn't be missed during inventory checks. There's obviously a high-level official involved."

Stanson held up a finger for pause and turned to an aid. "Have someone get President Aganine on the phone." He turned back to his audience. "Maybe we can get some help from him. Brad, what kind of naval presence do we have in the area?"

"The *Ronald Reagan* carrier battle group is in the Mediterranean."

"Do you need more?"

"No sir. One CBG is sufficient for any single target, or a package of three targets, for that matter. Give me locations and I'll make them disappear."

"All right, let's get to it, gentlemen. I'll talk to the Israeli Prime Minister after I've finished with Aganine. I want Hart and his missiles found and eradicated. Is that clear?" He looked around the room and to the videoconferencing screen for nods and got them.

"By the way, can anyone tell me where the hell my FBI director is?"

Around the room, heads shook and shoulders shrugged.

"He better be here within thirty minutes and have one hell of a story if he wants to keep his job. That is all."

10:25 AM CENTRAL DAYLIGHT TIME (LOCAL)
YELLOW CREEK

"Well that was really useful," I said to myself as soon as I was sure the link was dead. The most powerful men on Earth were thus far powerless to stop whatever was coming. I felt the weight of the situation bearing down on my shoulders one more time.

The feed cut back to Larry, who had already managed to build cluttered environs in the White House that rivaled his normal digs back in the Hoover basement.

"Matt, just wanted to let you know that the agents are

still working on your father's case. No luck yet, I'm sorry to say."

"Thanks, Larry."

"I think I've spotted something in this letter," Tark said.

"Are you serious?"

"I'm certain of it!" He was excited, puffing at warp speed; I could hear the soft cluck of his lips on the briarwood. "Put it on the big screen."

"Hang on a second." I routed the document to the display and Tark walked to it.

"I didn't break any fancy code," he said, pointing at the screen, "but take a look at the first letter of each paragraph in the body of the letter."

"Let's see, I come up with P – E –T – R – A. Petra?"

"Yes, Petra!"

"Meaning?"

"Petra is an ancient city in the Jordanian desert."

"You just earned my undivided attention. Is it inhabited?"

"I don't know what's going on over there now, but it was abandoned for centuries. Hidden in a canyon, buildings carved right out of the rock. It's slap dab in the middle of nowhere, Matthew, and next door to Israel."

"You might have just saved the day, Tark. If we're lucky, the world."

"I'm no savior, but I hope it helps. Think this is worth telling the President?"

"Your calls on this whole thing have been uncanny. How confident are you on this issue?" said the President.

"It fits, sir," I said. "I have no doubt he intends to hit Israel, and from a glance at the map, Petra looks to be as likely a launch point as any. I don't have figures, but I'm sure your people will confirm it to be within the range of those missiles."

Stanson turned to his aid and told him to get the CIA busy gathering intelligence on the area, then turned back to the camera. "Mr. Decker, I can't thank you enough for all you've done. When this is over I'd love to have you come spend a weekend here at the house."

"I'd be honored, Mr. President. May I ask what your plans are from this point in the operation?"

"Rich?" he said, talking to National Security Advisor Rich Henning.

"As soon as we wrap up this discussion I'll confer with CIA, but I think step one is to quickly re-task a hi-res bird or two for a look. Might want to move some drones into that airspace, as well."

"We have the latest and greatest on board the *Reagan*," Admiral Stockton said. "I'll get them airborne immediately. I can also mobilize a squad of Marines."

"Do whatever you see fit, gentlemen," the President said. "I want to be very clear on one point, however. It's not enough to stop the missiles. I want this man done away with. No media circus of a trial. Kill the sonofabitch."

"It goes without saying that I agree," Henning said, "but there's one big problem. We don't have any idea what he looks like. We have no pictures, and I do mean none. No fingerprints. Zero to identify him. We've talked to people who worked for years in Hardier Enterprises and not one soul has seen him in over twenty-five years. He's a phantom."

"He's no phantom," I said, "and I know someone who knows exactly what he looks like."

3:10 PM CENTRAL DAYLIGHT TIME (LOCAL) YELLOW CREEK

"I'm normally not a preachy kind of fellow," Tark said.

"Then why are you laying it on me so thick? You've made it abundantly clear you believe in God. I've made it just as clear that I don't. What's the problem?"

"You're walking right into harm's way, you could use some help, and I think you do believe."

If it had been anyone else essentially calling me a liar, not to mention annoying the hell out of me, I would have reached a breaking point long ago on this issue. But the truth is, I really liked Tark. Loaded with integrity and knows no fear, the kind of friend who has your back no matter what. He was Norman without the Labrador limitations. How could I not like him and give him a little room?

"Now my curiosity meter is pegged out. What would make you think I do believe?"

"You've always believed, you're just angry. You felt abandoned when your father got hurt and you never forgave God for it. That's a scary thing to fess up to, so you convinced yourself you don't believe at all. That's what I think, Matthew."

"With all due respect, my friend, you're off base. Your theory was true for the first year or so when I prayed day and night for God to heal my Dad, but when he didn't answer ... "

"You lost faith and quit asking."

"I stopped believing, and that's that. If he was real he would've answered."

"He answers in his time, not ours."

"I hear you, Tark, but we'll just have to agree to disagree on this one. Let me say this, though. You're a solid example of the human race and I sincerely appreciate your concern. I'll be fine."

"And what if you're not?"

"Hey, we all have to go sometime, right?"

"Yeah, but—"

"No buts, Tark. I'm no hero, but it's fallen to me to find and stop this asshole before he kills more people. If I have to die doing that, I'm okay with it. Really."

"At least think about what I've said."

"I'll do that."

"Good enough, and you take care of yourself. I'll hold down the fort here so holler if you need anything."

"Will do. I better get going." He shook/crushed my hand, then wrapped me up in a big hug. Time to go.

DAY SEVEN
MONDAY

And when he had opened the seventh seal,
there was silence in heaven about the space
of half an hour.
Revelation 8:1

62

4:15 AM GREENWICH MEAN TIME (LOCAL)
12:15 AM EASTERN DAYLIGHT TIME
TIME REMAINING: 14 HOURS, 1 MINUTE
SOMEWHERE OVER THE NORTH ATLANTIC

I can say without hesitation that Jana Fulton is the most beautiful woman I have ever seen in my life. The picture was breathtaking but it didn't come close to the real thing. The color of her shoulder-length hair reminded me of a canary yellow diamond I once saw in a museum collection of royal jewels. It was about the same color and sparkled wherever light touched it. Her eyes were bluish green—almost turquoise—her skin a creamy tan. She told me a female FBI agent in Omaha happened to be her size and loaned her the clothes she was wearing, a pair of blue jeans and a simple white cotton shirt. I tried not to stare but—no, that's a lie. I stared willingly.

The military brass in the Situation Room put up a brief argument when I suggested Jana—assuming she was willing—and I should make the trip to Petra. Very brief. Stanson was a man on a mission; protocols and rules were out the window as far as he was concerned and that was that. Jana did need to be there, of course, if they wanted to be sure the right man was dealt with since she was the only person known to us who knew what he looked like. As for myself, Hart had turned this whole affair personal and I'd earned the right to be included.

She had gotten a treat few civilians enjoy by being flown from Omaha to Memphis in the rear seat of an F-15. One of the helicopters that had brought in the RADIAC operators took me to Memphis, where we both boarded an FBI corporate style jet that got us to Washington in a hurry. We were met at Andrews Air Force base by Major Thompson and a small contingent of serious-looking soldier types. After several hours of briefing Jana and I re-boarded that same aircraft and were on our way.

I woke from a nap to see her gazing out the window at the blackness of night. "I'm very sorry about Brett," I said.

"Thanks. I'm heartbroken, of course, but our whole family steeled ourselves for the "Brett is gone" phone call long ago. He was wild as a buck. I hope that doesn't sound too cold, but I'm a practical, straightforward person." She unfastened her seat belt and turned to face me. "Enough gloomy talk for now. Tell me about Matt Decker."

I gave her the highlights, sans a few unsavory details like street fighting and strong-arm robbery. She asked a lot more questions and I gave a lot more answers. We moved from me to her and back and forth. I got the full story of the week she'd just been through and was amazed by the strength she had shown once the initial shock wore off. She was comfortable to talk to and it was a nice exchange. We lost track of time and got reminded when the sky outside started lightening as dawn approached.

"We better try to get a little sleep while we can," I said.

"Yeah, we might have a tough day ahead."

"That's probably an understatement. Night, Jana."

"Good night, Matt."

I switched off the overhead lights, pulled down all the window shades in the cabin, and looked across the small aisle at her one more time as she pulled a blanket up around her shoulders. Her very presence overwhelmed me. "Jana?"

"Yes?"

"I've never met anyone like you."

"What do you mean?"

"I only met you a few hours ago, but I feel like I've known you all my life." An awkward silence followed, the sort that takes place while one party watches the other try to lever a 10 ½-D from his mouth. She was the most fabulous example of womanhood I had ever seen and I just mucked everything.

In the dim light of the cabin, I couldn't tell whether she frowned or smiled. She said nothing. I resisted the urge to heave myself from the aircraft and fell asleep to the rush of jet engines pushing us toward Israel.

63

5:24 PM EASTERN EUROPE SUMMER TIME (LOCAL)
10:24 AM EASTERN DAYLIGHT TIME
TIME REMAINING: 3 HOURS, 52 MINUTES
TEL AVIV, ISRAEL

After landing at Ben Gurion airport in Tel Aviv, we were fitted in desert camo fatigues and escorted toward a very different kind of aircraft, a Chinook CH-46E helicopter. Its twin rotors were already spinning and the noise was deafening.

The marine walking us across the tarmac was a tank of a man. He nodded to Jana and shook my hand with a vise that would get high marks in Mississippi. "Sir, ma'am," he shouted over the roaring whoosh-whoosh-whoosh of the massive blades, "Colonel Mack Masters. We'll put you in near the front of the Shithook. The ride's a little better there. I understand you've been briefed already, and I'll bring you up to date at the staging area."

We climbed aboard, strapped in and put on helmets, and moments later left the asphalt in a pulsing roar of power. I looked around the spacious but full interior of the *Sea Knight* and counted sixteen marines, serious looking to a man, along with a cadre of formidable looking weapons and two FAST attack vehicles. They looked to be the newest version of what the Marine Corps calls an IFAV, short for Interim Fast Attack Vehicle. Shaped like stubby SUVs, the DaimlerChrysler vehicles matched our fatigues and were crowned with machine guns whose exact type I couldn't make out from a distance though judging from the size they were .50 calibers.

"Jana, you okay?" I said when I noticed she was tensed up with her eyes closed.

"I didn't mind the nice little jet we came over on, but I'm not wild about this ride." She grabbed my hand and held on tight. I still had the embarrassment from the plane gnawing at my psyche and holding her hand felt weird, but I wasn't about to push away a lady in need. She gave a quick tight smile and said, "Thanks."

"No problem." Thank you.

We rode in silence for the rest of the trip, which was under an hour. I felt the aircraft slowing and then descending as the pilot throttled the big engines back. Marines may be a raucous bunch when they're off duty, but these were on the clock and they were quiet and intense. The Chinook dropped down into a sandstorm of its own making and eased its wheels onto the hard floor of the desert. We stepped out and looked around to see an inhospitable landscape in every direction: dirt, rocks, and some small mountains that looked to be a few miles out.

While the Marines unloaded gear and the IFAVs, Colonel Masters took us aside and spread a map on top of a large rock. “This is the Petra area. We’re here, about five miles south of the target.” He pointed to a spot on the map. “We inserted a Recon team last night by HALO. They’ve scouted the area and report the presence of only a few personnel and they look to be local hires. That’s good news for us. Very bad news for them if they decide to make trouble.”

The engines whined to a stop and the activity around us increased as a small command post was set up. Masters continued, “Four men will stay here at the staging area. Until the area is secure, you’ll stay here, as well. Sunset’s about an hour from now. Once we have full cover of darkness, three fire teams will move from here in those two sand rails. Three more will approach from a similar staging area on the northwest side of the target, and three more from the northeast.

“Once we’ve established a wide perimeter, we’ll call in the air assault element, eight Blackhawks. They’ll provide cover as we move into the hot zone. Once we’ve secured the zone, one of the Blackhawks will fall back here and pick you up.”

“I hate to bring this up, Colonel, but are any defensive measures being taken around likely targets in case we don’t find him in time?”

“Yes, I’ve been advised that reliable intel indicates the targets to be Haifa, Tel Aviv, and Jerusalem. Israel has spun up the Iron Dome in all three locations.”

“Any idea where that intel came from?”

“No sir, that information was not provided.”

I nodded and Masters whistled to a marine who was carrying a case of ammunition and motioned him over.

When he arrived Masters said, "This is Gunny Sergeant Walt Cunningham. Once I leave here, he will be personally responsible for you. His orders will be to protect you absolutely from any and all threats. He will accompany you back to the target area aboard the Blackhawk. Sergeant, this is Mr. Decker and Mrs. Fulton." The sergeant nodded in our direction. "They will be your charge and from this moment they will not leave your sight."

"Yes sir!" Cunningham stood rigidly at our side, daring so much as a sand beetle to come our way.

"Any questions?" Masters said to us.

"None here," I said. He looked to Jana and she shook her head.

The desert sunset was spectacular. The sun slid into the horizon, leaving a fiery orange sky in its wake and casting a red glow over the barren landscape. The air cooled, going from stifling to pleasant and headed toward chilly within the space of a half-hour. I stood and stretched, then shook my head as I looked around.

"What?" Jana said.

"Look at this land. It's beautiful here in the colored shadows of sunset, but fact is it's nothing but one big slab of sand and rock." I pointed toward Israel. "Right over there lays a tiny sliver of land that millions of people have been fighting over for thousands of years. I've seen land worth fighting for; ever take a stroll through Yellowstone?"

"Always wanted to but haven't gotten around to it yet."

"It's incredible. Stunning beauty that'll literally take your breath away. But this?"

Cunningham stiffened when Masters walked up. "We're about to get underway. You can listen to a lot of the operation on the radios over in the command center if you like. Sergeant, these people are yours."

"Sir, yes sir!"

Masters pivoted smartly on his heel and left. We walked over to the command center, which was a tent with a table and a lot of communications gear. We listened for a couple of minutes as the order was given for the operation to commence. After that the exchanges were sparse and brief as the marines closed in on their unsuspecting prey.

64

7:10 PM EASTERN EUROPE SUMMER TIME (LOCAL)
12:10 PM EASTERN DAYLIGHT TIME
TIME REMAINING: 2 HOURS, 6 MINUTES
PETRA, JORDAN

I'm tracking three targets, Commander," the operator of the low-power radar console said.

"Position and speed?"

"Converging from the northeast, northwest, and south. Thirty kilometers per hour and slowing ... now stopped. Seven kilometers out, right at the limits of this system. I sure would feel better with a little more reach."

"Can you identify?"

"Not specifically. Land vehicles. Sand rails would be my guess."

"Very well. Make ready the perimeter and start sealing the doors. Do it quietly," the commander of the mercenary force said.

This is Kingworm. Ground teams report in," Mack Masters said into his headset microphone.

"Nightcrawler six."

"Nightcrawler three."

One by one, the nine Fire Teams responded.

"Fireflies, status," Masters said.

"Fireflies ready, Kingworm," came the response from the team leader of the air assault element as the eight Blackhawk choppers hovered at the ready several kilometers back so their engines couldn't be heard at the target site.

"Proceed to target! Proceed to target!" Masters said, sending a team of America's deadliest men toward their prey.

Commander, I now have multiple inbound bogies, count three on land and eight, repeat, eight, airborne!"

"Forget the 'quiet' part of the order. Emergency seal on all outer doors, now. Tell the perimeter to engage the ground targets as soon as they're in range. Raise the anti-aircraft positions and engage immediately!"

Kingworm, Firefly Leader. Our aircraft have just been painted. Taking evasive maneuvers!"

Masters couldn't believe what he was hearing. Recon had reported an undefended bunch of rocks in the middle of the desert and now the Blackhawks were being targeted with anti-aircraft radar? Less than thirty seconds earlier the eight Blackhawk helicopters, armed to the teeth, had roared overhead. The rock formation marking the target was dead ahead. Two massive overhead explosions detonated in rapid succession and his radio squawked again, "Blackhawks down, repeat, Blackhawks down! We've lost Fireflies two and four!"

Masters and the others in the IFAVs plowed forward at maximum speed, bouncing over the rough terrain. He ordered the Fire Teams to continue, then flipped a switch to monitor the communications between the Blackhawks.

"Firefly Leader, Firefly Eight. I've locked onto the origin of the SAMs and I am weapons-hot."

"Firefly Eight, Firefly Leader. Take out the SAMs."

The IFAV's were less than a kilometer from the target. The Blackhawks swarmed overhead like invisible wasps. Masters heard the shriek and saw two trails of fire arc to the ground, followed by an earthshaking explosion on top of the canyon fortress.

"Direct hit, site eliminated, paint is gone, repeat, paint is gone," an unidentified chopper reported.

"Kingworm, Firefly Leader. We need rescue here."

"Acknowledged, Firefly," Masters said before relaying the request back to the command post. He could clearly make out the canyon walls ahead through the night vision goggles that all the marines were wearing. They were no more than a few hundred yards away when the trail of fire coming toward them blinded him and everyone else before the night vision equipment could adjust to the unexpected bright light. The driver swerved and the incoming missile hit immediately to the right of the IFAV. The vehicle tipped to the left but settled back down and kept going.

"Enough of this crap," Masters said to his colleagues in the vehicle. "I'm calling in Spooky."

Our guard stuck to Jana and me like glue, even in the midst of the drama unfolding on the radio. With the airspace declared safe once more, the Chinook was spinning up to go to the site in a rescue role.

"Sergeant, did I hear them say Spooky's coming?" I said.

"Yes sir. Spooky's the code name for a specially outfitted aircraft, the—."

"AC-130U," I said. "Some military equipment I'm not terribly familiar with, like the Chinook. But my firm built the fire control software that's on the latest batch of 130s, the ones that went into service last year. A million lines of code. Took us four years to write it and marry it to the hardware."

"I'm impressed, sir."

"Thanks, Sergeant. Have you ever seen one in action? Up close?"

"No sir."

"I haven't either. We had a mockup of simulators set up in a huge hangar when we were developing the systems. We also did a lot of it through pure computer simulation, virtual reality modules."

"What exactly does this thing do?" Jana said.

"It shoots things. No, let me rephrase; it annihilates things. It's the most sophisticated ground-support weapons platform in the air, bar none."

"And where's it coming from?" she said.

"It left our base in Turkey a couple of hours ago. ETA at the target is ten minutes," Cunningham said.

The radio continued to broadcast the unexpected firefight. One of the crew from the Chinook came running into the command center/tent and said, "We have a problem on the rescue. Firefly Leader is reporting flares on the ground near the crash sites, so we know we have survivors. We can go get 'em, but that's about it. Our corpsman was on one of the IFAV units and sustained injuries. He's the only member of the team with medical training. We can't do anything for injuries beyond basic first aid."

"You don't have an aid station back at the staging area?" I said.

"This was a hastily prepared mission and we didn't expect this level of resistance."

The radio operator contacted the captain of the *Ronald Reagan* and apprised him of the situation. He said he'd get a medical team en route with all due haste, but their arrival would be at least an hour away.

"I'm a trauma nurse. I'll go," Jana said.

"Ma'am, there's no way I can allow you to go into a hot zone," the ever vigilant Sergeant Cunningham said.

"You want your colleagues to lie out there in the sand and die?"

"No United States Marine wants another one to die, lady."

"Then get out of the way or come along to protect me."

"Lieutenant," Cunningham said to the Chinook pilot, "as soon as Spooky arrives, let's go get our men."

Eight minutes later we got the call that the AC-130U was approaching the target. We left the ground in a mighty roar, the two massive rotors churning sand and dirt into a billowing cloud underneath us. The pilot and co-pilot wore helmets with night vision gear. The rest of us stared out at a black void for the first couple of minutes before the fires of the two crash sites came into view. The co-pilot worked the radio, keeping the airborne Blackhawks and the incoming AC-130U updated on our position to avoid a mid-air collision in the black skies, as the pilot eased the big bird down. A hundred feet off the ground he switched on a bank of floodlights on the Chinook that lit up the ground below like a football field.

Having seen charts of the area, I looked around and realized that we were no more than a hundred yards from the narrow slit that served as the entrance to Petra. I saw one of the IFAVs parked at the mouth of the opening. A firefight was in progress between the marines on the outside of the entrance and someone inside. I couldn't hear the guns over the din of the Chinook, but the muzzle flashes were fast and furious, providing a bizarre stroboscopic light show against the rock walls that surrounded the city.

Just as we touched down, the AC-130U, Spooky, passed overhead. The pilot throttled the engines on the Chinook back to an idle and we stepped out. We were halfway between the two crash sites, which were fortunately within fifty yards of each other. The pilot and co-pilot splayed an array of floodlights such that they lit the area in every direction. Sergeant Cunningham and Jana went right, carrying a field litter and medical kit. The co-pilot and I went left.

"Over here!" someone yelled, and we picked up the pace. Spooky droned overhead again, slowly circling the area.

"How many men were in these choppers?" I asked the co-pilot as we jogged.

"They were in attack configuration tonight, just two men each."

We got to the site and found one man cradling his dead friend in his arms. "Chrissake, he was just twenty-four years old. Got married last month. He's just a damn kid ... just a damn kid ... "

He looked like a kid. Baby face, smooth skin, looked like he could've just stepped out of a college classroom. Except for the gaping hole in his chest. The sand was thick with his blood.

"Shake it off, Dragon," the co-pilot said, obviously addressing the man by his handle. "This is battle, shit happens, and we have a job to do."

Dragon nodded.

The advice sounded cold, but I knew it was necessary. Soldiers didn't have time to grieve on the battlefield. That came later.

"What kind of shape are you in?" the co-pilot said.

"I think I have a broken leg, sir."

"We'll get you back to the Shithook then come back and get your buddy."

The tears had dried and he never made a sound as we picked him up and laid him on the canvas stretcher. It had to hurt like hell. He was back to hardened marine status. Or maybe it was just easier for him to deal with the physical pain as opposed to the emotional trauma of seeing half his young friend's chest missing.

We were about halfway back when Spooky engaged, and I almost dropped my end of the stretcher. The slow-flying aircraft was banked in a tight counter-clockwise circle around the city, firing out its left side. Its firepower on paper was impressive. Seeing it in person burned images into my mind I will never forget.

There were several streams of fire coming from different ports down the left side of the fuselage. One of them was a 25mm electric Gatling gun. As a targeting aid, every fifth round fired is a tracer that leaves a visible fire trail from the muzzle to its point of impact. The gun was firing so fast—1800 rounds per minute—that the fire trails were unbroken. It looked more like a laser than the firing of a conventional weapon, and it sounded like the high-pitched whine of an electric motor. The rest of the guns were spitting out plenty of lead too, but none compared to this thing.

Perhaps the most amazing thing of all was the precision with which these weapons fired. The targeting systems—my company's handiwork if this was one of the new AC-130U aircraft—were a technological marvel. Inside the plane, the fire control operators located their targets on television monitors. Thermal imaging television that could see through smoke, fog, dust, or rain as if it didn't exist. Once a target was spotted, the gunners locked onto them with a radar fire control mechanism that stayed locked on whether the target moved or not. The aiming of the guns was handled by computers tied into the radar and the television pointing systems. Even though the aircraft was moving, including normal bumps along the way, the guns in their isolated gyroscopic mounts stayed targeted exactly where the computers told them to be. The interior of the airplane was like the ultimate video game.

I kept plodding along with the stretcher, watching the awesome show as the firepower cut a surgical circle around the perimeter of Petra, destroying one defensive position after another. There was no return fire now. The defenders were running, trying to get inside caves or outside the circle of fire. From what I could tell, few made it to safety.

We loaded the injured marine into the Chinook and headed to the right where Jana and Cunningham had gone. We met them coming back toward the helicopter carrying an empty litter. Jana looked at me and shook her head. Add two more to the untold numbers of deaths this maniac was responsible for. The thought that we were probably no more than a few hundred yards from him sent a chill coursing down my spine.

65

7:53 PM EASTERN EUROPE SUMMER TIME (LOCAL)
12:53 PM EASTERN DAYLIGHT TIME
TIME REMAINING: 1 HOUR, 23 MINUTES
PETRA, JORDAN

After clearing the perimeter and moving inside the city proper, the contingent of marines–led by Colonel Masters–were ready to enter what looked to be a fortified compound built inside the caves. The Recon Force had formed a tight perimeter around the area and Spooky was loitering above just in case. Two of the Blackhawks had landed on the top of the canyon wall and had their front floodlights angled down, bathing the area in the blue-white glow of the massive high-intensity-discharge lamps.

Jana, Cunningham, and I were behind an outcropping of rock about fifty yards back from the main entrance when they detonated the C4 on three separate steel doors that were set into the rock wall. Of the thirty-six members of the Fire Teams who had originally converged on Petra in the sand rails, three had been killed and three more injured. The remaining thirty divided into three equal teams and muscled through the rubble into the compound after tossing in flash-bang grenades that would temporarily blind anyone inside who happened to be looking the wrong way, and quite possibly burst their eardrums if they weren't protected. We heard a lot of shouting but no shots fired. Five minutes later Masters came out through the main entrance and announced that the area was safe for us to approach.

When we got there he said, "I don't know how many kills there were outside, but we have six live prisoners from inside the complex. Ma'am, let me know when you're ready and we'll bring them out. Let me know which one he is. I have orders to isolate him and wait for a special transport detail to arrive."

Jana nodded and held her chin up, but I saw the fear in her eyes. She reached over and grabbed my hand. I gave a gentle squeeze and said, "It'll be okay, Jana. You're safe."

"Do it," she said.

Masters barked into his mike and the first one emerged through the opening, flanked by a marine on each side and another behind him. He wore a black tee-shirt covered in the red dust of Petra sandstone. He had close-cropped blond hair and a torso that looked like it would burst through the tight shirt at any moment. Masters looked at Jana and she shook her head.

The next one, also escorted by a trio of marines, looked like a local. He was dressed in Bedouin garb and might have had three teeth. He didn't look like the billionaire psycho type. Jana shook her head again.

The procession continued until five of them had been brought out, none of whom she recognized. "Get out there now!" I heard someone inside shout, followed by sounds of a scuffle. My heart was in my throat as I waited to see this animal who had wrought so much misery on me and the world. And whether my new marine friends knew it or not, I had plans to find out where my father was.

"Let go of me! You have no right to treat me like this, you cretins!" The marines didn't seem concerned about his rights as they drug him out by his feet. He was face down, clawing at the ground for something to hold onto and finding nothing. As they came through the opening I saw a slender man in what had been a solid white suit. His hair was black and wavy, his skin dark. Jana squeezed my hand harder and I heard her breathing quicken as he came more completely into view. He still had his back to us as he got up off the ground. Masters said, "Abraham Hart?"

"Yes, I am Abraham Hart." He dusted off his clothes as he turned around slowly. "And you will all die for what you have done here tonight!" He suddenly cut his crazy eyes directly at me and said, "And you in particular will die a thousand deaths in the depth of hell, Decker, you sniveling busybody!"

I let go of Jana's hand, walked over to him, and drew back to deliver my rebuttal to his latest prophecy. Jana caught my hand.

"No, Matt."

"After what he put you through?" I said.

"I've never seen this man before," she said.

"What? Are you sure?"

"Trust me, I know exactly what Abraham Hart looks like. I don't know who this imposter is, but it's not Hart."

Masters held a finger up for quiet and pressed against his communication earpiece. He listened for a few seconds and said, "We've been had. Not only is this not Hart; there's also no sign of a missile here."

66

12:09 PM CENTRAL DAYLIGHT TIME
1:09 PM EASTERN DAYLIGHT TIME
TIME REMAINING: 1 HOUR, 7 MINUTES
YELLOW CREEK

I am now very close to recovery of this file," Abdul said as he continued to blow through commands and code at a pyretic pace.

Tarkleton covered the mouthpiece of the phone. "Hang on, Abdul, I'm almost through to Matthew."

"This might be most important."

"I doubt it's more important than them being in the wrong place." Tarkleton paced. "Yes, I have to talk to him right now!" he shouted.

8:10 PM EASTERN EUROPE SUMMER TIME (LOCAL)
1:10 PM EASTERN DAYLIGHT TIME
TIME REMAINING: 1 HOUR, 6 MINUTES
PETRA, JORDAN

I was studying a copy of Hart's manifesto, looking for any clue, while one of Masters's men administered a sodium pentothal injection to the imposter in an attempt to glean information. The barbiturate had him happy and babbling, but that's it. Unlike the movie version of truth serum, the real thing reduces inhibitions but it does not eliminate self-control. The man was well-trained, probably to the point of having practiced under the influence of the chemical. It was a waste of time.

I was focused on two sentences near the end of the document that struck me as prescient.

You are henceforth warned that things are often not what they seem. Rely on my Word for your sustenance and survival.

Things had definitely turned out not to be what they seemed. Petra was an elaborate ruse, a distraction that worked to perfection. And the instruction in the next sentence to rely on his "Word," which I assumed to mean the Bible, seemed out of character since he had thoroughly trashed it a few paragraphs earlier. I felt certain that sentence was a clue, but without a Bible or Tark—

"Decker!" I looked around and saw a Marine headed my way with a handheld radio. "Some guy they've patched through from the States. Says he has to talk to you right now. Name's something like Tart."

"Tark?" I said, shocked yet not surprised.

"Matthew, we may have been—"

"Hart's not here. Neither are the missiles."

"I figured as much. I shouldn't have been so gullible as to miss the only logical place for him to be for his big finale."

"We're short on time. Where, Tark, tell me where!"

"Armageddon, of course."

"I thought that was more or less mythical."

"Oh, heavens no. Been the site of countless battles through the ages. It was located on one of the most important ancient highways in existence and—"

"Tark, I'd really love to hear all about it when I get back, but for now I just need to know where it is."

"Sorry. Its modern name is Tel Megiddo. Lots of ruins there that were being excavated until a few years ago when Israel had to clamp down so tight on everything. It's right at the mouth of the Jezreel Valley. The Israeli authorities can take you right to it, I'm sure."

"Thanks, I'll be in touch." I shut off the radio and handed it back to Masters. He heard enough of the conversation and was on his own radio by the time I finished with John. Jana had just gotten back from a restroom break in a cave—with Sergeant Cunningham faithfully in tow—and I brought her up to speed. "Are we going there?" she said.

"Yes," Masters said over the din of a Blackhawk that was settling down into the city between the canyon walls. "The four of us will go now. The other Blackhawks will load up with men and be right behind us. I've also called the Reagan and they'll have air cover in place by the time we arrive." We shielded our faces against the rotor wash sandstorm and climbed aboard the instant the chopper settled.

"How long will it take us to get there?" I said as we lifted off.

"We're right across the border from Israel now. Fortunately, the whole country's about the size of New Jersey. We'll be there in twenty minutes."

"We better be or there may not be a country left," I said.

2:02 PM EASTERN DAYLIGHT TIME
1:02 PM CENTRAL DAYLIGHT TIME
YELLOW CREEK
TIME REMAINING: 50 MINUTES

"Oh my goodness, James Lee Tarkleton, this file is not good."

"Put it on screen," Tarkleton said. He watched as the main display transitioned from a map of the Central region to an elaborate animation of Israel and the surrounding area.

The animation began with a simple overhead view of a map. A neon-red line then ripped from bottom to top, generally along the route of the Jordan River until it approached the top of the map, where it took a left-hand diagonal turn and raced across Lebanon to the Mediterranean. A label, also neon-red, faded into view: JORDAN FAULT. As soon as the line was complete, three yellow bull's-eye icons appeared along the line one at a time, pulsating in a short-short-long sequence.

Seconds later, a single spot—Tarkleton recognized it as Tel Megiddo—flashed three times. From the flashes came three missiles. They fanned out from the source, dotted lines marking their trajectory. The bottom missile flew directly toward the lowest of the three bull's-eye icons. The middle unit assumed more of an arc before angling back down toward its target, and the top one flew an arc that was higher still. The result was simultaneous impact on the three target icons.

The icons exploded and the map rotated into a three-dimensional view, as if the viewer were standing south of the area, able to see a cross-section of Israel and the ground beneath it, outlined by the now-pulsating red neon line. Flat along the top, representing the surface. A vertical line on the right edge extended down into the ground, then turned left—west—and deepened as it approached the Mediterranean. The overall effect was that Israel rested atop a wedge-shaped chunk of earth.

Suddenly the wedge broke loose from the land on the right, directly along the red line, and began a slide down and to the left. It moved slowly at first and then accelerated as the whole mass slid away from the continent on the right and into the Mediterranean Sea. A huge animated wave swelled and spread out, headed for the coastal areas that formed the oval basin of the sea.

The image faded to black. Until now the animation had been silent. Now a lone trumpet wailed and bright red letters filled the screen:

There was a great earthquake, such a mighty and great earthquake as had not occurred since men were on the earth. Revelation 16:18

The screen faded again, as did the trumpet.

"Dear sweet Jesus," Tarkleton said as the pipe fell from his mouth. It clattered onto the console, then rolled off and fell to the floor.

"We should tell the president, yes?"

A new voice said, "I'm doing the telling around here right now, assholes."

Tarkleton slowly picked up his pipe and sighed when he saw him. "What's the point in this, Rowe? Your horse is out of the race. Get over it," Tark said. Rowe had appeared behind them, filthy, stubbly beard, reeking of body odor, and holding a double-barrel shotgun.

"You people, especially Golden Boy, cost me a king's ransom. Get over it? Not likely. But tell me where I can find Decker and maybe I'll let you live."

"No problem," Tarkleton said, pointing with his pipe. "Go down this way about five thousand miles and hang a left."

"Don't be flippant with me."

"Decker's in Israel."

"For what?"

"Stopping your boss, you double-crossing slug."

"You're getting pretty cocky for someone with a shotgun pointed at him."

"I ain't the sharpest tool in the shed. Now what is it you plan to do? We seriously need to talk to the president or more innocent people are going to die, Rowe. You want more on your conscious?"

Rowe was fully involved in the conversation with Tarkleton now, pacing back and forth along the console, holding the shotgun in one hand. Abdul rotated his chair during one of the three-step passes when Rowe's back was to them, and stepped around the end of the console. He squat-walked quickly to the other end of the console and waited.

Rowe was staring at Tarkleton and didn't notice that Abdul wasn't in his chair. "I don't have a con—" Abdul connected a solid blow to his kidney. He spun around to face Abdul and Tark grabbed the barrel of the shotgun. Rowe squeezed the triggers and fired both barrels just as Tark pushed the muzzle upward. A cluster of acoustic treatment showered from the ceiling. The impact of the shot jarred Tark's grip loose and he fell back against the console. Rowe swung the butt around and caught Tark in the jaw; blood poured from his mouth.

Rowe reached into his jacket and pulled out two more 12-gauge shells. Abdul dove toward him and grabbed the barrels. Rowe had opened the gun and the spent hulls ejected. Abdul tried to wrestle the gun away from him as he fought to plug the new shells into the breech, but his thin frame was a handicap vs. the much larger Bob Rowe. Sensing the impending loss of his grip on the gun, he changed strategy.

First he let go of the rusty barrel. He immediately hit Rowe with a bull's-eye right hook, then knocked the shells away with his left hand and jumped to his feet. Rowe stood up too, digging in his pocket for a fresh load of ammunition.

"I'm gonna mop the floor with you, you little bastard!" Rowe said. Abdul's punch had been solid, opening a cut above the left eye. Blood was streaming down his face, making him look even more like a deranged monster.

Abdul saw Rowe's hand come out of the pocket with more shells. Now or never. He backed away and ducked behind a large support column near the middle of the room.

"No need to hide, little man. Come on out and take your medicine." A brief metallic ring sounded as he slammed the breech shut. He pulled back the creaky old hammers and made his way toward the column. When he reached it, he bent his knees to better absorb the recoil and quickly stepped around it.

Abdul squeezed the handle of the fire extinguisher and directed the Halon blast into Rowe's eyes. He screamed and started backing away, wiping at his eyes with his left hand and holding the shotgun in the right. The chemical fog hung in the air just long enough for Abdul, now the hunter instead of the hunted, to slip around behind his prey without being seen. He raised the fire extinguisher above his head and brought its heavy steel cylinder down on Rowe's head with every ounce of strength he could summon from his wiry 5'9" frame. It was enough. Rowe's legs melted like Jell-O and he fell face first onto the floor.

Tark pulled himself upright, smiled a bloody smile, and said, "Nice work, Abdul."

"Thank you, James Lee Tarkleton. Now we must talk to the president."

2:14 PM EASTERN DAYLIGHT TIME
SITUATION ROOM
THE WHITE HOUSE
TIME REMAINING: 38 MINUTES

"Someone please tell me this is impossible," President Stanson said when the animated presentation ended. His voice echoed slightly off the long table and the paneled walls, but no one answered. He slammed the butt of his fist down on the table. "It's a hell of a time for this group to turn into damn mutes."

"Sir," NSA Rich Henning said, "the truth is we don't know. It is, however, a certainty that this guy did his homework and it's likely he was the one behind the disappearance and subsequent murder of Dr. Hilton. We have to take it seriously."

"Ramifications?" Stanson said.

"I've been studying the documents that were attached to the file Tarkleton sent," Admiral Stockton said.

"And?"

"The Israeli land mass is thicker than the Med is deep so the whole thing won't exactly sink, but building and infrastructure destruction will for all practical purposes be total. Estimate loss of five million lives in Israel alone. Everything on the Med coast and one to two miles inland will be destroyed by the resulting wave. That kills a few million more people."

The president shook his head. Stockton flipped a page on the document in his hand and continued. "The waves will take out the Suez Canal. Repair will take years and the economic and political fallout from that will be devastating." He laid the document on the table.

"Is that all?"

Stockton's head drooped, an element of posture not native to the man. "No sir."

"Spit it out, man!"

"The Reagan, sir. Remember, she's in the Med, along with her escorts. Ten or twelve thousand of our finest men and women."

"The ships can't withstand the waves?"

"Sir, we're talking about a hundred thousand cubic kilometers of land sliding into the water. The resulting tsunami will be massive and it will be followed by a series of heavy aftershocks; no ship will withstand these waves."

8:44 PM EASTERN EUROPE SUMMER TIME (LOCAL)
1:44 PM EASTERN DAYLIGHT TIME
ARMAGEDDON (TEL MEGIDDO), ISRAEL
TIME REMAINING: 32 MINUTES

"Thank you for your continuing loyalty. You will be handsomely rewarded." Hart pushed a button to end the call and turned to the man on the other side of the small underground room. "It would seem we underestimated our adversaries yet again."

"What's the problem?"

"Decker and his squadron of military goons are on the way here."

"Just remember, I wanted to put surveillance and security measures in place here. We're sitting blind in a hole in the ground with no way to see what's going on outside and no defense against a serious threat. We should launch immediately."

"We will do no such thing. This operation will go forward at precisely the appointed time, you blasphemous buffoon!"

"Right," the man muttered to himself as he started keying the launch codes into a notebook computer. "I have waited my entire life for a chance to eliminate the Zionists and I will not wait."

Hart closed his eyes, breathing slowly, deeply. When he opened his eyes, he drew the Walther from the folds of his robe. The shot was well placed. The man's head flopped backward, his eyes still open with a bullet hole between them. Hart smiled as he thought about how easy it was to recruit bigoted zealots. The man had been a trusted Hardier employee, a hater of Israel, and a genius regarding military hardware. He hadn't even asked to be paid.

It disgusted Hart to touch the corpse but he had no choice. He removed the hands from the keyboard of the notebook computer and pushed him out of the chair. He sat down, checked the sequencing program, and entered the commands to close the launch tube the moron had opened. He switched off the lights in the room. All was in order. The countdown passed through eighteen minutes and continued its digital march to Glory.

Say again, Mr. President?" The roar of the helicopter was deafening, even with the noise-canceling headset, and I was sure I misunderstood him.

"Our previous intelligence was faulty. He's not hitting those three cities. He's aiming for the Jordan Fault, trying to cause an earthquake that will dump Israel into the sea."

Apparently I heard him right the first time. "We're coming up on Armageddon now, sir."

"Mr. Decker, you have to stop him. Millions of lives depend on it."

"I'll do my best, but I do hope there's a backup. What about Patriots? Or can Israel extend their Iron Domes?"

"Not enough range and we can't move batteries in time. I hate to sound corny, Mr. Decker, but our country needs you, the world needs you. Make us proud."

And with that he was gone. As promised, the U.S. Navy was patrolling the skies over the Jezreel Valley when we arrived. Masters was patched into the head of the Mossad, the Jewish state's famed elite intelligence agency, also known informally as "The Institution," the English translation for "Mossad."

The Mossad contact said the prime minister of course agreed to whatever measures deemed necessary in order to prevent a nuclear attack on his tiny country, but he also pleaded for destruction of the Tel Megiddo site to be an absolute last resort. Although the site hadn't been dug for several years, prior to that archeologists had declared it one of the most important excavations on the planet.

The Mossad had a finger in everything. Within minutes they managed to produce a detailed set of archeological diagrams for the Megiddo site. As advanced as military aviation had become, Blackhawks still didn't have fax machines or email, and my phone had no signal. This meant the charts had to be read by Mossad, then their interpretation passed on to us over the airwaves. With under a half-hour remaining, it was not an efficient way to work but it was all we had.

Masters took a call from a surveillance officer on the *Reagan* and learned one of the drones had been observing Petra, while the other kept a higher-altitude watch over Israel itself. The second one had been moved into position over the site as soon as the Armageddon/Megiddo theory was put forth, placing it there around fifteen minutes before us. The first ten minutes had shown nothing. The last five had gotten interesting. The officer reported that a hole in the ground had opened up, revealing what looked to be the business end of a missile inside. Chalk another one up for the old pipe-puffer.

In addition to the video equipment, the UAV was also equipped with a nosecone full of sensitive electronic monitoring equipment. That gear had detected the presence of faint, brief radio signals at the site. From analysis of those signals, the surveillance wizards believed they were coming from "handheld digital personal communication devices," Geek-speak for modern walkie-talkies or maybe even a cell phone.

The pilot pointed down and ahead. We were coming up on the site, tucked right in the mouth of the valley below. As we got closer the ruins came into view. So did the hole the Predator had picked up on video. The detection equipment in the Blackhawk showed no anti-aircraft threats, radar or otherwise. The pilot was vigilant nonetheless, with weapons hot and a ready hand in position on the fire controls. He eased the bird down near the hole and throttled the powerful engines down to an idle.

Masters led the way out, followed by Cunningham. Jana and I started to step out but Masters balked. "You folks need to stay here until some reinforcements arrive to clear the area."

"Like hell. I've fought this guy for seven solid days. He's here and I'm going after him," I said. I turned to Jana. "I do wish you'd wait here until we're sure it's safe."

She shook her head. "Nope. If anyone's worried about me, give me a gun, but I'm going in."

The pilot pulled a Beretta 9mm from his holster and handed it to her. "One in the chamber, safety's on."

"Got it," she said.

"Here," the co-pilot said, handing me his Beretta. "Full magazine but nothing up top."

I pulled the slide back and released it, smoothly chambering a round, then flipped the safety off and eased the hammer down. The thick grip told me that the sidearm was a fifteen-round model, a fact I found reassuring. Masters shook his head and said, "Let's go."

A low rumble sounded in the distance. Our companion Blackhawks were drawing near.

67

1:57 PM EASTERN DAYLIGHT TIME
12:57 PM CENTRAL DAYLIGHT TIME (LOCAL)
YELLOW CREEK
TIME REMAINING: 19 MINUTES

I got it," Abdul said as Decker's notebook whirred and clacked its way to life. As soon as the boot procedure finished he launched the email client. Tark watched over his shoulder.

"You have new mail," the notebook said.

"Oh no." Abdul looked at Tark.

"Let's see it," Tark said.

Abdul slid the patched-up machine to the side so Tark had a clear view:

```
Return-Path: <i14_696938@hotmail.com>
Delivered-To: x7ijljAweRRv
```

-deckerdigital:com-x7ijljAweRRv@
deckerdigital.com
X-Envelope-To: x7ijljawerrv@
deckerdigital.com
X-Originating-IP: [IP UNAVAILABLE]
From: i14_696938@hotmail.com
To: x7ijljAweRRv@deckerdigital.com
Transmission Time: 11:09 PM CDT
Subject: Spoils

Mr. Decker:

You proved to be an amusing and surprisingly resourceful adversary. With that in mind (although I find a reference to fair play laughable coming from a corrupt little weasel like yourself) I have elected to reward your meaningless victory by leaving be both your father and the Persian's family.

GAME OVER.

"He sent this last night," Tark said.

"Yes, I am seeing that. Should we call Matt Decker?"

"To tell him there's another email here? No, there's no point."

"But it claims Hart is not bothering his father, yet his father is gone."

"I saw that, but there's nothing Matthew can do about his father right now and he has enough on his mind. Right now I'm going to say a prayer for him. He needs it." Tarkleton bowed his head.

8:58 PM EASTERN EUROPE SUMMER TIME (LOCAL)
1:58 PM EASTERN DAYLIGHT TIME
TIME REMAINING: 18 MINUTES
ARMAGEDDON (TEL MEGIDDO), ISRAEL

We climbed up onto the mound on which the core of Megiddo was situated, then went down into an excavated pit to the "hole in the ground" described by the surveillance officer, and described it via radio to the Mossad agent who was studying the diagrams of the site.

"You don't have to describe it," he said. "We've managed to get a downlink from your UAV working and I'm looking at it right now. The controllers of the plane have brought it down to three thousand feet, and I can see the four of you at the edge of the shaft." There we stood in the middle of nowhere, at night, using flashlights to make our way around, and someone sitting in an office was watching the whole thing like a television show.

"Problem is, there's no missile in this thing that we can see. There's nothing here except stairs built into the walls. Some debris is piled up on the first landing of the stairway, about ten feet down, including a big tree limb with an offshoot pointed up. My guess is that's what was mistaken for the nose of a missile," I said.

"I understand," he said.

We looked around and saw nothing but more excavation pits and ruins of ancient buildings, none large enough or complete enough to conceal a nuclear missile that the experts had concluded was likely twenty-five feet in length. I had a sick feeling in the pit of my stomach that we were the only people at Megiddo.

"Mr. Decker, I have your surveillance expert connected now. He would like to speak with you."

"Go ahead."

"Decker, I don't know what the shaft is that you're looking at right now, but that is not the cavity we picked up with the UAV."

"It's the only shaft we've found."

"The other one closed back up around ten minutes ago."

"Can you guide us to it?"

"Do you see the shell of a building about a hundred feet east of where you are right now?

I was about to tell him we didn't have a compass when I noticed Masters climbing out of the pit with one in his hand. "Yes, headed that way now."

"The hole we saw is about ten yards beyond that shell."

I glanced at my watch. Twelve minutes. Out of the pit, I was running and looking but seeing nothing, when the ground suddenly felt springy under my feet. I stomped and got a faint hollow sound. "Over here!" I said.

Cunningham found a small camouflaged chopper tucked away in the shell we had just come by. We dropped to our knees and started digging, and quickly hit a metal surface that looked like aluminum in the glare of our flashlights. Ten minutes.

Within another couple of minutes we found the edges of the cover, which looked to be about thirty feet square. It was channeled in a metal frame flush-mounted in the ground. The whole assembly was covered with a clever mesh lid that held the topsoil and rocks in place for camouflage. All four of us tried to slide the cover open but it wouldn't budge.

"We're out of luck without tools," I said.

"A couple of my men on the inbound Blackhawks have emergency engineering packs with crowbars and small sledgehammers in them, and one man has a C4 kit," Masters said.

I could see the lights of the Blackhawks in the distance, headed to the site like a swarm of angry lightning bugs. "No good, Masters. This thing will have opened for the wrong reason by the time they get on the ground and the men get to us." I took his mike and keyed it up. "Gentlemen, if you don't have any more suggestions for us, we need to vacate the premises so those F18s up there can take care of this problem for us."

The Mossad agent's voice rose a notch. "We must find a solution! Tel Megiddo is perhaps the most important biblical archeological site in the world!"

"Do I need remind you it's your country that'll be nuked if this isn't stopped in the next six minutes?"

"Of course not. I am only looking for a way to stop it without destroying the site."

The surveillance officer cut in. "Decker, we've dropped the UAV to fifteen hundred feet and we're picking up something interesting."

I looked up into the starry sky looking for the drone but saw nothing and heard nothing as it circled quietly with its fuel-cell-powered electric engine. "Make it fast."

"The lower altitude has enabled us to localize those radio signals we were picking up earlier. There is a definite wireless link between the shaft you're standing on and another position at the site."

"You thinking it's a control link?"

"That's our best guess."

"Can it be jammed?"

"Maybe, but only by a Weasel and the Air Force doesn't have one in range."

A Weasel is an F-15 loaded with specialized gear for intercepting, interpreting, and disrupting electronic signals. "Too bad. Tell me where the other end of the link is."

"Go back to the first shaft you were at. The link terminates about two hundred feet due east of that shaft."

Masters, eying his compass, sprinted back down into the pit to the shaft, made a slight turn, ran again, then stopped. "Very good. He's standing dead on top of it," the officer said.

"He's standing in the middle of nowhere," I said, "Which means the link must be—"

"Underground! Of course!" Mossad Man said.

"Four and a half minutes, my friend," I said.

"The shaft was built in the eighth century BC by Ahab. At the bottom of the shaft is a tunnel. Two hundred ten feet long. It went to an underground spring outside the city, and allowed the inhabitants of the city to have a constant supply of fresh water while the city was under siege."

Mossad Man and Tark were obviously related, evidenced by their penchant for history lectures at the worst possible time. I ran to the shaft. "I'm taking the stairway."

"I go first and it's not negotiable," Masters said. "Then you, then the lady, with Cunningham bringing up rear guard."

"Whatever, go!" I said, and Masters readied his AR and hit the ancient stairway. The stairs had been carved right out of the rock walls of the shaft and were still solid. The shaft smelled old and musty, the odor growing stronger as we descended. We angled down into the earth for what seemed like a little over a hundred feet, and the last landing on the stairway opened directly into a tunnel. Mossad Man knew his stuff.

Masters signaled for quiet and flipped his night vision goggles down. We killed our flashlights and I moved in directly behind him. Jana held onto the back of my fatigue jacket. The tunnel was around eight feet wide and a little taller. Walking it was easy; someone had installed a raised wooden floor and handrails. The wood creaked and Masters slowed down, causing me to bump into him in the pitch blackness. I punched up the light on my watch dial. Two and a half minutes. I whispered the time remaining to Masters and he picked up the pace.

Hart heard the moan of the wooden bridge that ran through the tunnel. His enemies were approaching. Thank himself he was immortal, for people like these—especially the pesky and evil incarnate Decker—were probably low-minded types who would resort to physical violence at the drop of a hat. He watched the countdown on the notebook pass through two minutes. He stood and stretched. His robe was an elegant affair fit for a king, as he of course was. King of kings. Lord of lords. Yes indeed. He wrapped his hand around the Walther, faced the entrance where the tunnel opened into the room, and waited.

We could see a dim bluish glow just ahead at the end of the tunnel. Masters stopped just shy of the opening that led into what looked like a small cavern, and flattened himself against the wall of the tunnel. The faint light coming from the cave illuminated the end of the tunnel enough for me to see what Masters was doing. He maneuvered just his rifle around the corner while staying safely concealed. Only then did I notice the cable that ran from the gun to his headgear. He was using the Land Warrior system, the first high-tech weapons system to get down to the really personal level. The rifle had a tiny video camera underneath the barrel that relayed a picture back to a heads-up display in his helmet. In a battlefield scenario, text messages could be transmitted from command into those same displays. In the present situation, it meant Masters could look and fire around a corner without exposing himself.

I punched the light back up on my watch and showed him that we had ninety seconds. He nodded, slowly angled the rifle, and without warning unleashed a three-round burst that was deafening in the enclosed space. He ducked around the corner and I heard more shots that didn't sound like Masters's rifle. My ears rang and the smell of gunpowder was heavy in the air. I dropped to my belly and peeked around the corner.

Masters was down on his back, a dark pool widening under his left shoulder. A man was seated at a small table, tapping rapidly on a notebook computer. He was wearing–of all things to be wearing in a cave—a white robe. The light from the screen of the notebook gave the robe an otherworldly glow and I saw Masters wasn't the only one who had taken a hit. The left side of his body was facing the opening and the robe was so drenched in blood I couldn't tell what its source was. One thing I knew for sure: I was looking at Abraham Hart. I'd like to report that I was a picture of stoic heroism, calm and cool, but in reality I was terrified.

I rose to a crouch and turned the corner with the Beretta extended in firing position. "Get away from the computer!"

"Hello, Mr. Decker." The corners of his lips were turned up in something like a smile, his eyes bugged out and wild looking. The man looked demonic. "Hart, step away from the computer, now." At that moment, I was staring into the face of evil and I wanted to believe there was an opposing force to what I saw. *You've always believed, you're just angry.*

Masters moaned. Hart didn't move. He just sat there with a frozen look on his face I can only describe as psychotic. I aimed the Beretta and felt the cold metal of the trigger against my finger as I squeezed. The 9mm bucked slightly in my hand and Hart fell away from the table. I rushed to the computer and saw the countdown at 1:02. Hart was lying on top of another man who looked to be dead.

I heard Hart stirring behind me but ignored him. I'd rather die trying to stop the launch than live with letting it happen while I looked out for myself. Jana and Cunningham moved through my peripheral vision toward Hart as I studied the screen. *1:00*

The countdown was centered in a program window that contained only the countdown and two buttons, ABORT and RESUME. I clicked ABORT and got an ENTER PASSWORD prompt. Not again! *:58*

Cunningham had grabbed Hart and dragged him to his feet. He soon had him in front of me. "I need a password!" I said.

:53

My shot had grazed the back of his neck and the wound was oozing blood. "Thank you so much for bringing my whore back to me," he said when he recognized Jana. "She—" Jana slapped him, and the unthinkable happened. He caught her arm, twisted her around in front of him, and from nowhere came a small semi-automatic pistol that he pressed against her temple as her own gun clattered onto the hard floor of the cave.

:45

He was standing in front of and to the left of the table, his left side facing me, and Jana's back pulled tight against his chest as he held the gun to her head. Cunningham stood squarely in front of them, his finger on the trigger of his rifle. "Lower your weapon and release the lady," he said.

Hart threw his head back and cackled. "You mortal fools. I will release this whore at my leisure and after my pleasure."

:40

I had no choice but to concentrate on the countdown as best I could. I started trying passwords: REVELATION ... ACCESS DENIED ... ANTICHRIST ... ACCESS DENIED ... CHRIST ... ACCESS DENIED ... GOD ... ACCESS DENIED ...

:34

BIBLE ... ACCESS DENIED ...

"Mr. Decker, step away from the computer or she dies."

"Don't do it, Matt! Stop the missiles!"

"A noble whore. How very quaint."

In the space of a few seconds my mind, heart, and soul were wracked by what seemed like a hundred conflicting thoughts, emotions, and fears. Jana was more stunning than ever in the dim light, jaw set, defiant, unafraid, ready.

:27

ISRAEL ... ACCESS DENIED ... MESSIAH ... ACCESS DENIED ... ARMAGEDDON ... ACCESS DENIED ...

:21

"You amuse me, Mr. Decker. You sit in the very presence of God and yet you do not see." He cackled again.

:16

"Lower the weapon and release the lady, sir!"

Hart turned the gun and shot Cunningham in the throat as if he were shooing a fly. The poor Marine clutched at his throat in vain, trying to speak but only making a horrible gurgling sound as he fell to his knees and then crumpled face first into a pool of his own blood. Then the gun was back at Jana's head.

:08

I heard Hart cackle again and say, "You'll never get it, Decker, because you don't have it."

SATAN ... ACCESS DENIED ... DEVIL ... ACCESS DENIED ... I was out of time, and worse, out of hope. I was powerless to stop the launch, and probably powerless to save Jana's life or my own. After a week of hellish mental battles against a madman, I had failed. I'd never get it because I didn't have it. Was that one final cryptic clue? What didn't I have?"

:02

My fingers flew even as the thought was forming in my mind. F – A – I – T – H. Then the ENTER key. And as the countdown switched from :01 to :00, the screen flashed and said: LAUNCH ABORTED.

68

9:16 PM EASTERN EUROPE SUMMER TIME (LOCAL)
2:16 PM EASTERN DAYLIGHT TIME
ARMAGEDDON (TEL MEGIDDO), ISRAEL

Nooooooooooo!" Hart wailed like an animal when the countdown stopped, shoving Jana to the ground and turning the gun toward me. His mouth stayed open, still in the scream though the sound was gone. I kept my eyes on him but I could see Jana feeling on the ground for her gun. Mine was lying on the table beside the computer but there was no chance of getting it before he could shoot me from three feet away. Jana suddenly froze. She saw her gun, about six inches from Hart's right foot.

"What have you done with my father, Hart?" I said.

His eyebrows bunched up in a look of confusion. "Nothing, although I clearly should have exterminated the decrepit sloth and fully bastardized you."

"On top of being a failure, you're a liar," I said. Jana's hand was moving a millimeter at a time toward the gun.

"Believe what you will, you insignificant gnat. As I told you in my last email, I decided to spare his pathetic existence. In a way it is more satisfying to have you continue to grieve over him in the way you have for so many years, hopelessly."

"What email? You never answered my last message."

"Oh, but I did, little one."

The broken laptop. "I didn't get it." Jana's hand was halfway to the gun. He proudly claimed every other barbaric deed of the week, so why would he deny abducting my father?

"What now, Hart?" I said, trying to give Jana time to get the gun. Her hand was close. Almost there. Just as she reached for it, Hart slammed his foot down on top of it.

"Now you both will die. And you will spend an eternity suffering in the flaming pits of hell for the decadent evil you have perpetrated against me this day."

"Actually, I was wondering about you. What does a washed up, defeated, psychopathic, wannabe 'god' like you do now that you've had your butt kicked thoroughly by a mere mortal like me?"

His eyes raged and his nostrils twitched. Sweat rolled off his face and, along with large splotches of blood, plastered his robe to his body. As his blood pressure increased, the stream of blood from his neck grew stronger. "Defeated? Me, defeated by you? You are sadly delusional, Decker."

"Really? You know the bomb in Mississippi, your sixth seal? It was harmless. All you managed to do was break a few windows. Or Earth, Texas. You picked a blink-and-miss-it little town and had your ass handed to you by a posse of cowboys. And in case you haven't noticed, Israel is definitely not 'over.' You're not only a loser, Hart, you're a pathetic loser!" I threw my head back as he had done, and let out a roll of laughter that echoed through the cave and tunnel. I hoped to distract him long enough. I would soon find out.

He pulled the hammer back on his gun and said, "Prepare thyself for hell, sinner!"

"You first," Masters said just before he loosed a three-round burst of .223. The Land Warrior display in his helmet had let him keep his body and head perfectly still and slowly move the rifle into position. Hart fell face forward onto the table, three bullet holes in the right side of his head and looking as mortal as they come.

I stood up, reached down to Jana, and helped her to her feet. We looked around the room and found a switch by the tunnel entrance that bathed the room in light.

"Masters, let's get you out of here," I said. He barely grunted as I hauled him to his feet.

"I can walk. I'd really appreciate it if you could bring Cunningham out, though. If you don't feel like it I'll wait here with him until you can send someone back in."

"Not a problem, Colonel." That turned out to be a lie. Until that moment, all I'd seen in Cunningham was a gung-ho jarhead. Lying there on the ground, he looked like someone's kid. Dead. A sheer waste, like the incredible number of other people who had died within the past week. If I had been a little sharper, could I have saved him? I bent over to pick him up and salty tears fell from my face onto his. "Semper Fi," I said as I hoisted him onto my shoulders.

FOUR DAYS LATER

69

12:20 PM EASTERN DAYLIGHT TIME
OVAL OFFICE
THE WHITE HOUSE

Arnessy had a diabolical grin on his face as he leaned on the president's desk. "Here's how we play it. We already have Brandon in the can, and Justice is sure they can make a charge of treason stick. Now we don't have anything that we can actually charge Decker with, but that doesn't really—"

President Stanson was shaking his head slowly, looking at his buoyant chief of staff. "No."

"What do you mean? We talked about this. We may have gotten the madman but the people will want someone to blame for the breakdown that happened after the attacks. Decker's perfect."

"Have a seat, Dick."

Arnessy plopped down with an impatient sigh.

"This," Stanson said as he picked up a sheet of paper and dangled it between his index finger and thumb, "is my statement. I wrote it myself. Tell me what you think." He stood and handed it across the massive desk to Arnessy.

The look on Arnessy's face changed from giddiness to disbelief as he read the page. "You can't be serious!"

"Oh, but I am. I will present Mr. Decker with the Presidential Medal of Freedom next Monday. Israel's prime minister, along with the heads of state from a half-dozen other countries, will also be on hand to honor him with their respective highest honors."

"You're insane."

"And you're fired, *Dick*."

4:15 PM CENTRAL DAYLIGHT TIME (LOCAL)
YELLOW CREEK

My father was still missing and there were no leads. It was as if he ceased to exist. I was heading to the area with a team of private detectives. Power was restored across the nation and a pall of grief replaced the fear and panic. Congressmen and women blathered without pause on the news channels. America would be stronger, they said. She would be better. Her people did not give up and she did not cower. They pledged and promised ad nauseum to fix the shattered economy. The first day of Congress back in session was a show of Kumbayah bipartisanship. On day two it became clear the Republicans had one recovery plan and the Democrats another. Business as usual in the Beltway.

Los Angeles was anything but usual. The Governor, backed by FEMA, ordered the whole metro area evacuated so the unfathomable task of cleaning up could begin. The death toll from the chemical weapon attack was being estimated at 2.2 million, its aftermath beyond all comprehension. Decaying bodies bred disease and created an odor that could be smelled thirty miles away. Looters moved in to plunder the grisly ghost town and discovered that "no means no" when soldiers are enforcing martial law with unequivocal orders to defend the homeland against all enemies, foreign and domestic. Eight thugs were shot on sight and their erstwhile colleagues left en masse.

Hart's warheads were traced back to a general in Moscow who made a critical mistake when he checked the balance in his Swiss bank account on a wiretapped phone. The Russians opted for a swiftly assembled firing squad instead of years in court.

Yellow Creek was a mess but the cleanup was moving forward at a good clip.

I wanted to confront Abdul myself before putting him under a cloud of Fed suspicion that would follow him forever. I walked into the control room and found him at his console, hammering away at his keyboard. We were alone. "Got a second?" I said.

"Yes, Matt Decker." He was grinning from ear to ear. "Now I know not only a computer hero but a super hero, as well!"

"Abdul, drop the accent. I know." The toothy smile vanished. "You care to fill me in on anything before I bring the FBI up to speed on your multiple personalities?"

"How did you know?" he said in English that sounded more like Indiana than Iran.

"I'm more concerned with how Hart knew I was in the Middle East."

"I have no idea. He didn't learn it from me. I've never spoken to him; wouldn't know him if he walked in the room. You and I are on the same side, Matt. I'd like to think we could be friends. You really have been a sort of hero to me with all you've accomplished in technology."

"Friends don't deceive each other with bullshit play-acting, especially when the heat is on."

"I was working on my Master's at MIT when the terrorists hit the World Trade Center. Looking like an Arab, even though I'm really Persian, brought me a lot of grief. I understood why—didn't blame people for the way they felt—but it still got old. As time went by, I discovered that people accepted me a lot more when I played the part of an almost comical character. That's how the heavy accent came into play, and the dork persona just sort of became a natural for me. I love America. One of the happiest days of my life was when I finally became a citizen. I hope you'll forgive me for the charade. I was always on your side. Always. I'm sorry."

I knew he was telling the truth, felt it down in the bottom of my soul. I shook his hand and said, "Apology accepted. Think you'd be interested in talking to me about a job a little later?"

"Definitely."

"Great, I'll be in touch." We shook hands, then abandoned the silliness of man-acting and hugged each other.

I came to Mississippi eleven days earlier with notions of rednecks running amok and an eagerness to get in and get out. This visit was different. I was there to say goodbye to friends for whom I had developed profound respect, people I would be sad to leave behind.

Brett Fulton's funeral had been held the day before. Jana decided to stay at her parents' farm for a while. The land was gorgeous. We walked the fields and talked about ... well, about a lot of things. I left with her phone number and a kiss.

I visited the Tarkleton home and met Peggy, a petite beauty who obviously adored the man. He tried one last time to convince me that I believed, that I just hadn't been patient enough. He didn't get the job done, but I did listen, and finally, it was time to go.

After I bid farewell to Peggy, Tark and I walked out to my rental car and said goodbye, which involved another hug. Just as I pulled on the door handle, my cell phone rang. I pulled it from my pocket. "Hello."

"Mr. Decker?"

"Yes."

"This is Dr. Adderson at Alpine Village."

"You have news about my father?"

"He's safe and sound." Tears streamed. I covered the phone and told Tark, "My father is back!" He squeezed my shoulder and beamed one of those foot-wide smiles.

"Did you find out what happened, where he was?"

"Yes sir, can you hold on for a moment?"

"Sure." I wiped my eyes on the sleeve of my shirt and looked at Tark. "I'm so relieved to—"

"Matty?"

"What?" I said, cranking up the volume on the phone and pressing it harder to my ear.

"Matty, it's me, your father."

Also by Jerry Hatchett:

Pawnbroker,
available at Amazon and most other retailers
of fine fiction.

www.jerryhatchett.com

CPSIA information can be obtained at www.ICGtesting.com
Printed in the USA
LVOW01s2105230813

349377LV00034B/2124/P

9 780988 701243